In the mid-ninet[...] Arkansas were a hotbed of commerce and travel and played a huge part in the settlement of the West. Ms. Ashley brings us an exciting and romantic tale about a woman with multiple secrets who finds a treasure trove in the form of family connections she has been missing for most of her life. This new author does a great job with action and intrigue. Come along for the ride!

— Jenny Carlisle, author of the Crossroads series

Of Faith and Dreams is a delightful tale, shadowed by danger, mystery, and sprinkled with romance. Eliza Dawn and Justin pulled me into their world and held me captive until the last page. This debut promises more adventures to come, and I can't wait to tag along.

— Candace West, best-selling author of the Valley Creek Redemption series

OF *Faith* AND *Dreams*

LOST AND FOUND BOOK 1

TONYA B. ASHLEY

Scrivenings PRESS
Quench your thirst for story.
www.ScriveningsPress.com

Copyright © 2024 by Tonya B. Ashley

Published by Scrivenings Press LLC
15 Lucky Lane
Morrilton, Arkansas 72110
https://ScriveningsPress.com

Printed in the United States of America

All rights reserved. No part of this publication may be reproduced, stored in a retrieval system, or transmitted in any form or by any means—for example, electronic, photocopy, or recording—without the prior written permission of the publisher. The only exception is brief quotations in printed reviews.

Paperback ISBN 978-1-64917-376-8
eBook ISBN 978-1-64917-377-5

Editors: Amy R. Anguish and Heidi Glick

Cover by Linda Fulkerson, www.bookmarketinggraphics.com

All characters are fictional, and any resemblance to real people, either factual or historical, is purely coincidental.

NO AI TRAINING: Without in any way limiting the author's [and publisher's] exclusive rights under copyright, any use of this publication to "train" generative artificial intelligence (AI) technologies to generate text is expressly prohibited. The author reserves all rights to license uses of this work for generative AI training and development of machine learning language models.

*To my husband, Rodney, the love of my life—
there's no one I'd rather have by my side to navigate life's plot twists.*

Chapter One

March 30, 1849
Van Buren, Arkansas

A steamboat's low, moaning whistle wafted in from the river on a cool breeze as the horse stall door creaked open under Justin Hogue's easy touch. He haltered Dolly, leading the little dapple-gray filly to the stable yard. "What do you say we get some fresh air, girl?"

He had never experienced anything like the past several months. The city of Van Buren was incorporated only four years ago. His father had predicted rapid expansion, but no one anticipated growth like this. During the eight months since prospectors first flooded into town, Van Buren had more than doubled in population.

Would more prospectors arrive on the boats today? He raked his fingers along his stubbled jaw. Too busy with horses to shave, he was taking a liking to this rugged appearance. His chest puffed out a little when the fellas in town said it made him look like a man. At twenty-six, he was tired of folks teasing him he resembled a button of a boy and asking when he would grow up. What would Ma think of the stubble?

He winced. Ma was gone. Some days, it still didn't seem real. Pushing the thought away, he returned his attention to the stout filly.

"Hey, girl. Ready to get started?" Justin ran his hand along Dolly's silken neck and patted a couple of times at the withers before resting his hand momentarily. She remained still and relaxed. Turning his back to her head, he faced the rump and moved his hand across her hindquarters and down her leg. He gently squeezed above Dolly's fetlock, and when she lifted her hoof, he wedged it between his knees. Leaning his weight on her, he rocked back and forth slightly. After studying her foot, he released it.

"Your shoes are fine, girl. Just fine." Justin smiled, admiring his farrier work. "With any luck, you'll embark on a long journey soon."

Justin needed to sell seven horses before the first gold expeditions left town in twelve days. Though it was a lofty goal, it shouldn't be too difficult with so many prospectors seeking to outfit themselves with mounts and pack animals. If he could sell all seven, he would have enough money to purchase the land and building supplies to start his horse ranch. Only selling three would give him enough to secure the land. His heart swelled at the thought.

Moving to the back of the horse, he resumed his inspection of Dolly's hooves, though he didn't need to. He had checked them the night before. However, he wanted these horses to be comfortable in the hands of a new owner, so he made this a twice-a-day habit leading up to their sale. After that, it was up to the owner to build trust and familiarity.

He finished the process on the other side and grabbed a brush from the nearby bench.

"Let's get you brushed, sweet girl. Gotta be your finest today.

Remember what I told you. Stand tall, and don't be shy. You're strong and handsome, just like me." Dolly whinnied, tossing her head. Justin chuckled.

"Justin." His sister, Rebecca, appeared around the side of the stable. "Pa wants you to talk to a potential boarder."

He sighed. He'd told his father about his plans to meet a buyer. Pa probably forgot. That was a common occurrence since Ma's death. He wasn't sure if Pa was disremembering or perhaps wasn't paying attention. Maybe his father hadn't even heard him.

"I don't have time." He brushed Dolly. "Can you remind Pa I've got to get to a sale?"

"Remind him yourself." Rebecca tilted her head, narrowing her eyes. "You can't keep avoiding each other. I won't be your messenger for the rest of my life."

"Fine." Justin rubbed the back of his neck. "If the fella needs a room so badly, ask him to wait on the porch until I return."

"It's a woman."

"A woman?" Justin's eyes snapped to meet hers, and his grip on the brush tightened. "We don't board women. Send her to Bradley House. Why does Pa want me to talk to her?"

Rebecca shrugged. "You know Pa. He can't talk to women."

"Can't talk to women?" Justin scoffed. "He talked to Ma. He's got six daughters, for crying out loud. Can't talk to women."

"That's family." Rebecca put her hands on her hips. "You know he's afraid he'll hurt their feelings. Pa quit talking to Ivajohn, Cordelia, and me when we turned thirteen. He only began talking to Ivajohn again when the pastor started courting her. At any rate, I'm not telling this woman she must go. You're the oldest. I'd get Ivajohn to do it since she's the oldest girl, but she set out for Indian Territory this morning with Pastor Turner and the missionaries. They won't be back until later this week. That leaves you."

With a huff, Justin tossed the brush onto the bench. He'd have to shoot straight, that's all. Make it quick and get to the sale.

Justin followed Rebecca around to the front of the house. On the porch stood a young woman in a simple blue and brown plaid dress with no trunk or bag. Where were her belongings? Surely, Pa and Rebecca didn't allow her to set them inside, especially if Pa wanted to get rid of her.

"Good morning, miss. I understand you're inquiring about a room." He didn't bother getting her name as he stopped at the foot of the steps. No sense getting familiar when he intended to dismiss her. From the corner of his eye, he caught Rebecca making herself comfortable in a rocking chair. She wouldn't send the woman away but would watch him do it. "Unfortunately, we only board men here at Hogue House. You might check with—"

"Bradley House for women is full." She smiled, fingering the button at her collar. "The hotel is more expensive than I can manage. Anything will do. A bunk in the stable. I don't require luxuries."

He eyed her carefully. Creamy, unblemished skin, clean fingernails, delicate hands. She carried herself in a tall, stiffened manner. Though her dress was plain enough, it didn't suit her. It didn't even fit. Women in these parts wore their skirts above the ankle. It was more practical than the longer skirts of the east, but her hemline was nigh unto calf high. Surely, this outfit couldn't be hers. No bags, poorly fitting clothes. Everything about her read trouble.

"Bunkroom is mine." He raked fingers along his whiskered jaw. "Pastor is out of town, but Mrs. Pratt can find a church family to lodge you. How long will you stay?"

"No, no church families." She shook her head, light chestnut tendrils escaping her low bun. "Tried that once. Dreadful nosy. Caught the wife reading my journal."

"I'm sorry, miss." Justin checked his pocket watch. The tick-ticking propelled the hands closer to his appointment time. Better make dust. "Even if we boarded women, we've no space right now."

"That's not exactly true." The nagging creak of the rocking chair halted. Rising from the rocker, Rebecca broke her silence. "No one is in the lost and found room."

"The lost and found room." Justin chuckled. "There's no bed in the lost and found room. Besides, it's so packed with stuff you couldn't fit a body in there."

"I'll take it." The young woman stepped toward Justin, extending her hand.

Grinding his teeth, he hard-eyed Rebecca. He flicked the pocket watch open and clapped it shut again. Glowering, he held the timepiece in the air and let it drop, dangling from the chain. Rebecca shrugged.

"How much do the men pay?" She pulled a small pouch from a hiding place in her skirt waist and dug out some coins.

"We charge a dollar and fifty cents a week."

"I'll pay two dollars flat."

Rebecca's eyes widened. "You know the women at Bradley House only pay a dollar twenty-five, don't you?"

"Yes, but this is a terrible inconvenience for you."

"Hold on." Justin tucked the watch back into his vest pocket. "The hotel is too expensive, but you're willing to pay more than the men?"

"Well, yes. It's good business sense." She held some coins out to him. "I'm a seamstress. I'm following the prospectors, filling orders for new shirts, and mending work. The hotel asks for two and a quarter a night. So, two dollars a week is much better, and it's fair, providing for your inconvenience."

"Done. Put those away. We'll settle later." Rebecca grabbed her hand, pumping it heartily. "What will you do for a bed, though?"

"There are crates in the room?" She dropped the coins into the pouch and tucked it back into her waistband.

"Yes, several."

"If you have extra blankets, I can make a pallet."

"Rebecca, could I talk to you?" Lips pressed tight, Justin motioned to Rebecca to join him. They walked a few paces away, and he spoke in hushed tones. "We don't even know her name."

"It's Eliza. Eliza Dawn," the woman replied, smiling.

Justin's head swiveled, and he was momentarily caught in her alluring blue eyes. Then, shaking his head as if waking from a spell, he set his jaw and narrowed his eyes.

She ducked her head, lifted a slender hand, and cleared her throat. "My apologies. I didn't mean to interrupt."

Justin dragged Rebecca around the side of the house. "What are you doing? Didn't you say Pa wants me to get rid of her?"

"No, that's not what I said. I said Pa can't talk to women."

Justin crossed his arms. "Does he want me to get rid of her or not?"

"He didn't specifically say." Rebecca shrugged.

"Then what did he say—exactly?"

"He said, 'Have Justin deal with this.' And he did that waving thing with his hand. Besides, he's let you make all the boardinghouse decisions since Ma died." Rebecca clutched his arms above the elbows. "Justin, it's two dollars. Two dollars a week. Ollie and Nellie need shoes. Little Edie is bursting at the seams, and Simon shot up another two inches. Cordelia and I could get some nice calico to outfit the family with new shirts and dresses."

"If I make this horse sale, I can buy all those things."

"No. Absolutely not." Rebecca shook her head vigorously. "That's your ranch money. Ma told you not to let anything keep you from your dream. We are not using that money for shoes and necessities. Ma and I are the first ones you ever told about wanting to start a horse ranch. She warned me you'd wrestle with family obligations and let those dreams slip away. I vowed to make sure you kept your promise."

Justin wrapped his arms around her, pulling her close. She slumped into him, arms slack, shoulders quaking. He rested his chin on her head.

"It'll be all right."

"I miss her." Rebecca's voice trembled. "So much, every day."

"I know," he rasped.

"I wish I knew how to help Pa through the grief."

"I know."

Releasing his hold on her, he straightened his back and fixed a smile on his face. "We'll board this woman on a trial basis. Then, if it doesn't work out, we'll call on Mrs. Pratt."

"Can you sign her in?" Rebecca wiped a tear from the side of her nose. "It's time for me to start the noon meal, and you know how Pa gets if the meals aren't on time."

"Rebecca, I can't." Justin groaned. "I'm already late to this sale."

"Then, when you return. Please, Justin." Rebecca folded her hands underneath her chin. "You know I don't like the lost and found room. All that old stuff makes me a might uneasy."

"Fine then." Justin rolled his eyes skyward, releasing a long breath. "Keep her occupied until I return. Hopefully, it won't take long."

Justin returned to the porch. "Miss—I didn't get your family name. What was it?"

"I don't have a family." Glancing at her feet, Eliza Dawn cleared her throat. "Therefore, no family name. So, call me Eliza Dawn."

"Miss Dawn," Justin continued, trying to reconcile his manners with her unconventional moniker, "we'll lodge you on a trial basis. If it doesn't work out, we'll find a church family to help you. That's the bettermost we can do."

"I prefer to be called Eliza Dawn." Eliza Dawn turned to Rebecca. "I'm sure we can make this work. Since I'm paying extra, I don't intend to contribute to chores for the other boarders, if that's all right. But you won't have to do any of my wash or such. I won't bother you with my needs except for meals."

"It makes good business sense, considering you'll have to make a bed for yourself." Rebecca smiled, waving Eliza Dawn toward the door. "Would you mind helping me with lunch, however? I prefer Justin to show you the room when he returns from his business venture. I'm not fond of the lost and found."

"I suppose so." Eliza Dawn followed Rebecca into the house.

"I'm off to meet this buyer. Be back shortly."

Justin rode as hard as he dared. Pulling up short in front of Mooney's Mercantile, he slid off the pony's bare back. At the end of the street, his buyer rode off on another horse. He tilted his head to the side and blinked twice, questioning his vision. A sinewy, blond-haired fellow wearing a green plaid skirt waved to the buyer before mounting his horse and riding in the opposite direction. Justin grimaced as a sinking feeling settled in the pit of his stomach.

"Well, Dolly, perhaps you won't be going on that journey as soon as I hoped." Justin tied Dolly to the hitching post and scratched her between the ears. Then, taking the stairs two at a time, he reached the door of the mercantile. Glancing down the street once more, he shook his head. He entered the store and waited by the counter as Sam Mooney finished with a customer.

"Justin, I haven't seen you much lately." Sam's mouth turned up at the corners. "I guess you've been at it full chisel with your horses?"

"Yes, sir. I was set to sell that little dapple gray today." Justin hitched his thumb toward Dolly. "But the buyer just rode off on another horse. Any idea who that blond-haired fella is?"

Sam rounded the counter and peered out the window. "Reddish beard, short-trimmed?"

Justin nodded. "That's the one."

"Scottish emigrant, a prospector. Downright hard to understand." Sam retrieved a box of canned goods to restock some shelves. "Put a notice on the board out front. Has some horses to sell. Calls 'em Highland ponies and claims there's no finer pack animal."

"What's that thing he's wearing?"

"That skirt? Called it a kilt. Talkative fellow." Sam picked a can from the box and tossed it from one hand to the other, settling into a quick, easy rhythm. "Had to ask him to repeat everything."

"Just how many horses does he plan on selling?"

Sam shrugged. "Several, to hear him talk. Trying to sell enough to purchase a wagon and supplies. Gold rush has got people buying up everything."

Justin crossed to the window. Hooking his finger at the edge of the yellow gingham curtain, he drew it aside. Wagons lined the street, horses trotted at a leisurely clip, folks bustled from shop to shop. He wouldn't have missed the sale if he hadn't been distracted by that woman at the boardinghouse. Now, there was new competition with the owner of these Highland ponies. It wasn't shaping up to be a great day.

"You're staying busy." Justin returned his attention to Sam. "I guess gold fever is good for business."

"Yes and no. What folks aren't buying, they're thieving." Sam stopped stocking and turned to Justin. "Your Pa was right when he predicted this town would explode with growth. He was also right when he said lawlessness follows growth. So, tell your family and boarders to keep anything they cherish locked up, or they'll lose it."

"Will do. Say, Sam, did you happen to get that fella's name?"

"No. Ought to be on the notice outside." Sam shook his

head. "You still splitting time between the boardinghouse and Levi's?"

"Yes, sir. Only three stalls are available at the boardinghouse for my sale horses. Our family horses and the pastor's horse occupy the other stalls." Justin joined Sam. Picking a couple of airtights out of the box, he searched the shelves. He placed the cans with a clunk and grabbed two more. "Since I helped Levi build the new forge at his place, he was kind enough to let me build a temporary horse shelter with six stalls and a lean-to. It's not ideal, but I can stay overnight when I need to and keep more horses there."

"How many horses you got there now?"

"Four. Made good progress with them. They're well-grounded, ready to ride and pack." Justin grinned. "Of course, none of them are lacking in personality."

"Well, you ought to be able to sell plenty to these prospectors."

"Oh, sure." The image of Eliza Dawn in her too-short dress flashed in his mind. "Provided I don't have too many distractions."

"I always send anyone in the market for horses in your direction." Sam smiled, patting Justin on the shoulder. "It'll all work out. Listen, when you see Levi, let him know we miss having him and his forge at the boardinghouse. People fuss when I tell them where to find him now."

"I know what you mean. Folks still call on me for simple projects since I was his apprentice." Another distraction he didn't need. "They're a might sour about the distance. But you know Levi. If town grows too close to him, he'll move again."

Sam laughed. "I don't know what we'd do if he got too far away. Say, Simon stopped by one day after school. Said he's been doing some riding for you."

"That he has. That kid brother of mine is getting pretty good at trick riding. Although, I don't know why a person wants to do such stunts on a horse. As a kid, walking the ridge of the roof was daredevil enough for me." Justin placed two more cans and chuckled. "Course, now I think a man doesn't need to be any higher than a saddle, but I wouldn't risk my neck doing crazy stunts atop a moving horse."

"Well, that's all part of growing up." Sam paused to eye Justin. "Weren't long ago you were between grass and hay. Now, you're setting your own hook in this horse business. Wish your ma could see how fine a man you've become."

A lump settled in Justin's throat. "Thanks for the chat, Sam." He shook Sam's hand and strolled to the front door. "I'll check that notice board on my way out."

Outside, the notice board overflowed with announcements and advertisements. One, in particular, caught his eye. It read:

Seamstress Work
Shirts: $1.50
Mending: 50¢
Contact Eliza Dawn at Hogue House

Justin's brow furrowed, and he bit the inside of his lip. He found the notice he was searching for beside Eliza Dawn's advertisement.

Highland Ponies
Best pack animals this side of the Mississippi
Ewan MacKinnon, Scottish Prospector Camp, north side of town

MacKinnon. At least now Justin knew something about his competition.

Chapter Two

Eliza Dawn grabbed a handful of dough and squeezed. A sticky glop clung to her fingers. She squeezed again, and more dough clumped around her knuckles. Rebecca giggled, dipping a few fingers in a bowl of flour and pulling the dough free of Eliza Dawn's hands.

"You don't cook much, do you?" Rebecca scooted her over with a hip bump.

"No." Eliza Dawn smiled weakly. "Does it show?"

"Here, toss a little flour on top. Then fold and push down and away." Rebecca exampled the kneading motion. "Don't squeeze it. You'll overwork the dough, and the biscuits won't be light. Mr. Hildesheim, the German baker who boards here, taught us to make biscuits that aren't so hard. It takes a little more time, and sometimes it doesn't turn out, but it's worth it when it does."

"Thank you, Rebecca." Eliza Dawn picked bits of dough from her fingers and made another effort. She mimicked Rebecca's movement, glancing at her for approval. "You understand why I'm willing to pay extra for meals."

"Knead that dough gently until I tell you to stop." Rebecca

blew a strand of honey-colored hair from her eyes. "You're welcome to join me in the kitchen anytime. You get plenty of practice making three meals daily for eight siblings and half as many boarders."

"Nine children?" Eliza Dawn gasped. "How is that possible? It's so quiet."

"Four of us are grown, Justin, Ivajohn, myself, and Cordelia. Of course, Cordelia and Simon accompany the younger ones to school. Cordelia assists the schoolmaster. Simon is sixteen. He's not fond of school, but he's strappy, and walking through town with a little extra muscle at her side gives Cordelia some peace of mind. Little Edie is with Mrs. Pratt. She's four years old, the youngest." Rebecca retrieved a few jars from the pantry.

"I can't imagine what it must be like growing up in a household with so many children. You must've done an incredible amount of cooking, cleaning, sewing, and such." Eliza Dawn sighed. What a relief to be free of so many obligations to others. Who needed such entanglements?

"Noon meal is my favorite. With the young'uns at school, it's the boarders and us. Pa hasn't sat for dinner much lately. Mr. Hildesheim usually takes a lunch pail to the bakery. The pastor and Ivajohn have gone north. Captain Cobb and his brother have stayed on the steamboat this trip. Sometimes, it's just me, Justin, and Mr. Perry, the stone mason. Fascinating gentleman, when you can get him to talk."

"One of the boarders is a pastor?" Eliza Dawn forced a smile, keeping her voice light. If she had known Hogue House was home to a preacher, she would have found other accommodations.

"Yes, Pastor Turner has boarded with us for over four years. The church is finally building a parsonage, so he'll move out in the next few weeks." Rebecca waved a hand toward the window. "He and Ivajohn took a group of missionaries north and then into Indian Territory. They'll return later this week, just in time for Easter."

Rebecca turned, cocking her head to the side. "We're about the same height, wouldn't you say?"

"I guess so." Eliza Dawn shrugged.

"If you haven't any longer skirts, you can borrow one of mine." Rebecca picked up a potato and cut it into chunks. "Women here wear their hems ankle-high to keep them out of the dirt and mud. Calf high will have tongues wagging. Mind you, I'd wear britches if I could get away with it. They'd be far more practical for all my work here."

"You're kind to offer, but I can make do."

The front door creaked open and closed.

"Justin, that you?" Rebecca's bright voice rang through the house.

"It's me." The hard beat of Justin's bootheels preceded him. Then, momentarily, he appeared in the kitchen doorway with ledger in hand. He beckoned Eliza Dawn with a wave. "Sit, and let's get to business."

"What about the dough?" She turned to Rebecca, wiping her hands on her apron.

"I've got it. Go take care of business."

Removing the apron, Eliza Dawn joined Justin at the kitchen work table. He flipped roughly through the pages of the ledger. Was he upset with her? Had she done something wrong already? She shot a questioning glance at Rebecca, who shrugged in response.

She couldn't afford to lose these accommodations. Following prospectors meant lodging was limited everywhere she went. She had camped under the stars and enjoyed it until one evening when she narrowly escaped a run-in with a couple of ruffians. Plus, the nagging sense of being followed had plagued her since Alabama. If that were the case, she'd be more easily discovered at a boardinghouse for women.

Of Faith and Dreams

If she intended to continue this journey west, she needed to curry favor with Justin while she was in town. She still required a second horse to give the animals adequate rest on such a long trek, and, with any luck, she'd convince him to sell her one. And she would have to find someone with enough room in their wagon for her supplies.

"Eliza Dawn? That's all the name we're going to get?" Justin drummed his fingers on the page.

"It's all I've got."

Head down, he wrote her name in the ledger. He recorded the details of their arrangement as he spoke. "I didn't notice a trunk or any bags on the porch. No belongings?"

"Only what fits in my saddle bags."

Justin's head jerked up, brows knit together. "You have a horse?"

A slight shudder rippled through her at the sternness in his blue-gray eyes.

"Yes, of course. How else would I have gotten here?"

"You should have mentioned that earlier. So you didn't arrive by steamboat?"

Eliza Dawn shook her head.

"Stable is full." He slammed the book closed. "I'll speak with Mrs. Pratt. She'll know which families can stable a horse."

"No, please don't contact Mrs. Pratt." She seized his hand. "No church families. If I can't stay here, I'll negotiate my way into one of the prospector camps."

"Justin, we can't let her stay in the camps." Rebecca set her paring knife down and picked up a kitchen towel. Wiping her hands, she joined them at the table.

"What do you want me to do, Rebecca?" He threw his hands in the air. Standing, he shoved his chair under the table. "It's above my bend. We don't board women, and we have no stalls." His tone flattened. "Take your advertisement down from the board at Mooney's Mercantile. If you've placed one at the post office or elsewhere, take those down too."

Crossing the kitchen in quick strides, he departed out the back door by the cupboard. Eliza Dawn flew from her seat. Before she reached the door, Rebecca caught her arm.

"Best to leave him be a while. There's no talking to him when he gets like this." Rebecca gestured to the table, and they both sat. "Let him spend some time with the horses. We'll visit for a minute, finish the cooking, and then maybe we can approach him after dinner. Together."

Eliza Dawn nodded, wrapping her arms around her lurching stomach.

"Now, what is he talking about? What's this advertisement he mentioned?"

"It was impulsive and presumptuous of me." Eliza Dawn rubbed her hands over her face. "I put up notices advertising my seamstress work."

"Of course. How else would you get work?"

"I listed Hogue House as the place to contact me." Eliza Dawn tensed. Would Rebecca find offense like her brother? Spending the morning with Rebecca reminded her of a time when she was part of a family. She wrung her hands. "I didn't mean to offend. Hogue House was my last resort. If Justin hadn't agreed to let me stay, I planned to ask if I could rent workspace for a few hours every morning. I was being hopeful."

"I understand." Rebecca patted Eliza Dawn's hands. "We will work this out. It will be fine."

Later, during the meal, Rebecca and Eliza Dawn sat at one end of the table. Sitting at the opposite end, Justin didn't so much as look at her. Instead, he shared an ambling, relaxed conversation with Mr. Perry. When Rebecca spoke to him, he responded in terse, clipped phrases.

Eliza Dawn shifted in her seat, smoothing the napkin in her

lap. She fixed a bright smile and took a deep breath at a lull in the conversation. "Mr. Hogue, how did your sale go today?"

Justin's fork landed on his plate with a sharp clang. Keeping his back to her, his eyes stayed on Mr. Perry.

"I lost that sale." He turned, training his steely gaze on her. "Because of you, I was late. Rode up just in time to watch my buyer ride off on another horse."

"I'm terribly sorry. I didn't know." She broke eye contact, swallowing hard. "I wasn't trying to cause trouble."

"That distraction was not worth two dollars a week." Justin's jaw clenched. "That was a significant sale you cost me today."

"Justin!" Rebecca barked a harsh whisper.

Eliza Dawn excused herself, picked up her plate, and escaped to the kitchen table with Rebecca on her heels. Hands trembling, she set down the plate. She paced back and forth a few times. Then, turning to Rebecca, she slashed the air with her hand. "I *will* fix this. I will make it right, I promise."

"I'll be right back."

Eliza Dawn wrapped her arms around herself, rubbing her shoulders. She slumped into a chair as sounds of intense dialogue rumbled from the dining room. She couldn't make out the words. The front door creaked, and Mr. Perry called, "Back at suppertime." Voices in the dining room paused, resumed lower than before, and finally ceased altogether.

Justin appeared in the kitchen with the ledger. He sat next to her and flipped through the pages. "Let's begin again."

Eliza Dawn let out a sigh of relief. "Mr. Hogue, I'm so sorry about the sale. I can pay a little more, two twenty-five?"

"Two dollars is plenty." His back stiffened, and he crossed his arms. "You should have told me upfront about your horse and the advertisement. You don't want to tell me your family name, fine. But you will tell me about things that affect this family and the other tenants. Do you understand?"

"Yes. Yes, of course." She slowly released a shaky breath.

Rebecca skirted by on her way to do the dinner dishes. She squeezed Eliza Dawn's shoulder as she passed.

"Miss Dawn, I don't need to know your life's particulars. In fact, I prefer not to." He scratched her name into the book. "I can't afford the distraction right now. However, I expect you to have better discretion in the future about what to share with us."

"Absolutely."

"Where is this horse of yours?"

"I tied her to a post in the alley on the other side of the house."

"Why?" His eyes searched hers with an intensity that made her squirm inside. "You hiding something, Miss Dawn?"

"I am a woman traveling alone. I doubt I could fend off a horse thief, and I can't afford to lose that horse." She didn't dare tell him the real reason she kept her horse hidden.

He slammed the ledger shut. "Let's take care of your horse, and then I'll show you the lost and found room."

Eliza Dawn turned to Rebecca. "If you don't mind waiting a bit, I'll help you with those dishes."

"No need." Rebecca gave a reassuring smile. "Save some time for a chat later this evening once the younger siblings have nodded off, if you don't mind."

"That will be fine." She smiled. "Thank you. For everything."

Eliza Dawn led her horse from the alley to the stable. Justin worked the leather thongs loose, untying the saddlebags and dropping them on the bench. He removed the rest of the tack and showed Eliza Dawn where he stored the items in the stable. Then he scratched his head.

"I'm not fond of the idea, but I guess we can stable her in the old forge until I sell Dolly." Justin brushed her. "It's not a proper space for a horse. She might startle being in an unfamiliar place. I'll clear the tools and things out so she won't hurt herself if she spooks."

Eliza Dawn reached for the brush. "Here, I'll do that."

"You're paying for this service with those two dollars." Justin held the brush out of reach. "In fact, how about you get those two dollars right now."

She lifted a saddle bag from its resting place on the bench. A sachet of soap hung from one of the buckled closures. She brought it to her nose and sniffed. Lavender. How had it gotten there? Who would have left her such a luxury? Tucking it into the bag, she retrieved the money and handed it to Justin.

As he brushed, his shoulders relaxed. "What's her name?"

"Bonnie. I call her Bonnie the Beauty." She smiled sheepishly. She loved how Bonnie's chestnut face and socks faded to the lightest reddish-blond. "It probably sounds silly, but she is beautiful."

"It's fitting." He grinned, lifting and inspecting the horse's hooves. "You handle her hooves often? She's fairly comfortable with me picking up her feet."

"One of the prospectors showed me how. So, I try to do it regularly." She rubbed Bonnie's muzzle. "I can get her feet off the ground, but I don't know I'd recognize if something were wrong."

Justin summoned her to his side, instructing her on what to look for. The corded muscles in his neck smoothed as tension melted. His voice softened. His movements became more fluid. A gentleness replaced his harsh tone and starchy demeanor as he spoke softly to Bonnie.

"Tell me about you and Bonnie. What sort of things do you do together?" Justin patted Bonnie on the rump as he finished his inspection.

"I practice the usual asks with her, change in gait, staying while I walk away, that sort of thing. We do have one trick, though."

"Oh, what's that?"

"She'll lie down on cue." Eliza Dawn motioned for Justin to

step away from Bonnie. She removed the lead rope, handing it to Justin. Making eye contact with Bonnie, she straightened her arm at her side and held a flat hand parallel to the ground. She rewarded the horse by rubbing her nose and around her ears. Bonnie responded by standing when Eliza Dawn raised her hand.

"Good girl." She ran her hand along Bonnie's neck. "She'll do it even when I'm not looking at her. I make a *tsk*-ing sound, and she looks for my hand signal."

"That's a good trick. My brother, Simon, would love it. He's sixteen and teaches my horses to do trick riding." Justin reattached the lead rope and scratched Bonnie's belly. "She'll need to be reshod soon. I made new horseshoes yesterday and will be shoeing horses later this week. I'll take care of her."

"You *made* horseshoes?"

"Levi, the blacksmith, boarded with us, and I was his apprentice for a spell. That's how we came to have a forge." Justin tied Bonnie off and retrieved a bucket of oats for her. "I still make my own horseshoes. Now, Levi's moved to the edge of town. He allows me to stable some horses at his place. I pay for the space, of course."

"I feel terrible. You're already splitting your time between two stables, and I ruined your sale." She caught his arm. "I will make it up to you. I'll find a new buyer."

"What's done is done. Let's leave it in the past." He nodded toward the bench. "Get your bags. I'll show you the room."

Eliza Dawn followed him upstairs. At the top of the stairs, he paused.

"That end of the hall is boarders' rooms. Men only." He eyed her fixedly. Then, turning, he motioned to the other side. "These are the family rooms and the lost and found. You are to keep to this end of the hallway and your room when upstairs. Boarders are welcome to use the dining and sitting rooms downstairs. As Rebecca mentioned, she would be fond of your company in the kitchen if you want to visit."

"I understand."

When he opened the door to the room, she sucked in a quick breath, and her hand floated to her mouth. Her gaze drifted slowly around the space, soaking in the details.

"You still want it?" He chuckled.

"You weren't exaggerating. This room is full to the rafters." It was a labyrinth of stories waiting to be explored. Her pulse quickened. Her voice floated through the air, settling among the treasures. "This is delightful."

"This is a mess." Justin sighed. "Pa won't let us get rid of anything. Says precious memories could be attached to every item."

"He's right." She picked up a child's doll from the floor. A dull ache filled her chest. Smoothing the doll's dress, she nestled it among some blankets in an open trunk. "Well, this room suits me just fine."

"Do you have any idea how long you'll stay?"

"I'm not certain." She shrugged. "It could be days or a few weeks. Depends on when the prospectors move out."

"Where will you go when the forty-niners leave town?"

"I'll follow them west."

"You'll follow them?" Justin's eyebrows arched.

"Naturally. Prospectors are my business."

"That's wild territory, a hard place for a woman." Justin leaned against the door facing, his strapping frame almost filling the doorway. "Why don't you stay and do your work here?"

"Because there are plenty of wives, mothers, and church ladies to keep the town clothed, I'm sure." She rearranged things to create a pocket of space for herself. "Besides, I like an adventure."

"It's been my experience adventure has no trouble finding

people who put down ties. I didn't mean to pry." Justin scooted out the door. "I best get back to the horses."

"Oh, wait. Do you have the time?"

Pulling the timepiece from his pocket, he flipped it open. "Getting close to three o'clock."

"I'd better be heading out too. I'll finish making myself at home later."

"Where are you headed?"

"I've got to get to the mercantile before it closes."

"Do you have any longer dresses? If not, one of my sisters could lend you one."

She edged past him with a smile. "This will do for now."

"What do you need from the mercantile? I don't mind making the trip." Justin kept eyeing her hemline. "That way, you and Rebecca will have time to scare up a dress that might fit better."

"I want to browse the flannels. I like to choose supplies for myself." Eliza Dawn moved toward the stairway. "Now that I have a place to stay, I'll need to stock up on fabric and notions."

She couldn't tell him she intended to spend the rest of the afternoon at the pool hall observing the forty-niners. She couldn't tell him the real reason she was following them. If he objected to her hemline, he would certainly take exception to her true profession.

Chapter Three

Eliza Dawn strolled through town, taking in the same scene she'd experienced in every city on her journey west. Prospectors overwhelmed the mercantile, dry goods store, and livery. They spilled out of the gambling and drinking establishments. Prim women clutched reticules close and children closer, crossing the street to avoid revelry whenever possible.

She had gotten off to a rough start with Justin Hogue the previous day. In response to her nagging guilt over ruining his horse sale, she determined her top priority would be finding a new buyer for Justin. Once again, she would be the only woman moving toward the revelry in town. It was odd to be constantly in the middle of it yet never join in.

After awakening early to sew, she assisted Rebecca with breakfast clean-up so she could have the table free to cut fabric. Afterward, she sewed until dinner, leaving the afternoon to gather information on the prospectors and search for anyone interested in buying a horse.

Justin was living a life in motion when she arrived. But thanks to her, his business had ground to a halt, resulting in a substantial loss. She bit her lip. She envied those who could stay in one place without getting stuck. But, unfortunately, being in motion wasn't enough for her. She had to keep moving from place to place to keep her past at bay. Otherwise, it always managed to catch up to her.

Pushing away the thought, she glimpsed the sign overhead: Pool Hall. She slipped through the door and sat at an empty table near the center of the room. Gawking patrons were nothing new to her. A few men changed tables to sit farther away. More than once, she had endured a tense exchange with men opposed to her presence in these male-dominated venues.

The rhythmic tapping of billiard balls played sharply throughout the back of the room. The aroma of cigar smoke laced with notes of nutmeg, coffee, and bourbon hung thick in the air. The staccato laughter of a group of Scottish emigrants added interest to the thrum of easy chatter. Eliza Dawn singled out a nearby table of businessmen making plans.

"So's, I said to him, 'Mister, I'm westward bound, and I don't aim to look back.'" The burly, dark-haired man closest to Eliza Dawn set his drink down with force, sloshing the contents on the table. "'I don't give a rat's tail about this here letter. Keep it, and don't pester me no more.' You wouldn't think steamboat hands would be so bothersome."

"Well, I didn't encounter him, so he couldn't have stopped everyone passing by him. Never mind that." A short, stout older man stood and stretched. Then, stroking the gray streak down the middle of his dark beard, he eased into his chair. "I'd like to get one more horse, one that sits well. I stiffen up sitting on that wooden wagon seat for hours on end."

"Maybe we'll get a cushion for Gramps." The big ox slapped the table, laughing forcefully.

Eliza Dawn rose and approached the men. "Good afternoon, gentlemen."

The conversation halted as their eyes roved from the top of

her head to the hem of her skirt. Tugging at the hips of the garment, she tried to give the illusion of a longer skirt. Perhaps she should have lingered at Hogue House long enough to take advantage of Rebecca's offer for something more fitting.

"What can we do for you, miss?" The dark-haired man next to her straightened his bowtie.

"I couldn't help but overhear you may be in the market for a good horse." She gestured to the bearded man. "I've been staying at Hogue House, and Justin Hogue has some fine horses for sale."

"What does a pretty thing like you know about horses?" The man near her winked, catching her hand.

"Mr. Hogue has worked with my horse. He has a gift." She slipped her fingers free. "I'm sure you won't be disappointed with what he can offer."

"I wouldn't be disappointed with what you have to offer." The man's lips curled into a smile, exposing broad yellow teeth as he rubbed his hand down her sleeve and settled it at her waist. "Why don't you take a seat?"

Eliza Dawn's skin crawled. She pulled away from his meaty paw and smoothed her dress. "I wanted to share a tip on where to find a horse. That's all."

The man yanked her into his lap. "A tip on a horse isn't what I want from a girl like you."

"Turn her loose, Big Jim." Folding his arms across his chest, the bearded man leaned back in his chair.

"I'm just having a little fun." Big Jim took a long drag from his cigar.

Eliza Dawn struggled to free herself from his grip. He leaned close to her face with puckered lips, releasing curls of smoke. Wrinkling her nose, she recoiled. Her back pressed uncomfortably against the table edge. The other men laughed.

"Aye, lass, thir ye ur. Bin looking fer ye." A tall, muscular Scotsman slapped the table. "Didny ken where ye got off to."

He freed Eliza Dawn from her entanglement and tucked her close to his side. The honeyed glow of lantern light highlighted a faint hint of red in his unruly blond hair. His blue-gray eyes flashed as he wrapped his arm around her waist, pulling her uncomfortably close. Was she being rescued or newly entrapped?

"Relax, lass. Ye're safe 'nough." He whispered in her ear as he shepherded her away from the table. Then, removing his hand from her waist, he placed it gently on the side of her head. He kissed her temple and added, "Make a good shew of it."

Eliza Dawn laid her head on his shoulder and draped her arms around him.

"Back in a minute, lads." He called to his table as he escorted her out the door. The table erupted with whoops and whistles.

Outside, Eliza Dawn turned him loose. Stepping back, she straightened her shoulders and smoothed her dress. "I appreciate your help."

"Wis 'eh proper thing to do." He brushed wavy locks away from her face. "Feel lek I ken ye. Ye've shewed oop ev'rywhere we've camped since we left Georgia."

"You noticed?" Heat rose in her cheeks.

"Aye, lass. Ye're a difficult one no' to notice." His eyes flickered. "Ye're following us lek a stray pup, so the lads and I hev adopted ye."

"You've been leaving things on my saddle?" She raised her hand to her collar, fidgeting with the button. "Bags of food, sachets of soap."

"Aye, that'd be us. We call ye pup, but I imagine ye've got a more suitable name."

"Eliza Dawn. And your name so I can thank you properly."

"Name's Ewan MacKinnon."

"Mr. MacKinnon." She tipped her head. "My deepest gratitude for rescuing me. Please thank the lads for the gifts they've left along the journey. It's kind but unnecessary."

She turned to go, and Ewan grasped her elbow. Her breath caught in her throat.

"Call me Ewan. I'll be offended if ye don't. Hev ye bin to the bakery?"

Releasing a long breath, she relaxed. "The bakery? No."

"It's doon 'eh way. The baker makes a well tidy strudel." He flashed a warm, broad smile. "Permit me one more gift?"

She gave a nod, and he offered his arm. He grew taller as she placed her hand in the crook of his elbow. They strolled in silence a moment before he spoke again.

"Whit causes ye to be continually in oor midst?"

"Sewing." She caught her toe on an uneven plank in the boardwalk and stumbled. Ewan quickly steadied her. "I make flannels and do mending."

"Tis a long journey fer a little work. How mooch fer a shirt?"

"A dollar fifty."

"The lads and I will gi' ye two dollars a shirt." He pulled a wad of bills from his pocket. "How many can ye make?"

She blushed, pushing his hand away. "Oh, no. that's not necessary."

"It'll be necessary 'nough when we're a thousand miles from home." He held out the money.

"Payment on delivery, I insist." She pushed it back again. "I only make a shirt a day."

"A shirt a day. I'll hev five shirts then." He returned the money to his pocket and wheeled her into the bakery. "Five shirts ought to gi' ye joost 'nough free time."

"Enough free time for what?" she asked.

Ewan's wide smile reappeared. He held up two fingers to the baker as he spoke. "Fer more strudel wi' me, o' course."

Eliza Dawn laughed brightly. Ewan paid the baker and handed her the flaky pastry, awaiting her approval. Taking a bite, her eyes widened with delight. "Is that caramel?"

"Tis. Caramel, apple, and raisins." He ushered her out the door. "Brilliant, isn't it?"

"*Mm-hmm.*" She replied with a mouthful of pastry.

"Better get back to 'eh lads." He nodded toward the pool hall.

"Oh wait, when would you like to select fabric for the shirts?"

"I troost ye. Pick anything ye like. Will ye be all right on yer own?"

"I'll be fine, Ewan." She leaned close, placing her hand on his shoulder and pecking him on the cheek.

Turning to leave, her body slammed into something hard. Her gaze traveled slowly up the pressed white shirt front, landing on steely gray eyes. Justin Hogue. Her heart sank.

Clutching her arms, Justin pushed her back a step. The sticky caramel filling smeared as she wiped at bits of strudel smashed into his shirt. She glanced behind her. MacKinnon had vanished.

Chapter Four

Justin pressed his eyes tightly shut. Pursing his lips, he inhaled a deep breath and released it slowly. He turned loose of Eliza Dawn and opened his eyes.

"Oh, Mr. Hogue. I've made such a mess of your shirt." She rubbed frantically at the gooey filling.

He grasped her hands, instantly regretting it. His jaw flexed as he sought a place to wipe his sticky palm. Then, teeth clenched, he forced a smile. "I know you didn't mean to. It was an accident."

"Where were you headed?"

He gestured to the gray dapple tied to the hitching post nearby.

"Oh, no." Eliza Dawn shook her head vigorously. "No, not again."

He nodded.

"You're trying to sell that horse, and I've done it again."

"This time, it's just a ruined shirt." He released a puff of air. "Hopefully, the sale will go according to plan despite my appearance. So, who was your friend?"

She hesitated. "Oh, he's someone I bumped into."

"Interesting. He doesn't have strudel on his shirt."

There was a cozy familiarity in how Eliza Dawn had leaned into MacKinnon. Her kiss on MacKinnon's cheek hadn't escaped Justin, nor had the fact her advertisement was right next to MacKinnon's on the mercantile notice board. Hard to believe she had only just bumped into him.

"No." She cleared her throat. "He offered to buy it for me. He must come to the bakery regularly. He didn't tell the baker what he wanted, just held up two fingers and kept talking."

"To you."

"Well, yes. I was the only other person there besides the baker."

Eliza Dawn's decidedly informal manner with MacKinnon hinted at a relationship beyond a chance meeting and nagged at Justin. What if she intended to share information about his horse business with MacKinnon? What if her arrival at Hogue House as he was leaving to sell his horse wasn't simply happenstance? Had she and MacKinnon planned to delay him? How could they have known about the sale?

A petite woman with a lively boy hanging from her arm brushed by them. The boy waved his hand wildly as they passed. Justin nodded and smiled. The child pulled against the woman, drawing her toward the bakery until something else captured his attention.

"What did you talk about?" Justin asked Eliza Dawn.

"What did we talk about?" Her gaze followed the path MacKinnon had taken, and she sighed. "Strudel. And soap."

"Strudel and soap?" Justin tilted his head and shrugged.

"I guess you had to be there." She grinned.

Eliza Dawn's voice trailed off. A small covered wagon barreled down Main Street, the arched bows swaying wildly. Ahead of him, the petite young mother admired dresses in Brandt's Tailor Shop window. The small boy twisted free from her grasp and darted into the street. Pushing Eliza Dawn aside,

Justin raced toward them. Scooping up the child, he dove out of the way. He lay in a heap coughing, the boy cradled against his chest as a cloud of dust cleared.

The woman rushed over, gathered the boy tightly, and rocked him. Then, kissing him repeatedly, she set him on his feet.

"My baby. Thank you. I don't know what I'd do." The woman dipped at the waist and waved. "Thank you so much."

Eliza Dawn appeared at his side, out of breath and visibly shaken. "Oh, Mr. Hogue, you're lucky you weren't killed. Are you all right?"

Nodding, a deep, throaty cough tore through his body, rejecting the invasion of dust.

"That happened so quickly." She wedged her arms under his armpits, helping him to stand. Her arms shook under his weight. "I can't believe you got to that boy in time."

A twinge pricked his heart. If only he had been able to get to his mother as quickly. Bent over, hands on his knees, Justin strained to recover his breath. Eliza Dawn placed a hand on his back and patted. He raised a hand, gesturing for her to stop. She stepped back, and he straightened.

"I'm all right." He choked. "I'm all right."

Eliza Dawn bit her lower lip.

"What?" he asked. "What's the matter?"

"You look just awful."

He scanned his shirt front. Ground in dirt covered his clothes, caking together over the blob of strudel filling. He laughed.

"What's so funny?"

"I didn't even have a chance to taste that strudel." He chuckled.

She giggled, the concern fading from her eyes. "I hope the new buyer isn't scared off by the sight of you."

Justin checked his watch. "He's late. Probably a no-show."

"You should wait a little longer. I could join you." Eliza

Dawn motioned to a bench near the bakery door. "I'll buy you a strudel. You must try it."

"Which one did you have? Caramel apple?"

"It was delicious."

"I know. I've had it before." Justin strode toward Dolly with Eliza Dawn in tow. "That's Conrad's twist on a German tradition. Best strudel in the shop, though, is the one he invented. Hildesheim's Bakery is the only place you'll find it."

"Oh? What is it?"

"Muscadine." The corners of his mouth lifted as an image formed of Ma's surprised expression the day Conrad experimented with her muscadine preserves. "Nothing beats it. Better get one while you can. I don't know if Rebecca will make preserves this year with Ma gone."

"What happened to your Ma? How did she die?"

Her soft question triggered a pang in his heart. He stepped away, slapping at the dirt on his pants. Then, clearing his throat, he motioned. "Go on now. Get that strudel. Ask for a baker's dozen and have Conrad charge it to the Hogue House account. I'll see you at supper."

Justin swung onto Dolly's bareback and gigged her, turning her into the street. Once in the middle of the road, Justin squeezed his legs, urging the horse into a gallop. Wind ripping through his hair, images of his last moments with Ma flashed through his mind.

Her smile as she bade goodbye to Sam at the mercantile. The delicate wave of her hand as she gave him leave to talk to Daisy Warren. The crack of gunfire. Her crumpled body in the street.

Justin skidded to a halt, the Snow homestead a blur. He slid off the horse, the strength gone from his legs. Collapsing to the ground, he struggled to catch his breath. He wasn't sure how long he'd been there when Levi materialized.

"Wasn't expecting you this afternoon." Levi extended a hand. "Everything all right?"

"This woman at the boarding house, Miss Dawn, gets me sidetracked." Justin took Levi's hand and stood. "Got any advice on how to deal with that?"

"The last time I encountered a woman who threw my focus off, I married her." Levi laughed. "Now I have more distractions than I ever dreamed, and I wouldn't change a thing."

"How is little Mason?"

"He's into everything. Walking and talking more every day." Levi grinned, eyeing Justin up and down. "What happened to you?"

"Aw, it was nothing." Justin turned his attention to Dolly. "Guess I better rub her down. I cut dirt getting here."

"Will you be staying for supper?"

"No. Just needed to get away." Justin ran his hand through his hair. "Needed time to clear my head."

"Since you took care of these horses this morning, there's no work there to clear your head." Levi wagged a finger toward the stalls. "I'll help you take care of this filly, and then you can help me in the forge for old times' sake."

Justin led Dolly to the watering trough while Levi fetched a bucket of water from the well. As they rubbed the horse down, Justin delivered Sam Mooney's message and caught Levi up on the family. He also shared about the two failed attempts to sell Dolly.

When they finished, he emptied the bucket, turned it upside down on a fencepost, and followed Levi to the forge. It was bigger than the boardinghouse forge but exuded the familiar scents of hickory and smelt. Though the new forge had a couple of log stools and a coffee kettle, there was no table.

"Tell me about this woman." Levi pumped the bellows.

Justin blew out a puff of air. "You said we'd do some smithing to clear my head."

"Talk things out while you work." Levi picked up a pair of

tongs and handed them to Justin. "It's the best way to clear your head. I'm here to listen."

"She's barely been here a day, and she's already a pain in my hide," Justin grumbled. "From the moment she arrived, it's been trouble. It's her fault I lost the first sale, and I'm not sure she didn't also cost me the second one."

Levi raised an eyebrow. "Oh, how so?"

"Look at me." Justin motioned to his chest. "She ruined my shirt."

"She did all that?" Levi asked. "What'd she do? Wrestle you down and hogtie you?"

"No, she's not responsible for *all* of this." Justin waved his hand in front of his body. "She ran into me outside the bakery and smeared strudel on my shirt. The dirt is from an incident involving a runaway wagon."

"So, she bumped into you. Accidentally."

"I just get this nagging feeling she's hiding something."

"We all have our secrets. Things in our past that eat at us." Levi lifted a piece of hot metal from the forge, moving it to the anvil. "You and I both know what that's like."

"Yeah. Maybe that's all it is." Justin placed a piece of metal into the fire. He rubbed his neck and rolled his shoulders, dissipating the tension. "She was talking to one of those prospectors today. I think something is going on between them."

"What makes you think that?"

"He treated her to strudel."

"Well, that clinches it. When a man buys a woman a strudel, it's no light thing." Levi's hearty laugh filled the room.

Justin grimaced. "She kissed him."

Levi's jovial expression faded. "In public? And you saw this?"

Justin nodded. "On the cheek."

"Justin, it was probably to thank him for the treat." Levi grinned. "You like this girl. Is she pretty?"

"*Pfft*. Like this girl. She's trouble, Levi."

"Allie was trouble." Levi poked at Justin. Then he sighed. "Maybe we crave a hint of trouble in our lives. Just a hint, whether we realize it or not."

"Enough about Miss Dawn." Justin retrieved his piece from the fire. "Let's focus on the work."

"All right, all right." Levi set a couple of hinge plates on the table. "I need hinge pins for these."

"Sure." Justin lightly tapped the metal.

"Will you be able to sell enough horses to get the ranch going before the prospectors leave?"

"I don't know." Justin sighed. "It's not been going well lately. Even before Miss Dawn arrived. I'm beginning to question whether this is what I'm supposed to be doing."

"Stay the course unless you sense God showing you a new direction." Levi turned the metal piece he was working. "You know the Bible story of David. He was anointed king, but it was years before he took the throne. He experienced distractions, attacks, and times of great need along the way. Just because it's not working out doesn't mean it's not in God's plan."

"I guess." Justin tapped out a second hinge pin. "But how do I know if God is showing me a new direction?"

"That can be difficult to recognize." Levi added a nail to the pile in front of him. "When I need clarity, I seek out your pa, Sam Mooney, and Pastor Turner. They're always willing to pray with me and offer insights. I've helped Sam load his vegetable bins and stock many a shelf because it's easier to share my heart while my hands are moving."

Justin half grinned. "Is that what we're doing here?"

"Nah. We're just clearing our heads with some honest work." A broad smile broke through Levi's short, dark beard. He pointed to the pile of nails on the work table. "Help me finish up this order of nails for Captain Cobb. By the way, has he talked to you lately?"

"No. I guess the captain is busy aboard ship." Beads of sweat cropped up along Justin's upper lip, and he wiped his mouth on his shoulder. "He and his brother, Nute, haven't stayed a single night at the boardinghouse since they docked."

"He dropped by today. I was surprised because I told him I wouldn't have a box of nails ready until tomorrow and the whole order 'til week's end." Levi landed the hammer several times, continuing to shape the piece he was working on. Then he stopped to wipe his brow. "But he wasn't here to check on the project. Showed me a ring that was left behind on *The Resilient*. Thought I might be able to find the owner like Allie and I did with that nativity in '45."

Justin grinned, and his heart warmed at the memory of his part in the nativity search, bringing Allie and Levi together. "What did you tell him?"

"I told him I'm already married, and he ought to give it to you." Levi winked.

Chapter Five

Justin meandered down Main Street on Dolly's back. He studied the bustling figures along the boardwalk. Wasn't long ago he knew every man, woman, and child in this town. Now, he had to search diligently to find a familiar face. Approaching the mercantile, he spotted Sam speaking with a stout, older man out front. Sam caught sight of Justin and pointed. The man turned and, waving his hat, called out. "Mr. Hogue, a moment, please."

Justin hopped down, tied Dolly to the hitching post, and joined the two on the boardwalk.

"I'm in the market for a horse." The man stroked the gray streak down the middle of his dark beard. "I understand you have some for sale."

"Yes, sir." Justin nodded to the dapple gray. "I intended to sell Dolly today, but the buyer never showed. Would you like to have a look at her?"

"Perhaps another horse would be better." The man stroked his beard again. "I don't ride bareback."

"Oh, Dolly is saddle broke. I didn't put one on since I

planned to sell her today. She'll ride saddle and pack fine, though."

"How will she do on a trip across the country?" The man circled the horse, rubbing his hand along Dolly's back from withers to rump.

"She's reliable and calm. Doesn't spook easy." Justin scratched behind Dolly's ears. "I imagine you'll get excited before Dolly does."

The man raised a thick eyebrow.

"Not that you'd spook easy. I'm just saying Dolly will get you where you're going, and you'll enjoy her company."

The man lifted Dolly's lips, checking her teeth. Then, he raised her head and whispered, "Are you ready for an adventure?"

Dolly whinnied, shaking her head up and down. The man laughed. "I'll take her. One seventy-five will do, I suppose?"

Justin's eyes widened. Sam nodded vigorously in the background, mouthing, "Yes, yes."

"I'm only asking one fifty."

"Consider the extra twenty-five payment for the trouble."

"No trouble. We were in town anyway."

Justin took the money, and the man sauntered away with Dolly.

Justin scratched his head and rejoined Sam. "I don't know what to say, Sam. Thank you."

"Me?" Sam asked. "What did I do?"

"You pointed me out to him. Thanks for telling him about me."

"Oh, I didn't tell him about you. He came here asking where to find you." Sam crossed his arms. "I simply pointed him in your direction when I saw you coming into town. A good little blessing, you coming along when you did. Say, what happened to you?"

Justin sighed, glancing down at his disheveled appearance. "I had an unfortunate run-in with one of Conrad's strudels."

Sam laughed. "I've never known you to lose a fight with a strudel."

"It had a woman on the other end of it."

"You fought a woman for one of Conrad's pastries?" Sam chuckled. "I'm sure he would bake some special at the boardinghouse if you asked."

"It was that new female boarder. Miss Dawn was a little distracted coming out of the bakery and smashed the gooey thing into my shirt."

"She's the one who told that gentleman about your horses."

"I wonder where he ran into her. He's strudel-free, so it must not have been near the bakery."

"She approached him at the pool hall." Sam shook his head. "Takes a good bit of gumption for a woman to approach a man in a place like that. It's no place for a lady. I wonder what she was doing there?"

"She's why I missed that sale yesterday." Justin hung his head. "She felt bad about it and promised she'd find another buyer. Guess she's going to any lengths necessary to fulfill that promise."

"Maybe so. That fella said she's been in there before."

"That's odd. I thought she arrived in town just yesterday."

Sam put his hands on his hips and stretched from side to side. "She gets a sweet tea and sits alone for a while. Never spoke to anyone until she heard him mention he was in the market for a horse."

"I'll have to thank her. Still, I wish she hadn't gone to the pool hall." Justin shifted. "I told her not to trouble herself. Eventually, I was bound to make a sale with so many prospectors in town."

Sam hitched his thumb toward the storefront. "I better get back at it. Glad I caught you before that fella skedaddled."

Justin studied his feet a moment. Then, his gaze settled on Sam. He opened his mouth and closed it again.

"Was there something else?" Sam's eyebrow arched.

"Nah. Thanks again, Sam." Justin flipped open his pocket watch. "I've got enough time before supper to move Eliza Dawn's horse to Dolly's old stall. I'll talk to you later."

With a wave, Justin turned to leave.

"Justin. Justin Hogue. Hold up there."

Justin cringed at the familiar booming voice. He turned. Captain Hale Cobb was plowing a line straight for him. Usually, Justin enjoyed Captain Cobb's company. Cobb elevated storytelling to art with his rich voice and lively animation. But if what Levi said was true, Justin preferred to steer clear of Cobb today.

"Glad I caught you in town, my boy." Cobb clapped Justin on the back, unbalancing him. "I need your assistance if I may."

Justin raised his hands to chest level, palms facing Cobb. "I don't have the time to chat just now."

"Nonsense. Won't take but a moment." Cobb folded an arm around Justin's shoulder, pulling an envelope from his shirt pocket with the opposite hand. "Walk with me."

Cobb propelled Justin down Main Street toward the riverfront. Pushing the envelope into Justin's hand, he kept talking. "I've got this letter meant for one of those prospector fellows. Seems like you're just the man to deliver it for me."

"A letter?" Justin exhaled a sigh of relief at the envelope resting in his hand instead of the ring Levi had mentioned. "That's easy enough. Why don't you drop it by the post office?"

"Tried that. They won't take it." Cobb released Justin and pointed to the corner of the envelope. "It doesn't have that new-fangled, gummed stamp. Plus, the writing is badly smudged. No idea who the recipient is."

Justin chuckled at Cobb's reference to the five-cent stamp. Those stamps had been in use for two years now. Cobb's view of them as 'new-fangled' revealed his penchant for things staying the same. "How do you know it's intended for one of the prospectors?"

"Some fella gave it to Nute when we arrived. Carried it across four states." Cobb wagged his finger in the air. "He talked to someone in town who told him prospectors were arriving on the steamboats. So, he came to the river, and I guess my addle-brained brother was the first person he met, so he turned the letter over to that pinhead."

Justin closed his eyes and shook his head slowly. Nute wasn't known for his sharpness or attention to detail. But he was strong as an ox and determined to be helpful. "I don't reckon Nute got any more information from that fella?"

"You know Nute." Cobb shrugged.

"Yes, I do." Justin stared at the envelope. "Captain Cobb, I don't have time to get involved. I still have six horses to sell before these prospectors leave town."

"Great." Cobb slapped Justin on the back. "Take this letter. Show it around while you're conducting business. See who knows something."

"I guess I could ask around about it." Justin's chest tightened as he conceded. "But I'm not making any extra effort."

"Sure, sure." Captain Cobb dug into his shirt pocket. Pulling out a ring, he shoved it into Justin's hand. "This ring goes with the letter. Might not show that 'round right away. Somebody's apt to claim the letter to get their hands on it."

A lump caught in Justin's throat. Opening his fingers, his eyes widened. The piece of sterling silver jewelry featured a cameo with a relief of thistle. Justin's jaw dropped.

"It's a beaut, ain't it?"

"I can't be responsible for this. Or the letter." Justin stammered. "Finding the owner of this ring is much different from simply showing around a letter. That may be a precious keepsake. The owner needs to be found, and I don't have that kind of time."

Justin held the letter and the ring out to Captain Cobb.

Cobb pushed it back. "Son, I'm putting *The Resilient* back on the water tomorrow bright and early. You've got more time than I do. Find the owner or put it in the lost and found. Tell your pa I'm sorry I didn't get by for a visit this trip. Oh, and let Levi know I'll pick up my metalwork on my return trip."

Cobb disappeared as quickly as he had appeared.

Justin stared slack-jawed at the items in his hand. Pursing his lips, he folded the envelope, putting it and the ring in his breast pocket. He flicked open his pocket watch. There was still time enough before supper to resettle Bonnie into her new stall and get a fresh change of clothes. He would deal with the letter and ring later.

Chapter Six

Eliza Dawn scrawled words across the page quickly, capturing images that flashed through her mind. She had made a vital error in the pool hall earlier, judging those businessmen based on their appearance. She expected they would be more respectful of her than the raucous Scots. Unfortunately, her blunder landed her in a clutch she might not have escaped had it not been for Ewan MacKinnon acting as her sweetheart.

She scolded herself in her rush to judgment. Having been judged harshly, she knew how soul-crushing and debilitating it could be. It was the very reason she chose to live such a secretive life. And, though she vowed never to judge as she'd been judged, she'd broken that vow when she assessed the characters and dynamics of the two groups of men today.

Completing her summary of the day's events, Eliza Dawn closed the journal and pulled a few pieces of plain paper from her bag. She tapped the pages on the crate table. The directive of Mrs. Bly, her finishing school instructor, rang in her ears, "Always use perfectly plain paper, thick, smooth, and white."

This paper wasn't the quality Eliza Dawn preferred, but it was the finest quality she could come by this far west. So, pen in hand, she wrote, *In Pursuit of a Dream, Adventures of the Forty-niners, Part Two*.

At fifteen, she was devastated when her childhood best friend moved to Charlotte, North Carolina. But it was Eleanor's letters that first inspired her to write about the forty-niners. With Eleanor's blessing, Eliza Dawn had mailed her first piece featuring her friend's family story of tear-filled goodbyes to father and son. Dear Eleanor even suggested the pen name Edward Dodd. They were both shocked when newspapers in Charleston and Savannah picked up the piece and wanted more from the savvy gentleman writer.

After filling a couple of pages, she laid the papers across her makeshift bed to allow the ink to dry. She grabbed an envelope and a stamp from her bag. She'd post the article the next time she was in town to make her east coast newspaper deadlines. She was surprised when *The Courier* in Charleston and *Savannah Georgian* accepted her first article and requested a second installment. Fortunately, submitting the story by post instead of a face-to-face interview made it easy to pass herself off by her pen name.

Eliza Dawn folded a few more sheets of paper in quarters. Tearing them at the folds, she then stacked the pieces neatly together. Using a sewing needle, she poked through the layers in one corner, then the opposite corner, and finally used a winding clamp to widen the holes. Finding a length of ribbon, she threaded it through the openings. It was a suitable notepad. She'd have to wear her apron with the pocket tomorrow afternoon.

She fingered the hem of her skirt. Eventually, she would have to give more attention to her attire. Unfortunately, she was so busy finding a buyer for Justin's horse, observing prospectors wherever she could, sewing shirts, and writing she didn't have much free time. Rebecca had offered to loan Eliza Dawn some of her clothes, but she suspected Rebecca didn't have much either.

She rummaged through the lost and found. How all these belongings were left behind on the steamboats was mind-boggling. She fingered a collection of satin hair ribbons lying next to a wooden hairbrush in the tray of a steamer trunk, items easily misplaced and forgotten. But there were also oversized pieces, like furniture or entire chests. Who would leave such things behind? Yet the inattention of others might provide her with something more fitting to wear.

Pushing her way through to a wardrobe, she opened it. She wrinkled her nose at the musty smell. A bonnet caught her eye, and she picked it up. Blush-colored ribbon formed broad loops behind a wide brim trimmed in ivory lace. She smiled as she rubbed the ribbon between her fingers. It reminded her of a bonnet her mother had given her, one she'd left behind when she fled South Carolina. A lump caught in her throat. She returned the hat to its shelf and closed the wardrobe.

Turning her attention to a nearby trunk, she hoisted the heavy lid. Her breath caught as she viewed a collection of baby things. A quilted layette basket held a cream silk dressing gown, lace bonnet, quilted baby blanket, and rattle. Pain swept through her chest, her fingers hovering over the items.

There was a knock at the door, followed by Justin's voice. "Miss Dawn, are you in here?"

She jumped, dropping the lid of the trunk with a thud. "One moment, please."

Edging her way through the labyrinth of forgotten treasures, she reached her crate bed and quickly gathered the papers. She stowed them in her bag and shoved the bag behind the crates. After one more check to see nothing appeared out of place, she opened the door.

"Mr. Hogue, I wasn't expecting you."

"I heard a thump. Is everything all right?" Justin peered around the door.

Sincere concern graced his soft gray eyes. She hesitated to respond, unsure how he'd react to her nosing around the lost and found. He leaned uncomfortably close, surveying the room. She inhaled a slow, measured breath. The scent of sweet citrus, cedar, and leather filled her nostrils. Exhaling roughly, she pulled away from the door, away from him.

"Are you out of breath? Did something fall?"

"No." Eliza Dawn waved her arm across the cramped room. "I was sorting through clothes in these old trunks, searching for something better suited to my height. I know Rebecca offered the loan of some of her things, but I didn't want to trouble her."

He nodded, smiling. "Rebecca is the reason I'm here. She sent me to tell you supper will be ready soon."

He was no longer wearing evidence of her earlier mishap. The clean striped shirt he now wore made his gray eyes appear bluer.

"I'll be down momentarily."

"Don't be too long." Justin patted his belly. "I'm starving, and Rebecca will hold supper until everyone is at the table."

"I won't be long."

Pushing the door almost closed, she peered at Justin through the crack until he reached the top of the stairs. She pressed the wood until the latch clicked, turning her attention to a nearby crate. Lifting its cockeyed lid, she inspected its contents, hoping to find a suitable garment.

Across the room, a tuft of blue fabric from the sewing basket taunted her. It had been her nemesis from the first ragged seam she'd sewn. Yet, it was the best cover she could muster for her newspaper work. And here she was with five more shirts to make. She shook her head.

Rummaging through the crate, she spied a lovely blue print with small pale flowers. She checked the length by holding the skirt in place with one arm and the top with the other. Why did she have to be so tall? It hit two inches above her ankle, but it was a far cry better than the plaid she'd been wearing. It would have to do.

There was another rap at the door. She tossed the skirt on the bed. Still holding the top in place, she cracked the door open. Viewing Justin through the gap, she widened the opening.

"Yes?"

His breath caught. "What's this?"

"I found it in one of these crates." She folded the top over her arm. "It's a good two inches above the ankle, but the longest garment I've found."

"It sets off your eyes."

Eliza Dawn glanced away, and Justin cleared his throat.

"I forgot to tell you I sold Dolly today." Justin leaned against the door frame, elbow crooked above his head. A grin lightened his usually serious countenance. "To a man with a gray streak down the middle of his beard. You wouldn't happen to know how he learned about my horses, would you?"

"Word of mouth, perhaps." Her mouth went dry, and she shrugged. "Justin Hogue and his magnificent stock are the talk of the town."

"Listen,"—his face grew more serious—"that man told Sam you'd been at the pool hall before. It's not a safe place for you."

She stepped back, increasing the distance between them. Had Justin heard of the entanglement with the bearded man's associate? She rubbed her back, the satisfied smirk on Big Jim's ruddy face as he wedged her against the table's edge fresh in her mind. Surely, the older man hadn't mentioned the unsavory details during his business transaction with Justin. She swallowed hard.

Justin's jaw flexed. "Men tend to get unfavorable ideas about women who frequent places like that. Things can be pretty unruly here at the edge of Indian Territory. A lot of rough characters in town. Your safety is more important than my business."

Eliza Dawn cleared her throat. "I wanted to help. I felt so badly about making you late."

"I appreciate that. Honestly, I do." He leaned closer. "But you shouldn't put yourself at risk to help me sell a horse."

"It was no trouble. Really."

"He offered one seventy-five before I even quoted him a price." Justin's eyes glimmered. "That's twenty-five more than I expected."

She smiled and nodded. "Dolly is worth every penny."

"Said the extra was for the trouble. Not sure what he meant by that since Dolly and I were riding through town anyhow." Justin lightly squeezed her shoulder. "No more pool halls, in any case. Men in places like that forget their manners. I couldn't live with myself if I put you in harm's way."

"I appreciate your concern, but I can handle myself." She offered the assurance more for her benefit than his. Her job as a journalist required her to place herself in sometimes uncomfortable or extraordinary circumstances to follow these prospectors on their journey. If she planned to carry on her observations, she needed to frequent the same places they did, including pool halls, gambling establishments, and saloons.

"I'm sure you can." He smiled. "Meet you downstairs."

Eliza Dawn shut the door gently behind him, unsure what to make of his concern. Though it seemed genuine, she'd learned any interest a man showed toward a woman had more to do with business than a woman's personal well-being. If she explored Justin's motives, would she find an underlying connection to his bottom line? Still, the warm tone in his voice lingered.

What was wrong with her today? Casting judgment on strangers, allowing soft gray eyes and an alluring scent to trickle through a crack in her hardened façade. She'd have to do a better job of keeping up her defenses. She shook her head. It wouldn't do for a woman in her position to be swept away by her emotions. *A hearty meal and a good night's rest, that's what I need.*

Chapter Seven

Eliza Dawn descended the back stairway of the boardinghouse. The smell of freshly baked bread made her stomach rumble. Muffled voices caused her to pause at the bottom of the stairs near the kitchen pantry. Justin and Rebecca's familiar voices dotted the exchange, but a third voice, a smooth baritone, carried the conversation. Listening momentarily, she identified the voice as the elder Mr. Hogue's.

"Son, I don't understand why you agreed to board that woman. When I asked you to deal with this—"

"You didn't ask me." Justin's unyielding tone challenged. "Rebecca did."

"You know what I mean." Mr. Hogue's clipped words perforated the air. "When I asked you to deal with this situation, I presumed you understood we only board men. When have you ever known us to house a woman here who wasn't family?"

"Amelia Grace." Rebecca chimed in. "Amelia Grace stayed here for nearly a month."

"She was a teenager accidentally separated from her family at the wharf." Mr. Hogue's tone flattened. "She stayed in the room with you girls. So, we didn't have to provide a room dedicated to her."

"Miss Dawn doesn't have a room dedicated solely to her." Justin's voice was thick with tension. "She shares her room with every trinket ever abandoned on one of those steamboats. She's sleeping on a bed of crates and a pallet of blankets."

"That's exactly what I'm talking about. How will it impact our good name if word gets out that we didn't even provide a decent bed? And this business Mooney told me about her keeping company at the pool hall. How will that affect our reputation?"

Eliza Dawn grimaced. A knot formed in the pit of her stomach. She hadn't intended to create trouble for Justin, but she needed a safe place to stay for her and Bonnie.

"She felt terrible for making me miss my sale. That's all." Justin launched a defense. "She was searching for a new buyer, and she found one. I talked to her and don't think she'll frequent the pool hall anymore."

Eliza Dawn peeked around the corner. Mr. Hogue stood in front of the kitchen table, arms crossed. Justin faced his father squarely, arms crossed. The scene was like a street stand-off without the guns. Rebecca stood near the kitchen counter, twisting a towel.

"This horse business," Mr. Hogue gruffed. "That's another thing I don't understand. You could take over the boardinghouse business. Or, with my connections, I could get you onto the steamboats. Cobb would love to have you. Yet you are still playing at this horse mess."

"I know, I know. I could follow Levi into smithing too." Justin sighed in exasperation. "But I want to make my own way. I love working with horses. That's been my job since I was fourteen."

"Your job has been to help with boardinghouse chores as

we've seen fit. If your mother was here, she could talk sense into you."

Justin threw up his hands, turned away from his father, and paced a few steps toward the pantry. Eliza Dawn ducked into the recess, pressing her back firmly to the wall. Her heart thumped. She flattened her hand against her chest. Had he spotted her?

"If Ma were here, she would have talked you into boarding Miss Dawn, and you know it."

Eliza Dawn snuck another peek. Justin faced his father again, rubbing his forehead. A heavy silence hung in the air between the two men. She drew a breath deep into her chest. Without even trying, she made difficulties wherever she went. Here she was complicating the relationship between father and son. Perhaps it was a good thing she couldn't have children.

"Pa, you know it's true." Rebecca's soft voice cut the silence. "Ma helped everyone."

"I know it's easier to board only men or women." Justin's stance relaxed, hands on his hips, arms hinged loosely at the elbows. "I know you're more comfortable boarding men. But I believe Miss Dawn needs a haven right now. She doesn't need to be held accountable for our reputation, and she doesn't need to be judged."

"Ma would say we have an opportunity to minister to her hurts." Rebecca gestured with the dish towel. "And she's got 'em, I can tell."

"I don't think I can do that." Mr. Hogue's surly tone softened.

"Pa, we're not asking you to." Justin stared at his shoes. "Just help us provide a safe place for her to lodge."

Eliza Dawn pressed herself hard against the wall, a lone tear tracing down her cheek. She swallowed against the lump in her throat.

Their footsteps faded as the trio moved into the dining room. Wiping her cheeks and fanning her face, she waited a few moments before joining them. Then, entering the dining room, she sat next to Rebecca on one side and their brother Simon on the other. Justin sat across from her, elbows on the table and hands tented.

Once everyone was seated, Mr. Hogue offered the blessing. Immediately following his "amen," the clatter of utensils and comfortable chatter filled the air. Justin offered Eliza Dawn a tight-lipped smile as he passed the potatoes.

"Did I tell you I was able to move Bonnie today?"

She shook her head.

"Now that Dolly's sold, there's a stall for Bonnie in the stable."

Eliza Dawn shoved food around her plate with her fork. Laying down the utensil, she shifted the basket of rolls before her and rearranged the salt and pepper shakers. She bumped Simon's elbow and murmured an apology.

Perhaps it would be better for Justin and Rebecca if she moved out. She should ask Ewan about joining the Scottish camp. A few wives and children were among them, and they might be willing to take her in since they had already adopted her as their "pet."

"Miss Dawn? Did you hear me?" Justin interrupted her thoughts.

"*Hmm*? I'm sorry. I'm a bit distracted."

She bumped Simon again. She dipped her chin, indicating the disappearing space between them. Simon grinned under a mop of blond curls and shifted in his seat.

"Aren't you hungry? You haven't eaten a bite." Rebecca placed her hand lightly on Eliza Dawn's wrist. "Are you okay?"

"Oh, it's nothing. I've taken several new orders for shirts." She made tracks in the potatoes. "I'm just thinking of how to organize my schedule to complete them on time."

"You ought to have more time now you've finished helping me." Justin winked. "Pass me those field peas?"

Simon grabbed the peas and held them close to Eliza Dawn's face. Pulling her head back, she took the big bowl in both hands. A corner of her mouth turned up as she thanked Simon.

"Perhaps I will." She hefted the bowl across the table. "What were you saying about Bonnie?"

"Now that I've sold Dolly, I've moved Bonnie into the stable." Justin buttered his second roll. "Her stall is between Dale and Hershey. She's pleased as pie to have the company."

She smiled absent-mindedly.

"Are you certain you're all right?" Justin asked. "I imagined you'd be delighted to learn she's in a proper stall now."

Simon edged up under her elbow again. She shot him a warning glance, and he centered himself on his seat.

"Oh, of course, I am." Eliza Dawn took a sip of tea. Then, she leaned closer to Justin and Rebecca, whispering. "I'd like to talk with the two of you after everyone leaves."

The last of the diners left the table, wandering off to places unknown. Eliza Dawn rose to help as Rebecca cleared the supper dishes.

"Sit, sit. I'll get these. No chores. It's part of our agreement, remember?" Rebecca winked. "I'll fetch the strudel you brought home."

Justin took his attention off his supper plate. "Strudel? What kind did you bring?"

"Muscadine, peach, and," Eliza Dawn blushed, remembering the earlier mess on Justin's shirt, "the caramel apple with raisins."

"*Hmm.*" Justin pulled a face. "I don't know if we should chance it. I'm mighty fond of this shirt."

Her cheeks grew hotter. Justin patted his chest, and they both laughed.

Rebecca rejoined them with a platter of strudel and three dessert plates. She set the delicate plates in front of them. "What did I miss?"

"Oh, nothing. Miss Dawn got me into a sticky situation earlier today." Justin's playful manner set Eliza Dawn at ease about their earlier encounter. Perhaps she might find herself on steady ground with Justin if she could avoid sparking tensions between the two Mr. Hogues.

"I hope you don't mind using Ma's fine china. She and I used these for our evening chats after everyone cleared out of the dining room." Rebecca ran her finger around the edge of her plate. "Pa collected some very nice things for Ma on his steamboat travels."

"What did you want to talk to us about?" Justin asked.

Eliza Dawn blinked. "I'd like to make some changes to my living arrangements."

Chapter Eight

"Changes?" Justin exchanged a questioning glance with Rebecca. "Exactly what kind of changes do you have in mind?"

"You can pay a dollar fifty like the men if needed." A pillar of steam rose from the teapot as Rebecca filled Eliza Dawn's teacup. "For that matter, you could board here for the same price as Bradley House."

"I agree." Justin cut off a bite-sized piece of strudel with his fork. He eyed her intently. Her jaw set, shoulders pulled back, she was the picture of determination. "I know it may take time to get the word out to customers about where to find you. But we can work with you if you're not getting enough business."

Rebecca reached for Eliza Dawn's hand, and the somberness lifted slightly from Eliza Dawn's countenance. She smiled, squeezing Rebecca's hand.

"Oh no. It's not that." Pulling back, she rubbed her hands together. "My presence imposes a burden on the two of you. That was not my intention. It's time for me to find other accommodations."

"No, it's no burden." Rebecca situated a napkin in her lap.

"It's been nice having you. I know you hadn't planned on doing any chores, but you helped with biscuits yesterday and cleared the breakfast mess this morning. And I've enjoyed our chats."

"I only helped to have one of the tables for a cutting surface this morning."

"I don't care." Rebecca shot Justin a pleading glance. "You can't go."

He let the deep, sweet, slightly tart flavor of the rich, reddish-purple filling coat his tongue before coming to Rebecca's aid with a response. He longed for Ma's presence and learned savoring the tastes and scents he associated with her was the surest way to stay connected to her. Ma always knew how to help people, whereas he had more horse sense than people sense.

"I don't know what's prompted this." Justin put his fork down and pushed his plate back. "If it's about my shirt, you didn't cost me that sale today. Sometimes, buyers don't show up. That's business."

"Oh, I know that." Eliza Dawn fingered the handle of her teacup. "Occasionally, someone orders a shirt and never comes for it. Unfortunately, that is how business goes sometimes."

"Have we said or done something that makes you think we're put out with you?" He'd been too abrupt with her outside the bakery. Ma would have been disappointed in his attitude since she arrived.

"No."

"Then what is it?" Justin rapped his knuckles on the table in front of her. "Because we'll talk it out. You're not leaving unless we all agree it's the right thing. For all of us."

The pools of blue in her eyes deepened. "I know my presence creates tension between you and your father."

Justin cocked his head to the side.

"I was in the stairway before supper."

With a long sigh, Justin stiffened and straightened in his

chair like a plank, crossing his arms and feet. Rebecca gripped his shoulder, mirroring the tightness in his chest.

"Miss Dawn, you didn't create that tension. I assure you, it was there long before your arrival."

"Pa is struggling with Ma's loss." Rebecca released her grip on Justin. She picked up her teacup and fixed her gaze on its contents. "It has nothing to do with you. Not really."

"I know the tension between Pa and me is uncomfortable for everyone around us." Justin leaned forward, holding Eliza Dawn's gaze. "But if you can tolerate it, you should stay. Are we in agreement?"

Eliza Dawn's probing blue eyes held Justin's gaze for a long moment. Unwavering, he maintained eye contact. He had to convince her she wasn't responsible for what was happening between him and Pa. He'd created that divide when he'd left Ma's side moments before her death.

Eliza Dawn drew a long sip of tea. "Only if you're certain."

Justin glimpsed Rebecca's nodding head from the corner of his eye.

"We have an agreement. You will remain at Hogue House." He patted the table. "Now, I've got work to do before turning in. You ladies have a good evening."

Justin cleared his dishes, taking them to the kitchen. He glanced toward the dining room. Had he done enough to convince Eliza Dawn to stay? Ma would have gone above and beyond to welcome her. Perhaps he'd better give it a little more effort.

Justin grabbed his hat from the finial on the back stair rail. A light *tat, tat, tat* echoed behind him. He turned at the surprisingly familiar sound of Eliza Dawn's footsteps.

"Mr. Hogue, wait. You dropped something." Eliza Dawn held a grubby white envelope in her hand. "What's this?"

"It's a letter Captain Cobb asked me to deliver." Justin gripped the envelope, but she didn't turn loose.

"The letter I've heard some of the prospectors mention?"

"They've heard about it already?"

"I believe a few have, yes." She tugged at her ear. "I overheard some businessmen speaking about it. I was unaware you had it, but they mentioned someone was searching for the recipient of an undeliverable correspondence. What gave them the impression you're a steamboat hand? How long have you been searching?"

"Not me. Nute." Justin pressed his palm to his forehead. "He's Captain Cobb's brother. There's no telling how many people he ran his mouth to before the captain gave me this letter."

Eliza Dawn leaned close, tugging at the post. "May I?"

Justin hesitated, glancing at the letter, then at Eliza Dawn. He rubbed his whiskered chin. Slowly, he released his grip.

"*Hmm.*" Eliza Dawn ran her finger across the words. "It's in rough shape. It's understandable why delivery has been hindered."

"Captain Cobb carried it to the post office. They wouldn't take it since it doesn't have a stamp. But, of course, it's unlikely they could have delivered it anyway, as unreadable as the name is."

Eliza Dawn thumped the envelope. "I spend a significant amount of time around the prospectors."

"You do."

She eyed him warily. "I'm curious."

"About what?"

"Were you going to ask me to help?"

"Honestly, it crossed my mind, but I worried you'd spend more time at the pool hall if you knew about this letter." Justin toed the floor. "I felt bad about you spending time there to help me."

Eliza Dawn pursed her lips. "No matter." She brightened. "Plenty of prospectors visit Mooney's Mercantile for supplies.

You could simply tack it to the board outside the store. Someone is bound to recognize the handwriting."

"Won't work."

"I don't see why not."

Justin stared at her, muscles tense. He flipped open his pocket watch, glanced at it, and nested it again. Why couldn't he walk away? He could bow out and get to work if she had been anyone else. Sighing, he dug around in his vest pocket. He unfisted his hand to reveal the ring.

"I can't leave this on the board. Anybody might take it." Justin held it out to her. "It's to accompany the letter."

Eliza Dawn sucked in a quick breath and snatched it from his hand. Turning the sterling silver ring over and over, she moved to the kitchen table. Justin followed her. Pulling out a chair, she laid the envelope on the table and studied the ring. She ran her finger over the inside of the band. "Did you notice this?"

"No." Justin leaned over her shoulder for a better view. The letters *MSM* were engraved inside the band. "Could be someone's initials."

"What's this?" Rebecca nodded as she entered the room with the remaining dishes from the dining room.

"Oh, it's nothing." Justin reached for the ring, but Eliza Dawn pulled it away.

"*Tsk. Tsk.*" Eliza Dawn shook her finger at him. "A steamboat captain has entrusted a small treasure with a mysterious letter to your brother and charged him with delivering it to one of the prospectors."

"Which prospector?" Rebecca set the dishes in the washtub.

"No idea. Letter's damaged." Justin shrugged. "Information is unreadable."

"Captain Cobb gave it to you?" Rebecca sat next to Eliza Dawn at the table. "So, it's like the great nativity search of '45?"

"Nativity search?"

"Our friend, Levi, was caught up in the search for owners

of this nativity set that appeared in town just before Christmas." Rebecca beamed. "It's how he met his wife. Anyway, they searched the town over for the owners. That little nativity set inspired many of the town's Christmas traditions."

"What a beautiful story." Eliza Dawn held the ring close to Rebecca, pointing to the letters inside the band. "We've just discovered this engraving."

"Is it a clue that might help deliver it to its rightful owner?"

"Not likely." Justin bristled at Rebecca's notice. It would be tough enough to keep Eliza Dawn at bay without Rebecca's added curiosity spurring her on. Justin reached across Eliza Dawn, taking the ring back. "These probably aren't the initials of the letter's recipient."

"Then who?" Rebecca picked up the envelope, straining to make out the name.

"Could be the sender's initials." Justin dropped the ring back into his pocket. "Perhaps a family member."

"If it belongs to a family member, it could be generations old. They might be the initials of someone long deceased, making it more difficult for us to link it to someone in the present." Eliza Dawn pulled Rebecca's hand close, squinting at the words scrawled across the envelope. "I wish we could make out more of the writing."

Justin stiffened at Eliza Dawn's use of the words "us" and "we." He was on a short timeline to sell his horses. Having her caught up in this letter ordeal wouldn't do.

"What if it doesn't belong to a family member?" Rebecca returned the envelope to the table.

"What do you mean?" Justin asked.

"I don't know." Rebecca shrugged.

"It could belong to one of the forty-niner's sweethearts." Eliza Dawn turned to Justin, their noses nearly tip to tip. She sipped a breath and quickly returned her attention to the ring.

"What if one of these fellows proposed before he left, and this ring represents the answer?"

"Would that be a 'no'?" Justin pushed himself back from his perch over her shoulder. "Because I don't want to be the one to deliver that kind of news."

Eliza Dawn cleared her throat. "The fact is it could be anything. The ring could belong to anyone."

"You're right." Justin sighed. Straightening, he took the letter and the ring, shoving them into his vest pocket. "More pressing is I've got horses to sell. I don't have time to pursue this letter business."

"Let me help."

"Yes, Justin. Let her help you." Rebecca's tongue-in-cheek tone set Justin on edge. "Levi helped Allie, and look how that turned out."

He shot her a warning glare. Did she have designs on matchmaking? He set his jaw. She knew he couldn't be bothered with that right now. That should be the furthest thing from her mind since Dr. Ewing went west without her.

"I'm sure Miss Dawn doesn't have time now, do you?" Justin avoided eye contact with Eliza Dawn. "You're probably overwhelmed with your sewing business."

"Well, what will you do with the letter and ring if neither of us has time?"

"I reckon I'll put it in the lost and found room."

"I cannot bear the idea of that ring abandoned in there." She sighed. "It might be different if groups of prospectors had already left, but no one plans to leave for several more days. Ask Mr. Mooney if he'll keep it at the shop."

Justin shook his head. "Folks are pocketing items from the store left and right. Sam wouldn't want to risk someone walking off with the ring."

"He could keep the letter then."

"He has no more time to show it off than we do."

"Fine then." Eliza Dawn held out her flattened palm. "Give it to me. I will make time."

"No." Justin pressed his hand over his heart, guarding his vest pocket. "I guess we'll both have to make time because you're not doing this alone. But right now, I have work to finish up before bed."

Chapter Nine

"You asked her?"

"Of course, I asked her, Justin." Rebecca tied off the end of the thread and patted Ollie's middle. "There you go. That button is not coming off. Go ask Martie if she and Nellie are ready."

"And she declined?" Justin frowned.

"She said she's uncomfortable around 'church people,' as she calls them." Rebecca poked the sewing needle into the pin cushion and placed it into the basket. "Edie, come here and bring me those bows."

"We go to church. Does that mean she's uncomfortable with us?" Justin paced in front of her.

"No, of course not." Rebecca fastened a bow to the end of little Edie's plaited pigtail. "Stop squirming and put your dress tail down." Rebecca straightened Edie's shoulders and pushed her hand free of her hem. She affixed a bow to the end of the other pigtail. "She may be uncomfortable with you but has good reason to be. Doesn't she?"

Justin hung his head.

"You weren't very cordial her first day here. And, from what

I witnessed, you were only slightly better yesterday. So, if you want her to go to church with us, perhaps you should ask her yourself." Rebecca patted Edie on the behind. "Be a dear and go sit. We'll be going soon."

Justin's feet were stuck to the spot. Rebecca turned her full attention to him. The angle of her chin and stern eyes remarkably resembled Ma's no-nonsense warning glare.

"Go on. Get to it." Rebecca pointed to the front staircase. "And tell Cordelia to rustle up the older children. My lands, getting this family ready to go is much more difficult without Ivajohn."

"What about Pa?"

"In bed. Didn't come to breakfast. Again." She shrugged and folded her hands in her lap. "Would you check on him while you're up there?"

Approaching the foot of the stairs, Justin paused and glanced back at Rebecca. She silently reinforced her command with a nod of her head. The expectation in her eyes weighed heavily on him. She wanted him to talk to their father, to make things better. But he didn't know how. His father had lost the only woman he'd ever loved, and it was his fault. How could Pa ever forgive him for that?

He doubted he would do any better speaking to Miss Dawn. Rebecca had appeared in the bunkhouse before bed to give him her two cents. She scolded him for not being more hospitable. Being welcoming required a certain amount of openness and vulnerability. He wasn't sure he was ready to invite a new woman into his life or their home.

Justin trudged up the last few steps and paused, his gaze drifting from one door to another. Which should he knock on first? Neither choice was favorable. He took a deep breath and stepped down the hall. Then, landing three light knocks, he twisted the knob.

"Pa?" The word caught in Justin's dry throat. Allowing a

moment for his eyes to adjust to the dark room, he awaited a response.

"Told Rebecca I'd be down."

"Oh. I guess she didn't hear you." Justin's eyes settled on the lump in the bed. "We'll be ready to leave soon. Rebecca and Cordelia are rounding up the younger kids now."

"Five minutes."

Justin measured his breaths as he rubbed his thumb to and fro across the smooth surface of the door knob. "Pa, if you want to stay home, I understand. There are days I feel like I can't get out of bed—"

"Five minutes. Shut the door."

Justin gently pulled the door until it latched. Leaning his back against the door, he turned his face upward, eyes closed. *Lord—*

His heart ached profoundly, and he wanted to pour it out to God, but he had no idea what to say. He shook himself free of the moment and moved down the hall to Eliza Dawn's door. He glanced back to his father's room. Settling his gaze on the door before him, he took a deep breath. *This can't go any worse, right?*

He knocked softly. The door cracked open.

"Yes?"

Eliza Dawn's startlingly blue eyes blinked back at him. Her hair in loose waves framed her face and softened her high cheekbones. Why had he knocked on her door? He couldn't remember. *Speak. Or breathe. Don't just stand here.*

"Did you need something, Mr. Hogue?"

"I, uh—" Justin cleared his throat. "I wanted to invite you to church with us this morning."

"It's considerate of you to ask." As she closed the door, she caught the toe of Justin's boot. "But I have other plans. If you'll excuse me."

Justin followed her line of sight down to his toes. He pulled his boot back, caught her gaze, and smiled weakly. She responded with a smirk.

"What are you wearing?" He squinted at the wide-legged bottoms. Though the garment had two legs, it gave the illusion of a skirt.

"These, Mr. Hogue, are my riding pants. I'm spending the day with Bonnie. We're going for a ramble later."

"Do you think that's appropriate for a Sunday? Or any day?"

"That is precisely why I avoid church people." Eliza Dawn's scowl bored into him. "They are judgmental. Except for, perhaps, Rebecca. So far, she is unlike any other churchgoers I've ever met."

"Miss Dawn, I—" Justin rested his hand on the doorknob, head low. He closed his eyes. "Oh Lord, I've done this all wrong."

"Justin, help me." Cordelia emerged from the younger girls' bedroom, breathing hard. She had Ollie by the collar and Nellie by the hand. "Martie, c'mon. You look fine."

His muscles tensed at the tone of Cordelia's voice. Raising a finger to Eliza Dawn, he wrapped his other arm around Ollie's middle, drawing the ten-year-old close. "Please forgive me. Can we talk again later?"

"It's not necessary."

"Please."

She nodded and motioned for him to take Ollie down the hall.

As Justin and Rebecca finished loading everyone in the wagon, Pa appeared. His clothes were rumpled, and his vest was unevenly buttoned. Rebecca gave Justin a sideways glance, and he shrugged. Pa was going to church. What more did she want?

Ma's absence never stood out as starkly as it did on Sunday mornings. The music was missing from their lives. Ma's soft humming as she readied the family and heartfelt hymns floating on the breeze as she sang in the wagon. They arrived, eight

Hogues in the buckboard and Justin on his horse, Sugar Blue. They unloaded and filed into the church pew, filling a row.

Justin made eye contact with Rebecca to check they were all right. She patted Pa's hand. On Rebecca's lap sat Little Edie, wild strands angling from her braids. Only Ma could coax her still long enough for perfectly neat plaits. Nellie sat next to Rebecca. They knew better than to let Ollie and Nellie sit together. It was best to divide and conquer the twins.

Next to Nellie was thirteen-year-old Martie, who kept peeking across the aisle at Tommy Weston. Justin would ensure she sat beside him and Ollie on Easter Sunday. He smiled as Simon patted her on the head. Was he being the protective older brother? Cordelia faced the front, stiffly focused on the choir. He knew from experience Ollie's fiddling was scraping her nerves. He wrapped his arm around his youngest brother and placed his hand over the boy's fidgeting fingers.

They filled their usual roles, older siblings taking responsibility for younger siblings. Pa sat stoically at the end, as was his custom. It was the same, yet not. Something was ... off. Ma's absence left a hole bigger than the space left on their pew.

Breathe in. Breathe out. He closed his eyes. He'd never had to remind himself to breathe before. Opening his eyes, he forced himself to focus on the pulpit. Levi stood behind the podium, thumbing at the pages of his Bible. Justin had forgotten his friend had agreed to fill in while the pastor and Ivajohn took a group of missionaries north. He tuned in to Levi's words.

"Do not forget to entertain strangers because, in doing so, you might be entertaining angels." Levi came down from the pulpit. "It always makes me uneasy when Pastor Turner asks me to fill in. It took a long time for me to feel like part of the community. I carried many hurts with me, and I was afraid to open my heart to the town, to Allie." Levi motioned to his young bride, sitting in the front row.

"But you were patient with me. You kept drawing me in. You

included me in your town life, your celebrations and tragedies, your traditions and new endeavors. I finally realized God had a place for me here." He folded his arms across his chest. "I know the past months have been challenging. You've been overwhelmed by all the newcomers. Some of them dress differently than you. Some speak differently. Some have different customs. Many come bearing wounds from their past. Choose someone, just one person, and be welcoming to them. And then be welcoming to another ... and another. Be obedient in small acts of hospitality, and trust God is working far beyond you."

Levi's words were humble and gentle, yet they stung Justin's heart. The disappointment in Eliza Dawn's eyes during their earlier conversation ate at him. He tapped Cordelia, and she folded her arm around Ollie. He slipped out of his seat, down the aisle, and out the front door. A cool breeze washed over him, and he drank it in. *Lord, I can do better. Help me do better.*

Justin waited beside the wagon and Blue as the last hymn's final notes faded. Ollie ran to meet him, followed by an exasperated Cordelia. Simon rounded the corner, clutching Martie's hand.

"Ollie can sit by me next week." Simon gave Martie a slight shove toward the wagon. Then he leaned close to Justin and whispered, jerking his head toward Martie. "She should sit near the window on the other side of you. As far from Tommy Weston as possible. I'd hate to have to hurt that boy."

Justin grinned in agreement. "I'll keep that in mind."

"Slow down, Edie." Rebecca hitched her skirt, trying to keep up with the other girls. "Nellie, grab her hand before she falls."

Justin crossed to Edie in long strides. Sweeping her into the air with a toss, he caught her in his arms and settled her on his hip. The youngest Hogue squealed with delight. Justin kissed her forehead. She tickled his nose with the end of her pigtail as he hoisted her over the side of the buckboard into Simon's lap.

"You forgot this." Rebecca handed Justin his Bible. She extended her hand. "Help me up."

"Justin, I wanted to catch you." Levi sprinted toward them. "Could you have dinner with Allie and me?"

"I don't know." Justin scratched his head. "Stepped on my toes a bit, Preacher. You write that sermon just for me?"

"It's what God put on my heart." Levi gave Justin's shoulder a solid pat. "You know I have to address it in myself before I preach it."

"I know." Justin smiled. Levi's new habit of visiting the prospector camps in recent months came to mind. "Can I beg off today? I need to go home and practice what you're preaching."

"Glad to hear it. Give me a moment then." Levi tugged at Justin's arm, walking a few feet from the family.

"What's up?"

"I'm eager to hear about the letter."

"What about it?"

"Did Cobb find you?" Levi's eyes gleamed. "Are you searching for the owner?"

"Aw, Levi. This is not your way." Justin's face pinched. "You always plow straight to the point. You don't go on fishing expeditions."

Levi smiled mischievously. "I'm not sure what you're getting at."

"You want to know if I'm searching for the recipient *with Miss Dawn*."

"Well?"

Justin shifted. "Well, what?"

"Are you?" Levi rubbed his hands together. "Have you and Miss Dawn taken up the effort together?"

"If memory serves, you've reached out to men in the prospector camps." Justin rocked back on his heels. "You'd be doing us a tremendous favor if you'd ask around about it. I'm busy trying to sell horses, and she's trying to stay connected to her sewing customers."

"She's already committed, isn't she?" Levi shook his head vigorously. "But you're dragging your feet. What's wrong with you, man?"

"You know what's wrong. The last time I was interested in someone," a dull ache filled Justin's chest, "I lost Ma."

"It wasn't your fault. You know that." Levi rested his hand on Justin's back. "You have to forgive yourself."

"I don't know how." Justin averted his eyes. He cleared his throat. "Besides, what if Miss Dawn takes to frequenting the pool hall again in pursuit of the letter's recipient?"

"All the more reason you should conduct the search together." Levi patted Justin on the back. "It might be the best way to keep a close eye on her if you're truly concerned."

Chapter Ten

Eliza Dawn brushed her hair back into a low ponytail. Who did Justin Hogue think he was anyway? Who made him the authority on fashion and propriety? She slammed the hairbrush on the crate table, picked up a strand of ribbon, and tied her hair back. She needed to get out from under his watchful eye for a while.

She grabbed her saddle bag and headed out the door and down the back stairway. Bursting out the back door with a full head of steam, she stormed toward the stable. A rustling of leaves gave her pause. At the back corner of the house, a shrub shivered. She scanned the surroundings. The other shrubs and trees were still with no evidence of the slightest breeze. Was that the shadow of a figure rounding the corner? She shook it off. She'd always been told she had an overactive imagination, but she'd never let it get the better of her.

She opened the stable door slowly, still scanning the yard. Then, shrugging, she stepped inside and entered the tack room. She crossed to the shelf with the brushes and farrier tools, noticing a jar with a round brush on top. The brush resembled a shaving brush, only flatter and bigger around. She picked it up, grazing the stiff bristles with her finger. Scratched on the jar lid were the words "saddle soother." Picking up the container, she removed the lid and took a tentative sniff.

Eliza Dawn closed her eyes, drawing the scent deep into her lungs. The tension in her neck and shoulders eased. She breathed deep once more. Sweet citrus, cedar, and ... what was that scent? It smelled like—

"You left the door open."

She jumped, almost dropping the container. She straightened. Then she screwed the lid on tight and shoved the jar on the shelf, plopping the brush on top.

"Justin." She gave a curt nod. "I mean, Mr. Hogue. You're home."

He stepped closer, and she backed into the shelf. Leaning in, he stretched his arm over her shoulder. "Let me put these things back in proper order."

"In proper order?" Eliza Dawn cleared her throat. "You like things in proper order, don't you?"

"I wouldn't say I *like* it so much as that's what I'm *used* to." He straightened the brushes and saddle soother. "Levi is a stickler for order, and I guess he rubbed off on me."

Pulling back, Justin lifted her chin, and Eliza Dawn raised her eyes to meet his. She struggled to hold on to her earlier anger, but it drained away, leaving her lightheaded. What was in that saddle soother? Lifting his other hand toward her face, he swiped the underside of her nose with his index finger.

"Got a little saddle soother there." He wiped his hand on a rag hanging from the wall.

A plume of air escaped her lungs with a nervous laugh. "Yes, I guess so. What is saddle soother?"

"It's a special blend I made to condition the saddles and other leather tack." Justin moved to a larger storage shelf and pulled her saddle down. "You haven't had your ride yet, have you?"

"I was about to."

"You should come with us."

"Us?"

"Bwonco Bubba, where are you?" Four-year-old Edie peeked from behind the door. Then, spying Justin, she ran to him and wrapped herself around his leg. "I'm hungwy. Let's go."

Justin laughed as she pulled at his leg. He patted her head.

"Give me a few minutes. I've got to help Miss Dawn." Justin grabbed a pecan-colored Stetson from a hook on the wall and placed it on his head. "Simon and I are taking the younger children on a Sunday picnic. Come along. I'll get Bonnie saddled for you."

"Oh no, you don't have to do that." Eliza Dawn caught his hand and quickly released it. "I was going to take a ride in the hills. Find a pretty stream or an interesting patch of woods."

Edie grabbed Eliza Dawn's hand, and Eliza Dawn tensed. She pressed her lips into a tentative smile as the child pulled her away from Justin and out the door. "I hepped make a cake. It's gooood. C'mon."

"I've got just the place." Justin carried the saddle out the tack room door, edging past Eliza Dawn and Edie. Edie pulled Eliza Dawn almost off her feet, following Justin outside. He patted Edie on the head again. "Go help Simon load the wagon."

With a squeal, Edie ran off, and Justin chuckled.

"Honestly, Mr. Hogue, I was looking forward to some time to myself."

He slung the saddle up on a post and turned abruptly. "Haven't you been home alone all morning?"

"Well, yes. Or at least I think I have."

"What do you mean?"

"It's nothing. I thought I saw movement near the bushes earlier." She waved it off. "Probably a squirrel or something."

"*Hmm.* Always good to be vigilant around here. Edge of Indian Territory, jumping off point for prospectors. There's even been a few outlaw hideouts uncovered near Van Buren." His gaze sobered as he scanned the landscape. "So what do you say? Will you join us?"

"I'd like to explore on my own. I need some time away from town." She tucked a tendril of hair behind her ear. "I had in mind someplace less crowded."

"I understand that." He went back inside and opened the door to Bonnie's stall. Clicking his tongue, he signaled Bonnie to move forward. "C'mon, Bonnie the Beauty. Let's get you saddled up and riding pretty."

"Mr. Hogue, I insist." Eliza Dawn took hold of Bonnie's halter.

Justin placed his hand over hers. "Miss Dawn, I haven't been very welcoming to you. Our family invites people to lodge with us, usually men. This has been an uncomfortable undertaking for me, but that's no fault of yours. If I may, I've been terrible, and I'd like to start over."

"What brought that on?"

"Something my friend Levi said at church this morning." Justin cinched the saddle snugly around Bonnie's middle.

"I can't imagine what kind of comment would encourage such a change. Levi must have a way with words."

"It was a whole sermon."

"Well, you weren't wholly terrible. You were pleasant enough last night." Eliza Dawn smiled. "For about five minutes."

"That's fair." A sheepish grin spread across Justin's face.

He patted the saddle's seat and then offered his clasped hands as a foothold. Eliza Dawn placed her foot securely in his grasp, and he effortlessly hoisted her into the saddle. She and Justin rode their horses with the old buckboard following closely behind. About twenty minutes later, Justin slowed to a stop and turned in his saddle. He motioned for her to do the same.

"Mr. Hogue," the words came in a halting whisper, "it's breathtaking."

Justin dismounted and helped Eliza Dawn off Bonnie. He tied Blue and Bonnie to the wagon. Then, rejoining Eliza Dawn, he ushered her closer to the scene below. "Miss Dawn, I'd like to officially welcome you to Van Buren."

"You can see everything from here, can't you?" Eliza Dawn studied the horizon, wide-eyed. "Is that Main Street? And what body of water is this?"

"Yes, that is Main Street." Justin turned her slightly. "And, if you'll look this way, there's the Arkansas River and Lee Creek confluence. The steamboat just beyond is *The Resilient*, piloted by Captain Hale Cobb."

"Cobb? The captain who gave you the ring?"

Justin nodded. "He and his brother board with us sometimes when they're in town. They're getting a later start today than they intended."

Justin jogged to the wagon where Simon and Martie were helping the three youngest siblings out of the buckboard. He grabbed a blanket and spread it on the ground. Returning to the wagon, he retrieved a large picnic basket.

"Sit, sit. We'll let the children play a bit while we talk." Justin motioned to the blanket.

She sat next to him, folding her legs underneath her. "This is the best welcome I've had in any city on this journey."

"Miss Dawn, I want to apologize for my comment this morning. It wasn't my intention to be judgmental." He paused, rubbing his hand across his stubble and down his neck. "I was worried how others might react to your wardrobe. I intended to save your feelings, but my comment had the opposite effect."

"It's quite all right. But you should know, I don't mind being different, and I can handle most anything people might say." Eliza Dawn picked a tiny blue flower and tucked it into her hair. "However, I do appreciate what you were trying to do. And I apologize for being the source of frustration that led you to use the Lord's name inappropriately. I know church people are sensitive about that."

"I used His name inappropriately?"

"When you said, 'Oh Lord, I've done this all wrong.'"

Justin chuckled. "I know I said that out of exasperation—with myself, not you—but I assure you it was an honest prayer nonetheless. It was interrupted by all the commotion in the hall, but God knew where that prayer was going."

"And where was it going?"

"I can do better." His Adam's apple bobbed up and down. "Not on my own, but with God's help. Sometimes, I am overwhelmed by my shortcomings. I had the opportunity to finish that prayer while we were at church."

"Does God help you? When you ask?"

"I don't know." Justin shrugged. "Sometimes it seems like He doesn't. Other times, I know He does. Like today. It took courage to ask you for a fresh start. I haven't had much of that kind of courage lately. The kind of courage it takes to ask for a second chance."

They sat quietly as the clouds rolled along with the river. Peals of laughter erupted nearby as the children frolicked across the landscape. Justin opened the basket and pulled out tin cups and plates.

"Tell me a little more about yourself. How did you come to be so independent?" He lifted food items from the basket, arranging them on the blanket.

Eliza Dawn sized him up with a narrowed glance. "You'd prefer not to know my life's particulars. Except where it directly impacts you and your family. I believe that's what you said, isn't it?"

Justin's cheeks flushed, but he held her gaze. "I can be overly protective of my family. But perhaps my protective nature can withstand a bit of curiosity."

Eliza Dawn's heart flip-flopped. What she would have given for someone like Justin to be so fiercely protective of her. Instead, she had only gained his curiosity. Right now, his curiosity was the last thing she needed—the last thing she needed from any man.

Chapter Eleven

Mud spattered Justin's boots, the bottom of his pants legs tucked safely inside, as he led Hershey through town. Despite the proximity of the boardinghouse, Justin wasn't having much luck with potential buyers coming to him. Instead, he sparked more interest while parading the horses down Main Street. The problem was he could only do that with one or two horses at a time. If only there were a way to show off all the horses simultaneously. It would be even better if he could show them packing, working, and riding.

Passing by Conrad Hildesheim's bakery, Justin chuckled. He smoothed his hands down his shirtfront, free of Saturday's gooey mess. He warmed at the memory of Eliza Dawn's hand relaxing into his, her fingers soft and delicate despite the stickiness. He shook the memory from his mind.

Had he and Rebecca eased her concerns about staying at Hogue House? Or would the tension between Pa and him drive her away? He paused to scan Main Street. Would he run into her in town today?

Taking a deep breath, he stilled the fluttering in his stomach, though he couldn't quiet the curiosity she inspired. She must have a family name. Why didn't she want to reveal it? Why did she hide her horse in the alleyway when she arrived? Was she hiding from something or someone? Was she in league with MacKinnon? So many questions.

He rearranged his day to be at Hogue House this morning, half hoping she might reveal some answers or inadvertently drop some clues. He usually left before daybreak to work with the horses at the Snow homestead. Today, he worked the horses at the boardinghouse stable until the younger siblings and boarders left for the day. Then he joined Rebecca and Eliza Dawn for breakfast. He would head out to the homestead after dinner and return before supper.

Snap out of it, Justin. Why did his thoughts keep drifting back to Eliza Dawn? Why couldn't he keep his mind off her? This kind of distraction had endangered his mother. He couldn't entertain the diversion right now. Not only did it put the business at risk, but what if he hadn't spotted the boy in the street the other day? What if little Edie was with him and wandered in front of a runaway wagon while he was distracted by Eliza Dawn and her pastry?

He'd have to put a stop to his preoccupation with her. That's all there was to it. He'd buckle down and keep his morning schedule at Levi's. Simple enough.

Arriving at Mooney's, he tied Hershey to the post, pulled a cloth from his vest pocket, and wiped the mud from Hershey's legs and underside. He wanted to show off her unique bay-colored coat with the spattering of white on her belly and legs. Shaking the grime from the rag and tucking it back into his vest, he mounted the steps to the mercantile.

"G'morning, Justin." Sam's deep voice rang bright and resonant.

"You're in fine spirits this morning, Sam."

"Got a shipment coming today." Sam motioned toward the

waterfront. "A big shipment means these forty-niners are one day closer to leaving town. Maybe things will settle down some after that."

Justin laughed. "Always looking on the sunny side of things, aren't you?"

"You know me." Sam grinned, tucking a pencil behind his ear and closing the special orders pad. "You wouldn't happen to have any horseshoes you can spare, would you?

"I made some the other day, but only enough for the horses at Hogue House."

"I knew it was a long shot. Anything Levi might be able to spare would be appreciated. What brings you by today?"

"Hoping you could help me solve a problem." Justin lifted the shiny lid of a penny candy jar near the counter. He pinched a lemon drop between two fingers and popped it into his mouth. "Could you help bounce some ideas around? I remember you came up with some great ones the year that nativity showed up in town."

"I remember." Sam nodded. "That's when I began the tradition of live Christmas scenes in the shop window. I've done it every year since. Even that year I was so sick, with Allie's help, of course."

"A lot of the town Christmas traditions began that year. You and Conrad helped develop most of those ideas thanks to Levi and Allie's inspiration."

"Well, that little nativity set they discovered was quite moving. Conrad and I weren't the only ones to spark new traditions." Sam straightened items on the counter. "Don't know if I can help solve your problem, but let's try."

Justin pushed two pennies across the counter and took another lemon drop.

Sam scooted them back. "I've told you about that. You save Levi and me from wearing out the road between our two businesses by delivering things on your way home from there.

I'll pay you in lemon drops since you won't accept cash money from me."

"Aw, it doesn't make sense to charge you for delivering since I come by here twice a day." Justin pushed the pennies back again. "Besides, if you let me pay you, you'll save me from my sweet tooth."

Sam shook his head and scooped up the pennies. "Well, I can't guarantee I'll be able to compensate you for deliveries with my bright ideas, but what's your trouble?"

"I get more interest in my horses when people see them on Main Street. But I can only manage one or two horses at a time." Justin rubbed his stubbled chin. "I'm trying to figure out how to show them all off simultaneously."

"How many horses are you looking to show?"

"Six."

"Sounds easy enough. Tie three at my hitching post and three at Conrad's." Sam wagged his finger to and fro, indicating his store and the next-door bakery. "Levi and Simon could help you bring them over."

"I was hoping to show off their skills. You know, their ability to pack and work and ride well."

"You should ask Levi if you can hold an event at his homestead. You could parade the horses around, put them through their paces, and Simon could do some trick riding." Sam scratched his head. "Conrad bakes some fine loaves of bread, cakes, and special pastries for Easter. Perhaps he could cart some of his goods out there to sell."

A handful of men entered the store, scattering in different directions. A rawboned young fellow with curly blond hair held a list and sauntered to the far end of an aisle. Sam's eyes followed them through the room. He lowered his voice. "Better stretch my legs if you get my meaning."

"Of course. I'll join you." Justin followed through the aisles.

"I want to do my best to get these horses sold before the wagon trains depart for California next week."

"Excuse me. You say you've got horses to sell?" A sinewy fellow wearing a black bowler with a red feather popped his head over the shelves.

"Yessir, he does." Then, pointing out the window, Sam answered for Justin. "Yonder is one of his sale horses. If you don't like that one, he's got more."

"Mind if I take a look?" He twisted his handlebar mustache.

"Be happy to show her to you." Justin reached out his hand. "Name's Justin Hogue."

"Davis Whitmore." The man pumped Justin's hand and then followed him out the door.

"Mr. Whitmore, I'd like you to meet Hershey." Justin rubbed the horse's muzzle. "She's a sure-footed quarter horse, about five years old. She was skittish when I first traded for her, but I've worked with her. Now she's as steady as the day is long and versatile."

"That so?" Whitmore asked. "I do like her coloring. Pretty bay. D'you run her through a puddle of white paint on the way here?"

Justin chuckled. "Sure looks that way, doesn't it?"

"You say she handles well now."

"She's as settled and reliable as they come."

"I had a strawberry roan once. Beautiful mare." Whitmore circled Hershey, twisting one side of his mustache as he spoke. "You wouldn't happen to have anything like that? I miss that girl."

"What happened to her?"

"Stolen."

Eliza Dawn's peculiar behavior with Bonnie niggled at his insides, and he pushed the feeling aside.

"Whitmore." MacKinnon crossed from the bakery in long, determined strides. "Whit're ye doing wi' this horse?"

"You know I'm in the market for a horse." Whitmore completed his circle around Hershey. The mare stood still, one of her back legs cocked at an angle so the tip of her hoof barely rested on the ground.

"I ken ye spoke wi' me aboot buying ma horse." MacKinnon poked Whitmore's chest as he spoke.

"Relax, MacKinnon," Justin crossed his arms. "No problem in a man making sure he's getting the best horse for his money."

"Do I ken ye?"

"Hogue. Justin Hogue."

"Mind yer business, Hogue." Ruddiness rose in MacKinnon's cheeks. "A'm no' talking to ye. A'm talking to Whitmore."

Whitmore cleared his throat repeatedly. "Perhaps I'll pick up some Indian ponies along the way. But, right now, I best help my partners get supplies."

Whitmore retreated into the mercantile, leaving the stand-off between Justin and MacKinnon. Justin stroked Hershey's smooth neck. Her muscles were loose, relaxed, yet a keen awareness of MacKinnon shone in her eyes.

"You've run off a customer for both of us, MacKinnon."

"Tis 'eh second customer ye've taken from me, Hogue. A'll be putting a stop to yer business 'long as A'm in toon."

MacKinnon landed his palm sharply across Hershey's rump. The mare lifted her hind leg and clomped her hoof twice. Then she went still again.

"Are you threatening me?" Justin ground his teeth. He kept his voice level as he stroked Hershey's neck, more for his benefit than hers.

"Tis a promise." MacKinnon pointed to the notice board at the mercantile. "Get yer notice off 'eh board and stay oot o'ma way."

"Or what?" Justin loosened Hershey's reins from the hitching post.

"A'll tear it doon maself." MacKinnon removed his hand from Hershey, poking Justin in the chest. "In fact, how aboot I take care of it reit noo."

MacKinnon turned to walk around Hershey, and Justin pressed into her neck slightly. It was a familiar signal to the horse, indicating her to turn. Her head moved away from Justin as she swung her rump into MacKinnon, unsteadying him.

"Careful, MacKinnon. I don't think she likes you." A cockeyed grin emerged from Justin as he rubbed Hershey.

"Ye watch yerself, Cowboy." MacKinnon stormed the notice board, tearing down Justin's notice.

Justin brought two fingers to his forehead, waving the Scotsman off with a mock salute. Hershey nuzzled her nose into Justin's chest. He marveled at the change in her. She used to panic so readily, and now her steadiness kept him from getting riled. He leaned close to Hershey's ear, "Good, girl. You were calmer than I was."

Justin secured the horse and ducked back into the mercantile. Borrowing a pen and slip of paper from Sam, he wrote a new notice to replace the one MacKinnon had torn down. Tucking it into his vest pocket, his fingers brushed the letter. He grimaced at the reminder of his commitment to Captain Cobb. Better ask Whitmore and his partners about it while they still gathered supplies.

"Mr. Whitmore, could I ask you and your associates to help me briefly?" Justin leaned down the aisle where Whitmore was standing.

"I don't know." Whitmore's face scrunched up as he shrugged.

"May I show you a letter? It's intended for one of the prospectors, but the writing is smudged." Justin held the envelope in the air. "The recipient's name is illegible. Perhaps one of you might recognize the handwriting or some other detail?"

Whitmore gestured to his partners, who nodded their agreement. They joined Justin around the envelope, and Justin handed it to Whitmore. He studied it briefly before shaking his head and passing it along. Each man surveyed the envelope in turn before handing it back to Justin.

Justin returned the letter to his vest pocket. "If you gentlemen don't mind, could you spread the word about this letter? Perhaps someone expects it and will seek me out if they know it's arrived."

"We'd be happy to. News from home will be a long time coming from here on out. Correspondence from family is sure to be cherished." Whitmore, along with his men, resumed shopping.

Stepping out the door, Justin tacked his replacement notice on the board. As he turned to leave, he glimpsed MacKinnon entering the pool hall—with Eliza Dawn on his arm.

Chapter Twelve

Eliza Dawn caught Ewan's arm as he breached the pool hall door. The muscles in his arm tensed, and she withdrew her hand. Then, taking a step back, she excused herself. "My apologies. I didn't mean to bother you."

"Tis nae a bother, lass." Ewan grasped her hand and planted it firmly in the crook of his arm. "A wee bit o' surprise, tis all. But a welcome one."

"I wanted to give you an update on the shirts."

"The shirts? O'course. I want to hear aboot eh shirts." His brows knit together as he guided her in front of him.

"I've chosen blue flannel for all five shirts." Eliza Dawn glanced behind her as she glided through the tables.

"Ah, ye wis thinking about ma blue eyes, wis ye?" He winked.

"On the contrary, I was thinking about your Scottish flag, though this flannel is not quite the same shade."

"You know the Scottish flag?"

"My father loved flags, so he made sure I knew the flags of many countries."

"Thir's a man I'd lek to meet." Ewan guided her toward his table, but she paused. "Whit is it?"

"I was going to sit by myself at my usual table." She turned and pointed. "I only wanted to give you a quick report about my work."

"I dinnae think it a good idea fo' ye to sit alone following the incident the other day, do ye?"

"I'm sure I'll be fine. I want to continue my observations." She fidgeted with the button at her neck. "It helps me with my work."

"Whit do ye observe? Who has a shirt and who disnae?"

Eliza Dawn backpedaled as Ewan coaxed her toward his table once again. She could not allow herself such familiar contact with these prospectors. If she got too close, it might ruin the perspective of her story. Or would it? Perhaps joining them would allow her to ask some probing questions. But, of course, she would have to be careful not to raise any suspicion about her real reason for spending the afternoon with them.

Deciding it was worth the risk, she conceded and joined the lively Scots.

"Lads, A'd lek ye to meet Miss Eliza Dawn." Ewan introduced her, and, with a flourish, he gave her a twirl.

"Pup!" The chorus of men cheered as they rushed to pull out a chair for her.

Eliza Dawn's cheeks warmed. She thanked them while simultaneously trying to discourage their fawning over her. Then, anxious to get to her questions, she urged them to settle into their seats.

"I appreciate your kindness. Oh, and your gifts over the few weeks it took to journey to Van Buren." Eliza Dawn patted the air with her hands. "But please, please, sit."

When they calmed, at least as much as they were bound to, Eliza Dawn posed questions from her mental list.

"Ewan, how many are traveling in your group?"

"We hev better than eighty Scots in oor number."

"All men?"

"Aye, mostly. Thir ur a few families."

"Whit're ye asking aboot men and families?" A man with a thick, well-shaped beard asked.

Ewan jabbed the man's arm. "Naturally, she wants to ken who's unattached, Mal."

"Unattached?" Eliza Dawn's breath caught in her throat. For a moment, she feared the conversation might take an undesirable direction as it had with the businessmen the day before.

"Fer sewing. The few wives and older daughters among us ur no' enough t'dae all o' oor sewing and mending." Ewan patted her knee, and she was thankful she hadn't yet pulled out the scratch pad from her apron pocket.

"I'm so thankful for all you've done to watch over me, even though I only recently learned about your kindness. You must tell me all about yourselves." Eliza Dawn leaned into the table to address the group of just over half a dozen men. She beamed as they settled in rapt attention. "I want to know where you're from, how long you've been in America, what kind of work you do, why you'd travel to California when you've already come so far. I want to know everything."

"Ye dinnae ken whit ye're asking. The lads'll no' stop their blethering." Ewan chortled, slapping the table. "The gold rush will come full stop before they're done."

"Hoosh noo, Ewan." The bearded man pushed Ewan back in his seat. "A'll go first. Name's Malcolm Sinclair. Blacksmith by trade. Miss ma forge more than anny'hin. Whit I willny gi' t'hev hammer in hand agin."

"Blacksmith? Mr. Sinclair, I have a friend with a little used forge." Eliza Dawn leaned close, catching his hand. "I'd happily ask if he'd permit you to use it. Perhaps you could rent the space?"

"Where might 'is space be?" Sinclair leaned closer across folded arms.

"Hogue House. It's the boardinghouse where I'm lodging."

"A'd be doon reit grateful, i'ye dinnae mind."

"Happy to do it."

"Wouldn't get yer hopes too high, Sinclair. Hogue is no friend of oors."

Was there a story behind Ewan's comment? Sinclair launched into his tale before she could ask. She snuck the scratch paper from her apron. Keeping it hidden under the table, she jotted notes as each man shared his story. She shifted it back into her apron pocket or moved it to the opposite side of her lap whenever Ewan drew too close. Would she be able to read her writing when she returned to her room?

Halfway around the circle, she turned to ask Ewan to get her some sweet tea. When Ewan stepped away, she glimpsed a young man at a pool table in the back. The way he moved was oddly familiar, though a flat cap pulled low over his brow obstructed his face. Eliza Dawn studied him, and suddenly, his identity registered with her. She half rose from her seat.

"Where ye going, ma bonnie lass?" Ewan asked, returning with her tea.

"Pardon me, Ewan, but I think that's someone I know at the pool tables." Eliza Dawn took a step past him, and he caught her arm.

"Lek I said, I dinnae think it's a good idea fo' ye to be in here alone. Stay, talk with us."

"I can't. He's a boy, and he shouldn't be here." Eliza Dawn's gaze followed the lanky figure. "I must help him as you helped me the day you rescued me from my little predicament. It won't do for him to get in a tangle."

"A'll go with you." Then, he turned to his chums. "Back in a bit, lads."

Eliza Dawn pressed deeper into the smoky belly of the pool

hall. She kept her head down as her eyes surveyed the room. Despite her previous misstep with the businessmen, she had learned to avoid eye contact but remain aware in such establishments. Ewan followed closely behind with a hand on her shoulder, sending a clear message they were together.

Once they reached the pool table, Eliza Dawn paused and tilted her head to the side, peering under the hat. The figure edged away, slinking along the back wall and then around the opposite side of the table. Now, she had no doubt. He wouldn't be ducking her if they had never set eyes on one another.

"Simon, is that you?" She moved closer.

The figure grunted and sidled away again.

"Stop this tomfoolery. I know it's you." Eliza Dawn closed in from one side while Ewan flanked him on the other. She yanked the flat cap from the adolescent's head.

Simon Hogue hung his head. "Please don't tell Justin."

Holding Simon's hat in one hand, Eliza Dawn grabbed his ear and pulled him toward the door. Ewan again followed on their heels.

"Ewan, thank the boys for the gracious hospitality and convivial company this afternoon." She tossed over her shoulder. "Please explain I have a little problem to address and extend my apologies. I hope to visit with them again soon."

"I will, but who is this?"

"Let's just say he's a younger brother of sorts. I've adopted him as you and the lads adopted me."

Reaching the door, she held up a hand, indicating to Ewan not to follow them. Ewan caught her by the elbow. "When will ye return? I'd lek to ken ye better."

"I don't know." Heat rose in her cheeks. "I'm sure we'll bump into one another around town."

When would she be able to talk to Ewan again? Intuition told her his story would perfectly tie her article together. But it wouldn't do to give Simon any indication she'd be back at the pool hall.

She dragged the boy out the door and around the corner of the building, shoving his back against the wall.

She spoke in low tones through clenched teeth. "Simon Hogue, why aren't you in school?"

Chapter Thirteen

"I don't want to be at school." Simon set his mouth defiantly.

"You don't want to be at school?" She struck a stern tone. "Do you understand how fortunate you are your family still sends you to school at sixteen? Do you know how many boys must leave school at thirteen or younger to go to work?"

"But I don't like school." He averted his eyes from hers. His voice was barely a whisper. "I like you ... and you're here."

Eliza Dawn's breath caught. She blinked hard. How had she not recognized this? He wasn't edging closer to her at supper the other night due to the crowding around the table. He was sweet on her. Tightness ebbed through her chest.

She didn't know how to let him down without hurting his feelings. She couldn't imagine telling Justin without revealing how she discovered Simon's infatuation, which meant he'd know she had returned to the pool hall after he'd asked her not to. So, asking him for advice was out of the question. She also couldn't ask Rebecca for the same reason.

"Don't move." Eliza Dawn pressed her palm into the boy's chest as she leaned around the corner. She scanned the area. No sign of Justin, but Sam Mooney stood in front of the mercantile. "You get yourself straight back to school or go home."

"Are you going to tell Justin?" he asked in a thready tone.

"Aren't you worried I'll tell your father?"

"Pa don't pay no mind to what I do since Ma died." Simon toed the dirt. "Besides, Justin is meaner than Pa if he catches us misbehaving.'"

"Pa doesn't pay *any* mind." Eliza Dawn corrected. "Get yourself home. Stay out of sight between here and there, and I won't tell. Make sure Justin doesn't catch you, or I won't be able to help."

"Yes, ma'am."

She worried Simon might tell Justin everything if he ran into him.

"Miss Dawn?"

"*Hmm?*" Eliza Dawn stood guard, waiting for Sam to reenter the mercantile. She couldn't risk him spotting Simon in town since he and Justin spoke frequently.

"What were you doing sitting with those men?"

"I'm doing some sewing for them. We were talking about the work."

"Is sewing that interesting? Y'all were talking a long time."

"It can be interesting work."

"What were you writing on that paper under the table?"

Eliza Dawn's head snapped around. "What was I writing?"

He nodded.

"Underneath the table?"

He nodded.

"I was writing the details of their order. How many shirts, what colors, getting their measurements."

"Why were you hiding the paper? Why wouldn't you just put it on the table?"

Eliza Dawn swallowed. Her neck warmed, and she tugged at her collar. "Hiding it? Don't be daft. Did you see those men?

They weren't exactly neat with their food and drink now, were they? It's difficult to read notes when they have the midday meal slopped on them."

"Wouldn't it be pretty hard to read notes written under the table too?"

"Yes, well, with any luck, they'll be easier to read than food-spattered notes." Eliza Dawn peeked around the corner again. Still, no sign of Justin. Sam Mooney stepped back into the store. "I think the coast is clear. Get out of here, and mind you, don't come back to this pool hall until you're of age."

"Yes, ma'am." Simon nodded rapidly.

The adolescent took off like a shot without a backward glance. Eliza Dawn kept an eye on him until he was out of sight. Then she emerged from the hiding place and strolled Main Street.

She wished she had been able to finish collecting stories from the Scotsmen. Their accounts were fascinating. Many moved to America a little over a decade ago after being evicted from their homes in Scotland.

Ewan MacKinnon was most enjoyable, and Eliza Dawn was eager to learn his story. However, she couldn't help comparing him to Justin. They shared features: stubbled facial hair, a strong jawline, broad shoulders, and blue-gray eyes. But that was where the similarities ended. Justin's demeanor was decidedly formal, while Ewan's was less guarded and more playful. Yet, when Justin grasped her strudel-smeared hand, the pressure was firm and gentle, whereas Ewan's grip bordered on possessive.

"Miss Dawn."

Eliza Dawn turned as Justin slid off Hershey. She smiled at the timing.

"Mr. Hogue, what have you been up to today?"

"I brought Hershey to Main Street to show her off, and I visited with Sam Mooney at the mercantile a spell. I also spent some time at the saddler's." Justin walked, Eliza Dawn on one side and Hershey on the other. "Then I rode to the Snow homestead to work with my other horses."

"Sounds like a busy day. What did you visit with the saddler about? Are you in need of a saddle?"

"Got all the saddles I need. I figured folks in the market for a saddle might also need a horse." He pulled his hands free from his working gloves. "These prospectors will be looking to purchase anything related to mount and pack animals. That means I need to be a familiar face around the saddler, the feed store, the farrier, and so on."

"Makes sense." With a broad smile, she laid her hand on Justin's arm. "Perhaps we should mention the letter to the saddler."

"That's not a bad idea."

"We should go straight away. Where is it?"

Justin cleared his throat. "I don't have time to go back today. Perhaps tomorrow."

"You aren't just putting me off, are you?" Her shoulders drooped.

"I don't see how you can be so fired up about that thing. I'd think you'd be busy drumming up business." Justin shot her a questioning glance. "How did you spend your day?"

"Oh, I didn't do anything of particular interest. I spent the morning sewing as usual." She sighed. "Then I wandered Main Street all afternoon trying to entice folks to place an order for shirts."

The truth was she had more orders than she needed. She'd gained an order for mending before arriving at the pool hall. It would be waiting on her when she returned to Hogue House. If she took on any more sewing jobs, she wouldn't have enough time to finish another article for the paper back east before week's end. But she knew Justin would disapprove of how she spent her afternoon, and she certainly didn't want to let on about Simon.

"Oh, Justin. Justin Hogue." A short, rotund woman waving a silk handkerchief shuffled in their direction. "Justin, wait right there."

The woman's sing-song voice turned heads all along Main Street. Eliza Dawn caught the rise and fall of Justin's chest as his eyes darted rapidly. Was he searching for an escape? He rubbed the back of his neck. What sort of woman was this that she could elicit such an anxious response from him?

"Justin, dear, my butter churn is broken. Would you look at it for me?" The lady smiled sweetly.

"Good afternoon, Mrs. Pratt." He dipped his hat to her. Then, he grabbed Eliza Dawn and scooted her forward. "Have you met Miss Eliza Dawn?"

"Why, no, I don't believe I have." She shook Eliza Dawn's hand daintily. "Firm grip you have there, dear."

"She is staying with us until a room opens at Bradley House."

"Oh, I see." Mrs. Pratt's eyes widened under her thin eyebrows. "Isn't that ... unconventional."

"We considered asking you to help find a family she could lodge with, but we didn't want to trouble anyone so close to Easter." He cleared his throat, then turned to Eliza Dawn. "Miss Dawn, I'd like to introduce Mrs. Olivia Pratt. Mrs. Pratt is the most helpful person in town if you need anything while you're here."

Wrapping her arms around herself at the elbows, Eliza Dawn tipped her head to Mrs. Pratt. The woman beamed at Justin, patting him on the arm.

"Dear boy. Miss Dawn, I'm sorry, I didn't catch your family name."

"No family name." Eliza Dawn shot Justin a cross look. "No family."

"I'm sorry to hear that." Mrs. Pratt's countenance dimmed, and her voice dulled. "To be sure, Justin is correct. I am always happy to help whenever I can, so if you need anything, you can call on me."

"Mrs. Pratt, Miss Dawn is plying her hand at seamstress work. If you need any extra help, I'm sure she could oblige." Justin smiled and nodded at Eliza Dawn. "Her specialty is shirts and mending."

Mrs. Pratt laid her hand on Eliza Dawn's crossed arms. Then, the melodic quality returned to her voice. "I have two days' worth of mending I've meant to do, but I would be happy to send the work your way. That will allow me to focus more fully on Easter preparations. Which brings me back to you, Justin."

He winced.

"The butter churn. Would you look at it?"

"What's the problem? Did the dasher break in two?" Justin shifted as Hershey pawed the ground impatiently behind him. "Mr. Pratt can saw off an old broom handle to replace it."

"No, no. I have a new barrel churn. It's larger." She smiled at Eliza Dawn. "We had a minor incident while moving it, and the handle bent. So, it may need some blacksmith work."

"I'm sure if you get that to Levi, he could handle it quickly."

"I don't have time to take it by Levi's. I brought it to the mercantile and left it with Mr. Mooney. I know you're by there daily." She fiddled with her reticule. "I need it fixed straight away. Easter is in four days."

"Mrs. Pratt, I don't do blacksmith work anymore."

"Except for yourself, you mean. You do still make your horseshoes, don't you?"

Justin crossed his arms and pushed dirt around with the square toe of his boot. "Well, yes."

"Do be a dear and share those skills, won't you? Then, if you can't fix it, you'll be a sweetheart and drop it at Levi's when you go?" She patted his hand. She leaned close to Eliza Dawn and whispered, "Such a precious young man."

Just then, a gaggle of boys ran through the middle of their

conversation, bumping Mrs. Pratt and knocking her off balance. Justin caught her and set her upright. She fanned herself with her hand.

"My goodness. The boys have gotten rowdier since the town has become so overpopulated." She clutched at her collar. "Some of the older boys have taken to skipping school regularly to keep company with these ruffian prospectors."

Eliza Dawn donned her best poker face. She glanced from Mrs. Pratt to Justin. His eyes were set on the boys scampering down the street.

Mrs. Pratt raised an eyebrow and leaned uncomfortably close to Eliza Dawn. "We must all do our part to keep these youngsters on the right path. Don't you agree, Miss Dawn?"

Eliza Dawn nodded, saying nothing. Had Mrs. Pratt seen her dragging Simon out of the pool hall? Or hiding around the corner? Would Mrs. Pratt tell Justin if she had? Eliza Dawn buried her hands in the pocket of her apron.

"Do you mind if I leave the mending basket at the mercantile, and you can pick it up tomorrow?" Mrs. Pratt smiled.

"That will be fine." Eliza Dawn pressed her lips into a timid smile. "Thank you."

∼

"Did I roll my eyes?" Justin's gaze followed Mrs. Pratt as she disappeared into the butcher shop. "Please tell me I didn't roll my eyes when Mrs. Pratt called my name."

"Did you roll your eyes?" Eliza Dawn arched her eyebrows, her blue eyes widening. "Justin Hogue, why would you do such a thing?"

"Mrs. Olivia Pratt is a kindhearted soul, always ready to assist in times of need, but she never approaches me unless she has a task in mind for me to do."

Eliza Dawn laughed. "No, you did not roll your eyes. Not that I noticed."

Justin sighed. "Good. The urge was strong."

"Your eyes were darting to and fro like a trapped animal seeking escape, though."

Justin shook his head, lips pulled tight. "I have never been successful at escaping Mrs. Olivia Pratt. I always thought my mother helped her corner me. I don't know how she eludes my powers of observation." He sighed. "Well, I guess that's another thing I'll have to do I don't have time for."

"What else are you busy with? That you don't have time for, that is." Eliza Dawn tilted her head. "I know you're working with horses at the boardinghouse and your friend's homestead and trying to drum up customers. So, what else have you been up to?"

Should he mention the horse show? After seeing her with MacKinnon again, how could he be sure she wouldn't tip the man off to his plans? What if MacKinnon horned in on the event? Or worse yet, sabotaged it? Not knowing her relationship with the Scotsman, he best not divulge too much. Besides, with his luck, Eliza Dawn would want to make a grand announcement about the letter at the horse show, and they would be inundated with scores of men claiming it. He certainly didn't have time to weed through the opportunists to find a single man.

"Oh, nothing of interest. Folks around here often ask me for favors, is all."

"Tell them *no*." Eliza Dawn said matter-of-factly. "It's that simple."

"I wish that was true." He shrugged. "So, how about your day? Nothing of interest to report whatsoever?"

Would she come clean about going to the pool hall with Ewan MacKinnon? The image of her entering arm-in-arm with MacKinnon had set him on edge. What was she doing with him anyway? It was odd MacKinnon appeared out of nowhere while he showed Hershey to Whitmore, and then, less than five minutes after the encounter, she was on his arm. Justin swallowed the lump in his throat. It sure appeared as though she was in cahoots with his competition. He should ask Paulette Bradley if Bradley House was still full.

"Mr. Hogue?"

"*Hmm?*"

"I answered your question and asked if you were finished in town."

"Oh, I guess my mind wandered off. Yes, I'm headed home, and you?"

Eliza Dawn nodded.

"Would you like to walk together?"

Eliza Dawn nodded again.

"Justin," Eliza Dawn dropped his preferred formality, "I want to apologize again for asking about your mother the other day. I wasn't trying to pry."

"It's all right. I wasn't expecting it, was all." Justin's chest tightened, and he gripped Hershey's lead rope tighter. "We don't talk about it. The family, I mean. We don't talk about it."

"I understand. My mother died of smallpox, and my father died in a stagecoach accident." Eliza Dawn kept her eyes on her feet as she spoke. "My brother won't talk about their deaths."

"Thought you didn't have any family."

"I don't. Not anymore."

"What happened to your brother?"

"I honestly don't know." Her shoulders sank. She shoved her hands in her apron pocket. "He left. Perhaps I was too great a burden."

"That's difficult to imagine. From what I've observed, you're quite self-sufficient and independent." At times, Justin had disagreements and challenges with his siblings, but leaving them was unthinkable. "But that also means you do have a family name. You just don't use it. Why not?"

"I won't use the name of a family that doesn't want me. I go by the only name I can claim as my own. Eliza Dawn."

They turned off Main Street toward Cane Hill, leaving the hustle and bustle behind them. A steamboat whistle moaned in the distance. The laughter and chatter of children playing in yards nearby drifted on a cool, gentle breeze. Eliza Dawn gathered her shawl securely around her.

Justin studied her as they walked. Subdued, settled into her thoughts perhaps, she kept an easy stride alongside him. He was often overwhelmed by family. Overwhelmed but thankful. And here she was with no family to claim her.

A few wavy strands came loose from Eliza Dawn's low bun, gently cradling her face. The wind whipped a corner of her shawl from her grip. Justin caught the tail of it and wrapped it snuggly around her. Then he brushed the loose locks of hair behind her ear.

Her cheeks pinked. She paused and turned to face him. "If you ever want to talk about your mother, I'm willing to listen. Losing a parent is difficult."

"It is."

A few moments of quiet passed. The silence between them was like a warm blanket on a chilly evening. Unlike the unnerving silence that often settled between him and his father. A silence that weighed heavily with banishment and unforgiveness. Quiet moments with Rebecca were awkward and laden with expectation, as though she sought answers from him, but he had none to give. Yet here, with Eliza Dawn, the quiet brought peace and comfort.

"For a long time, I blamed myself for my father's death." Eliza Dawn sighed.

"Why? How could you possibly be responsible for a stagecoach accident?"

"My father was in such despair after my mother's death. Sometimes he was completely unaware of what was going on around him." She sniffed and cleared her throat before continuing. "A stagecoach lost control while making a turn. My father must not have seen or heard it because bystanders said he didn't attempt to get out of the way. The stagecoach toppled, crushing my father. If I had been there—"

"If you had been there, the stagecoach might have also crushed you."

"I can't help thinking maybe I could have pulled or pushed him out of the way. Like you did with the little boy."

"It's not your fault."

"That doesn't change how it feels, does it?"

As they walked, they drifted closer together. The back of his hand bumped against hers. She didn't withdraw. Justin drew in a slow, deep breath. An ache stirred in his chest, and he pushed it aside. He took her in with a discreet sidelong glance.

Hershey's muzzle shoved between them, nudging them apart. Justin drifted farther from her. What was he thinking, allowing himself to get pulled into her world like this? There was still too much he didn't know about her. He couldn't let his guard down. The risk was too significant to his business and, more importantly, his family.

Chapter Fourteen

Justin caught Bonnie's hoof and placed it on the hoof stand. He wiped his brow. He'd been wise to work on Dale's feet before hers. The yellow dun was prone to restlessness while being shod and had given Justin a run for his money. Bonnie, however, had been surprisingly calm. Eliza Dawn told him she'd made a habit of picking up her hooves, but he'd taken that to be a momentary thing. The gentle mare seemed well-accustomed to a lengthy three-legged stance.

He clinched the nails on this last hoof, then picked up the rasp. The stable door creaked open. His head popped up, but he couldn't see the door from his position.

"Need some help?"

Shuffling footsteps drew near. "There you are."

Pa stood before him, frowning. His eyes wandered the enclosure. He licked his lips as if preparing to speak, then went unnaturally quiet. This was the way of things between them since Ma's death. Justin longed for the easy conversations they used to have about nothing, about everything. It pained his heart Levi could still seek Pa's counsel on spiritual matters, but he and Pa could barely speak to one another. He swallowed hard, pushing the dull ache deeper. At least he still had his heavenly Father to talk to.

"Here I am, Pa. Did you need me?"

Silence. Pa sucked his teeth and exhaled roughly. His gaze met Justin's. Fatigue lined his eyes. Exhaustion weighted his shoulders. Justin knew the feeling. Smooth worn out. The kind of tired a body cannot sleep off.

"Pa?"

"I was at the saddler's earlier today."

"What were you doing there? We shouldn't have any tack in bad condition." Justin resumed his work with the rasp. "I check everything regularly."

"I know you do. You keep it in fine shape." Pa slipped his hands into his pocket. "Mr. Perry asked me to drop his saddle by for repairs."

"What's Mr. Perry doing with a saddle? He doesn't own a horse." Justin wiped his brow again. "Fella in Ozark shot his horse."

"Kept the saddle." Pa made a sucking sound against his teeth.

"Thought he'd have sold that thing by now."

"Loved that horse."

"I guess so. D'you need me to pick it up when Nicholas is done with it?"

"Naw." Pa shifted. Taking his hands out of his pockets, he crossed his arms.

Justin finished with Bonnie's hoof and set it on the ground. He moved the hoof stand to a corner of the oversized enclosure.

"Really ought to shoe these horses earlier when you've got better light. Take 'em outside."

"Normally do." Justin nodded. "Didn't work out that way today."

Justin brushed bits of hoof clippings, dirt, and manure from his farrier chaps. Removing the chaps, he hung them on a nail. He turned to his father.

"You didn't come out here to tell me that." Justin turned Bonnie, placing her between him and Pa. "Why are you here?"

"Nicholas says a fella in town is asking around about a strawberry roan. Might be one of them prospectors." Pa chewed his lip. "Says his horse was stolen and believed the culprit might be headed west, coming through here."

"And you think this is the horse?" Justin nodded at Bonnie.

"Didn't say that." He locked eyes with Justin. "But I reckon we don't know much more about this horse than that girl."

"I can't picture Miss Dawn as a horse thief."

"Not saying she is."

"What *are* you saying, Pa?"

"I saw her today." Pa shifted out of the doorway, allowing Justin room to maneuver Bonnie. "Going into the pool hall on the arm of some man. Thought you put a stop to that."

"That was my understanding." Justin walked Bonnie into her stall. He removed her halter, came out, and shut the door.

"Talk to her. Make sure she understands the conditions of living here." Pa moved toward the door. Pausing, he turned to Justin. "Because if I hear she's been at that pool hall again, she's gone." He slammed the door.

Justin doubled over, letting all the air out of his lungs. He raked his hands back and forth through his hair. That woman. Where was her sense of decorum? Her speech was refined. Her skin was milky smooth. Even the way she carried herself pointed to a person of some social standing. She ought to know better.

Justin returned to Bonnie's stall. She hung her head over the door and whinnied. He rubbed her forehead down the bridge of her nose. Resting his forehead against hers, her coat's earthy, sweet scent soothed his nerves as he spoke softly to her.

"Have you been thieved, girl?" Pursing his lips, he exhaled

roughly. He drew his head back, their Sunday ride playing in his mind. "When you're with her, it's like you've known her for years. Like it's not just her taking care of you, but you're taking care of her too."

Bonnie's head bobbed.

"I thought so. I don't want you to lose your cozy stall here, but if she doesn't stay out of that pool hall, that's what will happen. So, if there's anything you can do to help, better do it."

Justin scratched her behind the ears and left the stable. The bushes rustled nearby, but a quick glance before he entered the back door revealed nothing. Rebecca was stuffing a drawer with hand towels, and Eliza Dawn was sewing at the table.

"Pa come through here?"

"No, he left out the front door. He was going for a walk." Rebecca shut the drawer. "Do you need him?"

Perhaps Pa took a walk to cool down after their conversation in the barn. That might explain the noise outside. Justin shook his head. "We just spoke."

"Oh?"

Justin nodded toward Eliza Dawn. "About you."

"About me?" She raised her eyebrows.

"Pa caught you going into the pool hall today. You were arm in arm with that Scottish fella. The same one you were with coming out of Hildesheim's the other day." Justin rubbed his hand over his stubbled beard. "Thought you said he was someone you just bumped into."

Rebecca glanced at Justin, then Eliza Dawn. She ducked her head and busied herself with kitchen chores.

"Yes, and he ordered shirts for himself and four other lads. Today, I was following up with him about the order." She held up the blue fabric. "In fact, this is one of the shirts. Not that my business is any of your business."

"Lads? You know him well enough you're beginning to talk like him."

"I'll tell you what I know, Mr. Hogue." Eliza Dawn dropped the fabric in her lap, balling her fists around it. "I've known him about as long as I've known you. In that time, he has been welcoming, kind, and generous. Not once has he given off a judgmental air. But you have struggled to invite me in from the very first, despite what your mother taught you."

Though Eliza Dawn's comment left a bitter taste in his mouth, Justin couldn't deny Ma would have been more broadminded and benevolent. He was torn between a desire to embody his mother's heart for others and a competing desire to meet his father's expectations. Would it always be impossible to do both?

Eliza Dawn tossed the partially made shirt in her basket. She stood, pushed in her chair, grabbed the basket from the table, and turned to go.

"Where are you going?"

"I had hoped this arrangement would work. I needed it to work." She closed her eyes and let her head fall back, exhaling toward the ceiling. "But it's creating too much tension between you and your father and disrupting my way of doing business. So, I'll gather my things and leave straight away."

"What? No." Rebecca moved toward her but stopped short when Eliza Dawn raised a flattened palm.

"Rebecca, I cherish our time together, but it's come to an end."

"Justin, is this what you intended?" Rebecca propped her hands on her hips.

"Miss Dawn, it is not my desire that you should go." Justin placed two fingers at his temple, rubbing in a circular motion. "I would rather you allow Rebecca and me to help you develop other ways to connect with your customers. Ways that don't try my father's sensibilities."

The front door scraped open, and heavy footfalls drummed up the foyer stairway.

"I'm listening." Eliza Dawn held the sewing basket before her, her arms forming a stiff *V*.

"Well, I don't know." Justin kept massaging his temple. "For starters, maybe you could conduct follow-up meetings at another location, like Gray's Café."

"I imagine I would have to purchase a meal if I met my customers there." She tilted her head. "My customers would also be expected to purchase a meal and want me to pick up that expense."

"The gentleman who purchased Dolly told Sam you have a sweet tea at the pool hall. I'm sure Mrs. Gray would be fine with such an order." Justin shrugged. "Perhaps your customers wouldn't balk too much about purchasing tea. I'm sure it's less expensive than their beverage of choice at the pool hall."

Eliza Dawn eyed him narrowly. Was she considering the possibility?

"Some days you might have pie." He grinned. "To change things up a bit."

Her shoulders relaxed, and she smiled. "I'll think about it. Do you have more ideas?"

"You could have cake, biscuits, cornbread." Tapping his thumb to each finger, he issued the list.

She tilted her head, shifting the basket to her hip. "You know what I mean."

"I'm fresh out right now. Let's think of more tomorrow." Justin yawned and stretched. "For now, why don't we all turn in right here in this house? Except for me—I'm going to the bunkroom. But you'll stay?"

"For now."

~

"I'm so glad you're staying." Rebecca hugged Eliza Dawn. "One thing you'll have to learn is you can't just walk away. We talk things out here. Leaving is not the first step. It's the last resort."

Rebecca wiped the kitchen counters. Justin stood and stretched. He unbuttoned his vest, removed it, and dropped it into the laundry basket at the bottom of the stairs by the back door.

"The other thing you must learn is to be honest and upfront with us." He caught her gaze, and lowered his voice. "Pa wasn't the only one who noticed you entering the pool hall."

Her breath caught. "You?"

He nodded.

"But you didn't say anything."

"Didn't feel a need to address it right away." He opened his mouth as if to say more but turned to grab his Stetson from the stair rail. He tipped his hat on the way out. "See you in the morning. Sleep tight."

"I'm heading up." Rebecca squeezed Eliza Dawn's shoulder as she passed. "Are you coming?"

"I'm going to finish my tea." She rubbed her stomach. "Let my stomach settle before I go to bed."

"All right. I'll see you in the morning."

"Bright and early."

"Oh, I forgot to mention, a gentleman stopped by today with a bundle of mending. I cleared some space under the back stairs for your sewing business. It might be easier than finding a place for it in the lost and found room."

"Rebecca, you're so kindhearted." Eliza Dawn smiled. "I'm expecting another basket of mending from Mrs. Pratt. Will there be room for it as well?"

"Sure." Rebecca leaned against the door facing. "I'm glad you had the opportunity to meet Mrs. Pratt."

"She reminds me a little of the nosy church woman in Alabama."

"Reserve your opinion of her. Keep an open mind and give her time." Rebecca's eyes brightened. "I promise she'll surprise you. And in the best possible way. Salt of the earth, that woman."

"I'll have to take your word for it."

"One more thing." Rebecca walked to the laundry basket and pulled a skirt from the middle. "I hope you don't mind, but I had some solid blue fabric that matched your blue and brown plaid. I wanted to do something nice for you, so I added a few layers of ruffles at the bottom of the skirt. It can easily be removed if you don't like it."

Eliza Dawn took the skirt, blinking back the moisture in her eyes. "I don't know what to say." Returning to the kitchen table, she folded the skirt in her lap. She fingered the hem. It had been ages since she'd worn anything with ruffles. "It's lovely."

Rebecca joined her at the table. Laying her hand on Eliza Dawn's, she sighed softly. "I know there must be a story behind your skirt."

"I left South Carolina in a hurry, and the one outfit I had to my name was badly damaged early on." She ran her hand across the skirt. "This was given to me by a woman in Georgia, obviously much shorter than me. I'm thankful to have it."

"Why didn't you add layers to the bottom yourself?"

"I've been so busy sewing for others. I haven't given much thought to taking time to sew for myself." She shrugged. "I always push my needs to the bottom of the list."

"Leave the blue floral for me, and I'll make sure it reaches the ankle too." Rebecca smiled sweetly and patted her hands.

"You've already done so much. I couldn't ask you to do that for me."

"You're not asking. Let me bless you." Rebecca squeezed Eliza Dawn's hand. "It's all right to let others do for you occasionally. You don't always have to be so independent."

"I've had to rely on myself for a long time." Eliza Dawn

brushed a wavy strand from her brow. "I've grown accustomed to it."

"Well, you've got me now." Rebecca stood, giving her a gentle hug. "Don't stay up too late. Get some rest."

Eliza Dawn set her sewing basket under the stairs. The space Rebecca had cleared was generous. She laid her hand over her chest. Rebecca had made as much room for Eliza Dawn in her heart as in their home. Would she experience a tougher goodbye with anyone along this journey?

She turned to go up the back stairs, her toe stubbing the laundry basket. A glint of white in the middle of Justin's dark-colored vest caught her eye. She reached over, tugging at it. The grubby envelope sprang free from its entanglement. Her heart fluttered. She pressed the envelope to her chest. Tucking it under her arm, she picked up the vest and fished in the pockets. Hooking the ring with her finger, she pulled it out and dropped the vest into the basket. Smiling, she took the items to the table.

Placing the pieces before her, she picked up the unfinished cup of tea. She took a couple of sips and set the cup down. Examining the ring, she rubbed her thumb over the thistle relief. She'd seen images of thistle since she left South Carolina. Where? Among the prospectors? She searched her memory. Jewelry, saddles, gun handles, the list went on. She had encountered so many prospectors and townsfolk over her month-long journey.

How could it have only been a month since she'd left South Carolina? She rubbed her hands down her thighs, images flitting through her mind of a young house girl who'd met her at the back door with a change of men's clothes and the dark-skinned man who'd waited at the edge of the property with Bonnie. They'd risked so much to help her. Though she would always cherish them, she'd take their names to the grave to keep their connection to her escape from being discovered. Sighing, she returned the ring to the table.

Eliza Dawn thumbed the edge of the envelope. She had intended to ask the Scots about the letter, but the incident with Simon cut her time short. Simon. Her heart clenched. What would Justin do if he discovered Simon had followed her into the pool hall? Thank goodness Mr. Hogue hadn't spotted the boy, or he would undoubtedly have demanded her immediate dismissal.

She rubbed the back of her hand. The walk home with Justin had been pleasant. When his hand grazed the back of hers, she half-hoped he'd loop his pinky with hers. Sweet school girl desires. Hadn't she had enough of life to snuff out such thought? Even if she were free to act on such stirrings, she wasn't foolish enough to believe relationships were built on such romantic ideologies. Money and convenience. That's what men sought in a relationship.

Releasing a rough plume of air, she blew loose strands of hair from her face. She closed her eyes and rubbed the bridge of her nose. Resting her chin on her hand, she stared at the letter. She pulled it closer and picked at the edge of the flap. It was only tacked down at the center. A little steam might open it. She pushed it away. Better to resist her investigative tendencies. It might further upset the delicate balance between her and Justin. Instead, she'd be satisfied with visiting the saddler tomorrow and suggesting to him that reading it might reveal valuable information that could help them home the items.

She would mention the letter to Ewan tomorrow. But when and where? She'd grown accustomed to meeting him at the pool hall. The way the lads welcomed her today warmed her heart. Though she worried Ewan would discover her purpose, she enjoyed his closeness at the table and protective hand on her shoulder as they moved through the room. Sure, she could take care of herself, but she grew weary of doing it alone every moment of every day.

A heaviness settled in her chest. Besides that, she needed his story for her article. She picked up her tea cup and took it to the small washtub. Peering out the window, she caught movement in the bushes around the side of the house. Hadn't she heard Mr. Hogue come in while she and Justin talked? She leaned closer to the window, squinting. Nothing. She scanned the darkened treetops. Perfectly still. She studied the landscape's shadowed layers and dark lines. The bushes had gone still.

Chapter Fifteen

Eliza Dawn emerged from the back stairway to find Rebecca washing the dinner plates. Rebecca stared out the window, hands barely moving. Eliza Dawn walked over and rested her hands on Rebecca's shoulders. Then, propping her chin on Rebecca's shoulder, she gazed through the rain-streaked window at the blurry landscape.

"What's so interesting out there?"

"The West. Don't you think it's full of adventure?"

Eliza Dawn stepped back with a shrug. What an unusual daydream for a woman their age. Most daydreamed of husbands and families, not adventure. It was these little curiosities in Rebecca's character that endeared her so.

"I don't know. I've never been." Eliza Dawn gingerly pulled a plate from the too-hot rinse pan and bumped Rebecca to the side. "I'll dry."

"I envy these prospectors. Who knows what they'll experience during their travels?" The pitter-patter of raindrops slowed, and Rebecca drew the curtains closed. Picking up another plate, she dragged the dishrag across its smooth surface.

"Great mountains and rolling rivers. I hear there are buffalo out West. I can't imagine."

"There are mountains here." Eliza Dawn set the plate aside and took the next one from Rebecca. "And the river is just at the end of Main Street."

With a huff, Rebecca dropped the dishrag in the wash pan and turned to face Eliza Dawn.

"These mountains are mere hills, and that river is full of steamboats." She placed her elbows on the counter, propping her chin on her hands. "It's become too crowded here. I used to explore all along the river a few years ago, but now there's a risk of happening upon prospectors, wanderers, or outlaw camps."

"If you go west, you'll find more prospectors, wanderers, and outlaws." Eliza Dawn laughed.

"Thanks for the encouragement." Rebecca wrinkled her nose.

"You have a good life, that's all. You have people who love and appreciate you." Eliza Dawn placed another plate on the dry stack.

"That's true. But I feel drawn to something out there. It's more than wanting to experience something new for myself. I think there's some good I'm meant to do there." She sighed wistfully. "I keep praying I'll understand it better."

"But God doesn't answer your prayers. I understand what that's like."

Rebecca straightened. "I wouldn't say that. It's more like I'm in a season of waiting. I believe God *is* listening. But it's not about Him granting my wishes. It's about learning to trust Him, His timing, His yeses and nos. It's about learning to be in a relationship with Him. And, ultimately, that's what I want—more than I want to go west. More than I want relief from this congested town."

"These prospectors will clear out soon. I imagine some of the townspeople will join them." Eliza Dawn pointed to the plates in the dishwater and then held out her hand. "So, you'll have more time to explore your river banks right here in Van Buren."

Sighing, Rebecca pulled another plate from the hot, soapy water and slipped it into the rinse pan. "It won't ever be the same, though. It's forever changed."

"What's changed?" Justin appeared inside the back door.

"The town." Eliza Dawn gestured out the window.

"Was never going to stay the same." Justin slid his feet out of his boots, discarding them near the door.

"The river's changed too." Rebecca rinsed another plate and passed it to Eliza Dawn.

"And so has the weather." Justin grabbed a biscuit from the counter. "Rain seems to be letting up. Preserves?"

Rebecca dried her hands. She grabbed the preserves from the other side of the counter and handed the jar to Justin. He pointed to the utensil drawer. She stuck her tongue out at him, passing him a butter knife.

"Be careful. Your face will stick that way." Justin slathered the biscuit with a blob of gooey muscadine. "Then how will you get a fella?"

Rebecca grabbed the dish towel from Eliza Dawn and popped him with it. "I'm not after a fella, and you know it."

Justin's eyebrows shot up. "Don't start something you can't finish."

The interaction nipped at Eliza Dawn's heart. Why couldn't she and her brother share such easy banter and playfulness? These siblings were grieving the loss of a mother, but they still had these light moments. Perhaps she and her brother had endured more losses than a sibling relationship could bear.

"And you." Justin teasingly directed himself to Eliza Dawn, "You weren't going to do any chores around here."

"Oh, this is what I do for fun." Eliza Dawn snatched the damp towel from Rebecca, twirling it above her head.

"I'll make note of that." Justin wrote his note in the air.

"Don't ask Miss Dawn for entertaining ideas. She'll have you washing dishes."

"No, no." She wagged her finger at him. "Not washing, drying. Let's get it right."

"Got it." Justin directed his attention to Rebecca. "Wanted to let you know I'll be setting out to Levi's soon. Do you have errands you need me to run before supper?"

"I don't." Rebecca turned to Eliza Dawn. "How about you?"

"I'm sure Mrs. Pratt has left the mending basket at the mercantile by now. But I can collect that myself."

"I don't mind fetching it for you." Justin stuffed the last bite of biscuit into his mouth.

"That's sweet, but it will give me a reason to get out of the house."

"How are things going with the sewing?"

"I had plenty of work before I took on Mrs. Pratt's mending order."

"I'm sorry. I thought you needed more."

"It's fine. You didn't know."

Justin popped the last bite into his mouth. "I better scoot."

"Wait just a minute." Rebecca crossed the room to a dirty clothes basket by the back door. Pulling a wrinkled shirt from the top, she held it out to Justin. "Smell this. Tell me what you think."

Justin recoiled, narrowing his eyes.

"I'm not up to any chicanery." She shoved the shirt into his chest. "Just smell it."

Justin took the shirt, holding it up by the shoulders. "Whose is it?"

"It's Simon's."

Eliza Dawn's breath caught. She turned slowly, trying not to appear overly interested.

Justin buried his nose in the shirt. Scrunching his face, he jerked the shirt away. "What is that? Cigar smoke and horses?"

"That's what I thought." Rebecca nodded, propping her hand on her hip. "Now, where would he pick up the scent of horses and cigars?"

"Don't all boys sneak tobacco in some form or another?" Eliza Dawn forced a casual tone.

"Not Simon. He's not prone to following a crowd. Pa had a falling out with a group of tobacco farmers when he was steamboating back east. Forbids supporting those plow chasers in any way." Justin hung the shirt on the back of the chair at the kitchen table. "Do you know where he is now?"

"I assume he's at school." Rebecca returned to the counter, gathering a stack of plates to put in the cabinet. "But how can we be sure he's not off doing something else?"

"Wouldn't the younger children have mentioned if he hadn't been in school with them?" Eliza Dawn collected a pile of utensils to put away.

"Seems reasonable." Justin moved to help them. "I'd better ask him about it just the same."

A nagging clutched Eliza Dawn's chest. Simon's ashen face as he talked about the possibility of Justin discovering his misbehavior flashed through her mind. Would Justin be more understanding of the youth's innocent fixation on her than his hanging around the pool hall for fun?

"I don't know what's gotten into him." Justin rubbed his forehead. "These crazy antics since Ma." He took a deep breath, eyes closed tight. "Trick riding. Hanging out, who knows where?"

"He's a young boy who's lost his mother." A knot formed in the pit of Eliza Dawn's stomach as she pictured Simon falling in love, marrying, and having children, all without a mother's hand to guide him.

"Still, there must be consequences."

Eliza Dawn smoothed her apron, swallowing hard. "Justin, I

know where his shirt picked up the odor of cigars, and it's not what you suspect. It's rather innocent."

"Oh? How would you know?"

"I was in the pool hall yesterday."

"For the last time." Justin arched his eyebrows.

She cleared her throat. Her gaze cut to Rebecca, who was busying herself with kitchen chores, head down. *Looks like I'm on my own now.*

"For the last time." Her words came slowly.

"I hope we're clear on that. Nothing but trouble there."

"Can we get back to Simon, please?" Rebecca interrupted. "So, he skipped school to play pool?"

Eliza Dawn ducked her head. "Not exactly."

"What then?" Justin demanded.

"It seems Simon has cottoned to me."

"He's ... he's cottoned to you? And how would you know this?"

"Well, he's your kid brother. I'm not going to let him hang out in a pool hall knowing how you feel about it, now am I?"

"What did you do?" Rebecca folded her arms across her chest.

"I grabbed him by the ear and dragged him out. Then, I gave him a good scolding for not being in school. That's when he told me he doesn't like school but likes me."

Justin ran his hand through his hair and down his neck. He paced a few steps. Then he locked eyes with Eliza Dawn. "So, what I'm hearing is Simon figured out you've been spending time at that vile pool hall and followed you there?"

Eliza Dawn traced the wood grain on the counter, avoiding eye contact. "It seems so."

"That explains the cigar smell, but what about the horses?" Rebecca shrugged with her palms uplifted.

Justin returned to the counter, leaning close. "Do you see

how your being there complicates everything? I'm trying to look out for you and this family. I can't do it alone, however. I need you to cooperate."

His words tugged at her heart. "I hadn't considered my presence there would impact anyone other than me. Being around the prospectors in pool halls, saloons, and gambling halls has been the easiest way to conduct business with them. I go to them. It's how I work. I don't know if I can change that. Perhaps we should reconsider my lodging arrangements. If I stay in the camps, many of my customers would be at my doorstep."

"We're not back to that again." Justin slapped the counter. "Miss Dawn, we won't resign ourselves to your staying in the camps. He's not the first Hogue child to be sweet on a boarder." Justin shot a look at Rebecca, who scrunched her face at him. "We'll work it out, but I've got to get to Levi's right now. Do I have your assurance you'll stay put?"

She shrugged and nodded. "I'm going into town, but my things will stay put."

"No pool hall." He flicked open his pocket watch, waiting for her reply.

She pursed her lips. "Agreed."

Justin moved toward the door, grabbing his hat.

"Mr. Hogue." Eliza Dawn thumbed the button at her collar.

He turned, hat in hand, patting it impatiently.

"There's one more thing I should tell you." She bit the inside of her lip.

He released a haggard breath. "What's that?"

"While I was talking with the Scottish prospectors, one of them mentioned he's a blacksmith, and it's been weeks since he's had access to a proper forge."

Justin shrugged and patted his hat. "Okay?"

"I mentioned I had a friend with a forge that's not used much."

"You didn't." Justin rubbed his hand across his forehead. "Tell me you did not offer him the use of my forge."

"Well, no." She paused. "I told him I'd talk to you and see if you might be open to renting the space for the next several days."

"Great." Justin huffed, turned on his heel, and left.

Chapter Sixteen

"**M**r. Mooney, has Mrs. Pratt stopped in this morning?" Eliza Dawn drew aside the yellow gingham curtain in Sam's front window, scanning Main Street. The hustle and bustle of prospecting parties and townsfolk filled the road through town. Her gaze drifted from face to face, but none looked familiar.

In two days' time, she'd witnessed an inexplicable disturbance in the bushes at Hogue House more than once. She was inclined to attribute it to a squirrel or other wild animal, except similar oddities plagued her while lodging with a church family in Alabama. She was half-convinced someone was following her. Was it one of the Scots? Were they still trying to leave gifts for her even though she'd told them it was unnecessary?

Sam sidled up beside her, taking in the view. She smiled when he placed his hand tenderly on her back. There was such a warm, fatherly quality about the man. Had the kindly shopkeeper ever had children of his own?

"Won't do to look." He dropped his hand to his side. "She

comes by around one o'clock, usually on Tuesdays and Thursdays. Very timely, that woman."

Eliza Dawn forced a smile. She didn't know where she'd be at one o'clock, but it wouldn't be here. She wasn't up to making pleasantries with Mrs. Pratt today. She was thankful Sam was so familiar with his regular customers.

"Does Justin have a set time he comes by?"

"Used to come in at nine in the morning and four in the afternoon." Sam gathered candy jars from a shelf and took them to the front counter. "Still comes in twice a day, but the time is anybody's guess."

She turned to look at Sam. "What's changed?"

"Got a new boarder that's shaking things up." Sam smiled and tipped his head toward her.

"Me?"

Sam nodded as he refilled the jars with colorful candies. "That's right."

"I've disrupted his life, haven't I?" Eliza Dawn joined him at the counter. "It wasn't my intention to be a burden or cause trouble."

"I wouldn't call it a disruption. You've shaken him up a bit, is all." Sam patted her hand. "It's good to be shaken up now and again. Shake a jar of milk, you get butter. And who doesn't love butter?" A broad smile swept his face.

Her cheeks flushed, and she squeezed Sam's hand. Justin had certainly shaken her up with his saddle soother scent, ride to the bluff, and walk home from town. She half-believed his argument against the pool hall was based on concern for her safety as much as protecting their family's reputation.

She scooted a penny across the counter toward Sam.

"Encouragement is free here." He winked and scooted the penny back to her.

"What about lemon drops?"

"It's on me today." Sam scooped a bright yellow candy out with two fingers.

She nodded her thanks. "Mr. Mooney, if I needed to load up on supplies, how quickly could you put an order together?"

"You mean everything you need for your trip west?"

She nodded.

Sam scratched his head. "Might take a couple of days. You thinking about leaving early?"

"I haven't decided yet." She shrugged. "I might go ahead to Fort Smith and see if the men at the fort need uniforms repaired."

"Not getting enough work here?"

"It's not that." She paused, glancing toward the window. "It's getting time I go."

"Well, if you get a list together, I'll do my best to fill it." Sam patted the counter to get her attention. He held her gaze. "But folks are buying me out of things left and right. So, you don't be upset with an old man if there's some things we must wait on. All right?"

"I'm sure I can manage with whatever you're able to fill." She turned, pointing down the aisle near the window. "I'm going to browse for a few moments if you don't mind."

"Be my guest. Take your time. Be fine if you browse into the middle of next week."

Eliza Dawn ran her finger along the shelf by the window. Mooney's Mercantile was part of Justin's world. He was obviously more than a customer to Sam. In some ways, they acted more like father and son than Justin and Mr. Hogue. She glanced over her shoulder at him. Stick candy plinked in the jar as he filled it.

She fingered the yellow and white curtains, a homey flair for a store. A decorative metal piece hung on the wall. From Justin's friend, the blacksmith? A box of pastries from Hildesheim's rested on the counter. She'd grown more comfortable with this town than she intended. Her eyes roved the street. Mooney's was part of Justin's world, and she felt safe in it.

She picked up a sachet of lavender and inhaled deeply. Would she ever feel safe in the prospectors' world? The constant moving and uprooting. It didn't matter. She had to put more miles between her and her merciless husband. When she wrote Eleanor of her plans to leave with the prospectors from South Carolina, they concocted a plan for Eleanor to keep up with the Charleston newspaper. If Merritt Fairfax submitted an advertisement for a runaway wife, Eleanor would notify Eliza Dawn. She was sure her name would be slandered. Fairfax would likely accuse her of some immorality—adultery, theft, or the like—to save face amongst Charleston's elite. It would complete her ruination, and no man would ever want her. But where had the desires of men ever gotten her? Nowhere.

Unfortunately, Fairfax was at the top of the list of suspects who might be following her. Things would be more complicated if he'd chosen not to take out the runaway advertisement. It had been some time since she'd received any correspondence from Eleanor. If only there were some way to know for certain whether Fairfax was coming for her and her little quarter horse. She wouldn't allow herself to consider what he might do to her if he found her—or Bonnie.

Her eyes ranged the landscape once more. A mass of unfamiliar faces. She couldn't hide out in Sam's store all day. Fortunately, she'd already dropped her latest article in the post. Now, it was time to find Ewan. It was more important than ever that she continue her article series and stay as far ahead of Fairfax as possible. But first, she needed to explain to Ewan why she wouldn't be at the pool hall.

Depositing the sachet in its box, she pulled her shawl tighter and headed out the door.

"Miss Dawn," Sam called.

"Yes?"

"If you ask my opinion, Justin needs a little butter in his life." He grinned.

Her cheeks warmed. "I didn't ask, but thank you, Mr. Mooney."

Eliza Dawn stepped out to the boardwalk and perused the notice board. Reaching up, she trailed words on a notice with her finger: *Ewan MacKinnon, Scottish Prospector Camp, north side of town.* Gray's Café wasn't far. If she could catch Ewan, perhaps they could grab some pie, and she could get him to share his story. But if she couldn't get him to share, she might have to explore north of town later this evening.

"Well, hello." Ewan wrapped his fingers over hers.

She jumped at his sudden appearance.

"I see ye wis thinking aboot me." He tipped his head toward his advertisement.

"I was thinking I'd like to hear the story about what drew you to the gold expedition." She turned him towards the café.

He glanced over his shoulder, pointing. "I wis gunna meet 'eh lads. Thought ye wis too."

"Change of plans, Ewan." She smiled sweetly. "Let's have a glass of tea at Gray's Café or a sweet treat at Hildesheim's."

"Ah, it's aboot time ye warmed to me." A broad smile broke through his reddish whiskers. "But A'm famished. Willny ye let me buy ye a meal?"

"Oh, that's not necessary. I don't want to put you out."

"Don't ye ever do anny'hin fer enjoyment?"

A heaviness spread through her. Since her life turned upside down over a month ago, she hadn't done anything for the sheer enjoyment of it except ride Bonnie through the countryside. Not wanting to call attention to Bonnie, she refrained from sharing that detail with Ewan.

"My work provides enough enjoyment. I prefer to stay focused on that for now." She pressed a smile.

"Well, A've waited patiently to hev ye to maself, so A'd lek to make a meal of it." Ewan opened the door for her with a flourish of his arm.

She laughed. "A little gallantry will get you nowhere, Mr. MacKinnon."

"It's worth a try. I hev to pull oot all 'eh stops if A'm to best Justin Hogue." He guided her toward a table near the entrance.

"I prefer to sit near the kitchen if you please." She weaved through tables to the back of the room, preferring to sit in full view of the room and near an alternate way out.

"Ur ye ashamed to be seen wi' me?" Ewan half-joked.

"Of course not." She tugged at her shawl. "It's so much colder since the rain moved through. The kitchen might offer a little extra warmth."

"Ah, tis a cozy spot ye're looking fer." He pulled out a chair for her. "That bodes well fer me."

"Don't get any untoward ideas." She held up a flattened palm in warning.

"Wouldn't think of it." He scooted her seat forward. "I hev only gentlemanly intentions, I assure ye. May I?"

He indicated her shawl.

"I'll keep it, thanks." She pulled it closer around her shoulders, appreciating the barrier to the chill air.

An older woman with round cheeks and a bright smile appeared at their table. "Welcome to Gray's Café. I don't believe I've seen the two of you in here before." She glanced around the room. "But then I haven't seen narry one of these folks in here before." Her belly laugh trailed off.

"We're new to toon." Ewan folded his hands in front of him.

"I expect you belong to some prospector group or other."

"Aye, tis true 'nough."

"Well, such a lot of you has overwhelmed this town I've only one thing on the menu." She tapped the table. "Today is vegetable stew. If you don't like that, come back tomorrow. I'll have meatloaf."

"A'll take yer stew. Do ye hev hot tea?"

"Stew and tea." She nodded. "And you, miss?"

Justin's boyish grin flashed in her mind, accompanied by his words. *Some days you might have pie.* Perhaps it was time to change things up. "Do you have pie?"

"I asked ye to a meal, and ye're gunna hev pie?" Ewan's countenance grew stern.

"Settle down." She shot him a sidelong glance. "When I'm finished with pie, I'll have stew for dessert if I'm still hungry. You did ask if I do anything for enjoyment, after all. Today, I'll have dessert first."

Ewan beamed. "Bring 'eh woman pie."

"Peach or pecan?"

"Pecan, please."

"Back in a whistle." Mrs. Gray bustled away in a flurry.

"Now, what did you mean earlier about besting Justin Hogue?" Eliza Dawn propped her chin on steepled hands, smiling.

"Ye're lodging at his boardinghouse, ur ye not?"

"I am."

"Then he has an unfair advantage. He disnae hev to work as hard to gain yer attentions."

Heat rose in Eliza Dawn's cheeks. "I don't know he has much interest in my attentions."

"Then he's a fool." Ewan reached for her hand.

"Outta the way, dearie." Mrs. Gray bumped Ewan's shoulder with her hip, and he quickly withdrew his hand at the command, smiling politely.

"Pardon." Ewan leaned in, sniffing the stew Mrs. Gray was holding. "Smells as good as ma mother's cooking."

"Hot stew and hot tea for the gentleman." Mrs. Gray set a bowl and tin cup in front of Ewan. "And pecan pie for the lady." Her young assistant set a plate and cup in front of Eliza Dawn.

"The pie looks delightful." Eliza Dawn raised her fork in a salute.

"I took the liberty of bringing you hot tea, sweetie." Mrs. Gray was gone with her assistant before they could thank her.

"A'm interested in ye. Tell me aboot yerself." Ewan blew on his stew before taking a bite.

She cut off a small piece of pie. "There's not much to tell. I'd rather hear about you."

"Ma story is 'eh same as the rest of 'eh lads. Lost ma home, came to America, headed west." Ewan nodded at her. "Yer turn. Where ur ye from?"

"Oh, I just remembered. I wanted to ask if you have heard about the letter Justin is trying to deliver to one of the prospectors."

"*Mm-hmm.*" He grunted and nodded as he ate.

"Would you like to see it? I don't have it with me right now, but I'd love to show it to you."

"Not interested."

"You don't want to look at it? It could be from your family, assuming you have family."

"I do."

"Wouldn't they send you correspondence while you're apart for such a lengthy time?"

"They would not."

"Oh." Taking a bite of pie, Eliza Dawn chewed slowly. She set her fork down. "Why not?"

"Ma people cannae read, nor write."

Her stomach dropped. "Ewan, I'm sorry. I didn't think."

"Tis not a bother." He finished his stew and wiped his mouth. "One less thing to entangle me wi' Hogue."

She shoved a piece of crust around her plate. "I asked him about the forge, but I don't think he's favorable to an arrangement."

"I ken he wouldn't be."

"Is there something going on between you two?"

"Business puts us at cross purposes. Tis nothing to worry aboot."

A bear of a man stooped in the doorway, entering Gray's Café. He straightened, revealing a familiar black mop and yellowed teeth. Big Jim. Her stomach churned. She dropped her fork and grabbed Ewan's hand. Fishing coins from the pocket inside her skirt waist, she tossed them on the table.

"It's time to go, Ewan."

"But yer pie."

"It's time to go." She hissed through clenched teeth.

Ewan glanced toward the entrance as Eliza Dawn dragged him out the back door. "Is 'at bloke giving ye trouble again? A'll set him straight."

"No." She scanned the street. "I simply can't stand to be around him after the incident in the pool hall."

"Yer trembling."

"It's nothing." She squeezed his hand. "Thank you for dinner. I have an appointment. We'll talk later. I'll find you." She waved as she dashed up Main Street, not waiting for his reply.

Chapter Seventeen

Justin rode Rex at a canter, slowed to a trot, and then a walk. Bringing the stallion to a halt, he slid from the saddle and led the horse to the rail of the round pen. He removed the saddle, settling it on the top rail.

"Good boy." Justin rubbed Rex's face, moving his hands under his eyes and around his ears. "You've come a long way, ol' Bangtail. I remember when I couldn't get near you."

"What you've accomplished with him is impressive." Levi appeared at the edge of the pen.

"He's tested my patience. It took a while to curry the kinks out." Justin scratched Rex behind the ears. "Knowing the complete history of the horses I get my hands on would be helpful, but I have no doubt Rex had been mistreated. I wish I knew his breed. He's got some characteristics of a draft horse and some of a thoroughbred. Thanks for giving us space to work."

"It's been a pleasure to witness his progress." Levi ran his hand up and down Rex's forehead. "If I needed a horse, he's the one I'd choose. So steady now, and I love his white-masked face."

"He's got the look of a warhorse." Justin placed a crossbuck saddle on Rex's back and rigged him for packing. "This patch of black over his ears and chest resembles a helmet and breastplate. He's ruggedly handsome, for sure. Help me load these barrels."

"It would take me a while to save the money, but if a prospector doesn't snap him up, I'm interested." Levi attached a barrel to one side of the sawbucks while Justin loaded his barrel on the other side. "So, how is the search going for the prospector?"

"Search for the prospector?"

"The letter, Justin. Any luck finding the owner?" A cock-eyed grin crossed Levi's face. "Did you take my advice?"

"Ah, you want to know whether or not I've proceeded with Eliza Dawn's help."

"And did you?"

Justin rubbed one hand down Rex's neck and grabbed the top of the sawbuck with the other. He shook it back and forth, making sure it was secure. "I decided not to because she might get the idea to return to the pool hall and ask prospectors about it. I'm putting her off."

Truth was putting her off hadn't been that difficult. Not with Pa and Simon and their antics. They'd spent more time discussing her business habits than that letter.

"You should reconsider. It's a surefire way to keep an eye on her since you're so concerned about how she's spending her time."

"I hope she doesn't bring up the idea of going to the saddler today." He mounted Rex. "She mentioned it yesterday. It was a good idea, but I didn't have time."

"So, you're teaming up after all. Good man."

"Not so fast. We're not a team." Justin rode Rex around the ring, putting him through the paces with different patterns. "I told her we'd work together, but I don't plan to follow through. I'll find a way to back out. I don't have the time."

"You're a few horses shy of a herd, I'd say." Levi tapped his temple. "If it were me, I'd find a way to spend more time with her."

"Like you found ways to spend more time with Allie?" Justin laughed, recalling Levi's efforts to duck Allie during their infamous search.

"Hindsight does wonders. I'm a wiser man now." Levi chuckled. "So, what are you doing with the letter? How are you going to find the recipient?"

"Aren't you listening? I don't have the time for a goose chase." Justin dismounted, grabbed a rag from the rail, and wiped the pack rigging. He handed pieces to Levi, starting with the barrels. "I imagine I'll put the letter and the ring in the lost and found room."

"Isn't that Miss Dawn's room?" Levi hefted a barrel over the rail, setting it on the ground outside the round pen.

"Yes. What's your point?"

"Wouldn't she find the letter and move forward with the search?"

"No." Justin stopped what he was doing. He stared at Levi. "You don't think she'd do that, do you?"

"How you describe her, it seems like she has a strong sense of curiosity. I bet she spends a fair amount of time looking through items in that room. Probably sees them as treasures. Just a matter of time before she comes across the letter and ring if you stow them there. And if she's anything like Allie, she'll be across lots on the search before you know what's happened." Levi laughed.

"I guess I could keep them in the bunkhouse with me. I don't want it in sight, in any case. It'll make me feel obligated." He patted his vest. His brows knit together as he ran his hands down his front. He reached inside the pocket, wiggling his fingers.

"What's the matter?"

"The letter and ring. They're not here." Justin scratched his head, retracing his steps in his mind. He palmed his forehead. "I took my other vest off last night and dropped it in the laundry basket. It should have been right on top, but Rebecca pulled Simon's shirt out."

"I guarantee Miss Dawn gets her hands on them before you do. You should've put them in the bunkhouse when you got home yesterday. You put up a good fight, but it's time to throw in the towel and get on with the search."

Justin bit his lip and scratched his head.

"You trying to think of another way out?"

"Mentioning the bunkhouse ... I'm a clodhopper, Levi."

"Why?"

"When Miss Dawn arrived, I told her we didn't have a spare bed at Hogue House."

"That's true."

"Is it, though?" Justin scratched his head again. "We don't have a spare room, but your old cot is still in the bunkhouse and could be moved. It's piled with my stuff. That's one area I haven't kept in apple pie order since you've been gone."

"Well, get it straightened. Then, when you get home, you can offer her the cot and ask her to give you the letter and ring." Levi winked.

"If she doesn't mention them, I won't either." Justin shook his head. "I can't keep putting her off, and I can't tell her *no*."

"No is a simple enough word. Just say it outright." Levi smiled knowingly.

"There's something about her eyes, Levi. Like the other day, when I wanted to invite her to church. She opened the door. I got caught in those eyes, and I honestly couldn't remember why I was standing there." Justin put a bucket of oats down for Rex. Then he swung the saddle down from the rail and carried it to the tack closet. "Makes me feel like I'm not standing on solid ground."

"I've been there. Only days before Christmas, and it would not do Allie except we find the family the nativity belonged to." Levi hitched his thumb toward the house. "I couldn't look her in the eyes and stand by my 'no.' And I've never regretted it."

"Miss Dawn discovered initials inside the band of the ring. What do you think? Maybe you could show that around when you go to the camps again?"

"I think you need to enlist her assistance in this important undertaking and stop asking my advice about how to get out of it." Levi slapped Justin on the back and laughed.

"I don't know, Levi." Justin gathered more equipment. "I'm not sure I can trust her. She was arm in arm with that MacKinnon fella going into the pool hall yesterday."

Levi shrugged. "And?"

"When I ask how she spent her day, she said she didn't do anything of 'particular interest.'" Justin deposited the items in the tack closet and returned. "So, was she lying to me about going to the pool hall or being with MacKinnon? Or both?"

"Perhaps neither. Perhaps Eliza Dawn didn't find those things to be noteworthy parts of her day." Levi propped his foot on the bottom rung of the round pen. "Lots of prospectors spend time at the hall. So, it makes sense she might collect some customers by keeping company there."

"Or she could be giving MacKinnon the inside scoop about my business." Justin scratched his head. "I'm not the only one who saw her with MacKinnon. Pa did, too, and he wants me to cut her loose. One more misstep, and he'll dismiss her himself. What am I going to do?"

"*Talk* to her."

"I did. I told her what Pa said." Justin propped his hands on his hips. "I told her we both saw her. Then, this morning, she

Of Faith and Dreams

told me Simon was there skipping school. She should have shared that information last night. I don't know what to do about her."

"Talk *to* her, not *at* her. Take an interest in her business. Ask her who has orders with her. Offer to deliver for her." Levi rubbed Rex's shoulder. "So, what if getting the ranch going takes a little longer? You can sell horses long after these forty-niners dust out of town. On the other hand, Miss Dawn may not be here much longer. So, you better determine what you'll do where she's concerned and do it."

"Maybe, but there's one more thing."

Levi sighed. "What's that?"

"She told one of those Scottish prospectors she'd ask if he could use the forge."

"Wonderful. I've offered space here, but they're camped on the other side of town and don't want to get too far from the women and children they've brought with them."

"Wonderful." Justin's voice took on a biting tone. "It's not wonderful. That MacKinnon fella has made a rival of himself. You think I'll let one of his men move into my forge?"

"First, it's not your forge. Call it 'Levi's old forge' or 'the Hogue family forge,' but you wanted nothing to do with it besides making horseshoes." Levi narrowed his eyes. "Second, you don't have to let the man use it for free. He's willing to pay for a space. Just make sure you're asking a fair price."

"You're not suggesting I let the Scots use that space?"

Levi's brows pulled together, and he cocked his head. "Are you the same man who told me Sunday you needed to practice what I was preaching?"

"I was talking about Miss Dawn." Justin's stomach rolled.

Levi tucked his chin and arched his eyebrows. "Sermon doesn't apply to her only. Show the Scots some hospitality. You'll be the better for it."

"I'll consider it." Justin took hold of Rex's bridle. "But right now, I better get this ol' boy bedded down. Listen, Sam had an idea about how I could show these horses off, but it would require your help."

"In a heartbeat. I wouldn't have been able to build my forge out here if your family hadn't been willing to help me with that small space in town first." Levi followed Justin as he led the stallion to its stall. "What can I do?"

"Sam recommended I host an event here. Bring the boardinghouse horses out and show them all riding and packing. He even suggested I have Simon do some trick riding." Walking back to the round pen, Justin motioned for Levi to help him with the barrels. "Said I should ask Conrad to bring baked goods from the pastry shop."

"Good plan." Levi carried a barrel to the horse shed. He dusted off his hands.

Justin led Devil, a seal brown quarter horse, from his enclosure. "All right, Devil, you're coming along fine in the pen. Let's see if you'll respond in an open space."

"It's a shame he was given such an unfriendly name." Levi shook his head, pursing his lips.

"He does well so long as you don't use a harsh tone. Gotta keep it light, or he'll stubborn up." Justin walked Devil into position and signaled the horse to stay. "He's young enough. I'll change his name when I know his personality. He's responded well to retraining so far."

Justin moved several feet away from the horse and blew a high-pitched whistle. Devil nodded his head and snorted. Justin whistled again. Devil nodded and came to Justin. He rubbed the sides of the horse's neck. "Let's do it again."

"I tell you what, the way Simon rides him in the pen is nothing short of a miracle. He gets all the tricks out of this guy he gets from the others, plus a few extra."

"They have a bond, that's for sure. He does well in a small area but is a bit antsy outside the pen." Justin pointed at Devil's feet. "Notice how he's been a little shifty while we're talking? But it's still an improvement. He used to try to walk away as soon as he was beyond a fence rail. He's more well-mannered with Simon, but the goal is to be well-mannered with anyone."

"If anyone can get him there, it's you." Levi folded his arms across his chest. "I have an idea to draw more people out to your event. We'll put down the wagon sheet and have a shindig afterward. Let's do it Thursday."

"A dance? Day after tomorrow?" Justin grimaced. "I don't believe what I'm hearing. The town hermit offering to host a dance."

"Allie has been itching for a dance." Levi rubbed his hand through his hair. "Seems it's been far too long since the town last kicked up its heels. So, get the word out."

"I dunno if I'm up for it, Levi." Justin wiped his brow with his bandana. "It's mighty awkward dancing with my sisters every time we have a dance."

"You haven't danced with anyone besides your sisters since your Ma died. I suspect the girls are tired of dancing with you too. Except for little Edie." Levi chuckled. Then he released a heavy sigh. "It's time you forgave yourself. What happened to your Ma wasn't your fault. It's time to get out there and find a new dance partner."

"Who would I dance with?"

Levi smirked and swatted Justin's shoulder with his hat. "You know who."

Chapter Eighteen

"Afternoon, Sam." A bell jingled above the door. Justin removed his hat and turned, pointing. "What's this?"

"A little something to help me keep track of folks coming and going. I'm going to have to hire some help." Sam patted the counter before coming around to meet Justin. "Can't always be right here. Did you know John Slade is closing shop?"

"Closing the dry goods? Isn't he one of the busiest men in town now?"

"Got gold fever." Sam picked up a button from the floor, rolling it to and fro across the backs of his fingers. "Selling everything and heading west."

"Shame." Justin placed his hat on the counter and glanced out the window toward the dry goods store. "That button stray from its place on the shelf?"

"*Hmm?*"

"Somebody try to swipe it?"

"Oh, no. Likely came off a customer's shirt." Sam chuckled. "I find all sorts of things on the floor these days. Folks drop things or catch their clothes, and a button falls off. I keep things like this at the counter for a day or so. If no one comes for it, I sell it."

"Sounds like a reasonable policy."

"Especially now. Everyone is buying something." Sam placed the button in a glass jar on the front counter. "And I don't have room to store lost things. How much money do you reckon the boardinghouse loses on that lost and found room?"

"We do all right without renting that room." Justin toed the corner of an uneven floorboard.

"You'd do a might better auctioning off those left-behind items after six months or so. I reckon folks have moved on without a care if it hasn't been picked up in that time."

"Doesn't matter much now. Miss Dawn is paying to rent the room for the time being. Though it hardly seems fair since it's so cramped."

"I hear tell she pays more than the men do."

"Sam, do you think there's a problem with that?" Justin toed the board again. "The arrangement is she doesn't help with house chores like the women at Bradley House do. She takes care of her own needs, though, her laundry and such. It was her idea. You know, because of the inconvenience of lodging a woman at a boardinghouse for men."

"Sounds like good business sense to me." Sam moved along the aisles, straightening things as he went. "I don't understand why you didn't send her to Bradley House in the first place."

"No rooms available." Justin thumbed the brim of his hat. "Said she'd try to find lodging with the prospectors in the camps if we couldn't provide a place."

"Didn't you say she'd be going west with them? I reckon she'll end up in their camps soon enough."

"Well, we can't do anything about it once she leaves town. But you know Ma would've insisted on giving her a room." Justin sighed. "Pa, however, worries what it will do to our reputation."

"Don't worry about what people think."

Davis Whitmore appeared from a row of shelves with a box of canned goods. He nodded a silent greeting to Justin, and Sam followed him to the counter. Setting the box down, he took out his wallet, pulled out a banknote, and shoved it across to Sam.

"I believe that will cover everything."

"Indeed, it will." Sam slipped the note into his cashbox.

"I still have that Morgan horse if you're interested." Justin thumped his hat. A little fishing expedition might not reveal anything specific about Eliza Dawn and Bonnie, but he'd determine whether Whitmore was suspect.

Whitmore twirled his handlebar mustache. "How many horses do you have?"

"Six. I'd like to have them all sold by the time the prospectors set out if you know anyone interested in buying."

"I'll keep that in mind." Whitmore's dark eyes were difficult to read. "My heart is set on a strawberry roan—nice quarter horse about fifteen hands. I rode into town on a little palomino paint, but I best get another horse before heading west again. Sure do miss that roan mare. I'd love to have another like her. You'll let me know if you come across one like her. Strawberry roan mare, fifteen hands high?"

Now Whitmore was fishing. Justin maintained strong eye contact and a relaxed expression, though his stomach had just bottomed out. No doubt about it. This man was fixated on Eliza Dawn's horse. It had been two days since she'd ridden Bonnie to the bluff with him. Longer since she'd ridden Bonnie through town. With any luck, folks would think that little horse had moved on.

"Too bad I don't have a horse like that in my lot."

"His other horses are mighty fine." Sam recorded the sale in his ledger. "He's having a horse show out at the Snow homestead. Come take a look. Might see something that makes you forget all about your quarter horse wishes."

"Might do just that."

The bell jingled as a curly, tow-headed teen opened the door. He hitched his thumb as he spoke to Whitmore. "The gents are waiting."

"Good day, gentlemen." Davis twirled his mustache, picked up his box, and followed the boy out the door.

"Something's off about that fella, Sam. I don't like it."

"I've never known you to be wrong when you get a feeling like that. I'll be extra vigilant when he's around." Sam tapped his pencil on the counter. "I suspect that ruffian boy of shoplifting, but I can't catch him. He always comes in with that group of men, and it's too many for me to keep an eye on."

"How much of our conversation do you think Whitmore heard before he rounded that aisle?"

"A good bit, I imagine."

"Do you think he heard the bit about Miss Dawn?"

"Could be."

"Sam, I think Miss Dawn might be in trouble."

"How so?"

"I don't know. I don't have enough information to put it all together yet." Justin rubbed the back of his neck. "But I've got this feeling nagging me something fierce."

"Like I said, I've never known you to be wrong when you get a feeling." Sam patted the counter. "Best not ignore it."

"Yeah, but I don't know what to do about it." Justin raked his teeth over his lip. "I want to keep my family safe."

"What would your ma do?"

Justin exhaled roughly. "Ma would provide refuge. No matter what. Ma would minister to Eliza Dawn's heart."

"And she'd trust the Lord." Sam gave Justin a solid pat on the shoulder. "Do what your ma taught you. Trust God."

"I don't know if I can—"

The bell jingled, and a petite, stylishly dressed woman

entered. She smiled and nodded at Sam as she sashayed past him.

Sam straightened the counter. "Have you had a chance to speak with Levi?"

"I have. He immediately jumped on board with the horse show and added a little twist of his own."

"Oh?"

"You're not going to believe this." Justin leaned across the counter. "He aims to host a shindig following the event."

The woman leaned around a nearby shelf. "Did someone say 'shindig'? Is there to be a dance in town?"

"Mrs. Brandt never misses a dance." Sam winked.

"I'm having a horse show, but there's talk of following the event with a dance." Justin rubbed his thumb along the edge of the counter. "It's not certain, though."

"A dance." Caroline Brandt beamed as she rounded the corner with loops of ribbon in her hand. "Brilliant. And to what purpose is this 'horse show'?"

"I have several horses to sell. Gaining the attention of buyers might be easier if I show them working and riding. Sort of a preview of what they're getting."

"His kid brother will do some trick riding too. And Conrad will sell baked goods."

"Don't get ahead of yourself, Sam." Justin shook his head. "I haven't asked them yet."

"Just a formality."

"Could the tailor shop play a part? My father-in-law and I created more ensembles this year because of all the extra folks in town." Caroline placed the ribbon on the counter. "We haven't sold as much as we anticipated. Some prospectors are traveling with their families, but we rarely see the wives and little ones. This will surely draw them out for some entertainment."

Of Faith and Dreams

"I don't see why not." Sam beamed. "This is turning out to be quite the event."

Justin's breath caught in his throat. "I don't know, Mrs. Brandt. I'm unsure how the tailor shop would fit into it."

"We could have some women model a handful of our dresses before the dance." She gave a little twirl. "Then, folks will get an up-close look at the garments while the ladies are dancing. In fact, your oldest sisters would be perfect for showing them off." She turned to Sam. "And your niece, Allie."

Justin wiped his brow with his bandana, overwhelmed. "Well, that sounds like an all-day event, Mrs. Brandt. That's not exactly what I had in mind."

"Hold on there." Sam patted the air with his hands. "Think about it, Justin. An all-day event gives fellas plenty of time to look at the horses and make their decisions. You get a couple of fellas haggling over the same horse, and the price of that horse keeps going up. This could be very good for your business."

"That might well do." Justin drummed his fingers on the counter. "Mrs. Brandt, I'll ask my sisters. I'm sure Rebecca and Cordelia would jump at the chance. But Ivajohn is out of town with the missionaries. She wouldn't do it anyway. She'd say it's not fitting of someone engaged to marry a pastor to dress so fancily."

"I know Allie will do it." Sam snapped his suspenders.

"I don't doubt it." Justin smiled. "Levi said she's been itching for a dance. And I imagine she'd be pleased as punch to wear a new dress, even if she doesn't get to keep it."

"I'll be joining them. That makes four." Caroline patted the ribbon. "Can I put this on the tailor shop tab?"

"Of course." Sam turned the pages of the mercantile account book. He smiled broadly. "It'll be good to have another town event. Draws in folks who live farther out. Some we don't see often. Like the Humboldt family. Fine musicians in that bunch. Might invite them to play a song or two."

Caroline turned to Justin. "I'd like one more young lady to model our dresses. It's too bad Ivajohn isn't available. Do you know of anyone else who'd be interested?"

The bell jingled. They turned as Eliza Dawn entered. Caroline's smile widened.

"Mr. Mooney, did Mrs. Pratt leave a basket of mending for me?"

"Mrs. Brandt, this is Miss Eliza Dawn. She is staying with the Hogues." Sam tipped his head and raised an eye, signaling Justin to recommend her.

"Oh, yes. Miss Dawn does a bit of seamstress work." Justin met her and ushered her into the huddle at the counter. "She could assist you with fitting the dresses and be your fifth."

"Pardon me?" Eliza Dawn drew back with a quizzical expression. "I could be your fifth what?

"Model for dresses at the town dance." Caroline lightly tapped her arm with the cluster of ribbons.

"Oh, no. I can't." Eliza Dawn shook her head. "I am busy with sewing projects, and I've somehow taken on more work than I meant to."

"Nonsense. I have just the ensemble for you." Caroline circled Eliza Dawn, eyeing her up and down. "The dress is the fairest champagne, and the bonnet has layers and layers of ribbon trimmed in pale blue."

"It sounds delightful, but I'm afraid I must decline."

"If we sell the dress you wear, I'll give you fifteen percent and help finish your sewing projects."

"It's a tempting offer, but no."

"If you change your mind, I'm a few doors down." Caroline Brandt swept out of the store like a breeze.

"You should consider it." Leaning on the counter, Justin traced the brim of his hat with his index finger. "It would be nice to see you have some proper fun."

"Proper fun, *hmm*?" Eliza Dawn smirked. "Are you implying I normally have improper fun?"

"I don't believe you've had any fun since you've been here. All you do is work."

"Aren't we the pot calling the kettle black? And by 'we,' I mean you, of course." Eliza Dawn placed a penny on the counter and fished a lemon drop from the candy jar. "You work much later into the night than I do."

"How would you know that?" Justin plucked the candy from her fingers, a smile teasing the corners of his mouth.

She snapped the yellow confection from his grasp and popped it into her mouth. "I've seen your light on in the bunkroom. It casts a glow through my window that keeps me awake."

"I didn't realize it was troubling you. I'll get to bed a might sooner." Justin smiled. So, she had been staring from her room. He wasn't sure how he felt about that. "If you had signaled from your window, I would have known it was a bother."

"I wasn't looking." She fiddled with her collar. The corner of his mouth edged up in a half smile at her tell.

Chapter Nineteen

Eliza Dawn's cheeks warmed. Justin grinned like he'd caught her with her hand in the cookie jar. Why had she mentioned he was keeping her up at night? Not him, his light. Pressing her eyes closed, she inhaled deeply, trying to sort her muddled thoughts. Tugging at her collar, she turned to Sam. "Mr. Mooney, where might I find Mrs. Pratt's basket?"

"They're in the back. I'll get them for you."

"I'm sorry, did you say 'them'?"

"Yes, ma'am. Two baskets."

"There must be some misunderstanding." Eliza Dawn rounded the counter. "I was expecting one basket."

"She scratched out a note here. Says 'two baskets for Miss Eliza Dawn boarding at Hogue House.'"

"I see." Eliza Dawn tightened her jaw and frowned at Justin. "It's good I declined Mrs. Brandt's offer to flounce in fancy frocks. Unfortunately, I have less time for it than I imagined."

The bell above the door jingled, and a few men in kilts entered. They waved at Eliza Dawn as they passed. "Will we be expecting ye at th' pool hall later?"

Of Faith and Dreams

"I've got my hands full today." She smiled politely. "Not likely I'll make it, Malcolm."

Justin shot her a sidelong glance. "Looks like you know all the Scots well."

Malcolm rambled over and leaned on the counter facing Eliza Dawn. "I wis wondering if ye had time to chat with yer friend."

"Malcolm Sinclair, I'd like you to meet Mr. Justin Hogue."

Sinclair stretched out his hand. "Hogue."

"Sinclair." Justin accepted the gesture, pumping the man's hand twice.

Eliza Dawn tucked a stray strand of hair into her low bun. "Unfortunately, Malcolm, I don't think it's going to be possible for you to use the forge."

Justin lay a hand on her arm. "What she means to say is I have some questions. Perhaps we could talk later?"

"A'll be around." Sinclair nodded and returned to his mates.

Eliza Dawn gawked at Justin, mouth agape. She glanced from him to the Scots and back again. Who was this man standing before her? Just when she decided he was an easy read, he turned the page.

"You've taken on a lot of sewing projects, have you?" Sam asked. "You said you have your hands full."

She didn't answer.

"Miss Dawn."

She shook her head, uncertain how to interpret what had just transpired. She focused again on Sam and his question.

"I'm working on five shirts for the Scottish prospectors, plus a couple more. And I already have a basket of mending at Hogue House. If it's all right with you, Mr. Mooney, I must make two trips for these."

"Nonsense. Justin, could you give us a hand." Sam hitched a thumb toward the curtain behind him. "I don't want to leave the counter. Mind getting those two baskets just inside the curtain there?"

Justin returned to the counter with the two baskets, one stacked on the other.

Eliza Dawn sighed. "I don't know how I'll ever finish it all before leaving town."

"So, you really are leaving town?" Sam crumbled Mrs. Pratt's note.

"I go where the prospectors go." Eliza Dawn nodded down the aisle toward the Scots. "They are my business."

"Ever considered staying put somewhere?" Justin balanced the mending baskets on the edge of the counter.

"Once in a while, I consider putting down roots." Eliza Dawn stared at her feet. It was a lovely idea, but one she couldn't entertain for long. She couldn't risk losing Bonnie. "But it never works out the way I'd hoped."

"Don't lose hope. Trees that weather strong storms, lots of storms, grow stronger roots." Sam closed the accounts book and slid it back under the counter. "Find the courage to stay put through the storm, and you'll come out stronger too."

"That sounds nice, Mr. Mooney, but I'm not sure that's true for people." She folded her hands on the counter.

"Have you ever tried?" Justin shifted the baskets, edging closer to her.

"Sometimes you don't have a choice." Tightness gripped her heart. "Some storms uproot you, and there's nothing you can do about it."

"As someone who's been uprooted a time or two, I encourage you to stay put a while." Sam patted her hands. "God might replant you if you give Him time."

"Let's get these baskets loaded up for you. I've got to turn in at a reasonable hour this evening." Justin winked and grabbed his hat from the counter.

"See that you do." A warmth floated through her as she responded with a mock sternness. "I don't wish to be troubled by the light through my window."

"I've gotta shoe horses at the boardinghouse and finish smithing before breakfast tomorrow morning. Then I'll head to Levi's to update him on plans and follow up with Mrs. Brandt." Justin borrowed a length of rope from Sam and loaded the baskets onto Sugar Blue. "Shall we walk home together again?"

"I suppose so."

Eliza Dawn massaged tight muscles in her shoulder as they walked in silence. Sighting movement in the bushes the previous night and Big Jim in the café earlier left her tense. Now, there were two extra baskets of mending and the five flannels for the Scots. The deadline for her next article was looming, and she couldn't get Ewan to talk. Deep lines creased her brow.

She reminded herself to breathe.

"You're unusually quiet."

"*Mm?*" She rubbed her hands together, warming them.

"I said you're quiet. I'm surprised you haven't mentioned the saddler by now."

"Oh, I had forgotten."

"Probably for the best." He followed her with a sidelong glance. "It seems I've somehow lost the letter and the ring."

"Oh, you have, have you?" A small smile surfaced. "You should be more careful."

"I suppose you have them?"

"Perhaps."

"And I suppose you've wagged them all over town today searching for the recipient?"

"I have not." She pursed her lips and then released a long, quiet breath. "Not only that, but I refrained from opening the letter when I found it. But I suggest we read it. It might provide valuable information about the person for which it was intended."

"I don't like the idea of intruding into someone else's personal affairs like that." Justin shook his head. "If the choices are to talk to the saddler or open the letter, I prefer to talk to Nicholas."

"Could we leave it with him? Does he have a notice board?"

"No notice board. I doubt he'd agree to take possession of it. But I'm hoping he'll be willing to help get the word out. Perhaps the intended recipient will be expecting it. If so, they might seek me out if they learn it's arrived."

"Of course."

Eliza Dawn strolled beside Justin as he guided Sugar Blue through Main Street, avoiding the hustle and bustle of prospectors and street vendors. Every day brought more folks to town. New carts popped up on every corner, with vendors trying to make every cent off the prospectors before their departure. Corn, potatoes, cotton, baskets, anything a body could sell. Prospectors were jockeying to gather all the necessary supplies for the trip and perhaps a few luxuries if they could afford them.

Eliza Dawn's elbow bumped the gelding's muzzle, and he whinnied. Justin lay his hand on the bridge of the horse's nose and lightly pushed. The horse fell back a pace or two in response. A few steps later, he nosed between them again, nibbling at Justin's elbow with his upper lip. Eliza Dawn edged over to make room for the persistent animal. What was it these creatures found so irresistible about him?

"Not now, Blue." Justin pushed slightly harder against the horse's muzzle. "You'll have to wait until we get home."

"Wait? What must he wait for?"

"Sam slipped me a peppermint stick before we left the store." Justin patted his pocket. "Ol' Blue, here, smells it. He knows it's for him because Sam does this often."

"Isn't his name Sugar Blue?"

"Well, that's a mouthful. A little like Eliza Dawn. So I call him Blue for short."

"How did he get his name?"

"Sugar comes from his white coat, and Blue comes from his

eyes. Although, there are days I think I should have named him for his personality instead of appearance. In which case, I'd call him ornery." Justin chuckled.

"Oh, surely, he's not ornery. Just persistent."

"Call it what you like. Doesn't change the fact sometimes he and I don't see eye to eye." Justin scratched the bridge of Blue's nose. Then he fiddled with the horse's ear, and Blue shook his head in annoyance. Justin leaned over and blew in the gelding's ear.

"Stop that. You're irritating him on purpose."

"He was nagging me about that peppermint on purpose."

"How did you discover you enjoy working with horses so much?"

"I got a taste for it while caring for others' horses at the boarding house. I had to have a horse of my own." Justin patted Blue's neck. "Bought this ol' boy from a huckster and didn't know what I was getting. I wouldn't listen to anyone's advice. Had to have him."

"You make a good pair."

"It didn't start that way. I discovered I didn't know near as much about horses as I thought. But we've grown a good bit and learned to take care of each other." He strummed his fingers through the horse's mane. "Wouldn't trade him for anything now."

Justin looped his arm under Blue's chin and pulled the horse near in a side hug. Then he swapped the reins to his other hand, guiding Blue to walk in line with his outside shoulder. Had she ever seen a man so gentle with any living thing?

They walked on in silence.

Justin paused, plucking a dandelion from a nearby patch of green. He handed it to her as they strolled. "Looks like you could use some cheering up."

Taking the bloom, she smiled. Sam's words lingered in her mind. *Find the courage to stay put through the storm.* Where did one find that kind of courage? Lately, a light breeze was enough to blow her from one place to the next.

This was more than a light breeze kicking up between them. If only the forty-niners were leaving sooner. She needed to get out of town and away from Justin before things turned stormy, as relationships always did. Her head said run, but her heart told her to stay as if she were free to consider it. Courage was an expensive commodity, though. She wasn't about to waste it on the naïve notion this man was different from any other. Justin Hogue might have the gentlest hand she'd ever witnessed in a man, but his sense of right was unyielding. Besides, he was a businessman at heart like all the rest. He'd ship her home to Fairfax if he learned the truth about her marriage. And if he discovered she'd stolen Bonnie from her husband ...

Justin's pace slowed, and one of the baskets on Blue's side bumped him into her. He caught her by the waist to keep them both from tumbling to the ground. Folding into him, a deep breath flooded her senses with the fragrance of sweet hay and saddle soother. His gray eyes, full of concern, held her a moment too long. Her bearings were slipping. She pulled away, inhaling deeply. The odors of a well-populated town—dust, sweat, and horse droppings—steadied her senses.

Justin cleared his throat. "I feel terrible about Mrs. Pratt. She believes she's being extra helpful by sending more than discussed."

"It's okay. I led you to believe I needed more work. You were genuinely trying to help."

"I can do some mending, you know."

"What are you talking about?"

"I got you into this fix." Justin shrugged. "It's only fitting I should help get you out."

"You've done a lot of mending, have you?" Her mind formed an image of him with needle and thread in hand, and she laughed.

"What's so funny?"

"I had this mental image of you darning socks." She twirled the dandelion loosely between her fingers. "By appearances, you're better suited to anvil and hammer or horses."

"Well, I've got eight brothers and sisters. We've all had to pitch in with cooking, sewing, cleaning, and a thousand other things." He puffed out his chest. "You'd be surprised to discover what I can do."

"Jack of all trades, *huh*?"

"Something like that." Justin stopped suddenly. "Tell me my eyes are deceiving me."

His fists clenched. Eliza Dawn turned to see what caught his attention. Her skin prickled.

Chapter Twenty

"Hold this." Justin shoved Blue's reins into Eliza Dawn's hand. "I'll be right back."

In a few long, determined strides, Justin reached the storefront of the pool hall where young Simon stood, one hand over his brow, peeking in the window. With a yank of the collar, Justin pulled Simon off his feet.

Hauling the boy away from the establishment, Justin growled, "What are you doing here?"

"I, I, *uh*—" The stammering teen struggled under Justin's grip.

"Since you seem to be at a loss for words, I'll tell you what it looks like." Justin dragged Simon across the street. A tightness spread through his chest. He inhaled deeply, trying to quell his anger. "It appears you're skipping school to peer into windows where you've no business."

Justin shoved Simon toward Eliza Dawn and Blue. He took hold of Blue's reins, passing them to Simon. "When we get home, you'll have stable chores. After that, you'll help Miss Dawn and me with some mending. Then we'll discuss the rest of your punishment."

"You gonna tell Pa?"

"What would Pa do about it?"

"I don't know."

"I'll tell him. He needs to know because he's our pa." Justin sighed heavily. "However, I'll dole out punishment as I see fit, and I expect Pa will be fine with that. Now, do you wanna tell me what you were doing at that pool hall?"

Simon shook his head, lips clamped tight.

"That's all right." Justin shot a knowing glance at Eliza Dawn. "I figure I already know."

"You told him?"

"Rebecca found your shirt. It smelled of cigar smoke." Eliza Dawn shrugged. "I thought you might be in less trouble if they knew the truth instead of thinking you were up to no good."

Simon's cheeks blazed red. "You promised not to tell if I got straight home."

"I didn't promise. I agreed. And you agreed not to return to the pool hall." She pressed her lips flat, arching her eyebrows. "But here you are. I guess we both need to work on sticking to our agreements."

"What you did was wrong, and you know it. Don't you get sideways with Miss Dawn. You know what it means to be a Hogue in this town, the standards you're expected to live up to." Justin slapped his hand across his thigh, sending a cloud of dust flying. "We'll talk about this more when we get home. Until then, not another word."

Justin rolled his shoulders forward and back. Why was Simon pushing so hard against the boundaries since Ma died? He couldn't understand it. He allowed Simon to trick ride the horses he was training to give the boy an outlet, but it wasn't enough. It didn't help Pa had become so distant.

Justin glanced at the sulking boy, then at Eliza Dawn. Could there have been a worse time for such a striking woman to appear in their lives? He couldn't blame his younger brother for being enamored with her. After all, he couldn't stay his own thoughts when it came to Eliza Dawn.

Strands of soft chestnut waves had worked loose from her bun and gently framed her face. For Simon, the attraction was merely physical, most likely. Justin eyed her curiously. Something deeper drew him to her, a mysterious and profound sorrow. One he suspected had nothing to do with her parents' deaths.

She spoke freely about her parents. She could have been more forthcoming about her brother. But there was another story. One that had no words. A story that revealed itself only through subtle details and mannerisms.

Little oddities ate at Justin. Eliza Dawn's handling of the baby doll when he first showed her the room at the boarding house. She'd smoothed its dress and placed it delicately, intentionally, in a nearby chest of blankets, almost as if nesting a real baby. Yet she recoiled when Edie grabbed her hand as they prepared for a Sunday ride.

Plus, the matter of her hidden horse when she first arrived in town and her uneasiness about unseen figures in the yard. Then, there was her sewing business and the unusual amount of time she spent at the pool hall. Justin was sure all these things connected somehow. But he couldn't put the pieces together just yet. He massaged his temples with his forefingers.

"Are you feeling all right?" Eliza Dawn's quiet voice broke his train of thought.

"A minor headache. Nothing a soak in a hot, sweet bath won't cure. Provided I can find the time." Justin opened the gate of the picket fence surrounding the boarding house and motioned Simon toward the stable.

"A little honey in the tub is soothing. You should make time for that bath. I don't need help with the mending."

Justin grinned. "Miss Dawn, are you implying I'm giving off an unpleasant odor?"

His heart skipped at the pinking of her cheeks. She always seemed so poised. He enjoyed creating these little hiccups in her otherwise cool façade.

"I haven't gotten close enough to say how you smell, Mr. Hogue." She fidgeted with the button at her collar. "However, I did notice that curl of dust when you slapped your britches earlier. So, you might consider getting in the bath fully clothed and giving those garments a good soaping while you're at it."

Justin walked with her to the front porch and opened the door. "How about I get a change of clothes and save the washing for later? I'll help Simon wrap up these stable chores, and we'll join you shortly."

"Honestly, Mr. Hogue, it isn't necessary. I can manage myself."

"When you interfered with my horse sale, there was nothing doing, but you had to fix it. It's my fault your business is facing an obstacle, so I will make it right by easing your load."

"But you're overwhelmed as well. I don't want to add to your burden. That wasn't my intention when I sought a room here." Eliza Dawn went to the back stairs, where Rebecca had cleared space to store the mending baskets.

"Miss Dawn, we could go back and forth like this from now to eternity, which won't help either of us. How about you accept my help, and it'll save us both some time."

"But you're going to make Simon help too. Is that wise, given I'm why he was at the pool hall?" She pulled the original basket from its hiding spot.

"I'll carry that for you." Justin took the basket from her. "I've got to keep an eye on him, so if I'm helping, he's helping. Tomorrow morning, he'll work with me in the forge. Then we'll shoe horses here before going out to Levi's."

"He's not going to school?" Eliza Dawn's brow furrowed.

"Can't trust him to stay at school." Justin set the basket by the parlor sofa.

"But surely you can see the importance of sending him to school." Eliza Dawn clutched his forearm. "That's a rare opportunity for a young man his age."

"I agree. But if he's not *there*—never mind." Justin released an exasperated sigh. He hitched his thumb toward the stable. "We'll bring Mrs. Pratt's baskets in, but first, I better see that Simon takes care of Blue's saddle properly."

"Oh, the saddler." Eliza Dawn gasped. "After you spotted Simon, we forgot to stop by the saddler."

Justin's shoulders sank as he let out a heavy sigh. "It doesn't matter much. I don't expect telling him about the letter to help any more than telling Sam."

"We could always read the letter."

"Miss Dawn, we will exhaust every possible option before I agree to that."

"I don't understand why you're being so pigheaded about it. We should simply open the letter and read it. The damage to the envelope may not have affected the correspondence inside. We might be able to get a name and other information."

"Absolutely not. That would be an invasion of someone's private matters."

"Well, I don't see any other way."

Hard-headed woman. Justin had commented so to Rebecca, and she corrected him. Not hard-headed—determined. Hard-headed or determined, it was the one trait that made Justin's life more difficult. It's where they always got crosswise with one another. Simon would have stayed at school if she'd stopped frequenting the pool hall. If she'd listened and stayed away from the place, it would've been one less thing Pa held against him. And if she would just let go of this letter business, he could focus on his ranching plans.

"It's clear we're not going to resolve this right now." Justin scratched his head. "Let me get a change of clothes and check on Simon. We'll talk more later."

Chapter Twenty-One

"If we can knock these two baskets of mending out, would you reconsider Caroline Brandt's request?" Justin pulled the needle and thread nimbly through the side seam of a well-worn shirt. "Wouldn't you enjoy an evening in such finery as opposed to your riding pants?"

"*Hmm*, I don't know. Riding pants are quite comfortable." Eliza Dawn grabbed a sock from the basket near her chair. Attending a dance wouldn't help her with her newspaper pieces. It would be a waste of her time. "In all seriousness, Rebecca has both the skirts I've been wearing. She's added some length to the plaid and wanted to wash it. Then, last night, she offered to add to the floral I found. Besides, I still have so much to do."

"All socks go to Simon." Justin took the ragged sock from her, tossing it onto a pile at the end of the sofa near his brother. "What else do you have to do? Perhaps we could help."

"I don't mind helping, but I'm not darning any more socks after this pile." Simon placed the sock he'd finished on the tea table, laying needle and thread on top. Sitting back, he folded his arms across his chest. "Mrs. Pratt missed some of these when she did her wash."

"I reckon you'll be mending all the socks unless you'd like to muck stalls by yourself tomorrow." Justin handed him the needle and thread. Simon huffed.

Eliza Dawn pulled an apron from the basket and threaded her needle. "It doesn't matter. I don't have any use for dances and such."

"It could help you get to know more of the townsfolk." Rebecca appeared with a tray of cups, a teapot, and a honey jar. "Anyone care for a cup of hot tea?"

"There's not much point in getting to know folks when I'll leave soon."

"In six days by my count." Justin took a cup of tea.

He was counting the days. Eliza Dawn fiddled with the handle of her teacup. Was he hoping she would stay or eager to see her go?

"Must you go?" Rebecca offered a cup to Simon, who pushed it away. "We're just getting to know one another. I enjoy having someone to chat with after breakfast and supper when everyone else has gone their way."

"You have sisters."

"Ivajohn will marry before long, and Cordelia—" Rebecca drizzled honey into her tea. "Well, Cordelia is Cordelia."

"My clientele is going west. If I want to earn a living, I must follow."

"I imagine Sam Mooney would be willing to work with you. You could run some business through him like Levi does." Justin tapped the honey dripper against the edge of his cup before returning it to the jar. "People could place orders right there in the store."

"It doesn't make good business sense to stay." Eliza Dawn dropped the apron she was mending in her lap and took a cup. She drew a long sip. "Families manage much of their own sewing. The Brandts have a tailor shop. This town doesn't need my services. Not really."

"What about all of this?" Rebecca waved her hand across the room toward Mrs. Pratt's baskets.

"I suspect Mrs. Pratt was simply being generous because Justin made it sound like I was in dire need of work."

"Why is it then she had two full baskets of work available the moment you asked?" Rebecca crossed the room to the nearby credenza. She returned with a gray, toile-covered sewing basket. Pulling out needle and thread, she grabbed a pair of britches from one of Mrs. Pratt's baskets.

"I don't know."

"She's overwhelmed, that's why. Her brother is staying with them while his wife is in Little Rock caring for her ailing mother." Rebecca took a sip of tea. "I didn't realize she was overwhelmed until she sent these baskets. She's been watching little Edie during the day for me. She offered to do it while Ivajohn is away so I wouldn't be overwhelmed with boardinghouse chores."

"Now I feel bad about being reluctant to do some smithing for her." Justin sucked on his finger after poking it with the needle. "I'd forgotten about her brother staying with them."

"He's not very industrious," Rebecca whispered behind her hand to Eliza Dawn. "She said it's helpful to have Edie around to entertain Clementine, but I'll keep Edie here. Perhaps we'll have little Clemmie over some too."

Eliza Dawn's throat clenched at the idea of Edie being around during the day. At suppertime, there were plenty of people to create distance between her and the child, and her bedtime followed soon after supper. The only way Eliza Dawn could avoid the little girl now would be to spend her sewing time in the lost and found room. A hollowness rose in her chest. She feared she might never come to terms with the things in her life that could never be.

"Dawn." Rebecca patted her hand. "Eliza Dawn."

Eliza Dawn tuned into Rebecca's voice. "My apologies. I was

lost in my thoughts for a moment."

"What's on your mind?"

Eliza Dawn gathered the britches from Rebecca's lap. "I was wondering why you're sewing with us. I understand why the two of them are here, though I'm afraid I still have to disagree with it. But why on earth are you here? I know you have a heap of responsibility with the boardinghouse."

Rebecca took the britches back. "You pay more than the other boarders, and you've helped me a few times. So, I'll donate fifteen minutes an evening of sewing to even things out. I'm pretty swift with a needle and thread, plus it gives me some guaranteed time to visit. I figure I come out a little ahead in this deal."

Rebecca turned to Justin and Simon. "Now, what's going on here?"

"We're still working that out." Justin's gray eyes took on a steely quality. "I found him peeking in the pool hall window this afternoon."

"Simon." Rebecca tilted her chin and frowned. "What's come over you?"

He shrugged.

"Do you understand this is about more than skipping school?" Justin scooted to the edge of his seat. "We trust you to make sure Martie, Ollie, and Nellie get home from school safely. Do you understand that? You have responsibilities."

"What about Cordelia? She's at school, too, and she's older. Why isn't she responsible for walking them home?"

"You are both responsible for walking them home, and don't think I won't be asking her why she hasn't told me about your disappearing act." Rebecca wadded the britches and tossed them back in the basket.

"Aw, she didn't even notice. She's only got eyes for Mr. Sewell."

"Mr. Sewell?" Eliza Dawn tried to follow the conversation.

"He's the schoolmaster."

"Oh, I see."

"Well, Justin, what will we do about this?" Rebecca stood with her hands on her hips.

"This is none of my business, but wouldn't this be a good time to involve the elder Mr. Hogue?" Eliza Dawn tried to help Simon's case.

"Right now, it's easier if we handle this ourselves." Justin turned to Simon. "For the next week, you will stay home from school. Move your things out to the bunkhouse and stay with me. You'll be under my watchful eye at all times. Stable chores, mending parties, boardinghouse maintenance, whatever I tell you to do, you'll do it."

"But I—"

"I don't want to hear it. What I say stands." He turned to Rebecca. "Do you agree?"

"It sounds good to me." She shook her finger at Simon. "Be thankful Justin is doling out consequences, mister, because I'm ready to tar and feather you."

"Now, get yourself out to the bunkhouse and get bedded down. I'll be out shortly." Justin pointed to the door.

Eliza Dawn pressed her hand to her chest as Simon left the room, head hanging low. "I feel so bad. Like this is partly my fault."

"I reckon it is." Justin's straightforward comment caught her off-guard. "Just remember your actions have a far-reaching impact. That's going to be true even if you head west by yourself. You're never as alone in this world as you think."

"I'll remember." Eliza Dawn folded the apron and laid it on the basket near her chair. She picked up teacups, placing them on the tray. "I'll help in the kitchen before bed."

"That's not necessary."

The trio jumped at the sudden pounding on the front door.

Justin rushed to open it. Sam and Nicholas entered, supporting a large, bloody-faced man between them.

"There was a fight in the street." Sam struggled to get the words out through ragged breaths. "Fella's got a good gash on his cheek. Smells like he's had plenty to drink too."

"Why are they bringing him here?" Eliza Dawn followed Rebecca and the men to the dining room.

"Because the town doctor left us high and dry, and the barber is a might squeamish." Rebecca's words were clipped.

"What's Justin going to do for him?"

"I'm not going to do a thing for him." Justin grabbed a couple of sheets from the top of the china cabinet. He nodded at Rebecca. "She is."

Eliza Dawn's eyes widened. "What are you going to do?"

"First, I'm going to have a look at him." Rebecca pressed her hands down her apron front. "Eliza Dawn, I set a pot of water to boil to do the dishes earlier. Bring a bowl of boiling water and a bowl of warm water. Then fetch my sewing kit from the parlor."

Rebecca removed the tablecloth, and Justin folded two layers of bedsheets half-wise over the table. Rebecca nudged Eliza Dawn. "Hurry now."

Eliza Dawn left the room and hastily returned with the items requested.

"Gentlemen, get him on the table and hold him steady."

Sam and Justin hefted him onto the table, pressing his shoulders down. Nicholas draped himself across the man's hips.

"Eliza Dawn, I need you to hold his head steady."

Eliza Dawn moved quickly to the head of the table, grasping the man's head and turning it skyward. She gasped at the sight of his face. It was Big Jim. Her stomach clenched at the memory of her pool hall encounter with him, and she couldn't catch her breath.

"Are you all right?" Rebecca's light fingers on her arm steadied her.

"I'm fine." She wiped her brow on her shoulder. "I wasn't expecting such a sight, is all."

Big Jim groaned.

"Might not be as bad as it looks." Rebecca dropped a curved needle into the boiling water to soak. Then, she dipped a clean cloth into cooler water. "Injuries to the face bleed liberally, even when the injury is minor."

"That's good to know."

Eliza Dawn's mind raced. What if he opened his eyes? Would he recognize her? She buried her face in her shoulder as she stabilized his head.

Rebecca dabbed at the wound. "Are you sure you're okay?"

"I'll be fine."

Justin rubbed her shoulder. "You're doing great. Better than Augie."

"Augie?"

"The barber."

Big Jim groaned again, eyelids fluttering. Eliza Dawn's breath caught. She pressed her eyes shut. *Please, don't wake up. Please, don't wake up.*

"I'm going to start stitching, so I need you to maintain control of his head. Can you do that?"

Eliza Dawn nodded. "Wait. Shouldn't you give him something to ensure he doesn't awaken while you sew him up?"

"I can't do that since he's been drinking. I'll have to trust the four of you to hold him still, and we'll all do our best. All right?"

Eliza Dawn nodded again.

"Rebecca, will this take long?" A deep voice asked.

"If all goes well, you'll be out the door in no time, Nicholas." Rebecca smiled. "Can I trust you to resist your notorious sense of impatience? You're not going to let this bear loose on me, are you?"

"No, ma'am. Would never do that." He sucked his teeth. "Got a saddle I need to finish up tonight, though."

"I won't waste any time."

As Rebecca poked the needle through layers of flesh, her patient released a low, guttural moan. His eyelids fluttered. Eliza Dawn flinched, turning her head. She took a deep breath, searching her mind for a way out of the situation.

"Hey. Hey, you're doing great." Justin spoke softly, craning his neck to make eye contact with her. "Hold firm."

Eliza Dawn nodded, biting her lip. She was thankful the others perceived her reaction as a sign of queasiness in response to Big Jim's injury. Every time Rebecca pierced his skin with the needle, his eyes quivered. And every time, Eliza Dawn cringed, afraid he would open his eyes.

"That's three stitches." Rebecca dabbed at his face with the wet cloth. "I'm going to do seven more. Nicholas, you still with me?"

"Yes, ma'am. I'm with you 'til the end." The gentle giant smiled. "I'm hot-footing it out of here as soon as you're finished, though."

"I knew I could count on you."

"I take it they've done this before?" Eliza Dawn leaned close to Justin.

"Nicholas is handy to have around in these situations." Justin's breath tickled her ear as he spoke.

Big Jim's bloodshot eyes fluttered and flew open. His head jerked loose of Eliza Dawn's restraint.

"Hold him." Rebecca's words breached clenched teeth as she let go of the needle. "Hold him."

Eliza Dawn's heart leaped into her chest. "I'm trying."

Justin and Sam struggled against the large man's shoulders. An arm broke free, knocking Justin against the wall. Big Jim's thick, grisly hook dug into Eliza Dawn's ribcage. His eyes locked with hers as he spoke in a throaty, rasping voice. "Pretty little thing."

Chills ran through her. She struggled against his grip, seeking an escape. He climbed half off the table, Sam and Nicholas fighting to hold him down. Rebecca grasped his shoulder, trying to help Sam push him back to the table.

"Pretty." Big Jim growled again.

Eliza Dawn's stomach turned at the sight of the curved needle dangling from his cheek by a loose thread. She twisted, freeing herself from his grasp, but he caught her wrist before she could flee the crowded dining room. Her wrist burned as she turned it in his vise-like paw.

Justin, regaining his footing, pried her loose. Grabbing Big Jim by the collar, he landed a fist squarely across the man's jaw. Big Jim fell back, head lolling to the side.

Eliza Dawn's body went slack, her heart racing. Justin drew her close, her body shuddering in his tight embrace. Her breaths came in shallow gulps.

"*Shh.* It's okay. You're all right." Justin stroked her hair. "You're safe."

Nicholas cleared his throat. "Can we get back to it? I got someplace to be."

Rebecca released a nervous chuckle. "Of course, Nicholas." She turned to Eliza Dawn. "Now that Justin has sedated the patient, why don't you rest in your room? Justin can hold the man's head."

Nodding vigorously, Eliza Dawn pushed through the dining room and raced up the stairs, closing her door with a thud. She leaned her back against it and slid to the floor. Justin's warm whisper tugged at her heart. *You're safe.*

She rubbed her arms. For a moment, in his arms, the possibility fluttered in her heart like butterfly wings. If only she'd met Justin before her union with Merritt Fairfax. If only her father had allowed her to marry for love instead of giving her hand in a lucrative business deal. She longed to be sheltered and secure. But how could she ever feel safe without a family, a home, a community?

Chapter Twenty-Two

Eliza Dawn kneaded her arms as she paced through the cramped walkway of the lost and found room. Thready breaths made her lightheaded, and she pressed her hand to her chest, forcing herself to draw a deeper breath. Vibrating with frenetic energy, she shifted things around, searching for something to help calm her. She picked up the prospector ring and, rubbing her thumb over the thistle relief, counted the pointed edges of the leaves. One, two, three, four, five ... her breathing slowed. Six, seven, eight, nine ... the wooziness faded.

Sitting on the makeshift bed, she grabbed her journal and pencil from a nearby trunk. Flipping to a blank page, she steadied her hand. A jagged line appeared on the page. She set the pencil down, shook her hand, and took another deep breath. She attempted again to draw the image from the ring.

An eruption of discordant voices surged downstairs. Had Rebecca's patient thrashed free again? Her heartbeat quickened. Dropping the pencil in the journal's crease, she snapped it shut. She pressed her hand to her chest. She needed to get out. She needed fresh air. She needed Ewan's story.

Despite his gregarious personality, he spoke little about himself. Her attempt to draw him out at Gray's Café had failed miserably. The conversation had taken an awkward turn when she mentioned the letter, and she learned his parents couldn't read and write. He wasn't likely to openly share anything with her after that. Observing him while he was unaware would be better.

Another outburst of voices went up, followed by bumps and thuds. Justin's sedation hadn't lasted long. Scuttling her feet like a young, green broke horse, she edged toward the door. She pocketed the ring, a notepad, and a pencil on her way out. Sneaking down the back stairs and out the doorway unnoticed, she crossed the yard to the stable. The door to the tack closet hung open, and Justin's hat and light coat hung on the wall. She donned the coat and hat, tucking her hair inside. The smell of citrus, cedar, and leather warmed her. Grabbing a bridle, she headed to Bonnie's stall.

Bonnie's lips fluttered as Eliza Dawn fitted the bridle over the horse's head. "No time for a saddle, sweet Beauty. We're riding bareback tonight."

As Eliza Dawn led Bonnie out of the stable, the cool night air washed over her. She drew the crisp air deep, and her lungs relaxed. Breathing came more steadily. She guided Bonnie out of the picket fence. Whispering in Bonnie's ear, she grabbed a handful of mane and reins and hoisted herself onto the mare's back.

Upon her arrival in Van Buren, Eliza Dawn had ridden the outskirts of town to get an idea of how the prospectors had organized their camps. She'd limited her endeavors to town after securing the room at Hogue House. It had been days since she'd been by the Scottish camp on the north side of Van Buren, and she wasn't sure she could find it in the dark. She rubbed Bonnie's neck, thankful she could escape the Hogue property with her four-legged companion.

"C'mon, girl." With a sharp whisper, Eliza Dawn squeezed her legs against Bonnie's middle, and Bonnie took off at a trot.

The same chill air that had been such a relief as she left the stable bit sharply at her skin as they sped across the unfamiliar terrain. Her fingers ached from the cold. She wished she had grabbed Justin's work gloves from the tack room. She wiped a shoulder across each cheek periodically to warm them.

Heading slightly northwest from the Hogue place, her heart thumped in time with the hoofbeats underneath her. It wasn't long before she came into a clearing and could make out the outline of tents backlit by a fire's inviting glow. Too bad she couldn't walk into camp and make herself right at home in front of the flames.

She stopped short a safe distance from the tents and looped Bonnie's reins through a sturdy bush. Buttoning Justin's coat to the top, she appreciated its dark color and warmth. Crouching low, she padded to the back of the nearest tent and waited, straining to make out jumbled voices.

Several men were gathered around the fire, laughing and carousing. A rough twang and curled *R* characterized their brisk, tight speech. She was in the right place. Peeking around the corner of the tent, she searched for Ewan, but she didn't recognize any of the figures visible to her.

A long shadow grew between the tents, and she ducked back. A second man joined the first at the front corner of the tent where she hid.

"Did I tell ye aboot seeing Hogue today?" It was Malcolm Sinclair.

"Nae, ye didnae." Ewan's guttural voice was unmistakable.

"He wants to talk aboot 'eh forge." Sinclair sniffed. "He may be open to the idea o' renting space."

"Don't get yer hopes oop. When he realizes A've taken his notice doon again, he'll gi' ye the boot."

So, this was the way of business between the two men. Eliza

Dawn rubbed her hands together, blew warm air into them, then shoved them into her armpits. Ewan's advertisement was still on the board, so Justin hadn't responded in kind. She understood his reluctance to offer the use of the forge to the Scots if they were sabotaging his business. Yet, he'd still extended an invitation to talk to Sinclair.

"Aw, Ewan, you didnae. The man is trying t'earn a living. We hev come into his land and yer trying to poosh him oot. How is 'at different from whit wis done to us?"

"A'm not pooshing him oota his home. His family owns a boardinghouse with a forge. A've heard his father wis a steamboat captain. A'm sure the man could earn a living another way."

"I ne'er imagined ye to be the sort o' man who'd stand in the way of another."

"I willny be in his way long. Tis not ma intention to ruin the man. A'll sell ma ponies and go west to make ma fortune. A've got to do it for ma mother and father. Ye ken they're not in good health."

"I do, but I also ken yer father and mother wouldn't want ye to sacrifice yer integrity for their wellbeing."

"I don't want to lose them. They're ev'rythin to me." Ewan pulled a deep breath. "So, don't be surprised when Hogue denies ye."

"A'll talk to him all the same. I miss ma forge more than a wee bit."

"Good luck, mate. I'm turning in."

The flap rustled at the front of the tent, and Eliza Dawn held her breath. Horses whinnied on the other side of the circled tents. She quietly edged around the outside of the circle to a rough-and-ready corral. Shifting clouds unblanketed a silver moon. A soft blue-gray light shone across a herd of solid, well-balanced ponies.

She crept nearer, finding a few saddles balanced on saw

horses outside the pen. Slowly, she moved closer to check the designs stamped into the leather. The stamped figures resembled knots and circular labyrinths in patterns of three. But no thistle.

The clouds shifted, partially covering the moon. Something moved in the back of the corral, unsettling the horses. Eliza Dawn squinted. A figure launched over the fence. She sucked in a breath. Shaky legs propelled her toward Bonnie. She suppressed a desire to run so as not to alert the Scots to her presence but scurried quickly and quietly back to the bush where she'd tied her horse.

A flurry of activity churned around the fire as men ran toward the corral on the opposite side of the encampment. Eliza Dawn unlooped the reins from the bush and led Bonnie from the camp. With the Scots on high alert, she didn't want to make any unnecessary noise. She moved away from the clearing and toward a nearby tree line.

Just inside the tree line, she paused and turned toward camp. Using the trees for cover, she snaked along, trying to make out figures in the dim moonlight. The Scots were circling the horse pen, arms waving in the air. A short distance from camp, three figures on horseback drove four ponies toward the tree line. They broke hard against the line, keeping the ponies in the shadows outside the forested area.

Eliza Dawn held her breath and stilled Bonnie as they passed by her. She turned to see a few Scots riding bareback, drilling down on the bandits, when something hit her like a train. She fell. Bonnie spooked, dragging her through the underbrush. She released the reins and scrambled to glimpse what had rammed into her. In the distance, a figure was heaved onto the back of one of the thieves' horses.

She whistled for Bonnie and slung herself onto the horse's back when it neared. Breaking from the trees, she urged the mare to a gallop. She pulled her knees up high and leaned over

Bonnie's shoulders. The muscular quarter horse flew into action, gaining ground on the throng of riders ahead. The clouds shifted as she neared the double riders, allowing her to make out a black bowler on the horseman and a mop of golden curls on his rider.

She halted Bonnie, and all the riders sped past her. Turning, she disappeared into the woods. With Bonnie at a walk, Eliza Dawn lay breathless along the mare's neck, waiting for her heartbeat to slow. She rubbed Bonnie's silken neck. Hopefully, with her hair tucked up and wearing a man's hat and coat, none of the Scots had recognized her.

She pushed herself up in the saddle and squeezed her legs, prompting Bonnie to trot. She replayed the chase in her mind. Pale blond curls stood out. Had Simon followed her to the prospector camp after Justin had sent him to the bunkroom? Or did he leave to meet up with these horse thieves as soon as Justin dismissed him? It would explain the smell of horses on his shirt if he'd fallen in with them, but it was unthinkable.

A stinging sensation inched across her lower back. She reached around and discovered her shirtwaist pulled free of her riding pants. A chill crept up her spine as she recalled the scraping sensation while being dragged by Bonnie. The adrenaline rush must have quelled the pain until now. She flinched as her fingers raked across the raw, shallow wound running halfway up her back.

She needed to hurry back to Hogue House. With any luck, she could quietly stall Bonnie and find what she needed to tend the wound. A cleaning and light coat of salve and it ought to scab over by morning. But if Justin caught her, or worse yet, Mr. Hogue, she hated to think how things might go.

Chapter Twenty-Three

Justin shoved against the bunkroom door. It didn't budge. He banged his toe against the bottom, twisting the knob in both directions. "Simon. Simon, open this door."

There was a grunt followed by scraping along the floor. Simon's boyish face, topped by unruly blond hair, peeked around the door. He craned his neck from side to side before widening the opening, permitting Justin to enter.

"What's wrong with you?" Justin pushed past his lanky sibling with a sideways glance.

"Heard a lot of commotion out there a bit ago." He rubbed his hand through wayward curls. "So, I used your heavy Dutch oven as a doorstop. Got it from the cabinet in there."

"That might've provided some resistance, but it should have given way as hard as I pushed." Justin laid out his nightshirt and unbuttoned the one he was wearing.

"Oh, I took the lid off and wedged it under the door. Made sure it was good and tight."

"Well, everything is fine now." Justin shook his head. "It wasn't anything that would have put you in harm's way."

"It reminded me how things sounded when Ma—you know."

Simon shrugged. "I mean, how you described the sounds in the street after."

Justin eyed him quizzically. "I told you about that?"

"Just once." Simon sat on the chest at the foot of the cot across from Justin's. "You told me, Cordelia, Rebecca, Ivajohn, and Pa one evening in the kitchen. Before Ma died. While she was laying in the bed upstairs and couldn't talk to us."

"I don't remember sharing that. With anyone." Justin's chest tightened. His eyes stung. A bitter taste flooded his mouth. "I'm sorry I told you about it. I imagine there've been other times you've heard things that made you feel unsafe, especially since the population boon with these prospectors."

Simon nodded. "I'd call it a bust, not a boon. I don't like so many people here."

"Me either." Justin dropped to his bed. "Why don't you tell me when you're afraid?"

Simon hitched his thumb in the direction of the house. "I'm sixteen, and in there, I'm the big brother. I gotta be there for Ollie. Can't let him know I'm scared." He rubbed his knees. "Plus, you're way out here. It feels safer to hole up in my room when I'm scared."

"C'mere." Justin patted the bed.

Simon sat beside him.

"I'm sorry I caused this." Justin wrapped his arms around Simon, embracing the boy's narrow frame. He patted Simon on the back. "I'm sorry I didn't recognize it. I wish you'd told me what you were going through."

"We don't talk about it. Nobody talks about it." Simon pulled free of Justin. "Can't talk about it because we're all hurting. I don't want to add to someone else's pain by sharing mine."

"Is that what you think?"

"Well, yeah." Simon's breath caught. "Look at Pa. It's killing him. How could I ever add my hurt to his?"

A lump stuck in Justin's throat. He swallowed hard. "Listen. I want you to talk to me. I'm discovering talking helps. It doesn't make it worse. You understand?"

Simon nodded.

"Promise you'll talk to me?"

Another nod.

"All right, we better turn in. We've got a busy day tomorrow."

Simon moved across the room. "Hey, Justin?"

"*Hmm?*"

"When I was barricaded in here trying to focus on something else, I thought about Miss Dawn."

Justin pressed his eyes shut to avoid an eye-roll. Simon didn't need that right now. "I'm listening."

"Couldn't she use this cot instead of crates?" He patted the cot opposite Justin's. "It wouldn't be hard to move."

Justin grimaced. "Aw, the cot. Levi and I talked about that very thing. With everything going on, I completely forgot to offer it to her." Justin rebuttoned his shirt. "I should go up and check on her anyway. Why don't you get that folded up? I'll peek in, and if she's not asleep, we'll start moving crates. You'll have to make yourself a bedroll tonight."

"Sure thing."

Justin headed out the door and into the back of the house. He took the stairs two at a time. Arriving at Eliza Dawn's door, he paused, straightened himself, and tapped lightly. No response. He rapped slightly harder. Still no answer. He stepped back. Light shone under the door.

He opened it a crack. "Miss Dawn? Are you here?"

He peeked around the door. Blankets lay neatly across the crates. "Miss Dawn, you aren't trapped in this mess, are you?"

Pushing the door open, he waded through boxes and trunks in one direction. He turned and snaked a path to the window.

He opened it, stuck his head out, and glanced in both directions. No one in sight.

He trotted back down the stairs to the kitchen. Rebecca sat at the kitchen table with a cup of tea, perusing the pages of a large book.

"Have you been here the whole time? Since Sam and Nicholas left?"

"Yes. I've been going over treatment information in Ben's medical book. In case that Goliath returns with an infection." She sipped her tea. "I don't know if I'll ever be comfortable dealing with these situations in Ben's absence."

"Did Eliza Dawn come down? Have you seen her?"

"No. Isn't she in her room?"

"She's not." Justin rubbed his hand over his mouth.

"Do you think she left?" Rebecca rose, peering out the kitchen window. "Where would she go?"

"I don't know. I don't know what to think." Justin shrugged. "She seemed unsettled by that incident tonight. But if she was frightened, I would think she'd have shut herself in her room and barricaded the door."

"That's what I did." Simon appeared inside the back door with the cot.

Rebecca tapped a curled finger against her chin. "Maybe she went for a walk. She might have needed some fresh air after all that excitement."

"Maybe." Justin stood with his hands on his hips.

"Could someone have taken her?" Rebecca wrung her hands.

"Not without us seeing or hearing anything. Surely, she'd have made some noise." Justin paced a few steps and stopped. His lips pressed flat. A knot formed in his belly. "Unless she went willingly."

"Who would she go with?" Rebecca leaned against the counter.

"I've seen her in town with that Scottish fella, MacKinnon." Justin caught the inside of his cheek between his teeth.

Simon set the cot against the wall. "I saw her at the pool hall with one of those Scots."

"MacKinnon? Was it MacKinnon?"

"I don't know. Let me think." Simon scratched his head. "She called him Ewan if I remember."

"That's him. That's MacKinnon." Justin's muscles quivered as he balled and flexed his fingers repeatedly. "I bet she left with him."

"Justin, you're jumping to conclusions. You don't know that." Rebecca wiped her brow with her apron. "You should be worried about her safety instead of your suspicions."

Turning in a circle, Justin pounded his head with his fist. "I cannot protect people bent on putting themselves in harm's way. I don't understand that woman. What's in that obstinate head of hers?"

"Are you going to look for her?"

"I'll help." Simon hurried to the door.

"No. No, I'm not." Justin rubbed his forehead and then threw his hands up. "Where would I begin? The prospector camps? There are camps all around town. If she's with the Scot, I don't want to know. She *chose* to leave. What would I do if I found her? Drag her back here against her will? She didn't want to be here."

"You could reason with her, Justin. Convince her to return."

"No, Rebecca." Justin crossed his arms, heaving a sigh. "I've tried to reason with her. I've tried to convince her to stay. I've tried to befriend her. I'm not leaving this family vulnerable while I hunt her down in the middle of the night."

"Justin—"

He held up a finger. "Not another word about it." He motioned to Simon. "Bring the cot. If she chooses to return, she can sneak in as well as she snuck out. And, hopefully, she'll be thankful for improved sleeping arrangements."

Justin and Simon removed the first two crates, storing them in an out-of-the-way corner of the smithy. Simon returned for the third crate while Justin retrieved the cot from the kitchen. Pausing at the bottom of the stairs, Justin allowed his brother room to maneuver with the container.

As Simon passed, Justin caught his elbow. "After you put that in the forge, why don't you join Rebecca for a cup of tea? You don't have to go to the bunkroom alone. You can visit in the kitchen while I finish."

"I'll be all right."

"You sure?"

"Yeah, I feel much better since we talked." Simon propped his foot on a step and rested the crate on his knee. "Besides, it might be good to have a pair of eyes on the window if Miss Dawn returns. You'd miss her if she came in the window while you're descending the stairs."

"Sharp thinking." Justin patted Simon on the back. "Listen, if I don't catch her sneaking in tonight, don't let on that we know she snuck out."

"Are you going to follow her if she sneaks out again?"

"I haven't decided."

"I would."

"You are not to follow her *anywhere* anymore, young man. Do I make myself clear?"

"Yessir."

"*Yessir*. You make me feel like an old fogey." Justin smiled. "If she does sneak out again and I follow her, I'll wake you up. You can sleep on the sofa or in your bed. You don't have to stay in the bunkroom alone."

"That'll be good. Ollie gets scared sometimes too." Simon tilted his head, pulling his shoulders up. "I'd hate for him to be alone all the time. It's too bad we're outnumbered six to three by sisters."

"Tell Rebecca about Ollie so she can check on him." Justin winked. "Now get that box out to the forge."

Justin climbed the back stairs slowly, half hoping to discover Eliza Dawn coming in the door at the bottom of the stairway. It wasn't so much he intended to catch her, but he wanted to know she was safe. The idea of her with MacKinnon, after dark, turned his stomach. Aside from disregarding rules of etiquette and decorum, he'd not known her to do anything truly scandalous. But any sort of trouble could be waiting for her outside these four walls.

Justin closed his eyes. The terror on Eliza Dawn's face when the injured man dug into her side flashed in his mind. Did Ma have a similar expression when she realized she'd been shot? Did she have time to register what was happening before losing consciousness? If only he hadn't stopped to talk to the Warren girl. He shook the memory from his mind.

He scanned the room as he entered. No sign of Eliza Dawn. Unfolding the legs of the cot, his elbows bumped against crates or wardrobes every which way he turned. Snorting like a bull, he finally situated the core part of the cot. Ready to extend the head and foot pieces, he moved around to the side. He folded the head piece down first. The foot piece, however, was jammed. He pulled and pulled. It didn't budge. Standing on one foot, he draped the other over the top portion of the cot to provide leverage. The lower piece gave way with a mighty jerk, sending him reeling into a chest behind him.

Eliza Dawn's papers and journal sprawled across the floor. Justin stood, rubbing his elbows and backside. After soothing the soreness, he collected the papers. Studying the pieces, he shuffled them, trying to find the proper order. A title was scrawled across the top of one page: "In Pursuit of a Dream, Adventures of the Forty-niners, Part Three," by Edward Dodd.

Justin sat on the cot, papers in hand. Eliza Dawn's journal lay open at his feet. He picked it up, comparing the handwriting. It was a clear match. The words in the journal took shape. Realizing he was no longer studying her penmanship, he snapped it shut.

He returned to the kitchen, where Simon and Rebecca sat at the table.

"Decided to have a cup of tea after all?" He patted Simon on the back.

"I asked him to sit with me." Rebecca patted Simon's hand. "It's been a long time since we've had a chance to talk, just the two of us."

"I'm glad you're both here. I've changed my mind." Justin cleared his throat. "I *am* going to look for Miss Dawn. I won't approach her unless she needs help, but I want to know she's all right before I lay my head down."

"Why not approach her?" Simon shrugged.

"Because, if she's gone to the Scots, she's chosen where she wants to be."

"You mean she's chosen who she wants to be with." Rebecca's eyes locked with his.

"I won't interfere with her decision." Justin pursed his lips. "Get to bed soon. Don't want her feeling like a side show when she returns."

When Justin stepped out the door, the cool air surprised him. By his guess, the temperature had dropped from the fifties into the upper thirties. He rolled his shirt sleeves down on the way to the tack room. Empty nails hung in place of his hat and coat. He ran his hand through his hair, mumbling under his breath. Long strides brought him to Bonnie's stall. Empty.

Turning to Blue's stall, he grabbed the bridle from the hook next to the stall doorway and stepped inside. "Old friend, we've got to get up and dust. I need you rearing to go if things turn South."

He led Blue out of the picket fence and mounted. Turning northwest, he'd check the Scottish camp first. Deep in his heart, he hoped she hadn't gone to MacKinnon. But if she hadn't, that meant she was in trouble. The kind he wasn't sure he could bail her out of.

He clicked his tongue, and Blue picked up speed. He was glad Eliza Dawn had taken his hat and coat. Unfamiliar with the territory, he couldn't dismiss the possibility she might be lost. If so, it could take hours or even days to find her.

Justin paused, ears straining to filter through the trill of tree frogs and shrill whinny of a screech owl. Leaves rustled in the distance, followed by horse hooves drumming. He directed Blue behind a tangle of bushes and waited for the rider to emerge from the trees. Silencing his breaths, he tried to still the fluttering in his stomach.

The rider appeared from the trees, a small figure sitting straight in the saddle. Was it Eliza Dawn? With the rider wearing a hat and dark clothes, it was impossible to tell in the obscured moonlight.

Justin rubbed Blue's neck. "What do you think, ol' boy? Is that Bonnie? If only they'd come out of the shadows a little more."

The rider removed the hat, wiping forearm across brow. Then, the hand moved toward the back of the head and released long, wavy tresses. Justin turned Blue toward home and took off at a gallop.

Making good time, he stalled Blue and retired to the bunkroom. Simon, bedded down on the floor, had already extinguished the lamp. Justin unbuttoned his shirt with heavy arms.

"Justin?" Simon whispered. "Did you find her?"

"*Shh.* Go to sleep."

Chapter Twenty-Four

Justin warmed his hands over the potbellied stove in the old blacksmith shop. He was grateful Levi left behind the coffee pot when he and Allie moved to the homestead. Arms crossing his chest, he patted his shoulders and stomped his feet. A cold spell settled during the night, leaving a chill that was only bothersome if one stood still too long.

He poured coffee, grabbed a lantern, and moved to the work table near the forge. Wrapping his hands around the warm cup, he inhaled deeply. The warm scent of nutmeg and cinnamon soothed his soul. He'd return the spice jars before Rebecca found them missing. Ma added these extra indulgences around Thanksgiving, Christmas, and Easter. If only she were here now, he could talk to her about Eliza Dawn.

Heat rose in his neck as he remembered her disappearing act. With her returning from the northwest, it was a sure sign she'd gone to MacKinnon. Why? Were they plotting to interfere with his plans to establish a horse ranch? Or was there something more personal between them?

He had no idea what to say to her at their next meeting. She would know someone had been in her room since the cot replaced the crates. Would it escape her attention that her papers and journal had been disturbed? He hadn't meant to read the page in her journal, but what it revealed gave him pause. A heavy weight settled in his spirit. A glimpse into her world, the parts she kept hidden, replaced his anger with concern and compassion. He wasn't sure what to do, but he knew one thing for sure. If Ma were here, she'd provide refuge. Not only in her home but in her heart. In fact, Ma would start by praying for Eliza Dawn. Why hadn't he thought to do that before now?

He closed his eyes. "Lord, help Miss Dawn find her way back to You. Help me be a light that points to You, and our home be a refuge where she can rest in Your love—for as long as she'll stay."

He drew another breath of the spiced coffee and focused on Mrs. Pratt's churn. Unfortunately, closer inspection revealed damage to the handle, and the bar was also bent. He'd have to remove the whole assembly to fix it. He sighed, patting his hands on his knees.

If only Mrs. Pratt had left it at the mercantile with a request for Levi to repair it. She probably brought it to him for the same reason he hesitated to take it to Levi. Justin was capable and didn't want to impose upon Levi's family time. Levi and Allie had their hands full with little Mason. And now the dance.

A knock at the door disrupted the solitude. "Justin, are you here?"

Eliza Dawn, hands full, nudged the door with her toe. Justin hurried over and took a large basket and a small milk jar from her. He carried it over to the table by the stove, motioned for her to sit, and then took the shawl draped over her head. Her hair fell in loose waves around her shoulders, and his breath stilled.

"What's this?" Justin dipped his chin toward the basket as he hung her shawl on a hook near the stove.

"Breakfast. Rebecca planned to bring it to you when you

didn't come in. But she's busy cleaning, so I offered to deliver it instead." Eliza Dawn rubbed her hands up and down her arms.

"You didn't have to do that. Is it still raining? Your shawl seemed damp, but I heard nothing on the roof." He motioned overhead.

"It's a thick mist. Not enough to melt me." She grinned. "I wanted to thank you for the cot. I presume you did that."

He dipped his chin. "I only wish I'd thought of it sooner."

For the first time, an awkward silence hung between them.

"I wanted to ask before I brought it up, but I couldn't find you."

"Bonnie and I went for a walk." She straightened her skirt. "Had to get some fresh air. Felt like I couldn't breathe after all that ... excitement."

"*Hmm.* We didn't hear the door." He set the basket on the sitting area table.

"It was so chaotic. When I left, it sounded like you all had your hands full with the ... patient." She rubbed her hands together. "I didn't mean to cause concern."

"I checked the stable horses this morning. Bonnie must have thrown a shoe when you went riding." He eyed her carefully, looking for a tell, some sign indicating whether she was holding something back.

"I took a couple of passes down the road here at full gallop." She smoothed her hair. "Trying to calm my nerves. Running away without really running away, I guess."

Justin wiped the inside of a tin cup. "Would you like some coffee?"

"Please. How do you stand it in here? It's so chilly."

"Give it time. This little stove keeps the sitting area nice and cozy. It should dry and warm your shawl too." Grabbing the coffee pot, he poured her coffee. Then, he crossed the room to retrieve his mug before joining her at the table. "When that old forge gets to temperature, it's right toasty."

Her slender fingers encircled the mug. She closed her eyes and lifted the cup close to her face, soaking in the steam wafting off the top. "It smells delicious. Is that cinnamon?"

"And nutmeg. A little something special Ma used to do."

"So comforting." She took a long sip.

"It's a good way to ease into the day."

"Is that why it's so dark in here? You're easing into the day." She rested the cup on the table as her gaze wandered. "How do you see what you're doing?"

"Keeping the light low makes it easier to see the metal once heated. We open the windows if we need more light."

"We?"

"I'm not quite used to working in the forge alone." He chuckled. "I half expected Levi to come through the door when you opened it. Of course, Simon should appear any minute now."

"Seems like you had a good working relationship with Levi."

"Still do. We spend fewer hours of the day together, but we've got a good partnership." Justin rubbed his hand through his hair. "So, what did you bring this morning?"

"Not much, I'm afraid. It was a hungry crowd at the breakfast table. They didn't leave much behind." Eliza Dawn pulled the towel from the top of the basket. "A few biscuits, a jar of preserves, and some buttermilk."

"Muscadine preserves?" he asked.

"Your favorite." She smiled.

He grabbed the jar and a biscuit from the basket. "That'll do fine."

"Well, enjoy." Eliza Dawn patted the table. Then, rising, she proceeded toward the door.

"No need to rush off." He took a sip of coffee. "Unless, of course, you need to get to your sewing projects."

"I've got time." She returned to her seat.

Eliza Dawn sat quietly, sipping coffee while he ate. He

missed the easy silence they usually shared. So still and relaxed, no tension stirring up a desire to escape. Now, something rigid hung in the air between them. Words that needed to be said, but neither of them was willing to give breath to.

"Did Simon come to breakfast in the dining room? Do I need to save any of this for him?" He shifted as he spoke.

"Oh, no. He ate already. Have your fill." She wobbled on the stool, edging it closer to the stove. "I was surprised when you told Malcolm you'd talk to him about using the forge yesterday."

"Malcolm?" Justin's throat pinched tight at her use of the man's given name. "I'm surprised at how easily you use his given name. I was under the impression you didn't know these men well. They were just customers who buy shirts and pay for mending."

"Well, Mr. Mooney knows his customers well, doesn't he? He knows you usually come in at nine o'clock and four o'clock. That is, until recently." She averted her eyes. "He calls you by your given name."

"We've known one another a long time." He swished down a bite of biscuit with a sip of coffee. "However, he respectfully addresses his female customers as Mrs. or Miss no matter how long he's known them."

"I try to be personable. And sometimes, that means using a person's given name. There's nothing more to it than that." She shrugged. "So, will you allow him to use the forge?"

"I'm considering it." Justin dabbed preserves on another biscuit. "What are your plans for today?"

"I've got plenty of sewing to do, but I'd like to get out later if the weather improves."

"Guess I'd better get to work on this butter barrel." Finishing the last biscuit, he brushed the crumbs from his hands. He stood with his tin cup and moved to the work area.

"So, you won't take it to Levi then?" She followed him.

"Nah, it's not too bad. Should be able to fix it today. Of course, I'll have to make extra nails for horseshoes first." He pumped the bellows. "But we could get more rain if this cloud cover doesn't move out. Won't be much to do with the horses in this mess."

"Do you mind if I observe?"

"Not at all." He brought a log stool over. "I don't want to keep you from your work, though."

"I can't stay cooped up in the house all day. I'm used to getting out." Eliza Dawn retrieved her shawl. Folding the warm wrap snuggly around her shoulders, she made herself comfortable on the stool. "This will keep me from going stir-crazy."

"I know what you mean." He laughed. "I don't like staying in one spot too long. I guess that's one of the reasons I enjoy working with horses. Keeps me in motion."

Simon entered, grousing about the weather and the work. Justin pinched the bridge of his nose, closing his eyes tight. He released a slow, steady breath.

"Does your head still hurt? I'm sure you never got that sweet bath with all the excitement last evening." Eliza Dawn edged toward the door. "I can get the honey. A drizzle in your coffee might do."

"It's not that kind of headache. I'll be fine." He narrowed his eyes at Simon.

"Sewing is tedious work. I wish I had something that kept me in motion." She returned to the stool. "Why do we need that? To be in motion?"

A blanket of silence fell between them. Justin placed a length of metal in the fire. He sighed. "I don't know. What do you think?"

"I think it's the pain, the loss." She rested her chin on her hand. "If I'm still too long, the pain settles too deep."

"*Hmm*. You might be right." Justin gathered a few tools and organized them on the work table. He didn't need them all but wanted to keep his hands busy. The conversation was edging into uncomfortable territory.

"If I don't keep moving, the loss of my mother and father—and other losses—catches up to me." She rested one hand on her stomach, and with the other, she patted her chest. "It settles here, and I feel like I might be unable to breathe if I stay in that moment. Do you ever feel that way?"

"Mm-hmm." Justin turned his back to her, pumping the bellows again. A lump formed in his throat, and he swallowed it down.

"I feel like that sometimes." Simon's gaze stayed on his work, his voice quiet.

Justin glanced at Simon. "You do?"

"It's why I do stunts." Simon nodded. "I must concentrate hard so I don't fall off and get injured. I don't have time to dwell on the pain while I'm up there. Don't have time to feel it."

Justin paused, studying his brother's melancholy countenance. Taking a deep breath, he turned to face Eliza Dawn. Would she reveal what he'd already read in her journal? "What other losses have you experienced? Your brother?"

"And other people who walked away from me." She studied the shawl's fringe, splitting the threads with her fingernail.

"Why would anyone walk away from you?"

"Because they can't forgive me."

"For not being with your father when he died?"

"Not just that." A tear dropped into her lap. Her shoulders rose and fell, and then she stood. She brushed away another tear and, with it, the somberness. "Tell me about what you're doing here. What are these tools?"

Caught off guard by the sudden change, Justin fiddled with the tools. Eliza Dawn came closer. She picked up the first item. "What's this?"

"That's a pair of tongs."

"What does it do?"

"They grip the metal piece I'm working on."

"I could show her some things." Simon gathered the tools he needed.

"It's all right, Simon." Justin straightened the implements before him. "I've got it."

Huffing, Simon laid his equipment down on the table overly hard. Justin and Eliza Dawn stared at him. He met their gaze with a scowl.

"What else would you like to know?" Justin returned his attention to Eliza Dawn.

"What's this?"

"Also tongs."

Her head tilted, eyebrows pulled together. "They look different."

"They share some similarities. See this end here?" He pointed. "It's called the bit. On this first pair, the bit is straight. On that second pair, the bit is angled."

"Why?"

"Different bits allow you to get a different grip. To come at things from a different angle." Justin moved away. "I better get this piece out of the fire. You should have a seat for safety."

"Wouldn't it be nice if life were that way?" She took a seat on a stool by the wall. "If coming at your problems from a different angle was as simple as picking up another tool?"

"I hadn't thought of it that way, but yes." If only there were a tool that could help him come at things from a different angle with her.

Across the room, Simon donned a leather apron, slouched to the fire, and sifted through embers with the shovel. He returned the shovel to its stand and shoved the metal rod around. Poking it this way and that, he unnested the rod, exposing it to cooler temperatures.

Justin joined him and took the rod away. He repositioned the piece to get the appropriate exposure to heat. "You're piddling. Get to work. Finish that box of nails over there."

"Nails? What do I gotta make nails for?"

Justin arched his eyebrows in a warning.

"Fine." Simon moped.

"I expect top-notch work. Those nails are for Levi." Justin wiped his forearm across his forehead. "If they're not up to standard, you'll redo them."

"Why are you making nails for Levi? I'm just curious." Eliza Dawn rolled the fringe of her shawl between her fingers. "You've already taken on this churn that should've been brought to him."

"He's making nails because I know Levi taught him how before he moved." Justin pulled his pocket watch out and checked the time. "It's busy work, but Levi always has orders of nails to fill. So, it's busy work that won't be wasted. I'm making horseshoe nails. They're special for shoeing horses."

"Oh. I see."

Justin retrieved the metal from the fire and held it over the anvil. Then, using a hammer, he struck the part several times. Pausing, he studied his work.

"You missed your mark. You didn't hit that in the same place twice, you know."

"No, I didn't. It's not like hammering a nail into a piece of wood." He grinned. "I need to land blows up and down the length of the piece to get the shape I want. Shouldn't take long to turn this into nails."

"I imagine it feels good to do some work where you hit something repeatedly. That must help with pent-up energy and emotions."

Justin eyed her for a long time. Shoulders high, pulled up to her ears. From the cold? Or from the tension of deeper emotions? Had she built a dam to hold everything back as he had?

"Would you," the words came slowly, "like to try?"

"Could I?" Her eyes shone brightly.

"I don't see why not." He set the piece back in the fire, then crossed to the wall where Levi left a spare leather apron. "Levi left these aprons behind when he moved to the homestead. I offered to give them back to him. I think he secretly hopes when I see them hanging here, it will remind me of our days working together. He's asked me to work at his forge. I love making shoes for the horses, but I don't want to be stuck in the forge every day."

Justin motioned Eliza Dawn to him. "Lay your shawl on the stool."

He slipped the top strap of the apron over her head. A warm tingle worked through his fingers as he freed her silken hair from the leather loop. He rested a moment in the gaze of her clear blue eyes.

"Let me get a leather tie to pull your hair back." He broke away as she tied the apron strings behind her waist. "Wouldn't want it to get caught between hot metal and a hammer."

Eliza Dawn gathered her hair. He wrapped the thin leather around it. Then, swallowing hard, he patted her shoulders and guided her to the work table.

"It gets hot over here, so let me know if it's too much."

"I'll be fine." She smiled.

He carried the metal from the fire to the anvil. Standing behind her, his hand hovered over hers a moment before he clasped it, guiding her to hold the tongs in one hand. Then, he showed her how to grip the hammer and strike the metal with her other hand. She hit the metal with more force than he anticipated.

"Whoa, whoa. Easy there." Leaning over her shoulder to view the work, he coached her. "Not quite so hard. Loosen your grip."

She relaxed her hand into his, and her high, tight shoulders untensed, drifting from under his chin.

"Like this?" She turned her face toward his.

"Justin," his father's voice cut the air. "What on earth are you doing?"

With a clang, the tongs landed on the anvil, and the hammer dropped with a thud to the table. Eliza Dawn freed herself from him and hastened to the stool, gathering her shawl. She threw it around her shoulders.

"I'm making horseshoe nails before I fix Mrs. Pratt's butter barrel."

Mr. Hogue grimaced, hands on his hips. "Is that what you call it?"

"Not what I call it, Pa." Justin held up the metal rod. "It's what it is. Did you need something?"

Eliza Dawn rushed toward the door, pulling her shawl tight.

"A man here says he'd like to borrow the forge." The tension in Mr. Hogue's words was palpable. "Don't keep him waiting in this drizzle."

"Miss Dawn."

Eliza Dawn jumped at Justin's tight voice and turned. "Yes?"

"Better leave that apron."

A blush rose in Eliza Dawn's cheeks. She sat her shawl on the table and fiddled with the tie at the back of the smock. Justin came to her rescue, loosening the knot she had created. Handing him the apron, she bolted for the door. With his hand on her shoulder, he tugged her back. He untied the leather string in her hair. She escaped out the door.

"Didn't you give up smithing?" Pa's eyes narrowed as he challenged Justin.

"This is Mrs. Pratt's butter churn." Justin hitched his thumb toward the dismantled pieces. He drilled down on his words. "How often have you been able to tell Mrs. Pratt *no*?"

Pa nodded at Simon. "Why isn't he in school?"

"I needed an extra hand to take care of some repairs around here."

"Next time, check with me before keeping him home." Pa huffed, slamming the door behind him.

Simon laid down his hammer. "Why didn't you tell Pa about me?"

Justin joined him, laying his hand on the boy's shoulder. "I've already put you through the wringer with Mrs. Pratt's sock collection. And I'm not sure what Pa would do about Miss Dawn if he knew she was the reason you were at the pool hall. I'm afraid he'd put her out."

"She needs us, doesn't she?"

"We're the closest thing she's had to family in a long time." He patted Simon's shoulder. "Get back to work. I'll be back soon."

Chapter Twenty-Five

Eliza Dawn collapsed in a breathless heap on the cot in her room. Grabbing a stack of blank paper, she fanned herself. It would be a miracle if Mr. Hogue didn't put her out. How could she have been so foolish? Getting caught in what looked like an embrace with Justin Hogue and Simon right there across the work table. It's not like she didn't have enough work to keep her busy, what with the shirt order from the Scotsmen, the extra mending from Mrs. Pratt, and her article deadlines. She shouldn't have stayed after dropping off Justin's breakfast. Why had she lingered?

She released a long stream of air and patted her chest. It had been so long since she had anyone to talk to, especially about her grief and pain. She was tempted to tell him everything. She closed her eyes, remembering his breath on her neck and his hand's firm but tender grip over hers. The whole world faded away, and she was safe.

But she couldn't risk telling Justin everything. What would he think if he found out she wasn't with her father that day because she was angry with him? What if he knew she wasn't speaking to her father because he'd married her off against her wishes?

Her father had written a clause into his will, allowing his small empire to pass to her younger brother if she and Fairfax had no heir within five years of marrying. In the beginning, Fairfax had been charming and uncomfortably attentive. After her father's death, he'd grown increasingly volatile as the marriage progressed from month to month and year to year with no offspring. She edged her fingers inside her shirt, rubbing the circular scars where Fairfax had pressed his cigar into the flesh below her collarbone. Would Justin force her to return if he discovered she'd abandoned her marriage?

She flung the papers across the room and buried her face in her hands. Things always unraveled as soon as she grew comfortable. But this was more than comfortable. This was a crackling fire on a winter's night, a freshly baked pie on the window sill. It was what others might call home. Rebecca embraced her like family. Sam was warm and fatherly. And Justin. Her heart swelled at the discovery she wanted something more. If only she had met him before the decisions and actions of monied men had tainted her life. She drew her hand from inside her shirt and pressed the fabric flat over the disfigured skin.

She and Justin had gotten off to a rocky start, but the road between them was beginning to smooth. He didn't fill up every quiet moment. Rarely did someone appreciate a moment of silence as much as she did. Ewan MacKinnon certainly wasn't one to let a quiet moment linger. She shook herself free of these thoughts. "If only" thinking had never gotten her anywhere.

Rising, she weaved her way to the window. The sky was gloomy gray and indecisive, releasing a fine mist one moment and oversized, sporadic drops the next. She traced the path of a raindrop down the window. Had the weather not been so messy, she could have gone about her day as usual. But that was a problem in itself, wasn't it?

Even if the sun came out later, she'd have to be careful about going to the pool hall. She had respected Justin's wishes yesterday by meeting Ewan at Gray's Café. However, she still needed to glean any information she could from prospectors to complete her article series. Saloons, gambling halls, and pool halls were the likeliest places to find them loose-tongued and sharing the details of their lives and journey west.

Was there another place that would afford the luxury of time and overheard conversations among so many prospectors? These forty-niners were too quickly in and out of the livery and other businesses. She'd already had her fill of saloons and gambling halls on this journey, and there were bound to be more in her future the farther west she traveled. Pool halls were more tolerable.

She leaned against the window pane, staring at the soggy ground below. A strong wind blew a mislaid bucket against the side of the house. The trellis shook. The trellis. She had snuck out the back the previous night, and the conversation she'd overheard between Ewan and Malcolm Sinclair proved eye-opening and valuable. But she would not likely have another opportunity to walk out the door with most of the household distracted. The trellis, though, looked new and sturdy. It should easily hold her weight.

She rummaged through baskets and open trunks. She'd seen some men's clothes before. Where were they? *Here.* Snatching a wide-brimmed hat, a canvas duster, and a dark-colored bandana from the middle of a basket, she set them aside. They might come in handy if she could sneak away later.

After the episode in the forge, she'd do well to avoid Justin for a while, but if the letter and ring belonged to a prospector, she wanted to add the man's discovery to her newspaper stories. Perhaps she could sneak into the pool hall after dark dressed as one of them and pick up some helpful information. Or maybe she'd be lucky enough to spy the thistle image amongst them. If she could wrap up the mystery of this ring and get a few more details about Ewan, she should have two good stories to send in the post. She could leave a few days ahead of the prospectors and set out for Fort Smith, where she could await payment from the newspapers. Then she'd have enough money to finish the journey west.

Weaving her way back through the maze of forgotten effects, she paused at the trunk filled with baby things. She opened the lid, setting her gaze on the little gown. She rubbed the layers of fabric between her fingers. Pressing her eyes tight, a tear rolled down her cheek, and she wiped it away. If only circumstances had been different, she might not be here. If *she* had been different, her marriage might have survived.

Chapter Twenty-Six

Justin walked through the drizzling mist to the front porch. Malcolm Sinclair stood under the overhang, wearing a belt full of blacksmith tools. Justin shook his head and waved for Sinclair to follow him. In a jangling hustle, Sinclair was by his side. They ducked into the shop door, and Justin motioned for Sinclair to sit.

"Take your hat off. Warm yourself by the stove." Justin retrieved a tin cup from a nearby shelf as Simon tapped away at the anvil. "Coffee?"

Sinclair nodded, patting his arms. Justin passed him a cup and gave the man a moment to smother the cold. Sinclair took a few sips, slurping through the gap in his two front teeth.

He grinned from ear to ear. "Tha. 'At's a might better. *Tapadh leibh.*"

"Ta believe?" Justin's eyebrows knit together.

Sinclair laughed. "Thank you. Tis 'thank you' in ma home language."

"That's like no thank you I ever heard." Justin scratched his head and arched his eyebrows. He and Simon exchanged shrugs from across the room. "Sam said you fellas were a little difficult to understand. Said he had to ask MacKinnon to keep repeating himself the first time he visited the mercantile."

"Well, I don't mind repeating maself. Ye may hev to remind me to slow down." Sinclair chuckled. "Seems youse Yanks don't listen as fast as we speak."

Justin half grinned. "I understand you're looking to use the forge, Mr. Sinclair."

"Tha. I am."

"What sort of projects do you plan on doing? As you can see, the space isn't very large."

"No' a problem. A'll need to make horseshoes and nails. And, o'course, A've a long list o' repairs. Wagon wheels and hitches, tools and 'eh lek." Sinclair slapped some coins on the table. "I can pay white'er ye boarders pay daily or weekly. We expect to be here fer six to eight more days. A'll happily pay fer a week, and I willny ask fer 'eh money back if we cut oot early."

Justin raked his fingers through his stubble. "Mr. Sinclair, I'm not sure about this. There's been an increase in lawlessness and violence since the prospectors have come to town. You may be a fine man, but I don't know you, and I have a family to protect."

"I understand." Sinclair's countenance sobered. He reached into his vest pocket. "If I may, I'd lek to shew ye whit sort o' man I am."

Sinclair pulled a paper out and pushed it across the table to Justin. He picked up the paper, read it, and laid it back on the table. He hard-eyed the Scotsman.

"What is this?"

"I ken MacKinnon has bin taking yer advertisement from Sam Mooney's board. I guarantee A'll replace it ev'ry time I find it missing." He picked up the paper. "His pa wouldn't agree wi' his actions, so A'll be replacing yer notice whether ye and I come to an agreement or no."

Justin extended a hand across the table. "Mr. Sinclair, I believe we have come to an arrangement."

Sinclair grasped Justin's hand firmly and pulled him close. "Mr. Hogue, I only hev one more request."

Justin raised an eyebrow.

"Be fergiving of MacKinnon. His pa and ma aren't in good health. He's set on doing white'er it takes to better himself fer thir benefit."

"I understand." Justin's chest tightened. He'd have done the same for Ma if he could have saved her. "Thank you for stopping by. When would you like to get started?"

"If ye don't mind, A'll leave ma belt here. A'll go back doon to 'eh mercantile, hang yer notice, and get started when I return."

"I've also got some business at the mercantile, and if this rain will let up, I've got business elsewhere."

Sinclair stood and headed to the door. Glancing at the work table, he stopped and approached the anvil where Justin had been working.

"Whit's this?"

"One of the women in town brought a large barrel churn for repair. Thought I could fix the handle and be done with it, but the bar inside is also bent." Justin sighed. "It's not my intention to be a blacksmith, but I was an apprentice to a blacksmith for a while. People still bring me relatively small projects. I try to tell them *no* because I don't have the time. But this woman does a lot for the town and is tough to say *no* to."

"I don't want to take money oota yer pocket, but if you don't want 'eh work, A'd be happy to take it on."

"If you'd like the work, I'd be thrilled to pass it along. You'd be doing me a favor, Mr. Sinclair."

"Well, if we're going to hev sooch a partnership, call me Malcolm or Mal."

"Malcolm, you can call me Justin. And this is my kid brother, Simon."

"Whit a mop o' curls ye've got on ye." Malcolm pumped Simon's hand. "Bet ye've turned 'eh head o' more 'an a lass or two."

Simon grinned, his cheeks pinking.

Justin grabbed his hat and coat and opened the door. "I'll head to town with you. Simon, why don't you join us?" We'll see if we can get to town in the dry."

The fine mist hung in the air as the two Hogues and Sinclair walked to town. Justin and Simon were amused by Sinclair's rapid speech, rough twang, and unusual colloquialisms. Justin found himself asking Sinclair to slow down and repeat himself. Even then, he had difficulty understanding the man's unique turns of phrase. He'd lost count of how often he'd asked, "What do you mean by that?" Sinclair wasn't bothered by it. He'd release a hearty laugh and explain himself as best he could.

Sinclair reached the steps of the mercantile first, followed closely by Simon. Before Justin reached the steps, someone grabbed his shoulder, spun him around, and landed a fist across his jaw. He stumbled back, eyes watering, gripping his chin.

"D'ye think ye could steal ma horses last night and joost walk through toon today lek nothing happened?" Ewan MacKinnon bobbed in front of Justin with balled hands.

Justin shook his head, still reeling from the blow. "What are you talking about?"

"I ken it wis ye. Same hat, same coat."

"Back off, fella." Simon pushed past Justin, and Justin pulled him back.

"Ewan, whit's 'eh problem?" Sinclair wedged himself between MacKinnon and the Hogues.

"And to bring this lad into a life o' horse thieving." MacKinnon reached around Sinclair and shoved Simon's shoulder.

"Easy, Ewan." Sinclair's voice flattened. "Ye don't ken whit yer saying. I wis thir, and I didnae see them."

"I rode after 'eh scoundrels. A figure wearing this coat and hat and one with 'at curly head o' hair drove four o' ma horses away from oor camp. Hogue thir caught oop to his gang and stopped short, turning into 'eh woods lek a coward."

Justin's stomach clenched. Eliza Dawn had been wearing his hat and coat. So, she didn't ride out to meet MacKinnon. She wasn't with him. But if she wasn't there with him, what on earth was she doing? Stealing horses? How was that possible? When he'd discovered her, she was alone.

"MacKinnon, I know there's no trust between us, but believe me when I say neither of us was anywhere near your camp last night. You can ask Sam Mooney. He was at the boardinghouse."

"Bah," MacKinnon growled. "Mooney is yer pal. Ye think A'm fool 'nough to believe he wouldn't lie fer ye?"

"Mr. Mooney is as honest as the day is long." Simon pushed into the back of Justin, moving toward MacKinnon. Justin planted his hand in the middle of Simon's chest, shoving him back.

"Talk to the saddler then. He and Sam brought an injured man to the boardinghouse. The three of us held him down while my sister stitched up his face." Justin gave Simon another shove as the boy edged up underneath him again. "You hang out at that pool hall enough. You'll probably see my sister's handiwork on some bear of a man."

Sinclair grabbed MacKinnon by the shoulder. "How aboot ye join me, Ewan? Let's take a walk and cool off. Gi' them 'eh benefit o' 'eh doubt."

"A've got ma eye on ye, Hogue. I best not see ye trying to sell ma horses oot from under me." MacKinnon shook his fist as Sinclair shoved him toward the pool hall.

"Joostin, A'll check in wi' ye later."

Justin waved over his head as he pushed Simon into the

mercantile. The bell above the door clattered as they entered. Justin wiped his forearm across his brow and shifted his jaw from side to side.

"What was going on out there?" Sam leaned on the counter, eyeing the window.

"Seems like Simon and I have a couple of look-alikes in town stirring up trouble."

"That MacKinnon fella calls me a horse thief again, and I'll lay him out." Simon clenched his fists, thrusting out his chest.

"You'll do no such thing. You'll mind your *Ps* and *Qs*." Justin moved to the window and scanned the street. "Has Whitmore been by today with that young kid?"

"Haven't seen hide nor hair of his bunch."

"I'm curious as to whether they're still in town. If you see them, let me know." Justin returned to the counter. "But don't let on I'm looking. I don't want them getting spooked and hotfooting it out of town. Did Conrad bring the handbills for the horse show and shindig?"

"Sure did." Sam held up a stack of half-sheet-sized papers. "I've been passing them out all morning."

"Great. Give me a few of those, and we'll post them around town."

"You can drop one at all the usual businesses. I'm sure they'll gladly display it on their counter or in the window." Sam raised his eyebrows and peered down his nose at Justin, deepening his voice. "Just mind the both of you stay out of trouble while you're doing it."

Justin forced a smile. "Will do, Sam."

Chapter Twenty-Seven

Eliza Dawn searched for her sewing basket. Lifting the narrow cot, she rummaged underneath it. She turned in circles, checking the tops of trunks and furniture. Oh no. She pressed her palm to her forehead. She'd never brought it up after all the commotion the previous night. Opening her door, she peeked into the hall. All the doors were shut.

She slid out and edged down the stairs, spying around corners for Rebecca and Edie. She had managed to avoid contact with the youngest Hogue and further embarrassment with Justin by remaining in her room for the morning. A quick scan of the kitchen revealed an empty room. She tiptoed across the kitchen and into the dining room. Voices coming from across the hall made her pause. She quickly turned.

"Oh, Eliza Dawn, there you are." Rebecca's winded voice caused her to jump. "I was hoping I hadn't missed you on your way out."

Her heart lurched, and her hand flew to her chest. "You startled me."

"I need you to watch Edie for me. I've been called to the

saloon." Rebecca's brow furrowed, and she caught the edge of her bottom lip with her teeth. She unloaded household sewing items from her sewing box and searched through the bottom drawer of the china cabinet, pulling out various medical supplies. "They've sent word. Someone has been stabbed."

Eliza Dawn's eyes widened. "Stabbed?"

"Yes. I've got to hurry. You'll stay, right?" Rebecca latched the lid of the sewing basket. "I wouldn't ask, except no one else is home right now."

"No one? Where is everyone?" Eliza Dawn steadied herself against the china cabinet. "Rebecca, I am not good with children. Perhaps you could take her to Mrs. Pratt."

"Eliza Dawn, listen to me. I don't have time." Rebecca gripped her arm, locking eyes with her. "I don't know where Justin and Simon are. I don't know where Pa is. The same thing happened when Ma was injured. I was alone with Edie and couldn't get there fast enough. If one of them is hurt—" Rebecca bit back tears.

"Oh, no. You mustn't think that way. None of them would be at the saloon."

"It would be just like them to rush in and help break up a brawl." Rebecca hugged her and pulled away. "Take care of Edie. She's in the parlor. I told her you'd take care of her. I've got to go."

Rebecca hurried out of the dining room. A moment later, the front door creaked open and slammed shut. The house was disturbingly quiet. With nine Hogue children and Mr. Hogue, plus a handful of boarders, Eliza Dawn had become accustomed to a thrum of activity, including creaking doors and floors, the low murmur of voices during the day, sometimes wild chatter and horseplay before supper, and someone always going in or out. She walked through the dining room to the foyer and stood at the parlor's opening.

Edie's wide, innocent eyes met hers. Round, rosy cheeks

were pushed up by a broad grin. Eliza Dawn shuffled to the sofa and sat a short distance from the child. The little girl played with a well-worn rag doll, cradling it like a baby. A hint of sadness gripped Eliza Dawn's heart.

"Hello." Eliza Dawn forced a smile.

The child didn't look up. "Hello."

She searched for something to say. "My name is Eliza Dawn."

The little girl eyed her warily. Her grin had disappeared. "Bwonco Bubba calls you Miss Dawn."

"That he does." Eliza Dawn sighed.

"But I know you. You ate my cake at our picnic." She put the doll down and gazed pointedly at Eliza Dawn. "Did you like it?"

"Oh, yes. I remember that cake." Eliza Dawn smiled more easily. "I enjoyed it immensely."

"What is immensely?"

"Very much. I enjoyed it very much."

"I like that word. Immensely." She placed her hand on top of Eliza Dawn's hand. "Mr. Shine hepped me make it."

"Mr. Shine?"

"The baker." She patted Eliza Dawn's hand. "You know him. He lives here."

"Oh, Mr. Hildesheim, the baker. Of course."

She picked up her doll and handed it to Eliza Dawn. "I would like it immensely if you would bwaid her hair."

"Where did you get such a fine baby?" Eliza Dawn's throat pinched as she took the rag doll and weaved the pieces of yarn into a braid.

"Becca made it for me."

"Becca? You mean Rebecca?"

"She lets me call her Becca 'cause I don't have any *R*s." She pointed at the yarn pieces. "Tuck that piece in. Make it neat like Becca does."

"Naturally." Eliza Dawn finished braiding. She took the piece

Of Faith and Dreams

of string from the doll's wrist and tied off the braid. "There you go."

The child took the doll and smiled. "What else can you do?"

"Do you know how to write?" Eliza Dawn took the stubby pencil and notepad from her apron pocket.

"Not so good." She frowned.

"That's okay. I can write your name, and you can trace the letters." Eliza Dawn set the notepad on the tea table and called out the letters as she wrote. "*E-D-I-E*. Edie." She pushed the pad to the child. "Now you try."

"*E-D-I-E*. Edie." Her eyes searched Eliza Dawn's for approval. "Now, your name."

"Eliza Dawn." She wrote the words on a new page. "Your turn."

The little girl traced 'Eliza' and the *D* from Dawn. She stopped and tilted her head toward Eliza Dawn. Underlining the *E* and *D*, she said, "Hey, I have that too. We're the same."

Eliza Dawn swallowed hard and smiled. "Yes, I suppose we are."

The little girl popped up from her seat and threw her arms around Eliza Dawn's middle. Try as she might, Eliza Dawn couldn't keep a tear from springing free. It dropped onto the child's arm. The little girl reached up and wiped Eliza Dawn's cheek.

"Why are you sad?"

The words caught in Eliza Dawn's throat. "Because I always imagined I would have a little girl like you someday."

"Pa says I came to them on the wind." The little girl curled her fingers around Eliza Dawn's. "Do you want to walk to the wiver? We have lots of wind on the wiver."

Eliza Dawn hugged the child tightly. "That's very sweet of you to offer, but even wind from the river won't bring me a little girl like you."

"*Mm-hmm*." Mr. Hogue cleared his throat.

Eliza Dawn rose. "Mr. Hogue, I thought everyone was gone."

"I stopped by the saddler to pick up Mr. Perry's saddle." He stooped to avoid bumping his head on the parlor doorframe. "I've only just returned."

"I didn't hear you come in."

"I can see that." He smiled softly. "Looks like you girls were having a good time. Where's Rebecca?"

"Edie, I'll be right back." Eliza Dawn pulled Mr. Hogue into the foyer and spoke in a whisper. "She left suddenly. Her help was required at the saloon for a stabbing."

"I see." Mr. Hogue rubbed his hands together.

"I'm not very good with children." Eliza Dawn studied her toes. "I encouraged her to take Edie to Mrs. Pratt, but she said there was no time."

"Not very good with children. *Pfft.*" Mr. Hogue pursed his lips. "You're a natural from what I witnessed. The only person Edie is truly taken with is Justin. But it seems she's warmed to you right well."

"She is precious."

"Do you know if anyone went with Rebecca?"

"Not unless Justin or someone found her in town."

Mr. Hogue frowned under a wrinkled brow. He checked the time. "Could you stay with Edie a little longer? I want to make sure Rebecca is all right."

Her chest tightened. She drew a deep breath and exhaled silently. "We'll be fine. I'm sure Rebecca needs you."

The front door creaked open, and Rebecca stepped inside, removing her shawl. Eliza Dawn's shoulders relaxed, and the tightness in her chest eased. Rebecca glanced from Pa to Eliza Dawn and back again.

"Is everything all right?" Rebecca set her sewing kit on the entryway table. "Why are you standing in the foyer? Where's Edie?"

"She's fine. Thanks to Miss Dawn's watchful eye." Mr.

Hogue patted Eliza Dawn's shoulder. "Why, they've done up the doll's hair and practiced their letters. Miss Dawn will make a fine ma someday."

The heaviness in her chest made it difficult to breathe. She wrapped her arms around herself. She'd been called many things in her life. Daughter, sister, wife, friend. Stubborn, hard-headed, persistent, determined. Fetching, winsome, generous. Pretty little thing. It pained her to know she would never be called mother.

"I noticed the latch on the gate was sticking when I came in." Mr. Hogue shoved his hands in his pockets and moved toward the door. "I better take care of it."

"I noticed that too." Rebecca patted his shoulder as he passed by, smiling softly.

"Mr. Hogue, may I join you?" Eliza Dawn followed.

Mr. Hogue stiffened. "I suppose so."

They walked around the side of the house to a small shed, and Mr. Hogue retrieved an oil can. "What's on your mind, young lady?"

"I'd like to explain about this morning in the forge." She fiddled with the button at her collar as she followed him to the gate. "It was not my intention to behave so as to cast a poor light on Justin. We talked about life's unfortunate circumstances, and I commented that it must be good to do work that allows you to hit something repeatedly."

Mr. Hogue squirted oil into the moving parts of the latch.

Eliza Dawn cleared her throat. "Well, Justin asked me if I'd like to try striking the metal rod on the anvil. And I know this is very unladylike of me, but I've wanted to hit something for quite some time. So, I accepted his offer. I see now how inappropriate it must've appeared."

She held her breath, waiting for him to respond. He worked the latch repetitively to distribute the oil. Stooping, he oiled the gate hinges. Then he stood and worked the gate back and forth.

"You don't have to make excuses for Justin. He knew what he was doing." Mr. Hogue's gaze never left his work. He stooped and squirted more oil into the hinges. Standing, he quietly studied his shoes. He pulled his lips in and pushed them out a couple of times. Then, his narrowed gaze met hers. "Like to hit something, you say?"

She nodded.

"Just hit something, or would any kind of force do the trick?"

She arched an eyebrow over a sidelong glance. "I'm not sure what you mean."

"Got this set of throwing knives. Passenger in my steamboat days gave them to me." He walked to the shed and reshelved the oil can. Reaching up, he pulled down a box, removed a leather pouch, and returned the box to the shelf. "He was a huntsman. Taught me how to throw these things."

He handed her the leather pouch, and she followed him to the back of the shed. Unsheathing the knives, he dropped the bag on the ground. Holding the handles of two blades between his fingers, he took the third knife in his other hand, reared back, and flung it at a wooden target on the back of the shed. It stuck with a *thunk*.

"That is impressive."

"Well, I've had a lot of practice lately." He held a knife out to her. "Your turn."

"Me? Oh, no, I couldn't." She patted the air with her hands.

"Aw, now. You've plied your hand at smithing." He grinned. "You're about as ladylike as Rebecca. Here, now. Give it a try."

Mr. Hogue placed a knife in Eliza Dawn's hand. Taking her by the shoulders, he squared her with the shed. He took a step back and waited. She glanced back at him, and he nodded toward the shed. She pulled her arm back and pitched it forward. The knife stuck in the ground at her feet, and she frowned.

Mr. Hogue laughed. Shuffling back a few steps, he pressed his fanned fingers into his chest. He bowed his head. His voice softened. "I haven't laughed since—" He slid the blade from the dirt and wiped it on his pants. "Well, that's about how my first attempt went." He held her palm out flat and lay the knife across it. "First, you want to get a feel for how the knife's balanced." He wobbled it back and forth. "You feel that?"

She nodded. He motioned for her to grip the handle. Making a sucking sound against his teeth, he stood beside her, raised her hand near her ear, and held it still.

"Loosen your grip. You want to let it slide free when you release it." He rubbed her fingers. "Pull your hand back slightly and let go at the top of your arc. That'll keep it from going into the ground."

Mr. Hogue nodded at the board again. Eliza Dawn drew back and released the knife sooner. It hurled end over end, hit the shed, and bounced off. She exhaled deeply.

Mr. Hogue handed her the remaining knife. "You've played a fair amount of Graces, haven't you? Flicking the little hoop onto two sticks."

"I have. I was quite good at it." She straightened her back and smiled proudly.

"That's going to be to your detriment in knife throwing." He chuckled. "Keep your wrist straight. Don't flick it. Make it one smooth motion. And step into it a little."

She pulled the blade up near her ear and inhaled deeply.

Mr. Hogue leaned close, brushing her elbow. He whispered, "Don't hold your breath."

She exhaled and forced herself to breathe steadily. She drew back slightly and let the knife fly. *Thwack.* It wobbled as it protruded from the wall of the shed. Her heart leaped, and her mouth turned up in a bow.

"Oh, that was invigorating."

Mr. Hogue collected the knives and returned to her side.

"Now, I'm curious to know why a young lady like yourself wants to hit and throw things."

She sobered. "I find myself angry sometimes over the things I've lost."

He nodded as he stepped and threw again. "Understandable. But things can be replaced." He handed her a knife.

"When I say things, I mean my parents, my family, my home." She studied the ground and then fixed her eyes on the shed.

"Ah, I see."

Thunk. She stepped to the side, making room for Mr. Hogue.

"I guess that's why I've gotten so good at throwing these lately." He released the knife, and it landed solidly in the wood. "Mahala was the love of my life. I retired from steamboating to spend more time with her. I got an itch, a longing for the river. An injured captain asked if I'd make one more trip in his stead." He walked the length of the throwing lane and gathered the set. "I had just made port at Phillips Landing when it happened. I should have been here."

Eliza Dawn's heart slowed. "Mr. Hogue, what happened to your wife?"

"Pa?" Justin stepped around the side of the shed. "What are you doing?"

"Throwing knives. What does it look like we're doing?" Mr. Hogue picked up the leather pouch and stored the knives away. He handed the bag to Eliza Dawn. "You're welcome to borrow these any time you like."

He turned to go.

Eliza Dawn tucked the knife bag under her arm. "Mr. Hogue, do you sew?"

Justin's eyes widened.

Mr. Hogue gave her a sideways glance. "I've been known to thread a needle or two."

"We're having a mending bee in the parlor this evening." Eliza Dawn smiled. "I'd be honored if you'd join us."

"I'll consider it." With a nod and a grin, he disappeared inside the house.

Eliza Dawn's eyes met Justin's, and she quickly let her gaze drop to his shoes. "I thought you would be gone the rest of the afternoon."

"I heard about the stabbing. When I couldn't find Rebecca in town, I thought I'd better make sure she got home all right."

"You're a good brother." She clasped her hands in front of her. "She's lucky to have you."

"Do you still have the ring and the letter?"

"You know I do."

"Keep it out of sight. It doesn't leave this house." Justin lay his hand across hers.

Her brows furrowed with concern. "Why? What's going on?"

"Somehow, word has gotten out about that ring." He rubbed her hands. "That's what led to the stabbing. There's a lot of talk. Rumor is going around it's made of diamonds, rubies, and the like. These prospectors are chomping at the bit to get their hands on any treasure. Were you planning on going out today?"

"No, I must finish the last of the shirts for the Scots soon, and I still have a half basket of mending for Mrs. Pratt."

"Good." He rubbed his hands along her arms. "I brought Simon home. Tensions are running high in town. The closer it gets to their departure date, the more antsy and disorderly these fellas seem to get. I'm going to finish my business and be home. Save me a seat in your sewing circle."

Chapter Twenty-Eight

"I don't understand why she doesn't want to do it." Caroline Brandt spoke around the straight pins sticking out the side of her mouth as she pinned the hem in place. "I was sure she'd reconsider when I offered her a commission and help with her workload."

"I wish I had answers for you, Mrs. Brandt." Justin tapped the handbills on the tailor shop counter. "If you don't mind my asking, what's your opinion of Miss Dawn?"

"Why, she's the most stunning woman in town." She took a pin from between her teeth. "Gertie, you must stand still, or I'll never finish pinning this hem. No dress walks out of this shop until the hem is perfectly straight."

"Her appearance isn't exactly what I was getting at." Justin shifted, flipping his thumb along the edge of the papers. "She doesn't quite fit the image of a garden variety seamstress, does she?"

Caroline straightened, putting her hands on her hips. "Justin Hogue, what exactly *are* you getting at?"

"Mrs. Brandt, this is a tailor shop. You and your father-in-law specialize in finery." He raked his fingers through his stubble. "It shows in the way you speak and carry yourself. Miss Dawn speaks and carries herself like you, but her seamstress skills are more rudimentary. Doesn't it seem odd?"

"Well, now that you mention it, Miss Dawn does have an air of refinement about her that seems misaligned with her current situation." She motioned for Gertie to turn on the pedestal. "Her fingers are slender, elegant. There's a soft, flawlessness in her complexion. That's precisely why I want her to model one of our ensembles." She waved Gertie off the pedestal. "That'll do, Gertie. I'll have this ready for you by tomorrow morning."

Caroline returned the remaining pins to the pin cushion strapped to her wrist and joined Justin at the counter. She leaned close and whispered in a voice that took on a magical quality as she motioned toward the back of the shop. "She will be simply sublime in the attire I've chosen for her. Oh, Justin, what will it take to get her into my shop?"

"I honestly don't know." Justin shrugged. "Rebecca, Simon, and I helped with her projects last night. We plan to help again tonight. Pa may even sit in. But I have a sneaking suspicion she will decline even if all the work were completed tonight."

"Well, if I have anything to say, she will be at the dance tomorrow." Caroline drummed her fingers softly on the counter and grinned. "And she will be wearing my gown. You'll never look at her the same." She winked.

"I'll let Conrad know you'd like more handbills."

Justin shook his head and chuckled as he pulled the door of Brandt's tailor shop closed behind him. He was eager to learn whether Caroline Brandt's resolve would be any match against Eliza Dawn's determination. *Why, she's the most stunning woman in town*, Caroline's voice rang in his head. He couldn't disagree with her. The sudden urge to sew until his fingers bled to help the odds hollowed his stomach. When had this secret desire for

Mrs. Brandt's mission to be victorious settled on him? And why? He shook his hands. No matter. Eliza Dawn showed hardly any interest in the social event. He doubted she would agree to come even if he did sacrifice his poor fingers to help her complete her sewing projects.

He scanned the street for MacKinnon. The next time he encountered the Scotsman, he wanted to see it coming. Malcolm hadn't expounded on the situation with MacKinnon's parents, and Justin didn't want to pry. But after losing Ma, he wanted to help the man if he could. Justin took in the scene up and down Main Street. No sign of Ewan MacKinnon.

"Whatcha looking for, friend?" Levi appeared from around the corner.

Justin blew out a long stream of air, hands on his hips. "Whew, Levi. Don't sneak up on a fella like that."

"What's got you so jumpy?" Levi patted him on the back.

Justin stretched his neck from side to side. "That Scottish prospector, MacKinnon, thinks I was involved in a raid on his camp last night. He believes I stole some horses."

"What in the world would give him an idea like that?"

"Eliza Dawn." Justin nodded down the road. "Walk with me to the saddlery?"

"She told MacKinnon you stole his horses?"

"No. She snuck out last night wearing my hat and coat. Probably not meaning to look like me. She might've been trying to stay warm." Justin rubbed his temples. "No idea why. What's going on in that woman's head is beyond me."

"Did you ever make it to the saddler with her?"

"No. Things have been crazy. I don't know what's going on in this town."

"Come, now." Levi shoved his shoulder. "You know why she snuck out. She has the ring. She's on the hunt with or without you."

"That ring is going to be the death of me." Justin rubbed the back of his neck. "Did you know there was a fight at the saloon about it? They called Rebecca to stitch up a stab wound, and I wasn't with her. I've gotta get rid of that thing, Levi. I wasn't there to protect her. What if something had gone wrong?"

Catching Justin's sleeve, Levi stopped short. "Justin, you can't always be there to protect eight siblings and your pa. There are days you'll all have to go your separate ways. I know this will be hard to hear, but you'll have to trust God to care for your family."

"Like He cared for Ma?" Justin swallowed hard.

"Yes. Like He cared for your ma."

Justin cut his eyes at Levi like he'd pulled the rug from under him.

Levi squeezed his shoulder. "Your Ma had a personal relationship with Jesus, so she is assured to live for eternity in His love. Now, I know you wanted Him to save her life so she'd be here for you and your family, but He chose to take care of her a different way."

"Because I neglected to stay by her side." Justin kept his eyes on the ground.

"You couldn't be attached at the hip to your ma." Levi patted his arm. "You didn't neglect or abandon her. You stepped away to talk with a young lady, something men have been doing since the beginning of time. I want you to talk to Rebecca. Ask her how she felt about not having you around today."

"What good will that do?"

"It might help you see you're the only one who holds you responsible for these unexpected risks and dangers your family faces sometimes."

Justin toed the dirt. "I don't know."

"You've got to have a little faith. God will take care of this family and set you on a path to someday start a family of your own."

"I'm not so sure." Justin scoffed. "The ranch is how I was

going to provide for a family. With all the challenges running at me lately, I doubt I'll ever get these horses sold. If I don't, no ranch. In light of this saloon fight, I'm considering calling off the horse show."

"You're not calling off that show. You can borrow on my faith here." Levi pulled him into a side-armed hug. "We're going to follow through on this endeavor with faith. God will move you closer to this dream or give you another one. But don't let the distractions of this world push you off the path unless God makes it clear you should go another direction. Did you ever think these distractions might be part of the dream?"

"No." Justin shrugged. "That hadn't crossed my mind."

"Trust me. At times, it feels like everything is spinning out of control and the world is turning upside down. Instinct tells us to take control of those moments, to force them into some order. Instead, walk through your distractions and challenges, knowing what you can control."

"And what is that exactly? What can I control?"

"You. That's it. That's the whole list. Make pockets of quiet in your day to keep you focused on the Lord. Breathe in. Breathe out."

"Breathe and focus on the Lord. It's that simple?"

"I never said it was simple. Try it, though. Make room for your faith to grow. You have no idea what God can make of faith and dreams. Allie taught me that. He'll do more than you could ask or imagine. More than your wildest dreams."

"Well, I'll tell you what would be beyond my wildest dreams right now." Justin strode down the street. "I need to have a discussion with MacKinnon, but I'd rather not have a conversation with his fist again. So, Lord," Justin glanced skyward, "I need a miracle."

Levi smiled and patted Justin on the back. "Speaking of the Scots, what did you decide about the blacksmith?"

"Malcolm? We worked out an agreement. Actually, he's helping me by taking a project off my hands."

"A blacksmith project? What were you working on?"

"Mrs. Pratt brought a damaged butter barrel to me. Folks worry they'll take up too much of your time now that Mason is walking."

"Ah. I have plenty of work now with these prospectors, so it's good Malcolm was willing to take it on." Levi hitched his thumb in the opposite direction. "I've got to run some errands for Allie, but I wanted to catch you since I haven't seen you today. I fed and watered the horses this morning. Don't worry about coming by tonight. I'll take care of them since you'll be there all day tomorrow."

"Thanks, Levi."

More than you can ask or imagine. Perhaps Malcolm could help facilitate talks with MacKinnon. Until then, he'd better investigate the fight at the saloon. The quicker he could unload that ring, the better. If Nicholas couldn't help, he might have to yield to Eliza Dawn's request to read the letter. Showing that letter around town was stirring up the wrong kind of interest.

Justin pushed open the door to the saddlery. "Nicholas?"

The brawny man surfaced from a narrow closet at the back of the shop. "Ah, Justin. What can I do for you?"

"I'm hoping you can give me some insight into what happened at the saloon today. Were you there?"

"During the fray? You know better than that."

"No, no. With Rebecca. Were you there with her?"

"You know Doc Ewing gave me specific instructions before he left. If anyone ever calls on her in his stead, I'm to go with her. I have never failed to keep my commitment to the man."

Justin wiped his brow. "I know you haven't. It's just—"

"I know. You want your family to be safe. You wanted to be there." Nicholas inspected a set of reins. "This town may be busting at the seams, but those of us long-timers are still watching out for your family. Always will. Your ma was so generous to everyone."

Justin cleared his throat. "Sam claims the fight started over a ring. Could you tell me more about it?"

"Not much to tell. That big bruiser Rebecca sewed up tried to slice some young kid into bacon." Nicholas cut a leather strip several inches long. "Kid was fast, so the blade didn't do much damage. A stitch or two to each cut."

"Do you know more of the particulars?"

"That buster told the boy he'd find that ring and claim it for his boss. The boy said likewise. Neither knew how to shut his mouth, so they kept at it until the big fella pulled a knife. Kid's lucky he didn't pull a lead pusher."

"And that was it? Did they have any idea where to find it?"

"Nah. I tell you what. If I were the marrying kind, I'd like to find a woman as feisty as your sister." Nicholas set the strap down. "She told that bear if he were the reason for any more patients, she'd have me hold him down so she could yank out those stitches she put in. If he wanted to act an ugly fool, he could look an ugly fool."

"That sounds like Rebecca, all right."

"Yessir. She told those two they'd be better going about other business because you had the ring, and you're not about to let it go to anyone excepting the rightful owner." Nicholas clamped the spliced pieces of leather. "Said it wasn't of no value to them."

Justin's gut clenched. "She told them that?"

"That she did." He walked over and spit out the window.

Nicholas turned to face Justin, and a horse hoof shot through the window, narrowly missing his head. A raucous round of whoops and jeers went up. Then, there was a thud as hooves banged the outside wall of the saddlery.

They raced out the door and around the side of the small

shop. Davis Whitmore stood in the livery yard with a leafy tree branch in hand. He swished it a few times near a palomino paint and then pulled back, smacking the animal sharply on the rump. A hearty cheer filled the air as men lining the fence waved their hats. Whitmore raised the branch again.

Chapter Twenty-Nine

"Whitmore." Justin's voice cut through the din. "Put it down."

Whitmore's eyes squared on him, and the man struck the horse again. A rousing series of whoops erupted around the enclosure. Justin vaulted over the livery yard fence, rushing Whitmore. Bowling him over, they tumbled to the ground. Whitmore lost his grip on the branch, which cracked and snapped as they rolled over it.

Justin's heart raced as Whitmore swung at him and backcrawled on his elbows. A metallic taste flooded his mouth when Whitmore's knee banged his chin, and he growled. He dragged himself up Whitmore's body. At the periphery, he glimpsed a crowd clambering over the fence.

"Nicholas, push 'em back."

Nicholas was already scrambling over the fence. The stout saddler heaved men over the rail like rag dolls. "Get back, you roughnecks."

Justin's elbows dug into the damp earth while Whitmore landed dull blows around his ears. Within reach of Whitmore's head, Justin shoved his palm under the man's chin, forcing Whitmore's head back. Gaining leverage, Whitmore flipped Justin, landing with his hands at Justin's throat. Wheezing marked every breath as Justin struggled for air.

The pony stamped and lunged, edging closer to them. Justin's eyes bulged, heart pounding in his ears. Bucking and turning, the animal's back hoof caught a piece of Whitmore's shoulder. Justin used Whitmore's shift in weight to his advantage. Justin rolled while pushing Whitmore's shoulder into a rotation, causing Whitmore to land face down. Justin wrenched the man's arm behind him, ratcheting the pressure.

"Youse better get back."

Half a dozen Scots, including MacKinnon, closed in on the livery yard. A man in a red and black checked shirt grabbed a piece of the broken branch near Justin and moved toward the horse. MacKinnon jumped the fence and sprang to the horse's defense, snatching the branch and striking the man. The man recoiled and slunk back to the railing. MacKinnon's men helped Nicholas push back the crowd and clear the area.

MacKinnon shook the branch in the air as men scattered in all directions. "If we catch any o' youse beating an animal, we'll take a cane to ye. Get on. Be gone wit' youse."

MacKinnon stood by as Justin pulled Whitmore to his feet. Justin shoved Whitmore against the fence. MacKinnon closed in over Justin's shoulder.

"You've got a lot of nerve, Whitmore, asking me to find a horse for you when this is how you treat them." Justin pressed a finger into Whitmore's chest. "You'll not lay a hand to this horse again."

"It's my horse, Hogue. I'll treat it as I please." Whitmore snarled a grin under his handlebar mustache.

"Tell you what. I'll sky a copper for it."

"Flip me for it?" Whitmore let out a bark of laughter. "Child's play for a horse? Why would I agree to that?"

"Because if I lose, I'll find that strawberry roan you've been looking for."

"Strawberry roan?" MacKinnon nudged Justin's back. "You cannae flip on the roan, Hogue. I willny let ye."

Keeping his eyes on Whitmore, Justin lowered his voice, speaking out the side of his mouth to MacKinnon. "We've found ourselves on the opposite side of the fence more than once, MacKinnon, but you're going to have to trust we've got the same aim now." Justin addressed Whitmore. "So, what'll it be? I'll let that penny fly or turn you over to the Scot."

Whitmore's eyes darted from Justin to MacKinnon and back again. "Toss it."

Justin fished a penny from his pocket. "First, tell me about Merritt Fairfax."

"Where'd you hear that name?" Whitmore gritted his teeth.

"Don't worry about where I heard it." Words from Eliza Dawn's journal flashed through his mind. "Are you working for him? What's your relationship to the man?"

"He's my brother-in-law, and he's a powerful man. You'd do better to steer clear of me."

"Well, he ain't here now. So I'll toss this copper, and we'll finish our business." Giving the coin a flip, Justin said, "Call it."

"Tails."

The penny landed in the dirt, and the three men leaned in.

"Heads." MacKinnon shoved Justin's shoulder. "Och, I cannae believe it. Ye've come oop heads."

"Leave the horse and get back to your camp, Whitmore."

Whitmore climbed the fence, pausing at the top. "This isn't over, Hogue. I'm closing in on that strawberry roan. Shouldn't be more than a day or two before I reclaim what I came for."

Whitmore disappeared into the distance. Justin turned to MacKinnon, extending his hand. "I appreciate you and your lads charging in when you did."

MacKinnon stared at Justin's hand. "I didnae do it fer ye. I did it fer 'eh animal."

"I know." Justin pulled his hand and wiped his brow on his shirt sleeve.

"Ye shouldn't hev risked Eliza Dawn's horse to better yer business wi' this pony." Ewan tossed the tree branch to the ground. "An honorable man would've found another way."

"The risk in tossing the coin was minimal." Justin pulled the copper coin from his pocket and handed it to MacKinnon.

MacKinnon turned it over. "This coin bears 'eh same image on both sides."

"I took a chance Whitmore wouldn't think to inspect it before or after since he had his cage rattled." Justin grinned. "The only risk was Whitmore calling heads. Or the risk to my hide if Whitmore had seen both sides. I had to take a chance. It's the only way I could think to protect Eliza Dawn, her horse, and this animal."

MacKinnon guffawed and slapped Justin's shoulder. "We might be a bit more alek 'an I imagined. How many times hev ye used this coin to better yer chances?"

"This is the only time I've needed it. The stakes were too high." The palomino paint backed into a corner, still people-wary. "And you're right. We're more alike than you realize. Malcolm mentioned your ma and pa aren't faring so well. I want to help if I can."

"And whit would ye do aboot it?"

"I want you to show your horses with me."

"Joost because we've had a wee moment against a common foe, disnae mean A've fergotten ye were in ma camp, Hogue." MacKinnon's countenance turned sullen. "A'm missing four fine equines. And I still believe ye've taken 'em. Helping me sell a few willny make oop fer that."

"MacKinnon, I didn't take your horses, and I've only just gained this fine paint." Justin inhaled deeply. What he was about to say stuck in his throat. He pursed his lips and pressed on. "But I'm willing to give her to you. You're dedicated to your Highland stock and might not want to keep her. But you could sell her, and it would benefit you."

"Why would ye do that?"

"I lost my mother. If I could have done anything to save her, I would have." Justin gripped the man's shoulder. "I can respect you're doing everything possible to benefit your family."

MacKinnon pulled from Justin's grasp and slowly approached the horse. The mare raised her head. He took a step closer. Her ears pinned back, and her eyelids tented into an inverted *V* shape. He backed away, and the horse gradually relaxed with each step.

"A've heard aboot yer work, Hogue. How ye take unruly horses and turn them into mannerly stock." He returned to Justin's side. "A'm not going to be in one place long enough to help her, and I cannae sell her in good conscience."

"I'll take good care of her." Justin turned, propping his foot on the fence rail. He clicked his tongue. "I'd like to know more about the raid on your camp."

MacKinnon leaned on the rail beside Justin and squinted into the setting sun. "What do ye want to know?"

Justin clicked his tongue again. He took a piece of peppermint from his pocket and placed it on the nearest fence post. "I know you said there was a rider with a hat and coat like mine and hair like Simon's. Were you able to make out any features of the other riders? Anything distinguishing?"

"Curly hopped on a horse ridden by a man with a black bowler. Couldn't tell more 'an that. Why d'ye ask?"

"I've got a notion who's behind your horse theft." A gentle breeze washed over Justin's sore body as the pony edged closer to inspect the nearby treat. "Can you have some men camp in the woods near the boardinghouse tonight?"

"A'll move ma whole camp if it means getting those horses back."

The palomino lipped the peppermint off the post. Justin extended a flat palm with another minty treat. He turned slightly, leaning out and glimpsing the torn flesh on the animal's rump.

"No, just a half dozen. Dozen at best. Ask them to spread out and surround the house with their campsites. No fire. They need to be hidden. Even if Whitmore hasn't figured out where that horse is, he will have it out for me."

"Who is this Whitmore? Aren't he and his lads prospectors?"

Justin squared with MacKinnon. "I don't know much about him, but what I do know spells trouble for Miss Dawn."

"And Merritt Fairfax? Why did ye ask aboot 'at name?"

"He's also connected to Miss Dawn somehow. I don't entirely understand how." Justin pushed his hand through his hair. "I believe he's done her great harm in the past. He could've followed her here, although I've seen no sign of him. Yet."

"The lads and A'll do anny'hin fer Eliza Dawn. The lass is practically family."

"With help from you Scots, we can get to the bottom of this business and hopefully keep everyone safe."

"Aye, we'll go straight away and fortify 'eh boardinghouse." With a finger salute to the temple, MacKinnon climbed the fence.

Chapter Thirty

Eliza Dawn positioned a dining chair alongside the sitting chair in the parlor. Throwing knives with the elder Mr. Hogue—who could have imagined? She smiled and shook her head. The bigger surprise would be if he took her up on the invitation to join the mending bee Justin organized.

"What are you doing?" Justin walked in, a ragged mess like he'd been pulled through the mud.

"What happened to you?" She came closer. "Another wayward wagon?"

"I have been safe from wagons and strudels today." He offered a tired grin and wiped his brow. "Today, I am a defender of horses alongside Ewan MacKinnon, no less."

"Defending horses from what?"

"A group of men gathered around the livery yard today as a man beat a horse with a tree branch. Seems that's what passes as entertainment these days." Justin stretched his elbows back, pressing his shoulder blades together. "Turns out MacKinnon and I agree on the treatment of animals. He and his lads rushed in to help Nicholas push back the crowd while I subdued the abuser."

"It looks like he struck a good blow to your chin here." Eliza Dawn gently stroked the bruised area along one corner of his lips. Her heart fluttered when his eyes met hers.

"MacKinnon did that." Justin grasped her fingers tenderly, folding them into his, and rested their hands against his chest. "Earlier in the day. Says someone wearing my hat and coat made off with four of his horses and escaped into the woods. Can you imagine? Me? A horse thief?"

She glanced away. "No, I can't."

Her heartbeat quickened. Despite their moments at odds, Justin had been more tender and protective toward her than any man up to now. And how had she repaid him? By making life messier, by filling his days with challenges. Once he learned of her barrenness and abandonment of her marriage, he would view her as too much and not enough all at the same time. A lump caught in her throat.

He released her hand and pointed to the extra chair. "What's this?"

"An extra chair. In case your pa joins us."

"I wouldn't get your hopes too high. He's not been much for company lately, especially in a group." Justin motioned for her to follow him. "Walk with me to the stable. Rebecca will kill me if I sit on the furniture like this, and Simon is removing Bonnie's shoes. You can watch."

She followed Justin into the barn and stopped at the large open stall where Simon tended her horse. Justin ducked into the bunkroom, leaving the door cracked to be heard. Folding her hands behind her, she leaned against the stall wall.

"Surprising turn of events, Ewan coming to my aid this afternoon."

"Oh?"

"After we cleared the area, we had a somewhat gentlemanly conversation."

"Is that so?" Finding it difficult to resist the urge to peek through the crack in the bunkroom door, Eliza Dawn forced herself to focus on Simon's hands as he trimmed Bonnie's hoof.

"I guess I shouldn't have been surprised. Earlier, I had mentioned to Levi it would take a miracle to make way for a civilized conversation between us." A door creaked in the belly of the bunkroom. "I never expected it would come in the form of us taking the same side in a conflict."

"So, that was an answered prayer?"

"I suppose so. Doesn't clear me in MacKinnon's mind, but he's willing to extend some grace while we figure things out. Perhaps we can uncover his horse thieves if we work together."

"You're also extending him grace since he's removed your advertisements from Sam Mooney's board."

"You know about that?"

"I recently learned of it." She twirled a wavy strand at the back of her neck and then tried to tuck it back into place. "I don't know I would've been so generous if someone was trying to disrupt my business."

"I invited him to show his horses at Levi's tomorrow. Did you know his parents aren't faring well?"

Flip. He'd turned the page yet again.

"I might've heard something like that." She glanced at the bunkroom door. Justin was well out of sight. She refocused her attention on Simon and Bonnie. "He told you that?"

"Of course not. Malcolm told me. Says that's the root of MacKinnon's gold fever. He wants to provide better care for his folks. Explains a lot about his actions since he's been in Van Buren."

"Yes, it does." Her eyes drifted back toward the door. She glimpsed his muscular shoulders as his shirt waved overhead, slid down his arms, and into place. A tingle ran up her spine as she forced her gaze back to Bonnie.

In another moment, he was by her side. His green shirt intensified his soft grey eyes. He slid his hand into the small of her back, pulling her toward Bonnie. Her breath stopped.

"Let's look at her hooves. Simon, what do you say?"

"She tolerated me removing the shoes well." Simon ran his hand along Bonnie's back, patting her backside. "This back right hoof is a little tender. Maybe we should leave the shoes off, apply a poultice tonight, and check again in the morning?"

"I agree with your diagnosis and your treatment plan, sir. Care to look at another patient with me?"

Simon shrugged. "I guess."

The trio walked to the large enclosure at the opposite end of the stable. Again, Justin's hand rested in the middle of her back as he guided her down the stable's center aisle. She closed her eyes, enjoying the warmth of him near her. Inhaling deeply, she pushed the feelings aside. Would Sam have her supplies ready? She'd have to move on before she became used to his closeness.

Justin stopped at the tack room and grabbed a jar of salve. Continuing to the other large stall, he slid past Eliza Dawn and Simon. He handed the ointment to Simon and eased toward the palomino, slowly reaching out and laying his hand delicately on the mare's muzzle. He eased his hand across the animal's cheek and down her throat, shoulder, and back. When he neared her rump, she stamped her hind leg twice. Pausing, he pulled a piece of peppermint from his pocket. Using his free hand, he offered it to her. She steadied.

"Let me get some of that salve."

Simon opened the container and held it within reach. Justin dipped his fingers into the jar.

"Why don't you two step outside the stall in case she's not too fond of this?"

Eliza Dawn stepped to the other side of the stall wall,

holding her breath. Simon joined her. Justin dabbed lightly at the torn flesh. The mare turned her head toward him, but her body remained still.

"Simon, why don't you ease in here? Get a look at this." Justin waved Simon into the stall. Simon inched up beside him, leaning over his shoulder. Justin pointed at the torn flesh. "Looks like he struck her three times or more before we stopped him. Fortunately, the wounds aren't too deep. She won't need stitches. We'll keep her tied off here tonight. At this rate, I may have to ask Levi to help me install sliding doors so we can close these larger stalls."

He stepped into the center walkway with Eliza Dawn. "Well, what do you think?"

"Don't tell Bonnie I said this, but this horse is also a beauty. What's her name?"

"Didn't get that before we cleared everyone out. Might call her Polly. Polly the Palomino."

"I like it." She grinned. "Bonnie the Beauty and Polly the Palomino. I bet they'll be fast friends."

"Simon, make sure she has food and water she can reach and finish taking care of Bonnie. Then join us inside, and we'll find more socks for you to mend." Justin chuckled, and Simon smirked in return. He took Eliza Dawn by the hand and led her toward the house. "Listen, I wanted to talk to you about one more thing before the mending bee gets underway. Won't you reconsider Caroline Brandt's offer?"

"Dress up and go to the dance?" She shook her head. "I don't think so."

"Not even if we manage to finish all of your sewing projects tonight?" He held the front door open for her.

"I don't see what good it would do."

"So, there's nothing I can say?"

Her chest tightened at his plea. Try as she might to keep her distance, he was finding his way through the cracks in her walled heart. She'd have to leave soon, or they'd both be hurt. They turned the corner into the parlor.

"Miss Dawn, how delightful to see you again." Caroline Brandt sat on the sofa wearing a smart navy dress and stylish boots.

Eliza Dawn's eyes widened under arched brows. "Good evening, Mrs. Brandt."

She shot Justin a furtive glance. He shrugged and mouthed, *I didn't know.*

"Justin mentioned your sewing circle. Pardon me for showing up unannounced, but assisting is the neighborly thing to do whether you model one of my ensembles or not." She raised her sewing kit. "I hope you don't mind. Rebecca let me in."

Mr. Hogue entered carrying a tray of cookies, teacups, and honey, followed by Rebecca with a teapot. Simon, who'd snuck in the back door, was close on their heels.

"What's all this?" Eliza Dawn waved her hand over the tray as Mr. Hogue placed it on the tea table.

"Rebecca and I decided a sewing party wouldn't be complete without refreshments." Mr. Hogue handed her a cup, and Rebecca poured.

"I'm dumbfounded. I didn't expect such fanfare on my behalf." She patted her chest. "You shouldn't have gone through all this trouble."

"Now, how will we make you feel at home if we don't go through a little trouble." His baritone voice carried a new lightness. "Before you sit down, hand me a piece to work and a needle and thread. I'll take anything except socks or unmentionables."

Shocked expressions passed between them, followed by a lighthearted burst of laughter. They carried on lively conversation, the Hogue men sucking air through clenched teeth each time they pricked a finger. They talked of everything and nothing as though Eliza Dawn had always been there with them. In all her years, she'd never had this sense of family. Like she truly belonged.

Inhaling the scent of spiced cookies, hot tea, honey, and socks, she suppressed a smile. It would forever be the fragrance she associated with belonging. She inhaled again.

It could not last.

Chapter Thirty-One

Eliza Dawn closed her journal. She didn't want a single memory to be left behind if she had to leave Hogue House and Van Buren. Warm chats with Rebecca in the early mornings, Sam's fatherly advice, Edie's offer of a river walk, throwing knives with Mr. Hogue—she wanted to remember it all. She stroked her hand. Her fingers ached, longing for the steady beat of Justin's heart thrumming through her fingertips as he held her hand against his chest. She swallowed the desire. She couldn't leave town soon enough.

Placing the journal on the nearby trunk, she traced the band of the abandoned ring with her finger. Such a small item to stir up such interest, conjecture, and tension. Sitting cross-legged in the middle of the cot, she fluffed a pillow and stuffed it behind her, propped up against a wardrobe. She grabbed a stack of papers from the nearby chest and thumbed through the pages. Huffing, she tossed them back on the chest and picked up the modest treasure.

She dropped the ring on the blankets beside her and held the envelope to the lamplight. If only she could make out some detail from the letter within. She tapped the envelope against the trunk. In the aftermath of the saloon stabbing, tongues all over town were bound to be wagging. It would be an excellent time to visit the pool hall.

She rose and glided through the maze to the window. Lamplight shone from Justin's bunkroom. She couldn't take Bonnie, but she might sneak out unnoticed if she climbed down the trellis wearing the dark-colored men's clothes she'd found earlier. Returning to the cot, she quickly changed clothes.

Pocketing her notepad and the ring, she left the letter. She had no plans to speak to anyone about it. Best not to be seen at all. But given the chance, she could try to match the image on the cameo to images on other items.

Eliza Dawn shoved her hair into a hat and returned to the window. Slowly, she opened it. She leaned out, scanning the area. Ducking back inside, she reached across a stack of crates for a silver letter opener. She tucked it into her waistband, lifted one leg out the window, and found her first foothold on the trellis. Pulling her other leg down, she found another foothold. She glanced over her shoulder at the stable. No sign of Justin aside from his lamp. Her pulse quickened. If only she could take Bonnie with her, she'd feel safer. She took care of Bonnie, and Bonnie took care of her. She methodically picked her way down the trellis, reminding herself to breathe.

Was there time to go to the Scottish camp? Justin had filled in a few details from Ewan's story, but she still needed more. Gathering information on the man had turned out to be more complicated than she'd anticipated.

Her feet landed on solid ground. Better to set out for the pool hall and accomplish what she could there. Perhaps she'd find Ewan and some of the Scots still lingering. There wasn't enough time to traipse all over Van Buren before morning.

She walked to Main Street, avoiding pockets of moonlight. A block from the pool hall, she ducked onto a side street and around the back of the buildings. Tugging her hat low, she crept into the hall's back door and sat near the pool tables and dart boards. She surveyed the room. No sign of Ewan, or any of the Scots for that matter.

Rubbing the tips of her tingling fingers, she observed the overcrowded room. With double the patrons, the walkways narrowed and drinks swilled. A loud and lively racket radiated throughout the space. None of the faces were familiar. But she was a journalist. She could still take advantage of the situation even though her target wasn't present. In a quick study of the room, she discovered several men wearing rings and holstered weapons. A few had money pouches or wallets on their tables. Perhaps she could casually circulate the hall to spot any decorative elements displayed.

Eliza Dawn drew a deep breath, set her jaw, and imitated a manly walk. Keeping her head down, she glimpsed what elements she could as she passed through the crowd. She stuck her tongue in her cheek, hoping it resembled a chaw.

"You there."

Her heart froze. She held her breath.

"Hand me that drink."

Her lungs deflated as she passed the drink along. She skirted the back of the room, observing several items that sported floral or animal motifs and scrollwork. She worked her way between the billiard tables toward the regular tables where she usually sat. A scooting chair clipped her toes, causing her to bump into the man behind her.

"Hey, watch it."

She turned. Her gaze flitted upward. Her mouth went dry. Big Jim. She averted her eyes, then slinked through the crowd and out the back door. She hedged around the side of the building, pressing herself into the dark shadows. She stopped, her palpitating heart resounding in her ears. She gulped air. *You're fine. Settle down now.*

She rubbed her throat and slowed her breathing. A horse

neighed nearby, drawing her attention. It was tied to a hitching post with several others. She'd quickly check the saddles, and then she'd go.

Edging toward the front of the building, she waited for passersby to clear the area. She moved in and gently placed her hand on the first horse's rump. It remained calm, so she ducked between it and the next. A glance at the saddles revealed scrollwork on the first and the word ROSE stamped on the second. She slid her hand across the backside of the second horse. Calm. She slipped between the next two horses. She repeated the pattern down the row: five horses, five saddles, no thistle.

She shrugged and stood.

A vise-like grip clamped the back of her neck. Her feet left the ground. Eyes wide, she clutched and scratched at thick fingers.

"What d'you think you're doing?"

The arm folded, turning her toward her aggressor. In the pale moonlight, she could only make out yellow teeth under a dark mop of hair. He yanked her hat from her head.

"Pretty little thing."

Her breath caught. Jim.

"I knew there was something familiar about you," he growled.

Her eyes darted. A silent scream caught in her throat. Tremors tore through her flailing body.

Big Jim leaned close, spraying spit as he whispered loudly. "Hold still now, or I'll snap your pretty little neck."

Her body went slack at his words. Tears stung her eyes. Her breath shallowed.

"I've seen you on that strawberry roan. There's a fella mighty interested in that horse. Says it was stolen." He turned loose of her neck and caught her shirtfront, twisting it at the neck. "You don't look like any horse thief I ever seen."

She shook her head vigorously.

"Don't make me no mind, though." He spit in the dirt. "Fella's offering a pretty penny for a strawberry roan. Where's that little horse of yours?"

She steadied her mind with a few deep breaths. When she didn't answer, he shook her like a rag doll, bumping her into the last horse at the hitching post. Something gouged her side. The letter opener. Her eyes widened. She moved slowly, hoping not to draw his attention.

"Where is it?" He shook her again.

Her arm flew up, the letter opener slicing the air before the tip raked across Big Jim's face, catching Rebecca's stitches. He stumbled back, dragging her with him. Standing, he yanked her up when a dark mass hurtled through the air at them. They collapsed in a heap. A hand caught hers, dragging her to her feet and around the corner.

"Get on the horse." Justin's rough whisper spurred her on. She placed her foot in the stirrup, and he grabbed the back of her thigh, shoving her up. He flung himself up behind her and launched into a gallop. He didn't slow until they were in sight of Cane Hill.

Giving Blue plenty of slack, Justin pulled Eliza Dawn close. He whispered in her ear, "What did you think you were doing, fool woman?"

"I don't know. I've seen the image from the ring somewhere." She pressed her back against his chest, wanting to fold herself into him. "I needed—"

"Needed what?"

"Justin, I have something to tell you." She laced her fingers between his. "I'm not a seamstress. I mean, sewing is a cover. I'm a journalist."

His warm breath washed over her neck. "Edward Dodd. You write under a pen name."

She nodded. "There's more."

"Justin! Pa!" Simon's voice breached the barrier of the stable walls.

"Ha." Blue galloped the short distance at Justin's command. He slid off the horse. "Stay here. Don't move. This isn't worth a story."

Moments later, he and Simon emerged with a boy who resembled Simon.

"Simon, go inside and get Pa, Mr. Hildesheim, and Mr. Perry."

Eliza Dawn slid off Blue. "What are you going to do?"

"I'm going to take this young man to the sheriff. He was trying to take Bonnie, and I'll lay odds he was part of the outlaw band that raided MacKinnon's camp. I'll get Mr. Hildesheim, Mr. Perry, and Malcolm to ride with me while Pa and the rest of Ewan's men protect the boardinghouse."

"What? Malcolm?" She turned, peering into the dark.

"Fairfax's men, listen up," Justin shouted. He held the boy's hands behind his back. "This boy is going to the sheriff. Now is your chance to slither away. Make a move on me or this property, and you'll have a horde of Scots to contend with. Malcolm, join us."

"Fairfax?" Eliza Dawn's voice barely escaped her lips. "Wha—"

Simon reappeared with Mr. Hogue and the other men. Malcolm walked out of the nearby woods. Justin transferred control of the boy to Mr. Perry.

"You'll be all right." He pulled Eliza Dawn into his arms, kissing the top of her head. "You'll see. Everything will turn out fine. Get in the house and stay put. Ewan is out there, and if you try to leave again, he'll bring you back kicking and screaming this time." He smiled and mounted Blue.

Slipping into the kitchen, she retrieved a hand towel and dampened it. She eased up to her room. Sucking air through clenched teeth, she dabbed at her neck. She cleaned herself up in halting motions, discarded the men's garments, and donned her night dress. Her fingers lightly grazed the tender skin at the back of her neck, and she winced. Probably bruised. She would wear her hair down to cover it. Justin wouldn't think it ladylike, but he'd understand.

She lay down on the cot, pulled the pillow to her stomach, and curled her body around it. She'd rather be in a bed of hay near Bonnie as the sweet pony niggled her ear. Or camped under the stars with her as they'd done many times on this journey west.

A tear rolled down her cheek. So, it was true. Fairfax was coming for her and her beloved Bonnie.

Chapter Thirty-Two

"Justin, you got a moment?" Pa approached, coffee in hand, stopping at the post where Hershey was hitched. "I think it's time we talk."

"It's not the best time, Pa." Justin secured his saddlebags.

"What are you doing, son?" Pa's fingers tapped an anxious rhythm against the side of the cup. "Simon says you've loaded everything from the bunkhouse onto these horses."

"I'm moving on. It's past due." Avoiding eye contact with Pa, Justin rechecked everything, though he'd already checked twice. "My presence here is a danger to the family just like my absence was a danger to Ma."

"Your absence? Son, what are you talking about?" Pa's fingers stilled. His gaze fixed on the ground. "I was the one who was absent. You were there with her."

"No, I wasn't." Justin turned to face Pa. "I was right by her side when we came out of the mercantile, but I stepped away to talk to Daisy Warren. Ma stepped into the street without me. That's how she was caught in that shooting on-sight incident. Billy Kinder told everyone he'd shoot that Memphis stranger the next time he saw the man, given half a chance. Ma didn't see them and stepped right into the middle of it. If I'd have been by her side, I might have seen. I might have—"

"You might have been killed trying to save her."

"She was the love of your life. She was the strength of this family." A sick feeling settled in the pit of his stomach. He nodded toward the house. "I took her from them, from you. I can't live with that."

"Oh, son." Pa set his cup on the post and drew Justin to him. "I'm sorry I couldn't talk about it. I've been at odds with myself because I wasn't here that day."

"You trusted me to take care of the family while you were away." Justin's shoulders shook as he clung tightly to Pa. "I failed you."

"All this time, I thought you were blaming me for not being here, and you were blaming yourself instead." Pa rubbed his hand through Justin's hair. "We're both blaming ourselves for something neither of us could control. It's time we let it go, son." He pushed Justin back, his gaze unwavering. "You do your horse show today, and you come home tonight. You'll move out when you buy that ranch land and are ready to start a family."

Justin nodded.

"Now, what's the situation with this incident last night?"

"I haven't figured it out yet, but Eliza Dawn is in trouble." Justin studied his feet. He wanted to give her more but knew she wouldn't let him. "Having her here puts the whole family at risk. I want to help her but don't know what to do. I want to protect the family."

"You know your ma would've protected her. She doesn't have a family, and we have plenty enough to share. She'll remain with us until we can no longer convince her to stay." He patted Justin's shoulder. "I'll let her know you're ready to go."

Justin lightened the load from Hershey's saddle bags and removed the pack rigging from Dale. Simon brought saddles for

Dale and Bonnie. Eliza Dawn appeared beside Bonnie, and the knot in Justin's stomach tightened. He'd have to ask her about the journal. There was no way around it. Would she understand he hadn't meant to read the pages when it fell open?

Simon saddled Dale, while Justin saddled Bonnie. With God's help, the three of them could take care of things in town and make it to Levi's without any unpleasantness.

"She puffs out her chest. You'll have to tighten it again." Eliza Dawn pointed at the cinch.

"I know." Justin poked Bonnie in the ribs and gave the cinch another tug. He laced his fingers together, offering Eliza Dawn a foothold.

"Mr. Hogue said the rest of the family isn't riding out until after the noon meal."

"That's right." Justin nodded at Simon. "How you doing over there, little brother?"

"Everything looks good." He slid his hand under Dale's cinch. "Nice and snug. Ready to go."

"Is it wise for them to travel separately? Shouldn't we all go together?" Eliza Dawn leaned forward in the saddle.

"Don't lean so far forward. You're going to tire her out." Justin mounted Hershey. He took a deep breath in and held it a moment before exhaling. "I've got to trust they'll be all right here. Ewan's people are still guarding the house. They'll travel with the family and Mr. Perry."

"Why aren't you riding Blue?"

"Miss Dawn, you sure are full of questions this morning."

She relaxed back in the saddle. "I'm sorry. I'm just—"

Wavy lines creased her brow. Justin turned Hershey toward her. Coming alongside, he patted her hand. "Nervous. I know. We're going to take things as they come. First order of the day is to stop at the pastry shop. Conrad will ride out with us."

Justin gigged Hershey, bringing her to a trot. He shot Eliza

Dawn a sly, side-eye glance. "You stay away from that strudel when we get to Conrad's, and everything will be just fine."

A sheepish grin emerged as she brought Bonnie alongside him. "Brandt's Tailor Shop is right across from Hildesheim's. Could I pop in to see Caroline?"

"Thought you weren't going to participate in the dance."

"I didn't get the information I needed last night to post my articles today. It seems I'll need the commission Mrs. Brandt offered. And she was kind enough to participate in the bee last evening." She tucked wavy strands of chestnut hair behind her ear. She hissed when she grazed her neck.

Justin caught her hand. "Does it hurt much?"

"Not too bad." She grimaced. "As long as I don't touch it."

Plow a line straight to the point. That's what Levi would say. "Miss Dawn, I need to know about Bonnie. This is difficult to ask, but is she stolen?"

Eliza Dawn's eyes shifted. "My father gave Bonnie to me."

"There's no one else who could lay claim to her?"

She pressed her lips together and shook her head.

"I want to help you." Justin pulled his hand back, resting it on his thigh. "That's going to be a might easier to do if I know the whole of it."

"I'm not ready to talk about it." Her countenance dimmed. "I need more time."

"I'll give you all the time I can, but I'm afraid we may not have much." Justin cleared his throat. "When we get to the Snow homestead, we'll secure Bonnie in one of the stalls at my lean-to. We'll do everything we can to help you keep her."

"How much time can you give me with Caroline? Forty-five minutes or so?"

"The woman is mighty exacting about her hemlines. Will that be enough time?" Justin tied Hershey to the hitching post and helped Eliza Dawn down.

"I'm sure it will do fine."

"I'll stay with the horses."

Simon went to help Conrad load the wagon and, with a sweeping motion, Eliza Dawn disappeared inside Brandt's Tailor Shop.

"Justin. Justin Hogue." Mrs. Pratt's sing-song voice wafted across the street. Justin pressed his eyes shut. He couldn't leave the horses. There was nowhere to hide.

"Oh, Justin, dear. I wanted to thank you for sending the Scotsman with the butter barrel."

Justin hadn't even thought to ask Mal about the churn. Relief flooded over him. *I owe you one, Mal.* Mrs. Pratt took his hand in both of hers, patting lightly.

"Dearie, where is Miss Dawn?"

Justin nodded toward the tailor shop. "Just inside with Mrs. Brandt. She's getting fitted for a dress."

"Oh, joy." Her face beamed. "She's going to the dance then? And she'll be detained with Mrs. Brandt a spell?"

"Yes, ma'am."

"Some of the church ladies dropped by yesterday. They brought us a meal since I've had a little extra on my plate with responsibilities at home. They're so caring." She leaned in close to whisper. "We were talking of Miss Dawn and how hard she works to support herself. None of us like her having to follow the prospectors west to find work. So, we're taking up a collection. We do hope she'll consider staying in Van Buren."

"That's very considerate of you. I hope she'll stay." Justin glanced toward the shop window. "Please don't be put out if you give it to her, and she moves on anyway."

"We won't judge, but we will do whatever it takes to make her feel welcome."

"I appreciate that."

"Well, ta-ta. I'll see you at the dance." Mrs. Pratt waved her handkerchief in the air. She flashed a big grin over her shoulder.

"And I hope to see you dancing with someone other than your sisters this evening."

∼

As Eliza Dawn entered the tailor shop clutching her reticule, a quiver of unease ran through her stomach. "Mrs. Brandt, are you here?"

Caroline swept in from the back room, dark curls dangling like ribbons from her perfectly arranged bun. "Miss Dawn, call me Caroline. What a delight to finally have you in my shop. How can I help you? Please, tell me you've changed your mind about modeling one of my ensembles."

"Actually, yes, I have." Eliza Dawn folded her hands at her waist. "So long as I may make a few modifications of my own."

Caroline's brow knit together. "I don't know. We take a great deal of pride in our work."

"My modification will have little visual impact on the dress." She fiddled with the button at her collar. "I simply want to make some minor adjustments for comfort, and I'd like to add a ruffle along the bottom edge of the bodice for added flair."

"By all means, follow me to the back to check the fit, and I'll quickly make any necessary alterations. Then you may modify as you desire."

Caroline assisted Eliza Dawn with the gown. "My darling, it fits you like a glove. You will be the handsomest belle at the ball."

"Thank you, Caroline." Eliza Dawn pressed a smile. "Now, if I may."

"Yes, of course."

Caroline left the needed supplies with Eliza Dawn and returned to the front. Eliza Dawn took off the gown and redressed in her clothes. She stored the skirt in the box Caroline provided. Working carefully, she tore out some stitching and removed a piece of boning from the bodice. She quickly but neatly attached the ruffle around the bottom edge. Picking up her reticule, she pulled out the silver letter opener. She slid the narrow blade into the boning channel. It was a perfect fit, and the ruffle covered the short handle nicely. She returned the letter opener to her reticule and stowed the bodice in the box, replacing the lid. She carried the box to the front with her.

"Caroline, will you bring the boxes, or should I ask Mr. Hildesheim if he has room in the wagon for this one alongside his baked goods?"

"Don't you worry about it. My father-in-law and I will bring everything this afternoon."

"I look forward to seeing you then." Eliza Dawn smiled. As she turned to leave, she breathed a sigh of relief.

Chapter Thirty-Three

Justin leaned, arms folded, across the top rail of the round pen as Simon performed stunts on Cowboy, a bay thoroughbred. Simon spun around the saddle horn and then stood in the saddle. Applause filled the air. Gripping the saddle horn with his right hand, he dropped off the left side of the saddle and reached his left arm in front of Cowboy's neck. Making a finger pistol, he shouted, "Bang! Bang!" He repeated the trick hanging from the opposite side. The crowd roared.

"I love that trick. He must have some great arm strength." Levi joined him, propping his foot on the lower rail.

"His right arm is stronger than his left. Did you notice that little hitch when he dropped off the right side?" Justin removed his hat and waved away curls of dust as Simon raced by a little too close. "Not as fluid as he's capable of with his right arm."

"If that kid can shoot as good as he can ride, he'd make a great lawman someday." Levi winked.

"I'd rather him stay away from guns." Justin put his hat back on. "I think Pa feels the same after what happened to Ma."

"Allie and the ladies are in the cabin getting gussied up. You ought to hear the chatter in there."

"How's Miss Dawn?" Justin patted his hands on his elbows. "She was rather anxious this morning."

"Seems more relaxed than when she arrived." Levi clapped as Simon vaulted side to side across Cowboy's back. "Man, that kid gets better and better on these horses. Will he ride Devil today?"

"Nah. Devil has come a long way, but I'd rather not chance it." Justin raked his teeth across his lower lip. "I don't know where this Whitmore fella is, but I know he's coming for Bonnie. I'd hate for Simon to be in the middle of a big figure with Devil and a peck of trouble crop up. Told him we'd play it over-careful. He'll finish out the round on Star."

Simon trotted out of the ring, and Justin hopped the fence. He raised his arms high, patting the air to quiet the crowd. "Ladies and gentlemen, Simon will perform a few more tricks. Then Levi and the boys will lay the wagon sheet, and we'll start that dance. You saw the Scottish Highland ponies earlier. Don't forget, Ewan MacKinnon is at the other round pen if you're interested in a fine mount or pack animal. I'll be joining him after the show."

Justin looked to the pen's entrance, where Simon signaled he was ready. "Now I give you Mr. Simon Hogue on Chestnut Star."

Justin hopped the rail and returned to Levi's side.

"Hey, Levi, I noticed a horse fitted with a saddle that had a thistle image stitched into the seat earlier today, but I didn't spot a rider anywhere in sight." Justin crossed his arms. "Have you seen a saddle like that when you've been out visiting prospector camps? You have any idea who owns that horse?"

"*Hmm*, no. Can't say I've seen it."

Justin shrugged. "It was worth a shot."

"Listen. Give me a dance or two with Allie, and then I'll relieve you so you can get a dance with Eliza Dawn." Levi patted

Justin on the back. "Simon and I can answer questions about the horses. We won't make any deals without you, I promise."

"I don't know, Levi." Justin hooked his thumbs in his pockets. "I don't know if I should ask her. Who's to say she'd want to dance with me?"

"You're going to follow through on this endeavor with faith, remember?" Levi's brown eyes sparkled. "Embrace some of the distractions."

"I never pegged you for a matchmaker, that's for sure."

"Love changes a man." Levi grinned.

Thanks to Simon's trick riding, Justin received immediate offers of more than two hundred dollars for Cowboy and Star. He was speaking with a man about Dale when MacKinnon approached. MacKinnon waited until the man wandered away to observe the stock.

"The lads sold six o' ma ponies afore I finished shewing 'eh animals. A've got a couple o' blokes bantering back and forth o'er five more. Tis a good day. I cannae thank ye 'nough." MacKinnon extended a hand to Justin.

"It's my pleasure. Glad to help." Justin shook his hand. "Any sign of Whitmore?"

"No' that we've noticed." MacKinnon's gaze roved the grounds. "Maybe he's thought better of it."

"Nah. He's biding his time, is all." Justin licked his lips and pulled his hand through his whiskers. "I bruised his ego, laying him out in front of all those men yesterday. And he wants that strawberry roan. He's coming. I can feel it."

"Well, A've got more 'an a dozen Scots here and a dozen or so around the boardinghouse."

"Ewan, I appreciate everything you've done in the past twenty-four hours." Justin toed the dirt. "Last night could have gone very badly."

"We've bin looking oot for Pup—Eliza Dawn—since Alabama. We're not aboot to stop now."

"Justin." Levi appeared with two tin cups of coffee and offered one to MacKinnon. "Are you ready for that dance now?"

"Where's Simon? Wasn't he going to help you?" Justin glanced around for his younger brother.

"He's a bit distracted at the moment."

"He stopped to talk to a girl then."

"Not exactly." Levi sipped his coffee. "Tommy Weston was making eyes at Martie. So, he's tied up being the protective older brother."

"It's tough being outnumbered by sisters six to three. Always gotta have your guard up." Justin chuckled. "I believe I'll do a bit of hovering myself. I'll be a bit more covert and exercise my powers of observation from the dance floor."

Justin walked through wagons and straggling individuals toward the shindig on the other side of Levi's cabin. Examining clusters of people, he approached the wagon sheet. He had to remain vigilant amid the merriment. The last rays of a shimmering sun played on the horizon as laughter and lively music hung in the air. Men were lighting lanterns around the gathering area.

Caroline Brandt sashayed to the center of the crowd, her deep red dress swaying as she moved. She held her hand up and clapped a few times. The crowd parted. She clapped another pattern until the group fell silent.

"Good evening, ladies and gentlemen. Brandt's Tailor Shop is featuring five elegant gowns at tonight's festivities. These ensembles are available for purchase. We will begin this waltz with five couples to allow you a closer look at the fit and movement of our fine apparel. If something catches your fancy, approach me during or after the dance, and we'll arrange for you to pick it up at the shop tomorrow."

She nodded to the crowd, and Rebecca stepped forward in an emerald green gown. "Our first gown is worn by Miss Rebecca Hogue. Why don't you give a little twirl, Rebecca?"

Rebecca whirled, coming to rest with a flourish of her arms. Her relaxed smile warmed Justin's heart. He hadn't seen her smile like that in quite some time. A sense of relief washed over him when Pa emerged from the crowd and took Rebecca's hand. Not only was he free from dancing with her, but he didn't have to worry about the gentleman claiming her dance.

"Next is Miss Cordelia Hogue, a true beauty in pale blue." Mrs. Brandt motioned for Cordelia to turn. Mr. Sewell, the schoolmaster, appeared at her side before she'd finished. Though Justin enjoyed the sparkle in his sister's eyes, he would have to be watchful of the overeager teacher.

"Mrs. Allie Snow is modeling the fairest lavender gown, and joining her is a familiar face. Please give a hand to her uncle and mercantile owner, Sam Mooney. Sam, I understand we have you to thank for presenting the idea that inspired today's events. Why don't you give Allie a whirl?"

Justin tiptoed, searching the crowd. He couldn't find her, the one he longed to behold. His pulse quickened. Was something wrong? Had something happened to her?

"And last, but certainly not least, Miss Eliza Dawn, a vision in champagne trimmed in blue. Doesn't it make her mesmerizing eyes sing?"

Coming from Mrs. Brandt's opposite side, Eliza Dawn floated to the center and curtsied, spreading the gown wide, bowing her head low. Justin's breath caught. His heart stilled. She stood, and her gaze combed the crowd. Who was she searching for?

Mrs. Brandt slipped up beside Eliza Dawn. They exchanged a whispered conversation. Mrs. Brandt returned to her spot. "Ladies and gentlemen, Miss Dawn will be sitting out this round. She would delight in lively conversation." In a playful aside, she added, "Gentlemen, I beg of you, don't bother her unless you have something interesting to say."

Justin pushed his way through the crowd. Hesitating before

the two women, he gazed intently at Eliza Dawn. Caught up in those eyes, he lost the words he'd practiced in his head.

Mrs. Brandt cleared her throat. "Mr. Hogue, may we help you?"

He stumbled over his words. "I'd like to—may I—can we talk?"

Mrs. Brandt grabbed his hand, placing it in Eliza Dawn's. She patted his fingers. "Oh, dearie, just keep your mouth shut and dance."

The crowd went wild with whoops and whistles. Heat rose in Justin's cheeks as he slid his fingers around her waist, and the first notes of the waltz lilted on the breeze. As the intro played, the men led the ladies into position.

Eliza Dawn held his gaze with an intensity that matched his. He drew her close, erasing the distance between them, and the tension in her narrow frame faded as he delicately guided her around the other couples. His heart swelled with every rise and fall of the waltz as they turned smoothly around the floor.

"Have you been looking?" Justin whispered in her ear.

She stiffened. "Looking?"

"For the thistle image?"

She let go of the tension with a nervous laugh. "Oh, that."

"What else?" Justin grinned mischievously. "I mean, I didn't have to ask to know you've been looking at me."

"Your modesty is astounding." She blushed. "I've been a little preoccupied. I hate to admit I'd forgotten about the ring."

"I noticed a saddle with a similar thistle image." He enjoyed the old familiar curiosity that lit her eyes once again.

"You've found him then?"

"No. There was no one around the horse when I discovered the saddle." He guided her around other couples. "I've asked around, but no one has seen the saddle before. I couldn't keep hunting for the rider. I needed to help Simon with my horses, and I haven't encountered that horse since."

Of Faith and Dreams

"Justin, do you think we will ever find the recipient of these items?"

"When the dance is over, I'll ask the owner of the saddle to come forward." He lightly squeezed her hand. "If that doesn't work, I will accept your recommendation to read the letter."

"You will? You'd really do that?" Her eyes sparkled.

He made an *X* over his heart. "Cross my heart, we'll read it together."

"Thank you, Justin." She beamed.

"I'll bet you're praying right now no one steps forward." He smiled. "Praying you get the chance to read that letter."

The light in her eyes dimmed. "I don't pray. I used to, but I don't believe God answers prayer. Leastwise, not mine."

"He's answered mine—through you. I owe you a debt of gratitude." Justin lightly changed the pressure in his hand, guiding her around Pa and Rebecca.

"Oh?"

"Because of your willingness to discuss your mother and father, I've been more open with Simon. We're starting to share how we feel about losing Ma."

"I'm glad to hear it." Her lips turned up at the corners. "He's going to be fine, you know. He's surrounded by a loving family."

"And I don't know what you said to Pa, but it was magic."

"I didn't say anything really. He needed to talk about your ma, and I listened."

"I thought he blamed me for Ma's death."

"Why would he blame you?"

"Ma and I left the mercantile one day, and before we crossed the street, I stopped to talk to a young lady outside the store. My mother stepped into the road, not realizing Billy Kinder stood yards away on one side of her while the man who killed his brother stood not far on the other. Kinder fired the shot that killed my mother."

"Oh, Justin." Her fingers folded over, and she rubbed the back of his hand.

"I shouldn't have left her side."

"You couldn't have done anything to save her." Her eyes welled up. "Your pa blames himself for being on the steamboat instead of home with her."

"Eliza Dawn, I don't know if I can protect you." He pulled her closer, squeezing her hand. "But I promise I'll do my best. Tell me about Bonnie. Tell me the story you've been holding back. You can trust me."

She opened her mouth to speak when there was a tap on Justin's shoulder. Simon pressed his lips together, his mop of curly blonde hair hanging in his eyes. He inhaled deeply and leaned near Justin's ear.

"May I have a dance?"

A broad smile broke across Justin's face. "With me? I'm not that desperate."

"No, with her." Simon pulled a face.

"You'd have to ask her."

"Miss Dawn, may I have a dance?" Simon's cheeks pinked. "Not as a boy who's sweet on you, but as a friend?"

"How could I refuse such a request?" She dipped her chin demurely. "As a friend."

Justin stepped aside, offering her hand to Simon. "We'll dance again later?"

"Of course." Her eyes shone brightly.

Justin moved to the edge of the crowd. Simon's eyes followed his feet, moving in jerky, halting motions. Eliza Dawn leveled Simon's eyes with the gentle lift of two fingers under the boy's chin. Her lips mouthed *one-two-three, one-two-three* as she adjusted Simon's frame. Justin smiled. For the first time in over a year, he considered the possibility things might be okay again one day.

His eyes followed Eliza Dawn around the wagon sheet, and

his heart lifted. What would it take to convince her to stay? *I'm a journalist*, she'd said. She was following a story, not the seamstress work. Was there a story here she could follow? A story that would make it worth her while to stay in Van Buren?

A hard thump landed between his shoulder blades. He turned to face Malcolm. Breathy and red-faced, Malcolm tried to speak.

Justin patted him on the back. "Slow down. What is it?"

"MacKinnon." He gasped. "The horses."

"Catch your breath. I'll be right back." Justin raced to Pa's side, interrupting the dance with Rebecca. "Make sure everyone stays here. There's trouble at the round pens."

Chapter Thirty-Four

"Shut 'at gate." Ewan MacKinnon's gruff voice cut through the chaos.

Justin and Malcolm rushed to Ewan's side. Justin stepped onto the bottom rail of the pen and, hinging at the waist, peered into the fresh blanket of darkness. "What's going on? Something's happened to the horses?"

"The gate was left open, and some of oor stock got oot." MacKinnon motioned for Justin and Malcolm to follow as he rounded the corral. "As far as A've bin able to tell, three o' yers and three o' mine ur gone."

"What happened? Who left the gate open?"

"Tis ma fault. I shoulda shut doon sales when it neared dark." MacKinnon rubbed his forehead and paced a few steps. "I let those hagglers interested in ma stock hang 'round and 'eh one looking at yers. Then suddenly, thir were half a dozen men here asking Levi and me aboot 'eh horses."

"That still doesn't explain who left the gate open." Justin tilted his head back, eyes closed, and blew out a long breath. "And where are the rest of the Scots?"

"The three men interested in oor horses must've hidden amongst the stock when 'eh others appeared to talk wi' Levi and me. Those newly arrived men fired oop, making offers and creating a stir, so 'eh lads moved 'round us in case Levi and I needed help. The other three must hev opened 'eh gate when 'eh lads left their posts 'round 'eh pens. Now, 'eh lads hev gone after 'eh horses."

"Where is Levi?"

"He and Mal went to find ye."

"We split oop when we reached 'eh crowd." Malcolm turned, pointing toward the shindig. "Maybe he's still trying to find ye around 'eh wagon sheet."

"The dance." Justin hit his forehead with the round edge of his fist. "Whitmore's men may have stolen the horses, but it's also a diversion to draw me away. Ewan, get your men back here as fast as you can. Don't worry about the stolen horses. We'll get the sheriff to sort that out."

"Consider it done." MacKinnon patted Malcolm's shoulder. "Ye check 'eh crowd. Thir's bound to be more lads from camp at 'eh dance. Gather any ye find."

Justin sprinted back through wagons and the crowd. He grabbed a man by the shoulders, pushing himself higher to view faces in the group. Moving through the gathering, his eyes darted from person to person. He bumped into Olivia Pratt.

"Mrs. Pratt, have you seen Eliza Dawn?"

"Justin Hogue, where are your manners?" She waved a lace handkerchief in front of her face. "You didn't even say excuse me."

"Mrs. Pratt, she may be in trouble. Do you know where she is?"

"The last time I saw her, she was coming off the dance floor with Simon. That was after Caroline Brandt's waltz."

Justin brushed through the crowd, continuing his search.

Ahead of him, Rebecca's green dress stood out at the center of a small knot of men. Justin pushed his way through.

"Rebecca, have you seen Eliza Dawn?"

"She was with Simon after the waltz." Rebecca lay her hand on the side of his face. "Justin, you're flushed. What's wrong?"

"She's in trouble. If Simon is with her, he may be in trouble too." Justin grasped Rebecca's hand. "I must find them."

"Let's ask Pa. He was speaking with Simon after the waltz." Rebecca led Justin through the crowd toward Pa.

"Justin!" Levi's voice cut through the music and chatter. "I've searched everywhere for you. There's trouble—"

"I've already spoken with MacKinnon. Eliza Dawn and Simon are missing." Justin clutched Levi's arm. "Fetch the sheriff. Tell him a band of horse thieves crashed the shindig, and a young man and woman may have been taken. Ewan is gathering the Scots as we speak. The sheriff can deputize them if he needs help."

Levi's eyes darted heavenward. "Lord, help us. I'll return with the sheriff in tow."

"I'd appreciate it if you'd continue that prayer as you ride after him. Take Rex."

Levi disappeared in the crowd as Rebecca dragged Justin through huddles of people engaged in lively conversation. They found Pa visiting with Sam and Allie.

"Pardon the interruption." Rebecca gave a polite nod. "Pa, after you spoke to Simon, did you see where he or Eliza Dawn went?"

"They danced a reel together. I don't recall seeing them after that, now that you mention it."

"Some of the horses have been stolen. They might have taken Eliza Dawn and Simon. I'll get Devil and search for them." Justin clenched and unclenched his fists. "Levi has gone for the sheriff, and MacKinnon is gathering his men. Keep the music going, and don't let anyone wander off. I don't want to give these horse thieves any indication we're coming for them."

Justin's heart sank. Whitmore would be lying in wait for her if she'd gone to check on Bonnie, as he suspected. And Simon would be following her into a trap.

Chapter Thirty Five

"Miss Dawn, where are you going?" Simon jogged to catch up to Eliza Dawn.

She stopped, propping her hands on her hips. "Simon Hogue, haven't you gotten into enough trouble following me? Haven't you learned your lesson by now?"

"But Pa said we're not to leave the gathering place." Simon grasped her hand, tugging her toward the celebration. "You can't be running off by yourself. We've got to get back."

"I'm just going to check on Bonnie." She shrugged herself free. "It'll only take a moment. A quick peek. And I'll thank you kindly to stop following me."

Simon's eyebrows drew up in the center, and his lips flattened.

"Oh, stop." Eliza Dawn took hold of his shoulders and turned him toward the festivities. "Don't give me those watery blue pools under basset hound eyebrows. The pleading puppy eyes will get you nowhere. Now get on back, or I'll find you a never-ending pile of socks."

"Yes, ma'am." Simon moped, dragging his feet as he went.

Plodding along, he glanced over his shoulder. She hardened

her expression and pointed. He slipped between Conrad's pastry wagon and the chuck wagons. Satisfied he was seeking refreshment instead of following her, she continued along the path to the lean-to. As she rounded Levi's forge, Bonnie whinnied, and Eliza Dawn's stomach muscles tensed.

Had Bonnie picked up her scent on the wind, or was her trusty companion alerting her to an unknown presence? She paused at the back of the forge, listening and squinting into the inky darkness. The last time she'd seen Merritt Fairfax was the night he'd branded her with his cigar. A fire burned in her belly. She didn't know how she would respond to the man, but she couldn't let him take Bonnie.

She crept across the small strip of yard between the forge and the makeshift stable. Bonnie hung her head over the stall door with a snort. Scratching the mare around the ears, Eliza Dawn made a cooing noise.

"Hello, girl. I'm here." She laid her forehead against Bonnie's. "It's you and me against the world, my beauty."

"Aw, now, isn't that precious?" Davis Whitmore stepped out from behind the lean-to.

"What are you doing here, Davis?" Eliza Dawn turned to face him, Bonnie lipping Eliza Dawn's shoulder. Eliza Dawn caught some movement from the corner of her eye. For a split second, a thread of moonlight highlighted blond curls. Her gut clenched. That boy. Why had he doubled back?

"You were always a sucker for fairytales, weren't you, sister dear?"

Simon bumped against the forge, and Eliza Dawn's heart froze.

"Did you bring a friend?" Davis scanned the area.

"It's probably the wind rattling through the forge there." She shrugged, playing off the noise. "I'll ask again, Davis. What are you doing here?"

"I've come to take Bonnie."

"She's not yours." Eliza Dawn lay her hand along the mare's muzzle. "Father gave her to me as a wedding present."

"Which means she's not yours either." He twirled his handlebar mustache. "She belongs to Fairfax, and he will pay me a pretty penny when I return her."

"I'd sooner die than let you take her."

"Don't force my hand." Davis pulled a revolver. "There's more than money at stake here. Fairfax will make me partner when the horse is returned. So, it's not simply a monetary reward but a chance to better myself. You were supposed to be my ticket to betterment if you'd only produced an heir for the man. The one thing women have been contributing since the beginning of time, and you couldn't do it."

A dull ache radiated through her chest. "If you're going to kill me, stop talking and do it. For all my independent nature, it's the one thing I've been unable to take care of myself."

"I'm serious, Eliza Dawn. Don't tempt me."

"After praying for years for a child, I stopped and prayed instead for God to let me die. I finally gave up praying for anything when He didn't answer." Her muscles went slack, and her hands dropped to her side. Numbness swept through her like a frigid wind off the river. A cold, childless wind. "I have no family, no friends, no community. I'm adrift in the world. Bonnie is all I have. So, if you're going to take her, just shoot me."

"No, that's not true." Simon sprang from the shadows of the forge. "Miss Dawn, we're your family."

"Simon, what are you doing?" She held a hand out toward him. "Get out of here."

"I heard Pa tell Justin." Simon's voice trembled. "He said you don't have a family, but we have plenty enough to share."

Whitmore trained the revolver on Simon. "You shouldn't have come out here, kid."

"Davis, put the gun away. He's a mere boy. No threat to

you." Eliza Dawn's heart raced. She edged closer to the boy. "Simon, get behind me."

The musicians struck up a lively tune. Whoops and hollers filled the air.

"I can't afford to leave any witnesses." Davis cocked the revolver.

Eliza Dawn stretched out her hand. "Simon, now."

The music heightened. Simon's fingers brushed hers. Hooking her fingers into his, she yanked. Davis pulled the trigger. The crack split the air. Simon released a yelp of pain. Eliza Dawn rolled to the ground with the boy in her arms.

"Simon. Simon, answer me." She shook his heavy form. Something moist and sticky coated her hand. She heaved his torso to her chest, tears staining her cheeks. "Simon."

Bonnie's stall creaked open. Eliza Dawn flew at Whitmore, landing multiple blows on his back. His arm swept around, and as he half-turned, he caught her by the hair. Twisting his hand, he forced her to her knees.

"Ha." He waved a hand at Bonnie. "Ha. Move."

As the horse exited the stall, he slapped her rump, prompting her to flee. Eliza Dawn swung her arms wildly as he held her at arm's length. Releasing her, he let his hand fly, the back striking her face. A flash of pain splintered through her. Her head lolled as he jerked her to her feet. A metallic tang coated her inner cheek.

"My men better be able to find that horse." Davis pointed the gun at Eliza Dawn. He waved the gun toward the end of the lean-to. "Get up. Move."

Legs wobbling like a new foal, she rose. She placed a hand against the wall, steadying herself. The gun barrel dug into her ribs with each thrust of Davis's hand. He propelled her to the far edge of the horse stalls. She glanced back at Simon's motionless form. *Lord, please don't take him. Not for my sake, Lord, but for Justin's.*

"Whistle." He shoved the gun into her side. "Call her back."

"She's not going to come." Her legs buckled, but she caught herself. "Why did you send her off?"

"Couldn't leave her in the stall and had another problem to deal with." He jabbed her again. "Whistle."

Eliza Dawn's attempt to whistle came out thready and weak. Blocking out the high-spirited sounds from the dance, she focused on the outlying area behind the forge and the lean-to. A faint rustling came from something stirring in the nearby trees. A twig snapped.

Davis prodded at her back. "Whistle again."

"She won't come, I tell you."

"No matter. You're all I need." Shoving the gun into her side, Davis closed his other arm around her neck. "I'll get that filly before the night is over, though. I want the satisfaction of taking everything from you."

"What are you talking about? I have nothing. Except Bonnie."

"Fairfax is not done trying to get what he needs from you. He promised me a place by his side in Father's company if you'd give him an heir, so I've followed him across the country to help him retrieve his wayward wife and stolen property."

"Don't make me go back to him." Her throat ached. Her voice scraped. "Please, Davis."

"Don't you worry, sister dear." His hot breath sent a chill through her. "You're only returning to Fairfax long enough to sign Father's and Fairfax's companies to me."

"I don't have the power to do that."

"You will when Fairfax is dead. I've been lacing his tea with arsenic. He won't last much longer." His voice was low and haunting. "You'll be there to witness his last breaths. And after you sign everything over to me, I'll answer your prayers, sister dear. It'll appear as though you've poisoned your husband and then killed yourself."

The barrel of the gun dug into Eliza Dawn's side. "Now, why don't you give one more whistle?"

~

Justin led Devil, a seal brown stallion, through the stand of trees surrounding the northeast side of Levi's property. He halted at the crunching underbrush and snapping limbs nearby. Though the moon was bright enough, a small cloud bank and leafy treetops made it challenging to see. His eyes ranged through the shadows. A large mass moved nearby. A barely audible whinny wafted in the air. Bonnie.

Fishing a peppermint from his pocket, Justin eased around Devil. He threw the candy in Bonnie's direction. Nose to the ground, she wiggled her lips as she searched the undergrowth. She munched the sweet treat, and Justin tossed another piece closer to himself. Bonnie sniffed the earth. Reaching toward Devil's saddle, Justin grabbed the rope hanging from the saddle horn.

"Hey there, Bonnie the Beauty." He slid up next to her, looping the rope around her neck. "How did you get out here? Did Eliza Dawn cut you loose? Whitmore getting too close?"

She neighed softly. As he tied her to a tree, she niggled at his pocket. He breathed a chuckle and scratched around her ears. Lightly, he pushed her muzzle away.

"That's enough for now. I've got to find Simon and Eliza Dawn."

Justin took advantage of the music and the crowd, using them as cover when the volume increased and falling still as the noise level grew softer. He hedged inside the tree line, angling for a better view of the lean-to. Devil followed closely, barely visible even at such close range.

The clouds shifted, and moonlight flooded the landscape. The hairs lifted on the back of his neck. Eliza Dawn stood with

Whitmore at her back at the end of the stable nearest him. His eyes roved the area. Simon lay face down on the ground, unmoving. Justin's stomach dropped.

His knees went slack, and he shouldered a tree for support. He forced himself to take slow, deep breaths. *Trust in Him always. Pour out your heart to Him, for God is our refuge.* He repeated the words until his mind stilled.

He surveyed the scene again. Tilting his head, he squinted. Had Simon moved? Eliza Dawn whistled, and Bonnie responded, but Justin kept his gaze on Simon, whose knee pulled up toward his side. Justin sounded the whistle he used only for Devil. The stallion's ears perked. Justin whistled again. Simon's fingers lifted off the ground and fell back to earth, a signal the younger Hogue understood Justin's plan.

"Listen, boy. I'm sorry I didn't trust you with Simon in the show." Justin pulled Devil's face close to his. "But now is your big moment. You've got a special bond with him. I need you to go get him."

Justin left enough slack in Devil's reins for the horse to move freely but secured the ends to keep them from dragging and catching on anything. The clouds moved slowly. *Come on. Come on.* He silently urged the clouds into place. A dark shadow fell across the landscape. He set Devil on a path for Simon with a tug and a whistle.

The dark stallion's hooves thundered. Whitmore's gaze searched the horizon. Justin held his breath. As Devil neared the small structure, Simon scrambled to his feet. The boy returned the unique whistle call, helping the horse locate him quickly. He hoisted himself onto the dark horse with one arm, circled the stable, and shot through the shadows on the other side. Whitmore fired. Simon dropped off Devil's back, hanging from the saddle. Whitmore fired again and again.

Devil disappeared into the trees. Simon lifted himself into the saddle and lay across the horse's back. Devil slowed to a walk and returned to Justin. He carefully eased his brother from the saddle, resting him against a tree.

He pulled Simon into an embrace. "Are you okay? Are you hurt?"

"I've been shot. Whitmore shot me." Simon cradled his arm. "I don't think it's bad, but it hurts. I'm sorry, Justin. I lost consciousness for a bit. I didn't know what to do when I woke, so I stayed down."

"You did fine. You're safe." Justin ruffled Simon's curls. "That's all I could hope for. Could you ride Bonnie around the pens and back up to the dance?"

"I think so."

"Good. Find Rebecca straight away and have her take care of that arm." Justin fashioned a halter from the rope he used to secure Bonnie. "It's not ideal, but get going. Stay well in the shadows. Her light-colored middle will give you away, especially in the moonlight." Justin folded his hands together as a footing.

"Wait, Justin." Simon stepped back.

"What is it?"

"Four shots. Whitmore fired four shots."

"So, he's got two left. Good to know."

"Colt Baby Dragoon." Simon shook his head. "A five-shot revolver. One shot. He's got one shot."

Justin lifted his brother into the saddle, uttering a silent prayer as Simon slipped away into the night.

Chapter Thirty-Six

"Show yourself, Hogue." Whitmore shoved Eliza Dawn forward.

Justin didn't respond. He hadn't been by Ma's side. The cost was her life. He wanted to be at Eliza Dawn's side, but the consequences could be dire if he went to her now. Every fiber of his being screamed *go*. But a voice within said wait.

He surveyed his surroundings. The barn, a rain barrel, the forge. If he waited for the right moment—

"All right, boy, I know Simon is your favorite." He pulled the horse's muzzle down to meet his forehead. "But I could use your help. I need you to stay put and be nice and quiet. Then, when I whistle, come at us full split. Like your old self, wild and angry. It's a lot to ask, I know. Understand?"

Devil's head bobbed, and he released a soft snort. Justin shrugged. "I don't know if you understand or that's just a habit, but there's so much at stake here. I'll give you peppermint every day for a week if we come out of this alive." Justin scratched his muzzle and down the sides of his neck.

He gave Devil the sign for stay. When the clouds drifted in front of the moon again, he made for the barn, treading lightly.

The clouds stalled, and he dashed to the rain barrel. Rays of moonlight shone through as the cloud separated into wispy ribbons. He peeked around the barrel. Whitmore had an arm around Eliza Dawn's neck, and, with his other hand, he waved the Colt revolver haphazardly into the night. Justin settled his back against the barrel, waiting for more cloud cover.

"Hogue, come out and bring Bonnie with you."

The Lord is good, a refuge in times of trouble. Be her refuge, Lord, not mine alone. Justin glanced around the side of the barrel. Eliza Dawn clutched at Whitmore's arm. Clouds rolled in front of the moon.

Justin crept to the front of the forge and ducked inside. He picked up the poker from the rack of fire tools. Edging out and around the other side, he stole a glance around the corner. Whitmore's back was to him. Eliza Dawn struggled to keep her feet under her as Whitmore pulled her against himself.

Cloud cover floated in once more. Ever so softly, Justin moved toward the opposite end of the lean-to from Whitmore and his captive. Once there, he pressed his back against the wall, releasing a deep, silent breath. The whoosh of blood pulsed in his ears. He needed to get on top of the lean-to without Whitmore noticing. He needed a miracle.

The clouds parted, and light washed over the landscape once again. A trace of movement by the forge caught Justin's eye. A figure leaned briefly into the light, out of Whitmore's line of vision. Malcolm Sinclair's woolly profile was a welcome sight. The Scotsman had turned out to be a fast friend, earnest and ardent, a gift from God when Justin least expected one and most needed it. Mal saluted with two fingers. Justin studied the landscape. Had Ewan and Malcolm managed to gather more of the Scotsmen?

The music, cheering, and applause swelled. The clouds suppressed the moon. A stiff breeze whistled through the trees. The minor miracle he needed. Justin hooked the poker at the edge of the stable's roof. He used a short stack of firewood as a step and lifted himself to a sitting position atop the stable. The music lulled, and he froze.

"Hogue. I know you can hear me." Whitmore's voice resonated with a sharp, foreboding tone. "This is your last chance to show yourself."

The music kicked up again, joined by a chorus of loud, off-key voices. Justin grabbed the poker and crawled across the roof. He perched quietly above Whitmore.

~

ELIZA DAWN'S heart beat erratically. She closed her eyes, taking a deep breath. Citrus and cedar. Her skin tingled with a sense of Justin's presence. She opened her eyes, scanning the horizon. Was he out there? Somewhere in the near distance?

She pawed at Davis's arm around her throat, trying to create a distraction as much as ease the pressure. With slow, diminutive movements, she slipped the fingers of her other hand under the edge of her bodice. A series of gentle tugs freed the letter opener from its hiding place. She carefully flipped it so the blade extended from the pinky side of her fist, keeping it tucked close to her abdomen.

Clouds curtained the moon. A shrill whistle broke above her. Thundering hooves echoed the pounding of her heart. She searched the horizon but could not find the animal. Hammering hoofbeats drilled down on them. Davis shouted and waved the revolver. Suddenly, the dark steed was upon them. The massive horse reared up, hooves pawing the air. The stallion screamed.

Eliza Dawn plunged the letter opener into Davis's thigh. He growled in pain, and Eliza Dawn twisted free from him. The stallion reared, trumpeting fiercely. She backed away.

A faceless figure dropped down, brandishing a metal rod. The dark form dropped the rod over Davis's shoulders, pulling

Davis against him. Rays of moonlight broke through the clouds. Justin. He made a *ft-ft* sound, and the fierce stallion retreated. Justin grabbed Davis's gun hand and yanked, dislodging the weapon. She jumped to retrieve it.

Davis elbowed Justin in the gut, and they both went down. Justin lost his grip on one end of the rod. They grappled over the implement, and Davis wrestled it from him. They rolled, and Davis straddled Justin, pushing the bar against Justin's throat. The veins in Justin's neck corded, his eyes bulged.

"Davis!" Eliza Dawn pointed the revolver at her brother.

His eyes bore into her as he snarled a laugh. "You don't have it in you."

"Don't I?"

Justin shoved the pointed end of the poker, grazing the underside of Davis's chin. Coming back across his body, he pinned Davis in the dirt, landing a right hook. Dazed, Davis's body went limp. Justin rolled Davis over, and, catching Davis's hands behind his back, Justin pulled him to his feet.

Eliza Dawn squared with Davis, thrusting the revolver toward him.

"Dawn. Eliza Dawn." Justin tugged Davis farther from her. "Put the gun down."

"He's been following me since Alabama, or longer." Her thready breath produced a fleeting, misty cloud in the cool night air. "He won't stop."

"Pup. Ye're not alone." Malcolm appeared at the edge of the forge. "We willny let him hurt ye."

The gun shook faintly in her quavering hand. Close by, horse hooves beat the ground. Several riders surrounded them, wielding weapons. Davis rolled his shoulder, hitting Justin in the chest.

"Better turn loose of me, Hogue. You're outnumbered."

"Whitmore, best keep quiet until we diffuse the situation." Justin pursed his lips. "Because you'll be the first to go down."

"She won't do it."

"Don't test me, brother dear." Eliza Dawn pulled the hammer back and stepped closer.

A chorus of clicks peppered the night as Davis's men raised their weapons.

Malcolm issued a piercing guttural cry. "*TAMHAS.*"

Ewan MacKinnon emerged from the wood line on horseback with several Scots. More appeared from the area near the round pens. Men on foot rushed toward them from the direction of the shindig. MacKinnon pulled up short near Davis's men, brandishing a rifle.

"Better ease yer fingers off and drop yer pieces to the ground, gents." Ewan's lips curled. "Or my lads and A'll not wait for 'eh sheriff to arrive."

One by one weapons fell to the dirt. Malcolm joined Justin and took control of Davis. Justin moved closer to Eliza Dawn.

His fingers lightly grazing her arm, he whispered, "Give me the gun."

"She's not the woman you think she is, Hogue." Davis spat in the dirt.

"I know enough." He leaned into her line of vision. "Give it to me."

She shook her head, sucking in a breath.

"God-fearing man like yourself oughtn't have anything to do with a married woman and a murderer," Davis sneered.

Tears welled in her eyes, and she swallowed hard.

"I'm not buying the lies he's selling."

Her eyelids fluttered as her gaze shifted from Davis to Justin.

"Do you hear me? I don't care what he has to say." Justin held out his palm. "Put the gun in my hand."

"I can't." She whispered. "He won't stop until he has Bonnie."

"She's right." A disturbing smile broke across Davis's face.

"Fairfax isn't about to lose a horse and the opportunity to have an heir to the same woman."

Eliza Dawn pushed past Justin. Leveling the revolver at Davis, she pulled the trigger. The hammer slammed against the cold metal. Davis's eyes snapped shut, his broad frame shuddered. An unsettled silence infused the air.

Eliza Dawn leaned close to Davis, her lips near his ear. "Three shots or four. You couldn't remember, could you, brother dear?"

She turned, placing the weapon in Justin's hand. Her legs collapsed, and Justin caught her.

"I've got you."

She smiled weakly and clung to him. "Where's Simon? Is he all right?"

"Hopefully, he's with Rebecca and Pa." Justin took his jacket off and draped it over her shoulders, squeezing her close. "My guess is they've taken him home already, and they're waiting to hear from us. Let's go home and get some rest."

Chapter Thirty-Seven

"Justin." Pa pushed open the bunkroom door. "Mr. Sinclair is here. He's fired up the forge. Thought you might want to know."

"Thanks, Pa. I'll come talk to him." Justin gently tugged a shirt over his achy torso, buttoning the front. He followed Pa out the bunkroom door and through the stable into the yard. A bay-colored Highland pony stood tied to the hitching post. It nickered at Justin's approach. Justin walked over to give the horse a good scratch. The image on the seat of the saddle caught his eye. He smiled as he rubbed his hand across the ornate thistle stitched into the durable leather.

The forge door gave easily under his touch. Mal stood pumping the bellows. Justin nodded and grinned. He crossed to the stove and poured a cup of coffee.

"I see you started with a fresh pot of coffee." Justin took a sip.

"Disnae ev'ry good blacksmith make coffee afore he makes anny'hin else?'

Inhaling deeply, Justin moved to the work table. Setting the cup down, he stared at Malcolm.

"Whit are ye looking at me fer?"

"Aren't you here early, Mal? All things considered?" Justin tapped his cup.

"I don't ken when A'm gonna hev another crack at a forge." Malcolm placed a length of metal in the fire. "A'm gonna soak oop ev'ry moment I can."

"That horse outside, is it yours?"

"Tis."

"I noticed a thistle on the saddle."

"Aye." Malcolm adjusted the rod.

"I saw that saddle yesterday, but it was on another horse."

"Nae. No' that saddle." Malcolm took the rod from the fire and moved to the anvil. "Tis mine and mine alone."

"But it had that exact thistle design."

"A'm not 'eh only one with 'at design."

"You know others with similar saddles?" Justin raked his hand through his scruff.

"Do I ken others?" Malcolm chuckled. "Near ev'ry man in oor group has a saddle bearing that image."

"Thir's less 'an a dozen whose saddles don't bear a thistle." Ewan MacKinnon stepped forward from where he'd been leaning against a broad support beam. He lifted his tin cup in greeting.

Justin's smile faded. "Ewan, I didn't see you. D'you ride double on Mal's horse?"

"Nae, we unhitched a small wagon oot back." MacKinnon thumped his cup. "I saddled 'eh pony because A'm no' staying long. A'll be leaving fer Levi's soon."

"Of course. You brought the wagon to haul the metal." Justin raised his cup. "Guess I need a little more coffee. How many Scots are traveling with you?"

"Close to eighty, no' counting 'eh small number o' women and children." Malcolm hammered the red-hot metal. "Why do ye ask?"

"No reason." Justin sipped his coffee. "Why do so many display that image on their saddle?"

"Tis 'eh national flower of Scotland." MacKinnon swirled the contents of his cup. "Represents 'eh Scotsman's bravery, strength, endurance, resolve, and honor. Tis a symbol of oor protection."

"Did Eliza Dawn happen to mention the letter we have? The one intended for a prospector?"

"She offered to shew it to me." MacKinnon stared into his cup. "But ma people cannae read or write, so I didnae bother to look."

"Mal?"

"The lass didnae mention it to me. But ma folks don't read or write either."

"Oh, I see." Justin walked over to the sitting area table and set down his cup. "I'm going to check on Simon and Eliza Dawn. I'll talk to you in a bit."

"Hogue, I'll join ye." Ewan followed him to the door.

Justin and Ewan left the blacksmith shop, pausing near Malcolm's horse.

"Hogue, I owe ye an apology." MacKinnon laced his fingers through the Highland pony's mane, detangling the strands of hair.

"An apology? For what?"

"Fer taking doon yer notice." MacKinnon toed the dirt. "The thistle represents oor honor, and I hevnae bin very honorable in ma dealings wi' ye."

"You were thinking of your family's well-being. I can respect that."

"Despite ma behavior, ye extended an opportunity to ride yer coattails. Ye didnae hev to let me take part in yer event."

"For all the good it did." Justin rubbed the back of his neck. "We closed less than half our sales yesterday, thanks to Whitmore and his men."

"We've had some blokes stop us in toon this morning, asking fer a chance to make an offer. That's why A'm going oot to Levi's." His eyes squared on Justin. "If ye'd troost me, A'd lek to return 'eh favor. I want to help sell yer remaining stock. I willny take less 'an a hundred seventy-five fer any o' them."

"Yesterday, I had to trust you with my life, MacKinnon." Justin swatted MacKinnon's shoulder. "I believe I can trust you with my horses. I'll join you at the Snow homestead this afternoon."

As MacKinnon rode away, Levi entered the front gate. Justin crossed the yard to meet him.

"What are you doing out and about so early?" Justin climbed the steps with Levi.

"I wanted to check on your stunt-riding brother and Miss Dawn." Levi removed his hat and tapped his fingers on the brim. "Plus, I thought Miss Dawn might gain some peace of mind hearing the sheriff has rounded up the rest of her brother's crew."

"That's good news." Justin offered a tired smile.

"There's more." Levi caught his arm. "What Whitmore said is true. Miss Dawn is married. And that's not all."

Justin held up a flattened palm. His stomach knotted. Married? So her brother had been telling the truth. Was there any truth to the other things Whitmore had said about Eliza Dawn? His breath slowed. What would Ma advise him to do now? A warmth spread through his chest. Ma would remind him love bears all things. Ma would continue to provide refuge and give Eliza Dawn a voice. She'd allow the young journalist to tell her story.

"Levi, when I prayed God would save Ma, it was a selfish prayer. I wanted her to be well *with us*. It never occurred to me she'd be free from not only physical pain but all pain once she was in heaven. And that would be better for her." Justin raked his short whiskers. "I recently said a prayer for Miss—Mrs.—

Dawn, asking God to help me be a light that points her to Him and our home, a refuge where she can rest in His love for as long as she'll stay." He folded his arms across his chest, taking a deep breath. "I've tried to welcome her into my home, my heart, and yet not overstep. The past day or so has been difficult because I realized I want her to stay. But I won't be selfish this time. She's only here for a season. I've known that from the start, married or not. My prayer is God will be her refuge wherever she goes."

"But Justin—"

"Please, Levi, I don't want to discuss the rest of her situation without her present."

Justin held the door open, allowing Levi to enter first. Heading to the dining room, they nodded at Mr. Perry as he passed on his way out. They found Rebecca and Pa sitting with Simon around the table. A plate loaded with bacon, eggs, and burnt toast sat before the boy.

"Looks like your appetite is doing well." Justin chuckled. Standing over Simon's shoulder, he patted his brother's back.

"Can't get enough. I'm starving." Simon shoveled a forkful of eggs into his mouth while he was talking.

Levi removed his hat before addressing Rebecca. "How's the injury?"

"I packed the wound and bandaged it last night. I wanted to wait until I had better light before I stitched it up." Rebecca pushed a small portion of eggs around her plate. "It looks to be fairly superficial, though. Another inch and the shot might have missed him completely."

"Seemed like a good bit of blood last night." Justin tousled Simon's hair, and Simon shrugged away.

"By the time you saw him, he'd done a little stunt riding to escape Whitmore." Rebecca grimaced. "I'm sure that aggravated the wound."

"What's this, Rebecca?" Justin picked up a piece of burnt

toast. "You burnt the toast this morning? That never happens. You all right?"

"Eliza Dawn did that. Said she needed to keep busy and wanted to help with breakfast."

Justin pulled a used napkin from one of the other place settings. He reached to set the toast aside, but Simon grabbed it.

"Eliza Dawn made this for me. I'll eat it and be thankful." He returned the toast to his plate, folding a piece of bacon into his mouth. "She saved my life. She told me to go back to the shindig, but I doubled back. If I'd listened to her, I wouldn't have been shot."

"Where is she?"

"I couldn't convince her to join us." Rebecca pulled her head toward the kitchen. "She's sitting at the kitchen table by herself."

"Rebecca, could we talk for a moment?" Justin nodded toward the foyer, and Rebecca followed him.

"I've been struggling with the idea I must always be here to protect the family." Justin rubbed his chin. "Levi suggested I ask how you feel when I tag along or show up when you are called to doctor folks."

She bit her lip and took a deep breath before answering. "Honestly?"

He nodded. "Honestly."

"Sometimes I wish you hadn't come along." She shrugged. "Don't get me wrong. I'm thankful to have you when there's not enough muscle in the room to hold down a patient. But sometimes, you're too protective, and it gets in the way of my ability to do the job. And other times, I can't focus on the task at hand because I'm worried about you, worried I'm putting you at risk, dragging you into these situations. Sometimes I need to go alone. Besides, Nicholas always shows up. I'd rather not have my family in harm's way with me."

"I didn't know. I appreciate you telling me." Justin scratched his chin. "I'm going to check on Eliza Dawn."

Crossing into the dining room, he grabbed a piece of bacon from Simon's plate. He waved it at Levi. "Shall we?"

Levi stepped around the table. "Excuse me. I want to talk to Eliza Dawn. I'm going to reassure her she doesn't have anything to fear from her brother anymore."

Eliza Dawn sat sipping coffee in front of the kitchen window. Tiny droplets of water gathered to form narrow rivulets trailing the glass. Levi sat in the chair next to her while Justin stood behind her.

"How are you doing this morning?" Justin placed his hands on her shoulders with a tender squeeze.

"I'm all right." Her soft voice took on an unusual reticence.

"Are you sure?" Justin leaned around, pulling her hair back. His muscles stiffened at the sight of the crimson bruise along her jaw and the dark bluish-purple bruise at the back of her neck. He wanted to pull her into his arms and safeguard her. But she wasn't his to protect. He'd have to trust God with her, just as he was learning to trust God with his family. "You ought to be sore."

"I brought that on myself, now, didn't I?"

"You were taking a stand for things that were important to you." Justin pulled out the chair on the other side of her. He took her hands in his. "I'd have done the same."

"Miss Dawn, your brother and his men won't be a problem for you any longer." Levi set his hat on the table. "The sheriff rounded them all up with the help of the Scotsmen he deputized. They'll stand trial for multiple counts of horse theft."

"Mr. Snow, I appreciate your reassurance, but we both know capital punishment for horse theft is a myth. They may serve some time, but they've got money in their corner. It's just as likely their release will be bought. If a vigilante mob had captured them, there would have been a hanging. I don't desire their deaths, but I fear it's the only way to gain a sense of peace."

"Miss Dawn, there's more." Levi rubbed his hands together. "The sheriff found your husband's body."

She blinked hard. "His body? He's deceased? You're certain?"

Levi nodded.

"Davis told me he'd been administering arsenic in Fairfax's tea." Her breath stalled.

"One of Whitmore's men has confessed to purchasing arsenic at Whitmore's instruction. Another told the sheriff Whitmore shared the plan with him." Levi's brows pulled together. "Miss Dawn, you are widowed, and your brother will stand trial for your husband's murder."

She slumped in her seat, covering her mouth with her hand. She closed her eyes, remaining silent for several moments. "It's over? It's really over? And Bonnie is mine?"

"Miss Dawn, I believe everything is yours."

"Everything?"

Levi nodded. "Everything."

"Are you all right?" Justin took her hands in his again.

"I'm fine. I plan to pick up supplies and head west immediately."

"Head west?" Justin's stomach lurched, and he drew his hands back. "Levi, would you give us a moment."

"Of course." Levi patted Justin's back as he left.

"Why are you leaving so soon?"

"I put Simon in danger last night."

"That's not how Simon sees it. He said you made him return to the dance, but he doubled back. Says you saved his life."

"Justin, you've cautioned me repeatedly about my impact on others. You've told me my actions affect others beyond myself."

A tear rolled down her cheek. "Simon could have been killed because I put my desire to protect Bonnie before his safety."

"He chose to follow you after he was told not to."

"I lied to you." She turned to face him. "Bradley House wasn't full. Fairfax would too easily discover me at a boardinghouse for women. I lied to you about Bonnie being stolen. Father gave her to me, but because of the marriage, she is—was—Fairfax's property." Another tear escaped.

"You didn't know who to trust. I understand that." He yearned to make her stay. "You can't leave. What about the letter? We haven't finished the search."

"Oh, Justin." She rolled her eyes. "Let's face it. We'll never find the prospector that letter is intended for."

"What if I told you I narrowed it from one thousand men to less than a hundred just this morning?"

She studied his face. "You did not."

"I certainly did." He knocked his knuckles on the table. "Did you know Malcolm has a thistle stitched into the seat of his saddle? In fact, it seems most of the Scots do."

"So, how do we determine which Scotsman it belongs to?"

Justin shrugged and half grinned. "Guess we'll have to read the letter. Do you have it?"

"It's upstairs."

"Best run up and get it. I'll put a pot of water on to boil."

Momentarily, Eliza Dawn returned with the letter and ring. She sat down at the table, fit the ring over her thumb, and studied the image. Her soft chestnut hair fell across her shoulder, covering her bruised neck. Though dark shadows settled under her eyes, they were as mesmerizing as the moment they'd met.

"What do you think will be in the letter?"

"I can't even guess." Tiny bubbles formed in the bottom of the pot.

Levi ducked his head in. "What can't you guess?"

Of Faith and Dreams

"What's in this letter." Eliza Dawn held it up.

"Ah, so you're finally going to open it?" Levi took it, squinting at the front.

"Yes. Why don't you join us?" Eliza Dawn motioned to the chair beside her.

"I've got to get back." Levi handed the envelope to her and grabbed his hat from the table. "Allie is a little nervous about being alone with the baby at the cabin since last night's mayhem."

"Thanks for coming out to check on us. I'm meeting MacKinnon at your place later today." Justin waved him off with two fingers.

Levi tipped his head, donned his hat, and retreated to the dining room to make his final goodbyes. Justin motioned to Eliza Dawn. Picking up the letter, she joined him at the stove.

Justin sighed. "Here goes nothing."

He passed the letter back and forth over the pot, gently lifting the edge of the flap. Little by little, the gummy flap released its hold. He slipped the paper from the envelope and handed it to Eliza Dawn.

"Me? You want me to read it?"

"It was your idea."

She unfolded the paper and read:

Dear Tamhas,

I hope this letter finds you well and you haven't made it too far on your journey. My name is Dr. Pettus. Your father asked I write to you on his behalf. I have spent several days at your mother's side as her health rapidly declined. Her condition was beyond my help. You should find with this letter your mother's ring. Before she passed, she requested the ring be given to you with a reminder the thistle represents resilience, strength, resolve, and protection. Wear it in remembrance of your mother's undying love.

Regards,

Dr. John E. Pettus

"Tamhas is the word Mal yelled last night when he signaled the Scots to surround my brother's men."

Justin stroked his chin. "The ring's owner is much closer than we ever imagined."

Chapter Thirty-Eight

"Are you going into town before you head to Levi's?" Eliza Dawn joined Justin in the tack room. A mid-morning nap had done her good, and the drizzling rain had given way to blue skies.

"I hadn't planned on it." Justin grabbed Blue's saddle and shuffled past her. "Why do you ask?"

"I have some deliveries to make." She picked up the jar of saddle soother and removed the lid, inhaling deeply. The fresh, woodsy scent quieted her spirit. "Three baskets of mending, the box with Caroline Brandt's dress, and shirts for the Scotsmen. I was hoping to avoid making multiple trips."

"That would mean hitching up the wagon." Justin shuffled back by her, hefting the saddle onto its resting place.

"I don't want to burden you." She quickly fastened the lid and returned the soothing ointment to its spot on the shelf.

"It's not a burden." Justin took her hands in his. "I quite like the idea of you riding next to me in a wagon. It does require a little different preparation, though. I'll hitch the wagon and load it."

The tightness in her chest eased. She hated to admit it, but since her encounters with Big Jim and battling her brother for Bonnie, riding through town alone triggered a vulnerability she could no longer stomach. She wasn't sure how she would make it to the fort, traveling alone when she couldn't even manage a ride through town. But the sooner she left, the better it would be for everyone.

She picked up the jar of saddle soother and sniffed again. Dabbing her fingers in the ointment, she applied it to the back of her hand. Could she sneak it into her saddlebag before leaving town? It was just the thing to help her hold on to the afternoon spent with Justin at the bluff, walks home from the mercantile, blacksmithing with his arms around her. She breathed deeply once more and sighed.

"Careful there." Justin reappeared with a blanket and a small basket. "You're going to get that on your nose again."

She smiled. "What's this?"

"What's it look like?" Justin handed her the blanket and basket.

"A blanket and a basket. But why—"

"Honestly, I hope Sam tells you he can't fulfill half your supply order. I hope he can't fill any of it." Justin bit his lip. "But if you're leaving tomorrow, I've got to make all the moments I can. So, I'll escort you around town, and you can ride to Levi's with me to deliver shirts to MacKinnon. But then we'll ride out to the bluff and admire the sun on the river until it's swallowed up by the West."

"Oh, Justin, I don't know. Maybe it's best—"

"I spoke with Mal while you were napping. He explained about Tamhas." Justin ushered her out to the wagon. He patted his vest pocket. "I have the letter and ring and know where to find our prospector."

Justin helped her into the wagon and settled in beside her. He took her hands in his, and a tingle ran up her spine. Sweet citrus and cedar warmed the air between them. She held her breath. He gazed into her eyes.

"Dawn, delivering this letter will be the most challenging thing I've done all week. It'll be the most difficult thing I've done since Ma died, telling another man he's lost his mother." He held her fingers to his warm lips. "So, don't deny me my moment at the bluff. Because tomorrow, when I must bid you farewell, will be another trying day. And after that, life will be full of difficult days missing you. All I'm asking for is one memory of watching the sun fade away with you before you go off chasing it."

Her heart grew heavy, and she fell silent. Fairfax was dead. Davis had been arrested. Bonnie was hers. Yet her past still wormed its way through her. She couldn't shake the need to outrun it. If only things were different. The silence between them was more solemn than usual, carrying a certain finality. Justin sat impossibly near, taking hold of her hand, and an old familiar longing kindled within, a longing that would never be satisfied.

She didn't want to go in when the wagon stopped at Mooney's Mercantile. Instead, she wanted to stay by Justin's side. She yearned for a forever moment.

But when Justin offered her his hand, she took it and stepped from the wagon. The world seemed somehow different, duller, a hazy gray. Like so many cold, misty days, not bothersome enough to bring life to a halt but dreary enough to drain the life out of them.

Justin handed Eliza Dawn a mending basket and stacked the remaining two. Her feet heavy like anvils, she trudged into the mercantile and set the basket on the counter.

"Miss Dawn, I didn't expect you'd be out and about today after all the commotion last night." Sam tapped his pencil on the counter.

"I've finished these baskets of mending. Those two go to

Mrs. Pratt." She pointed at Justin's baskets. Then she pulled her notepad from her apron pocket and flipped through the pages. "I've misplaced the other woman's name, but her husband should be by to pick up her mending."

"Not a problem. I know who it goes to." Sam smiled, lightly resting his hand on hers.

"Would it be possible to pick up my supplies tomorrow morning?"

Sam's gaze drifted from Eliza Dawn to Justin. He cleared his throat. "Well, now, I told you it's mighty hard to complete these large orders. Everyone is buying up the town. And what they're not buying—"

"They're stealing. I know, I know." She pulled her hand away. "Whatever you have available will be fine. I'll be by around nine."

The bell above the door jingled. Olivia Pratt bustled into the store. Her face brightened when her eyes met Eliza Dawn's.

"Oh, dear Miss Dawn, what good fortune this is." She beamed as she pushed past Justin.

"Mrs. Pratt, aren't you a little off schedule? It's Friday." Justin set the baskets on the floor next to the counter.

"That brother of mine is eating us out of house and home. Bless his heart." Mrs. Pratt lifted an empty potato sack. "Mr. Mooney, I'll be filling this toe sack." She turned to indicate the baskets. "I see you've brought the mending baskets. Very timely."

Mrs. Pratt fished in her reticule, pulling out bank notes. "Here you go, dearie. Thirty-seven dollars."

Eliza Dawn's jaw dropped. She pushed Mrs. Pratt's hand away. "Mrs. Pratt, mending is fifty cents a basket. You only owe me a dollar."

"Oh, child. We take care of one another around here." Mrs. Pratt extended the money to her. "I'm paying two dollars for the mending work. You have no idea what a help that's been while my brother stays with us. And the thirty-five dollars is a gift, a collection from several families. We hoped to make it possible for you to stay in Van Buren, but if you must go, it should help you on your journey."

"Mrs. Pratt, I can't accept this. It's too much." Tears welled in Eliza Dawn's eyes. Even though she had no intention of availing herself of the inheritance gained from her father and husband, it seemed wrong to accept charity from others. "I honestly don't need it."

Mrs. Pratt spoke with a stern tone. "You must accept this. It is a gift from many folks who'd like to bless you. I dare say blessings are likely to be few and far between the farther west you go."

"Please, tell them I am overwhelmed by their generosity." Eliza Dawn smiled at Mrs. Pratt's hand, resting tenderly on hers as she accepted the gift. What was it Rebecca had said? *She'll surprise you in the best possible way.*

She turned to Sam, offering the bank notes. "Mr. Mooney, may I apply this to my order now?"

"You may not." Sam pushed her hand away. "Anything could happen between now and tomorrow. Since your order is only partially filled, it could be I'll need to pull items to complete other orders. I don't want to fool with the bookkeeping of returning money. Pay me in the morning."

"All right then. I guess we'll visit Mrs. Brandt." Eliza Dawn hugged Mrs. Pratt. Her gaze floated from Mrs. Pratt to Sam and back again. She hated to leave. Could people really be this bighearted? God truly fashioned church people here unlike any others she'd met before. "You are the salt of the earth, both of you. I won't forget you."

She followed Justin toward the door.

"Miss Dawn," Mrs. Pratt called after her, "Would you consider joining us for Easter services?"

"I was planning on leaving town early tomorrow morning." Eliza Dawn smiled. "But I'll think about it."

"Well, if I don't see you, take care of yourself and try to visit us again."

A knot formed in the pit of Eliza Dawn's stomach as she carried the box across to Brandt's Tailor Shop. After her encounter with her brother, the dress was ruined. It was a good thing Sam hadn't taken the money she offered. She'd need to compensate Mrs. Brandt for the loss.

Justin held the door open as she entered.

"Mrs. Brandt, are you here?" She peered toward the back room.

"Just a moment." The mumbled response came from the back. Moments later, Caroline Brandt poked her head into the hall. With a mouthful of pins, she beckoned, "Miss Dawn, come back. Come back."

She gave Justin a furtive glance. Hesitantly, she carried the box down the hall to the ever-elegant Caroline Brandt.

"Good afternoon, Mrs. Brandt."

"Miss Dawn, such a delight to see you out today." Caroline now held the pins in her hand. A young lady stood on a fitting pedestal wearing the green skirt from the gown modeled by Rebecca the previous evening. Mrs. Brandt reached up and lightly stroked the bruise on Eliza Dawn's face. "My goodness, what an ordeal you have experienced."

"Mrs. Brandt, I've brought the gown." Eliza Dawn held out the box.

Caroline clasped her hands together with a clap. "Lovely. You certainly were the belle of the ball, just as I had predicted. It's unfortunate you endured all that barbarianism at the end."

Eliza Dawn cleared her throat. "I have to tell you something about the dress."

"Oh, let me get your commission." Mrs. Brandt placed a

hand on the young lady's arm. "Josie, don't move. I'm not finished pinning that hem."

Eliza Dawn gripped Caroline's arm, halting her. "You cannot pay me for the dress."

"Why ever not?" Caroline's eyebrows arched.

"It's ruined. It's a complete shamble." Eliza Dawn released a heavy sigh. "I'm sorry, Mrs. Brandt. I'll pay you for the dress."

"Nonsense. I know all about the condition of the dress. Stay right there, Josie." Caroline prompted Eliza Dawn to follow her. "Miss Dawn, every woman visiting my shop this morning wanted your dress. You were so delightfully enchanting. I've explained the little I knew about the details of its destruction. In each instance, the customer chose another gown and paid the asking price plus half. They have requested I use the surplus to help you. They have purchased hats, gloves, parasols, and more."

Caroline Brandt grabbed the cash box under the front counter. "What I have for you, my darling is a twenty-five-dollar commission, plus fifteen dollars as a kindness collection. I pray your travels are light and you find it in your heart to return to us soon."

Caroline blew a kiss as she hurried down the hall. Dumbfounded, Eliza Dawn returned to Justin's side. He offered her his arm, and she rested her hand in the crook of his elbow.

"Leaving is going to be harder than I anticipated."

Chapter Thirty-Nine

With a flick of his wrist, Justin popped the reins, urging Blue to pick up speed. Dale was a better wagon horse, but Dale and Hershey had been stalled at Levi's with Rex and Devil after the shindig. Justin and Ewan, exhausted from the run-in with Whitmore, took advantage of Levi's offer to overnight their horses at the Snow homestead rather than trying to move them during the night. They didn't want to risk an ambush since some of Whitmore's outfit were still at large. So Blue rambled along awkwardly.

Justin had made this trip a thousand times on horseback and by wagon. Never had it seemed so agonizingly long. Eliza Dawn hadn't uttered a word the entire way. She hadn't shifted when he'd settled close to her, so he'd laced his fingers snugly through hers.

Justin pulled the wagon in front of Levi's cabin. Levi was already out the door to meet them. Eliza Dawn handed Levi the brown paper-wrapped package containing the flannels for the Scots, and she took Justin's hand as she climbed from the wagon.

"Ewan is at the round pens. He's been getting to know Rex

and Devil." Levi handed the package of flannels to Eliza Dawn. "I'll have Allie make some tea and meet you out there."

Justin nodded. He took the package from Eliza Dawn and offered his arm. She wrapped herself tightly around his arm as they walked to the pens together.

"Joostin." MacKinnon's voice surged with energy. He pulled a thick money bag from his chest pocket, waving it at them. "Am I glad to see 'eh two o' ye."

A heaviness weighed in Justin's heart. When prospectors flooded into Van Buren, he'd had one goal: avoid distractions and sell his horses. He hadn't intended to befriend any newcomers or get to know them. Yet, over the coming days, he would lose newfound friendships and love all at once.

MacKinnon passed the money pouch to Justin and then hopped the rail of the round pen. MacKinnon rubbed his thumb across Eliza Dawn's cheek.

"It disnae look too bad, lass." He smiled, lifting her chin. "Ye'll be all reit. Hev ye seen 'eh Pratt woman in toon? She had a little surprise fer ye."

"How did you know?" Eliza Dawn's brows knit together.

"She wis in and oot of 'eh mercantile half a dozen times afore I left this morning." MacKinnon patted the dust from his pants. "Mentioned some of 'eh toonswomen took oop a collection hoping ye'd stay here. So, 'eh lads and I took oop a collection too."

Ewan took the money bag from Justin and pulled some notes loose. "Here's forty dollars."

"Ewan, you didn't have to do that. I don't need the money. Really." Eliza Dawn motioned for him to keep it. "Well, I do need the money for the flannels."

"Aye, that's another ten." He leafed another note from his pouch.

"That's not what I meant, Ewan." She pursed her lips.

Eyebrows knit together, head tilted, her silent plea failed to enlist Justin's assistance. "Take thirty back."

"Cannae do it. The lads and I agree ye deserve a proper home." He rubbed his hand through his wild blond hair. "Ye shouldn't be following a boonch o' ragtag prospectors across 'eh country."

"Ewan, truly, I do not need the money. My situation has changed dramatically." She shoved his hand back. "Please keep it. Your need is far greater."

"Stubborn lass. We're aware of 'eh change in yer circumstances. But how long will it be afore ye hev access to sooch an inheritance? It'll take time." A broad smile broke through his reddish whiskers. "The lads will string me oop if I return with a single cent of it."

"Justin, I don't have room for all this. I'm embarrassed to ask." She dug all the notes from her apron pocket. "But could you carry this for me?"

Justin counted the money. "One hundred twenty-seven dollars. Putting it in my wallet."

"No' so fast, Hogue." MacKinnon held up his hand. "That wis from 'eh lads. A've sold a good number o' ponies. So A'd lek to contribute more." MacKinnon peeled off several notes and handed them to Eliza Dawn.

She flipped through them. "Two hundred dollars? Ewan, no. I must draw the line."

"Ah, now. Ye're practically one of us. Take the gift." He turned his attention to Justin. "I wis only able to sell Hershey today. Rex, Devil, and Dale ur still here." MacKinnon counted out more notes, passing them to Justin.

"That's two-hundred fifty dollars." Justin counted. He pulled more paper from his wallet, handing it to Eliza Dawn. "Take this. It's three hundred."

Eliza Dawn's eyes bulged. "That's six hundred twenty-seven dollars. What am I supposed to do with all that?"

"That's for you to decide." Justin arched his eyebrows. "Perhaps you should pray about it."

"That's whit ma mother would say." MacKinnon stuffed the money bag into his vest pocket.

"Mine too." Justin lowered his head.

Eliza Dawn fanned the money. "Perhaps I will. God did answer a prayer I uttered recently."

"You prayed?" Justin's eyes widened.

"Yes. For Simon." She paused. "I prayed, asking God not to take him from you when Davis shot him."

Justin swallowed hard. "Thank you. I'm grateful."

"You're welcome."

Justin smiled. "You're free to do anything you like. Live anywhere you like. Put down fresh roots."

"Oh, I don't know about that." She straightened the money and handed it to Justin. "It is something to think about, though. Hold this for me until we get back to the boardinghouse."

MacKinnon extended his hand to Justin. "Hogue, A'm thankful we reconciled. Wish we'd teamed oop sooner. A'll be taking 'eh few ponies I hev here back to camp, and then we'll be busy readying ourselves to move oot early next week. I may not see mooch of ye afore we depart. Thanks for ev'rything."

"Ewan, before you go, I must insist you give the letter entrusted to us your attention."

"Told ye afore, Hogue, ma people cannae read nor write. Neither can I."

Justin retrieved the ring from his pocket. He held it out to MacKinnon. "Do you recognize this ring?"

MacKinnon's breath stopped short. Slowly, he reached out and took the ring from Justin's hand. He stroked the thistle image. "I don't understand. How did ye get this?"

"May I read the letter?" Justin held up the envelope.

MacKinnon nodded.

A deep ache swept through Justin's chest as he read the

letter. He wished he could change the words and make a new reality to spare Ewan MacKinnon's heart. Justin swallowed hard, pressing his eyes shut before reading the last lines.

"Before she passed, she requested the ring be given to you with a reminder the thistle represents resilience, strength, resolve, and protection. Wear it in remembrance of your mother's undying love. Regards, Dr. John E. Pettus."

Ewan buckled. Justin caught him and eased to the ground with him. The proud Scotsman shook in Justin's arms. Justin's skin prickled at the memory of crumbling in the street beside his mother.

"Ewan, I'd like you to stay with my family for a while." Justin's low voice trembled. "Levi will take you to the boardinghouse. Mal is waiting for you. The two of you can get a good night's rest in the pastor's room. When he returns, he can room with Mr. Perry."

Eliza Dawn knelt, hugging Ewan from behind.

Justin drew a deep but shaky breath. "Is there anything else I can do?"

"A've got to return home. A've got to take care o' ma father."

"Mal said that's what you'd want. He's already started making arrangements for the trip home."

Levi appeared at Justin's side. Together, they helped Ewan to his feet and walked him to Levi's wagon. They provided extra support as he climbed into the buckboard.

"I'll check on you at the house later." Justin patted his knee.

Levi clicked his tongue, setting the wagon in motion. Justin stood with his arm around Eliza Dawn as Levi and Ewan disappeared.

Chapter Forty

The sun edged across the sky as Justin spread the blanket overlooking the river. He motioned for Eliza Dawn to sit and retrieved the little basket from the wagon. Pulling the cloth lining aside, he revealed the contents.

"Strudel." Eliza Dawn laughed. "After everything I've put you through, you'll trust me with strudel." She shook her head. "I don't know, that's a very nice shirt you're wearing."

He leaned close. Her skin tingled as his warm breath fell softly on her neck. "I'm willing to chance it. A clean shirt is overrated."

Her insides fluttered as though a rabble of butterflies had been set free. Her breath caught. The sun blazed a trail like melted butter. Justin's fingers grazed hers as he handed her a sweet pastry.

"One thing puzzles me." He took a bite of strudel. "Whitmore carried a five-shot revolver. How did you know it was only loaded with four shots?"

She covered her mouth while she spoke as his question caught her mid-bite. "Father taught him to load a gun with one less shot than it holds if he planned to carry a loaded weapon. That way, he wouldn't accidentally shoot his foot off."

"Still seems like a risky roll of the dice, you pulling the trigger."

"Of course, I couldn't be entirely sure he still practiced what Father taught him." She smoothed her skirt. "I'm glad he hasn't learned to control his impetuous nature. That's what made him second guess how many shots he'd fired. Pulling the trigger would have been much less satisfying if he'd known for certain he'd fired four shots." She paused. "I have a question. Did you know about the money collected on my behalf before we left the boardinghouse?"

"I knew about Mrs. Pratt's collection and my money. Mrs. Brandt and Ewan surprised me. Any thoughts on what you might do with it?" He popped the last bit of strudel into his mouth.

"It's been so long since I had a choice. I don't know." She nibbled at her flaky pastry.

He gazed intently at her. "Would you like me to pray with you about it?"

"I don't know. I know God answered my prayer about Simon." She shrugged. "But that prayer wasn't for me. I don't know if God would answer my request on my own behalf. Besides, I'm not sure I know what to pray for."

"Surely there's something you've dreamed of."

"Only two things. I dreamed of writing and having a family."

"You *are* writing, and you can do that anywhere."

A light breeze caught her hair, and Justin gently tucked it behind her ear.

"Yes, but I have to pretend to be someone I'm not."

"And what about family? Is that the prayer you believe God left unanswered?"

Eliza Dawn nodded. She swallowed against the barbed sensation at the back of her throat. She couldn't share her other unanswered prayer. Lifting the cloth from the basket, she placed the remainder of the strudel inside and covered it.

"I struggled with the fact God didn't save Ma. I believed He didn't answer my prayer." Justin's chest rose and fell deliberately. "Levi challenged that recently. It's not that God didn't save Ma. He didn't save her the way I wanted Him to. I wanted Him to save her here—for me."

Pressing her eyes tight, Eliza Dawn bit back tears.

Justin took her hands in his. "It's not that God hasn't answered your prayers for a family. It has taken longer than you'd hoped and is not what you imagined."

"What do you mean?" Her voice quivered.

"I've asked for several things since Ma was shot. First, I asked for her healing, and God did that. Just not this side of heaven. I've prayed for a way to help my family through the grief." He stroked her hand. "You were the answer to that prayer. Your willingness to talk with me about your losses. Your ability to connect to Pa and Simon. You opened doors for our relationships to heal. Doors we couldn't open alone. I sought a way to deal with the distractions and competition that challenged my business, and you introduced me to Mal. That man has been a fast and faithful friend. He handled Mrs. Pratt's smithing project. He paved the way for Ewan and I to overcome our rivalry."

His gaze shifted from her to the setting sun. "God has been working in my life all along. It's not how I would have done it. I would have plowed a line straight from my hard work to a horse ranch, free of distractions. But He accomplished so much more than I imagined. He took care of the deep, tender things, the eternal things—and those are the things I would have missed if I hadn't been distracted."

He lifted her chin, his gaze meeting hers. "God has been working in your life too. Can't you see it? The family God has built around you? The way He provided refuge here?"

A knot loosened in her chest. Rebecca had been like a sister to her from the very start. Teaching her to cook, encouraging and supporting her through tense times with Justin and Mr. Hogue, lengthening skirts, and sharing hopes and dreams. Sam, though warm and fatherly, had also gently challenged her to stay when she wanted to run. She had bonded with Simon and Pa. Even Mrs. Pratt and Caroline Brandt had embraced her. And little Edie's tender concern made it possible to mourn the loss of the child that could not be and embrace the love of a child who wasn't hers. This was a family, unlike anything she could have asked for or imagined.

"Yes, I can see that now. God raised a family around me when I wasn't looking. When I least expected it." She blinked back tears.

Justin brushed the hair back from her face. He pulled her into his arms. "I don't know what family will be like for you in the future, but I know I want to be part of it."

Her tears flowed freely. He pulled her into his arms. How could she make him understand she couldn't give him what he wanted?

"Justin, you'll want a family someday, and I can't give you that."

"Don't you see you've already given me that?" He held her at arm's length, his gray eyes probing the depths of hers. "I'd lost Pa. I'd lost Simon. Because of you, we've found each other again. Because of you, we're going to be okay."

"But what about children?"

"Is that still your dream? Do you still want to have children of your own someday?"

"Yes." She choked the answer.

"We'll hold that dream in open hands and allow God to shape it however He sees fit. As Levi says, He'll move us closer to this dream or give us another one. Either way, I want to hold all my open-handed dreams with you."

He drew her close again. As she nestled against him, the sun sank lower. Her heart slowed. She thought of the men whose stories she'd been writing. She couldn't allow them to fade into nothing. History needed to know the good intentions, the hopes and dreams, the lust and greed, all of it.

"Justin, I need to follow these stories. I'm not sure why, but I do." She placed her hand on his chest. "I don't know where life will take me after that, but for now, I need to go west with the prospectors."

"I thought you might say that." He sighed. "I can't bear watching you chase the sun tomorrow without me. But if you can wait four or five days when the first groups of prospectors are set to leave, I'll go with you."

"Go with me? What about your horse ranch?"

"I started building my stock by purchasing horses from owners who believed their horse had a behavior problem. Every horse I've owned, I came by dirt cheap because the owners believed they were trouble." He rubbed his hand through his wavy hair. "I can do that again. I love retraining horses. Shouldn't be too difficult to find riders headed west on ponies who need a better owner."

"Justin, I've caused you so much trouble already. I can't take you away from your family and your dreams."

"Levi says we crave a hint of trouble. I agree, and you're the kind of trouble I'd like to get used to."

Justin pulled her to her feet and led her to the bluff's edge. The low-hanging sun colored the golden ribbon of the Arkansas River flowing through the valley. He knelt on one knee at her feet, and her heart swelled.

"Justin, what are you doing?" she whispered.

He took her hand in his. "I know this flies in the face of convention seeing as how you've only just been widowed—"

"Our marriage was never what a marriage ought to be. I wasn't a wife. I was a prize, an incentive."

"A prize isn't what I'm looking for." He lightly brushed the back of her fingers with his lips. "I want a friend—a love—someone who's not afraid to dream with me. And I don't want to hold on to any dreams I can't share with you. We can travel west together, and we can always return home to family. If you'll have me, I can't think of a better way to begin this adventure than with you by my side as husband and wife. Eliza Dawn, would you marry me Sunday morning after church?"

"On Easter Sunday?"

"Is there a better day to start an adventure of faith and dreams?"

"No. It's perfect."

Justin stood and drew her into his arms. His lips met hers in a lingering kiss. Then, wrapping her in his arms, he freed his pocket watch and flipped it open.

"Did you have somewhere to be?" She lifted her eyes to meet his. "Are you late again?"

He snapped it shut and smiled. "I'd say I'm right on time for once."

Epilogue

March 31, 1850
Angels Camp, California

The hum of tumbling water and the trill of birds echoed the peaceful sunrise on Angel's Creek. Eliza Dawn stoked the fire and made a pot of coffee. She exhaled her warm breath, a mist on the cool air. Fingering the sachet of lavender soap looped on her saddlebag, she smiled softly and pulled a worn envelope from its interior.

Justin returned from the creek and sat beside her. He pulled her close, kissing her temple. "A brisk wash in the morning gets my blood pumping. How soon will you be ready to leave for Ney's Ferry?"

"I thought I'd ease into the day. Spend time reflecting on where we've been and how far we've come."

He pointed to the letter in her hand. "You rereading his letter?"

"I was about to." Eliza Dawn slipped the paper free of its enclosure. "I'm so glad Dr. Pettus befriended Ewan when he returned to his father. It's been a joy receiving word from him."

"And gifts." Justin thumbed the lavender sachet on her saddlebag. "I suppose I ought to be jealous the man still sends you such gifts."

"Oh, it's not from him alone. He writes of a handful of Scots who returned home with him." She patted Justin's knee. "Seems they truly do think of me as family."

Justin scrunched a blanket behind him and leaned back against the log, folding his arms behind his head. "All right. I'm ready. Tell me again how the lads are doing."

"Well, Mal and Ewan have partnered. Ewan's Highland ponies are growing in notoriety in their part of Georgia. Together with Mal's smithing skills, they've started a livery and small horse ranch." She cut her eyes. Justin's chest rose and fell. His eyes remained closed. "Dr. Pettus is teaching Ewan to read and write. In fact, he's written a bit in this letter himself. Not the whole, but a bit."

Justin wove his arms around her again, nuzzling his cheek against the crown of her head. "Remind me what it says, the part Ewan wrote himself."

"Tell that apple pie husband of yorn to write once ye've returned home as Mal and I plan to drive half a dozen Highlands his way. A gift from ma father, who's doing right fine."

She tilted her head to the side, taking in the slight upward turn of his mouth through his scruffy beard.

"Justin, I'm sorry you've had to put off your dreams of a horse ranch." She laced her fingers through his, resting her head against his shoulder. "It can't set well that Ewan is doing exactly what you had hoped to do."

Justin pressed his lips together, then sighed. "I'd be lying to say I don't have a touch of envy, but then I think here I am doing what he had hoped to do. I've come west, and—though it wasn't our purpose—I've tried my hand at prospecting and even came up with a nugget or two. It's not a fortune. I'm guessing you didn't include that in your letter to Ewan."

"No. You asked me not to, so I didn't mention it."

"He seems happy. I don't want him to wonder what he might have missed."

"Speaking of that,"—she twisted to face him—"did you read Mrs. Pratt's letter?"

"Yes, I know she hoped we'd be home by Easter. But here we sit." He squeezed her hand. "We'll make it to church with them soon enough. And, Lord willing, we won't miss another Easter with family in Van Buren."

"She writes the sweetest letters, though she occasionally asks about hemlines out here." Eliza Dawn giggled. "I've assured her mine have gotten no shorter." She pressed her eyes closed, settling her mind on their predawn walk. "I look forward to attending church with the whole Hogue brood, but I can't imagine an Easter morning finer than this one. The cave we came across this morning with the large boulder resting to the side of the opening fit so perfectly with your scripture reading."

"Happening upon that certainly brought that passage to life." Justin rubbed his thumb across the back of her hand. "It makes me feel childish for questioning His timing sometimes. If He knows when to place a cave and boulder in our path, He'd know the best timing for a ranch."

"And children." Her eyes drifted to their joined hands.

"We've encountered children along our path. And you've nurtured every child, whether it involved tending a scraped knee or blessing their family with food, clothes, money, or encouragement. You've taught girls to read and write and sew. You've taught boys manners, when and where to pour out their energy, when to sit still and hold their tongues, and when to make a stand."

"I owe you a debt of thanks for recommending I use my inheritance to improve the lives of children. I hadn't planned on touching any of it. It didn't feel right, knowing the wheeling and dealing done to amass such wealth. Much of it at my expense."

She pulled his arm around her middle. "You reminded me God can use all things for good. Using what was so damaging to me to help children provides a degree of healing to my soul. But I do still long for a child in my life."

"You just wait until we get home." He squeezed her. "Edie will be hanging off your skirts nonstop."

"I want a child we can call our own." She sighed. "I love Edie. And I'm grateful for her. Honestly, we have a beautiful life, although I've witnessed things on this journey west I hope never to experience again. But I do wonder if children will ever be part of our story, part of our home."

He turned her hand over. "That's a dream I'm still willing to hold in an open hand—if you are."

A half-smile graced her lips. "As long as I'm holding it with you, I can keep my hands open to that dream."

Justin leaned in and kissed her forehead. "I love you, Dawn."

Her cheeks warmed. She whispered, "I love it when you call me that."

"I'll always call you that. It suits you. You're a new woman with a new dawn on the horizon." He stood, offering her his hand. "But it's time we get going. I want to get to Crescent City. We'll stay the night so you can post your last article about the prospectors in the morning. Then we'll resupply and start for home."

"I'm so thankful Mr. Clarke at the *Arkansas Intelligencer* agreed to publish my articles, knowing I'm a woman. Mr. Mooney is such a dear to have introduced me to him before we departed." She took Justin's hand and wiped the dirt from her skirt as she stood. "I'm fine with the fact he asked me to use the name E.D. Hogue. I like that better than Edward Dodd."

"I'm sure Rebecca's recounting how Edie delights over it every time she shows her your name in print helps." His broad grin lit his eyes. He mimicked his youngest sister. "E.D. We're the same! So, my name is in the paper too."

"I can't wait to get home and squeeze that little sister of yours." Eliza Dawn picked up her blanket and shook it out. A twinge pricked her heart. "Justin, will you tell Rebecca we found Dr. Ewing?"

"No." Justin's movements slowed as he helped load the remaining items from around the campfire. "He asked me not to, and I'll respect his wishes. He's not the same man she knew. But you and I can continue to pray for him. That's a man who needs to find home again."

Justin flicked his pocket watch open.

"Are we on a rigid schedule?" Eliza Dawn propped her hands on her hips. "Late already?"

"We are most definitely late for something significant I forgot to mention."

"Oh, what's that?"

Justin pulled her close to him, his lips hovering over hers. A tingle ran up her spine. "One more kiss before I swing you up into this wagon headed for home."

THE END

Acknowledgments

A writer's journey is sprinkled with so many encouragers, helping hands, educators, friends, and family that it can be challenging to know where to begin when thanking them. Naturally, there is a fear of leaving someone out, especially when my love of writing dates to grade school, and my obsession with reading began before I was old enough to go to school.

God bless my mother, who was my first reading teacher and, when I was older, volunteered in the school library. She introduced me to my first and favorite fictional hero—Katie John, a curious and adventurous tomboy much like me (thank you, Mary Calhoun, for creating her!). My father was a great storyteller in his own right, and together, they taught me stories can take you anywhere.

A long line of educators followed my mother. Virginia Wright cultivated a desire to read. Jana Workman and Matthew Sego read captivating books aloud in class. Katherine Gault introduced me to haiku poems, which sparked the realization that we can play with words. Melinda Chase taught me to take critique like a champ and encouraged me to explore writing far beyond the classroom. Pat Eggburn and Martha Matthews continued to help hone my writing voice.

In my adulthood, I found an incredible writers' group in the Arkansas Chapter of ACFW. With their help, I discovered my writing process, learned to write a plotline straight through, shared many prayer requests, and so much more. But most of all, I want to thank them for sitting in the deep places with me and for the laughter. Shannon Taylor Vanatter, Tara Johnson, Linda Fulkerson, Kathy Vernich, Jenny Carlisle, Jolene Staker, Debbie Archer, Rosie Baldwin, Suzanne Bratcher, Candace West, and so many others—you rock!

Along with a great writers' group, I've been blessed with some incredible and affordable writers' conferences within three to five hours of home—special thanks to Midsouth Christian Writers in Collierville, Tennessee, and KenTen Writers Group for hosting. I've made meaningful connections with so many other writers through these events. The KenTen Writers Retreat is where I met Kathy Cretsinger, a publisher with a heart for new writers. I still have the coffee mug you gave me, "Writing is my superpower!"

Then there are the 501 Fictioneers, a sweet writing fellowship that grew from a novella partnership. Thank you, Jenny Carlisle and Ellen Withers, for creating the most beautiful debut opportunity in *A Gift for All Time* and for your kindness, encouragement, support, and friendship. I can't wait to write with you again.

To my editor, Amy Anguish, I'm so thankful you push back when I test the limits with my characters. You make me a better writer, and I am deeply grateful. And your stories make me a better person. To Linda Fulkerson, my publisher, you're a blessing beyond words.

I couldn't have made it this far without some dear friends. Melissa Nesbitt, Kathy Vernich, and Susan Davis have explored life and faith with me. I'm thankful for your incredible sense of curiosity and adventure and your ability to sit in hard places and do hard things. Melissa, I continue to be amazed by how "twin" we are, even though our lives are very different. You challenge me in the most loving and needed ways. Kathy, you never fail to check in and make sure I'm staying afloat. Susan, I cherish your ability to take the next step in faith. And your willingness to turn bank vaults into time machines.

To my guys—Rodney, John, and Quinn—I owe you so much. You've made space for writing in our lives. You listen to all my crazy what-ifs. You're my preferred search platform (lol). You've cooked, cleaned, and cheered me on. I would never make it to "The End" without your love and encouragement. I love you more than words can express. You have no idea.

I'm thankful for my Grandpa Rebel and Grandpa Bradford, both incredible men of faith. Thank you for those last words, Papaw Rebel, "Don't let anything get in the way, including the devil himself." And thank you, Grandpa Bradford, for cherishing my words and being my biggest fan.

And, to my friends and animal lovers who helped name Justin's horses: Meggan Harris (Sugar Blue), Lynlee Preator (Bonnie), Emily Scott (Dolly), Candace West (Hershey), Melinda Steele (Dale), Amanda Ivey (Rex), Haley Danielle (Cowboy), Melissa Nesbitt (Star), and Wendy Hancock (Devil, originally El Diablo).

Praise God, who does exceedingly more than I could ask or imagine and who is always working even when I can't see it or make sense of it. I am blessed. Even in the hard things.

About the Author

Tonya B. Ashley is an award-winning writer who loves a thread of adventure, whether in story or in life. Along with her publication credits as a devotional writer, she received first place in an ACFW First Impressions contest for mystery and suspense.

She and her firefighter/paramedic husband are the parents of an adult son, also a firefighter, and a school-aged son. With experience as a 911 dispatcher and volunteer firefighter, she enjoys all sorts of adventures, including hiking trips well off the beaten path.

Also by Tonya B. Ashley

A Gift for All Time

A Collection of Three Christmas Novellas

by Tonya B. Ashley, Jenny Carlisle, and

Ellen E. Withers

A beautiful hand-carved nativity set travels from its original home in Germany to a riverboat in Van Buren, Arkansas, in the mid-1840s, then to Mexico, Missouri, at the beginning of the American Civil War. More than a century later, it resurfaces in a tiny town in the Arkansas River Valley.

Three stories tell of the impact this treasure has on the families who own it. God's love survives tragedy, turmoil, and even abandonment. His love is the gift for all, for all time.

This collection includes the novella, "Once Lost, Now Found," by Tonya B. Ashley.

https://scrivenings.link/agiftforalltime

You May Also Like ...

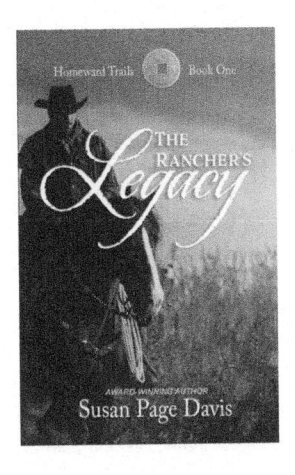

The Rancher's Legacy—Book One
Will Rogers Medallion—Copper Award Winner

Matthew Anderson and his father try to help neighbor Bill Maxwell when his ranch is attacked. On the day his daughter Rachel is to return from school back East, outlaws target the Maxwell ranch. After Rachel's world is shattered, she won't even consider the plan her father and Matt's cooked up—to see their two children marry and combine the ranches.

Meanwhile in Maine, sea captain's widow Edith Rose hires a private investigator to locate her three missing grandchildren. The children were abandoned by their father nearly twenty years ago. They've been adopted into very different families, and they're scattered across the country. Can investigator Ryland Atkins find them all while the elderly woman still lives? His first attempt is to find the boy now called Matthew Anderson. Can Ryland survive his trip into the wild Colorado Territory and find Matt before the outlaws finish destroying a legacy?

Get your copy here:

https://scrivenings.link/therancherslegacy

Love's Twisting Trail

Trails of the Heart—Book One

Stampedes, wild animals, and renegade Comanches make a cattle drive dangerous for any man. The risks multiply when Charlotte Grimes goes up the trail disguised as Charlie, a fourteen-year-old boy. She promised her dying father she'd save their ranch after her brother, Tobias, mismanages their money. To keep her vow, she rides the trail with the brother she can't trust.

David Shepherd needs one more successful drive to finish buying the ranch he's prayed for. He partners with Tobias to travel safely through Indian Territory. David detests the hateful way Tobias treats his younger brother, Charlie. He could easily love the boy like the brother he's always wanted. But what does he do when he discovers Charlie's secret? What kind of woman would do what she's done?

The trail takes an unexpected twist when Charlotte falls in love with

David. She's afraid to tell him of her deception. Such a God-fearing, honest gentleman is bound to despise the kind of woman who dares to wear a man's trousers and venture on a cattle drive. Since her father left her half the ranch, she intends to continue working the land like any other man after she returns to Texas. David would never accept her as she is.

Choosing between keeping her promise to her father or being with the man she loves may put Charlotte's heart in more danger than any of the hazards on the trail can.

Get your copy here:

https://scrivenings.link/lovestwistingtrail

Scrivenings
PRESS
Quench your thirst for story.
www.ScriveningsPress.com

Stay up-to-date on your favorite books and authors with our free e-newsletters.

ScriveningsPress.com

Made in the USA
Middletown, DE
21 March 2024

51401072R00186